The Innocent Spy

THE INNOCENT SPY

Laura Wilson

FELONY & MAYHEM PRESS • NEW YORK

All the characters and events portrayed in this work are fictitious.

THE INNOCENT SPY

A Felony & Mayhem mystery

PRINTING HISTORY
First UK edition (Orion, as *Stratton's War*): 2008
First U.S. edition (St. Martin's): 2009
Felony & Mayhem edition: 2012

ISBN: 978-1-937384-09-8

Manufactured in the United States of America

Printed on 100% recycled paper

Library of Congress Cataloging-in-Publication Data

Wilson, Laura, 1964-
 [Stratton's war]
 The innocent spy / Laura Wilson. -- 1st U.S. ed.
  p. cm.
 ISBN 978-1-937384-09-8
 1. Motion picture actors and actresses--Crimes against--Fiction. 2. Great
Britain. Metropolitan Police Office. Criminal Investigation Dept--Fiction.
3. Great Britain. MI5--Officials and employees--Fiction. 4. Fascists--
London--Fiction. 5. World War, 1939-1945--England--London--Fiction.
I. Title.
 PR6073.I4716S77 2012
 823.92--dc23

            2011049915

To Jane Wood, with much gratitude

ACKNOWLEDGEMENTS

I am very grateful to Professor Sue Black, Mark Campbell, Tom Donnelly, Emma Dunford, Claire Foster, Freeway (basset hound), Jane Gregory, Jane Havell, Maya Jacobs, Helen Lloyd of the National Trust, Fenella and Huon Mallallieu, Jemma McDonagh, Dr John Manlove, Claire Morris, Michael O'Byrne, Sara O'Keefe, Christine and David Ratsey, David Roberts, Sebastian Sandys, Margaret Willes, and June and William Wilson for their enthusiasm and support.

The icon above says you're holding a copy of a book in the Felony & Mayhem "Historical" category, which ranges from the ancient world up through the 1940s. If you enjoy this book, you may well like other "Historical" titles from Felony & Mayhem Press.

———————⚬•⚬———————

For more about these books, and other Felony & Mayhem titles, or to place an order, please visit our website at:

www.FelonyAndMayhem.com

or contact us at:

Felony and Mayhem Press
156 Waverly Place
New York, NY 10014

Other "Historical" titles from

FELONY & MAYHEM

The Innocent Spy

CHAPTER 1

A child saw her first.

June 1940, Fitzrovia: five o'clock, and the sky overcast. The boy, six years old, had been running half-heartedly up and down the empty street, pretending to be an aeroplane, but it wasn't much good without the others. He'd been delighted when his mother came to take him away from the farm, with its pig-faced owner and the huge smelly animals that still chased him, snorting and steaming, through nightmares. His mother, smothering for the first few days, had soon tired of him under her feet and turned him outdoors to play, and three months on, with most of his friends still evacuated and his old school requisitioned by the ARP, he was bored.

He picked up a stick and ran it up and down the iron railings in front of the tall houses, then turned the corner and, sighing, sat down on the kerb and pulled both his socks up, hard.

Raising his head, he saw a sack of something draped over a set of railings further down. It hadn't been there when he'd run down the road after his dinner, he was sure. He dawdled along for a closer look. It wasn't a sack, but a woman, impaled on the sharp black spikes. He stared at her, uncomprehending. Face down, her dress was caught up round her waist, and he could see her drawers. He extended a finger and poked her shoulder. Under the slippery material, she felt scraggy and bony, like the meat his mother sent him to fetch from the butcher's. She seemed to have two lots of hair, one short, brown and stiff looking, on the back of her head, and the other, longer and yellow. This top hair had slipped forwards, hanging down on either side of her face so that he couldn't see what she looked like. He considered this for a moment, then looked down at the pavement, where a number of little round white things were scattered. He picked one up and rolled it between his fingers—hard and shiny. A sweet? He put it in his mouth, sucking first, then testing it against his teeth. It felt slightly rough when he bit it, but tasted of nothing. Spitting it into his palm, he squatted down and peered up at the face between the long yellow curls.

In shadow, upside down, one eye stared back at him. The other was closed—a long, lashless slit like a wound, its outer corner pulled upwards, as if by invisible thread. Then, with a groan, the mouth opened, a black, cavernous O, to swallow him whole.

He screamed. Someone else screamed, too, and for a moment he thought it must be the woman, bent on eating him alive. Then feet pounded towards him, and in a confusion of shouts, gasps and police whistles, an unknown hand pressed his head to an alien bosom. Howling and thrashing in terror, he was carried away down the road, pounding at his rescuer, the single pearl still clutched in his left fist.

CHAPTER 2

The barrage balloons were shining in the evening sun. DI Ted Stratton squinted up at them. He felt, as he always did, comforted by their rotund, silvery serenity. Despite everything, he thought—first Norway and Denmark, then Holland, Belgium, and now France, like dominoes—it was hardly a picture of a country at war. For Stratton, the word conjured up bullet-riddled scarecrows sprawled across the wire in No Man's land, even though the Great War had ended too soon for him to be called up, leaving him unable to tell whether he was glad or sorry. That had been his brothers' war; the eldest had died. It had come as a shock to realise that, at thirty-five, and in a reserved occupation, he'd be too old for this war—for the time being, at least. He was fit enough, strong and muscular, but he certainly looked his age; a broken nose and a great deal of night duty had given him a battered, serviceable appearance. In a way, thought Stratton, this war's everybody's, even the nippers'. Terrible that it should have come to this, but exciting, that sense of something happening, of being poised in history, alone, at the very centre of the map, of the world tilting on its axis: shall we be next?

As he passed the sandbags at the hospital entrance, Stratton thought of the rumours he'd heard about the local authorities stockpiling thousands of papier-mâché coffins, and thought: soon.

Middlesex Hospital, emptied the previous September of most of its patients to make room for as yet non-existent air-raid casualties, was still quiet. Stratton's footsteps echoed on the stone stairs as he descended to Dr Byrne's underworld—the mortuary, lavatory-tiled, harshly lit and smelling of decay and chemicals. The pathologist was seated at his desk, writing notes. 'Is this an official visit?'

Stratton shook his head. 'Curiosity.'

'Won't take long, will it?'

'Just a few minutes.' Stratton neither expected nor received the offer of a seat. He'd met Dr Byrne a couple of times, and the man's manner was as chilly as the corpses he filleted. He even looked dead—not cadaverous, but there was something cold and doughy about his pale skin that suggested a freshly washed corpse.

'It's about Miss Morgan.'

'The suicide? Body's at the police mortuary.' Dr Byrne paused to knock out his pipe before shuffling through a stack of papers. 'What do you want to know?' he asked aggressively.

'Isn't it unusual, a woman throwing herself out of a window?'

'No. Women do it. Didn't she leave a note?'

'No, nothing.'

'Worried about the invasion. I've had a couple of them in the past month. Neurotic types.'

'I was wondering about where the body fell. It was the fourth floor, and the area's not that wide...I was surprised she didn't land further out, in the road.'

Byrne shrugged. 'Depends how she jumped.'

'What about her underclothes?'

'What about them?' Byrne looked at him with distaste.

'Were they clean?'

'I've no idea. She hadn't soiled herself, if that's what you mean.'

'Would you say she took care of herself?'

'She was reasonably clean.' Byrne glanced at his notes. 'Lot of scarring on the face...Burns. She'd had a skin graft. Not a very good job, by the look of it.' He looked up. 'Lot of paint. Prostitute, was she?'

Stratton tried not to sound as annoyed as he felt. 'I imagine she hoped that heavy cosmetics might hide the scars. As a matter of fact, she'd been in films.'

'There you are, then. Artistic type. Highly strung. As I said, the injuries were quite consistent with the manner of death. Now, if there's nothing else...'

Stratton marched back upstairs, irritated at the man's way of reducing everyone to a type. Just as well he didn't have to deal with living patients. Stratton wondered if Dr Byrne was married, and then, firmly suppressing an image of him in fumbling coitus atop an equally corpse-like wife, went out into the street.

As he strolled back along Savile Row—even after years out of uniform, his internal pacemaker was still set at the regulation 2½ mph—Stratton thought about his first suicide, a young man who'd put the muzzle of a gun under his chin and blown most of his head into the walls of his outdoor lav. He remembered the drops of blood falling from the wooden ceiling onto his back and neck as he'd bent over to look, and a larger one on his hand that turned out to be a piece of brain. There'd been chips of skull embedded in the boards all round the toilet, pink and white, like almonds on an iced cake. Stratton had been twenty-five then, the same age as the poor bastard who'd killed himself. They'd found a note saying he was suffering from an incurable disease. Turned out he was homo-sexual—he'd gone for treatment, but it hadn't worked. Stratton remembered what one of the older coppers had said about it being unusual for a nancy to use a gun. 'They normally do it like women: gas or pills, and clean underwear.' The same officer had told him that the most violent way women did it was with carbolic—'bloody painful, burns your insides out'. Everything Stratton had seen since had confirmed these rules, until yesterday. Clearly, female jumpers weren't as uncommon as he'd thought, and the underwear was inconclusive...Nevertheless, the feeling that something wasn't quite right continued to nag at him. Not that there was much he could do, it wasn't his case. It wasn't anybody's. As far as his superiors were concerned, the thing was over and done with.

Stratton breathed in the familiar station smell of soap, disinfectant and typewriter ribbons. Ballard, the young PC who'd dealt with Miss Morgan, was by the desk, admonishing Freddie the Flasher. 'I've got a weak bladder, there's nothing they can do for it, on my life...' Stratton grinned to himself: there was one in every district. Female exhibitionists, as well—there'd been one at his first posting who'd never closed her curtains when she undressed for bed. Every night at 11.30. Good looking woman, too. He'd watched her several times, a few of them had. Not that he was proud of it, but...

He waited until Ballard was finished, then nodded at Freddie's retreating back. 'Poor old sod. He can't be having much fun in the blackout.'

'No, sir.' Ballard suppressed a grin.

'You found Miss Morgan, didn't you?'

'Yes, sir.' Ballard grimaced. 'I won't forget her in a hurry, I can tell you.'

'Who was with you?'

'PC 29, sir. Arliss.'

'I see.' Fred Arliss, one of the old, horse-drawn brigade, was so incompetent that 'Arlissing around' had become station slang for ballsing something up. Stratton wondered if Ballard knew this yet, but decided not to enlighten him.

'Did either of you notice anything unusual about her?'

Ballard frowned. 'I don't know if you'd say it was unusual, but there was one thing that did strike me when we moved her—she didn't have her teeth in.'

'Didn't she?'

'No sir. Made me wonder if it wasn't some kind of accident. The window was wide open, not much of a ledge, and if she'd been leaning out...It's only a thought, sir. It just seemed to me a shame if the coroner said it was a suicide when it wasn't.'

'Certainly rough on the family.'

'She didn't have any relatives, and her husband's dead. Died in a fire. That's how she got the scars on her face. The young chap she lived with told us.'

'Young chap?' Stratton raised his eyebrows.

'Nothing like that, sir.' Ballard reddened. 'He wasn't... well...he wasn't normal.'

'A kiss not a handshake, you mean?'

Ballard looked grateful. 'Something like that, sir. It was like talking to a girl.'

'Oh, well...' Stratton shrugged. 'It takes all sorts. How are you finding it at Beak Street?' Ballard, like most of the young policemen, lived in the section house. Stratton had lived there himself years ago, when he had his first posting at Vine Street. Tiny cubicles, and never enough blankets in the winter. 'Don't suppose it's changed much, has it?'

'I shouldn't think so, sir. Do you remember her, in the films?'

'Can't say I do.'

Stratton thanked Ballard and returned to his desk to shake his head at a heap of paperwork about the Italians they were supposed to be helping to round up for internment. Bloody ridiculous, he thought, staring at the list of names. It came from MI5, and they hadn't screened anybody so, basically, every Gino, Maria and Mario who'd come to Britain after 1919 was for it, even if they had sons or brothers serving in the army. Not to mention attacks on Italian businesses...Admittedly, it was an easy way to get rid of some of the gangs, although, with the Sabini Brothers safely out of the way, the Yiddishers and the Malts would have the run of Soho, which would mean shifting alliances—accompanied by a fair bit of violence—until everyone settled down again. Not that the Jews were having an easy time of it, either. Stratton sighed. It wasn't the criminals he felt sorry for, it was the poor bastards who were trying to make an honest living and getting bricks chucked through their windows. Not to mention all the stories in the papers about Jews profiteering and evading the call up.

He tried to concentrate, but the missing teeth bothered him. Byrne hadn't thought to mention it. But if Mabel Morgan had painted her face, why hadn't she put in her teeth? Surely that would come first. Stratton had his own teeth, and he'd never tried applying lipstick, but it had to be easier with them than without them. He tried to shrug the problem away, but it kept coming back. On the way home, he made a mental note to ask his wife if she remembered Mabel Morgan. Women were better at things like that.

CHAPTER 3

Joe Vincent stood at the window of his flat and scrubbed Mabel's teeth with a nailbrush. He'd tried using her toothbrush, but the dentures were coated in a grey, slightly furry accretion that the softer bristles couldn't shift. He wasn't really surprised; they'd never been immersed in any liquid other than water—and saliva—and she'd always been lazy about cleaning them. The work did not disgust him; he was grateful to be able to perform a last, small task for her. He'd spent most of the day staring at her things, unable to believe that she wasn't coming back.

He gave the teeth a final swill in the bowl and laid them out to dry on a sheet of newspaper. Why hadn't she been wearing them? And why not the fox fur jacket? She'd told him once that she wanted to be buried in it—'Unless you can lay your hands on a mink, dear.' They'd told him at the hospital it was suicide, but he couldn't believe it. He hadn't seen her in the morning—she liked to sleep late—but the night before, when he'd gone to the pub after his shift at the cinema to escort her home through the blackout, she'd been fine. Tight, as usual, but quite happy, reminiscing about her days on the set with Gertie and Bertie, the child stars known as the Terrible Twins ('I wanted to strangle the little bastards, dear. We all did.'). He knew she had a habit of leaning out of the front window and throwing her keys to her few visitors to save walking down the four flights of stairs, but if she'd toppled out doing that, someone would have seen her—unless she'd just thought she'd heard someone and leant out too far trying to see who it was... The window'd been wide open when he got back and there was no guard-rail, so it was possible. But then, why were her keys still in her handbag? All the same, it must have been an accident. She'd be the last person to take her own life, he was sure. There'd be an inquest...The thought of a suicide verdict was unbearable; surely they'd let him say something? After all, he'd known her best.

At least she'd been wearing her wig. Her real hair had been doused so many times with chemicals that it had snapped off and had to be cut short. They hadn't thought to straighten the wig at the hospital—she'd been lying there with it cocked over one eye. He'd adjusted it as best he could without causing her further pain, and sat holding her hand, numb with shock. Then he'd heard her whisper, 'Joe...' She'd died after that. He'd asked the nurses whether she'd said anything else, but if she had, none of them had heard it.

He looked down at the railings below, then drew back, feeling nauseous, trying to wipe away the image of her stomach impacting on the deadly spikes, the lethal prongs spearing her flesh and puncturing vital organs.

He wandered back to Mabel's room, took a framed photograph from the mantelpiece and blew on it to get rid of the dust. Huge, wistful eyes, rippling blonde hair (still, at that time, her own), a heart-shaped face and a rosebud mouth: sheer beauty. It was taken in 1920, when she'd come third in the *Picturegoer* survey for the 'Greatest British Film Player', before the fire that scarred her, and before the work dried up, leaving her, by the time of their meeting in 1937, almost destitute. Joe had been just six in 1920, but his aunt Edna, who'd brought him up, had been an avid picturegoer and had taken him and his sister Beryl to see everything. Beryl had longed to be an actress, but she didn't have the looks. Joe had got those; eyelashes wasted on a boy, Auntie Edna had always said, and as handsome as they come. She'd been pleased when he became a projectionist—it got her a weekly free seat at the Tivoli, where he worked—although she'd fantasised about him being up on the screen.

He sat down in the rumpled wreckage of Mabel's bed, clutching the photograph. He hadn't known about the scars until he'd met her. Her career had been over for several years before the fire that had marked her face and killed her director husband, and she was already forgotten. He'd read about how she'd been discovered, aged eighteen, in 1911, but he'd been shocked the first time he'd heard her speak: a Cockney accent, not far off his own. 'They wouldn't have me in the talkies, dear. I couldn't do it. They wanted people from the stage, who could speak right.'

They'd met in a café. He'd been sitting over a cup of tea, minding his own business, when he'd noticed her. She'd been seated—deliberately, he realised later—next to the wall, beside a sign that read 'Eat Here and Keep Your Wife as a Pet', and there was something about the flawlessness of her right profile that seemed familiar, though he couldn't for the life of him think why. Staring into space across an empty table, there was something undefeated about her, in the tatty grandeur of her clothes and the defiant bravado of her jauntily angled hat. He didn't think she'd noticed him until the manageress, who'd been glaring at her for a quarter of an hour, had approached and asked her, loud enough for everyone to hear, to pay up and go. He'd thought she was going to leave, but, halfway to the door, she'd come up to his table and said, without ceremony, 'Can you spare a fag, dear?' Seeing her full-face for the first time, he'd been caught off guard, embarrassed by his gasp at the sight of her damaged cheek and the circle of shiny, raw skin round her sealed eye. Hastily pushing the packet across the table—only three left in it to last the day—he'd lit a match for her. He thought she would leave then, but she'd lingered, watching him, apparently quite oblivious to the glowering manageress, until he'd felt compelled to ask if she'd like a cup of tea.

'Thank you, dear. Now the old bitch'll have to put up with me, whether she likes it or not. I'm Mabel.' She'd extended a hand as if she expected it to be kissed, and Joe, blushing, had obliged. The manageress had slapped down the cup between them, slopping tea into the saucer. 'None of that here,' she'd snapped, and marched back to stand guard over her urn. When she was out of earshot, Joe's new companion had leant across the table and said, 'What's your name, then?'

'Joe.'

'You're a kind boy. I don't suppose you remember me, do you dear?'

Unsure, he'd blurted, 'Did you know my aunt, Edna Vincent?'

'I don't think so, dear, I meant from the pictures. I suppose it's not likely.' She tapped her temple. 'I got this in a fire. They gave me new eyelids, but they don't work.'

'Were you in pictures, then?'

'That's right, dear. Mabel Morgan.'

He'd stared openly then. Of course he knew her! She was burnt into his consciousness through a thousand afternoons watching her melt into the arms of barely noticed leading men. It wasn't until later he'd started to look at them; as a young boy, he'd watched only the actresses ('looking for hints, ducky,' as a sympathetic chum had said later). And now she was in front of him, a phantom made flesh.

'I do exist, you know. Some might say it's a mistake, but still…' She stuck out her arm. 'Go on, pinch me if you don't believe me.'

'But…why are you here?'

'Nowhere else to go, dear.' She indicated a large, battered suitcase, which Joe hadn't noticed before. 'Lost my room.'

'Your hotel room?'

'No, dear. Where I live.'

'But…' He'd paused, not wanting to offend her. It was hard enough to reconcile the lustrous beauty of the silent screen with the blemished, Cockney reality, even though he could see they were one and the same, but he'd always thought that film stars—even film stars who no longer made pictures—lived in mansions like the ones he'd seen in newsreels. Embarrassed, he'd changed the subject. 'The first picture I ever saw was one of yours. *David Copperfield.*'

'I died in that one. I did a lot of that, swooning and dying. I enjoyed that, especially the suicides. I was very good at those.'

'Like *The Passionate Pilgrim.*'

'Oh yes! Aubrey Manning had to lay me down on a tomb. We filmed it after lunch, and his breath stank of sardines. Worse than the dog it was.'

'Which dog?'

'Oh, you won't remember that one, dear. *Old Faithful*, it was called. First one I ever did. I had to keep on kissing this great big dog. Mind you, I got along with him, despite the...' Mabel fanned her face with her hand. 'It was the director I couldn't bear. Henry Thurston. There was this one moment, dear...' She leant across the table. 'I had to look frightened, you see, and he kept saying it wasn't good enough, so he said, "I'll give you a fright," and he undid his trousers and took it out. Scared me half to death. I was only eighteen, I'd never seen one before.'

Joe had been captivated. He'd used up the last of his money buying cups of tea while she talked, and then he'd taken her back to see his landlady. Mrs Cope, who liked Joe because he didn't cause trouble, had seemed willing—for a small consideration on the rent—to accept his explanation that Mabel was a relative, fallen on hard times, and allowed her to share his tiny flat.

And now she wasn't here any more. She'd never be here again. Joe laid the photograph on her pillow and went to her chest of drawers, where he opened her jewellery box and fingered the few items she hadn't been able to pawn, then kissed the wooden pate of her wig-stand and, turning, ran his hands along the shoulders of the four dresses that hung from a rope strung across one corner of the room. He slid his favourite, a fine red wool, off its hanger and inhaled its scent before taking off his dressing gown, stepping into the dress, and zipping it up at the back. He was slim enough for it to fit, although the fabric across the chest, unsupported by breasts, sagged and puckered. For some reason it was the sight of this, as he stood in front of the mirror, which brought the tears.

'W hy do you wear knickers?'

Stratton and Jenny were alone in the kitchen of the small, semidetached mock-Tudor house they occupied in the north London suburb of Tottenham. Sunday lunch was over, Jenny's two sisters and their husbands had departed to their homes up the road, and the washing up was done. Stratton was leaning back in his chair in a way forbidden to the children before they were evacuated because it weakened the joinery. Jenny was standing between his legs, her plump buttocks resting against the edge of the table. She folded her arms under her breasts and frowned slightly, considering the question. 'What do you mean, why?'

Stratton pulled on his cigarette, exhaled, and squinted at her through the smoke. Jenny Stratton's soft skin and round, dimpled face made her thirty years seem more like twenty-one. She had big green eyes, chestnut brown hair and a curvaceous body. After eleven years of marriage Stratton still watched the way that other men—including his brothers-in-law—looked at her, and felt a secret thrill of pride.

'I'm not trying to be funny,' he said. 'I'm curious.'

'Well,' Jenny's frown deepened. 'I wear them because they keep me warm, and they're comfortable—I'd feel strange without them. And they make me feel respectable.'

'You don't need to be respectable now. There's no one here.'

'Except you.'

'Except me. So if you come upstairs, I can keep you warm, and make you comfortable.'

Jenny raised her eyebrows. 'What, now? We've only just eaten.'

'It's not like swimming. And even if it was, it's been a good hour...'

Jenny looked around the kitchen as if there might be some objection hidden amongst the crocks and canisters, then stood upright and undid her apron. 'Why not?' she said.

Jenny laid her head on her husband's chest. 'All right, are you?' he asked, putting his arm round her.

'Oh, yes. Only...'

Stratton knew what was coming. It crossed his mind that she'd only agreed to come to bed in order to soften his mood for another onslaught about the children.

'I know we've talked about it,' she said, 'but—'

'We're not bringing them back, love. It isn't safe.'

Jenny twisted round to look at him. 'Nowhere's safe, is it? Not now. Not if the Germans come.'

'We don't know that they're going to come. And even if they do, Pete and Monica will be safer in Norfolk.'

'The Germans'll go to Norfolk, won't they? It's not that far from the coast, where they are. I keep imagining...What if there's an invasion and I never see them again? Or if they're killed, or...I think about it all the time, Ted. At least if they were with us we'd know, wouldn't we? We'd be together, and even if...if...'

'Don't, Jenny.' Stratton stroked her hair. 'We've got to give them a chance.'

'A chance to do what?' Jenny wriggled out from under his arm and sat up straight, her voice rising. 'To get killed? Or go to prison, or be slaves?'

'That won't happen.'

'How do you know it won't happen? Don't you care what happens to them?'

Stratton sat up. 'Of course I do. That's why they're staying put.'

'The Lever boys are back, and the Bells—'

'And they're running up and down the street all day, causing trouble. Pete and Monica need to be at school.'

'Doris wants to fetch Madeleine.'

Stratton sighed. Doris was Jenny's favourite sister.

'What about Donald? What does he think?'

'He's being as pig-headed as you are.'

'We're being sensible. I know you're worried, love, but honestly, they're best off where they are. There's kids being evacuated all the time, now.'

Jenny levered herself off the bed, and, turning her back on him, put on her dressing gown.

'We know they're being looked after properly now, at this new place,' said Stratton. 'I know it was bad, before—'

'Don't, Ted. I'll never forget when we saw them that first time. That horrible woman! I felt like a murderer for letting them go—'

'But we got it sorted out, didn't we? And this time they're happy. You said that yourself.'

'That Mrs Chetwynd sounds far too posh for us.' Jenny rounded on the mirror and started jabbing hairgrips back into place. 'With her big house...She'll turn them into little snobs. We won't be good enough for them any more.'

'Is that what's really worrying you?'

She spun round to face him, bashing the back of her hairbrush against the edge of the dressing table. 'She's got a castle in her garden!'

'It's a keep.'

'I don't care what it is! She's got servants, and...everything.' The last word was thickened by tears. As Jenny wrenched open the door, Stratton scrambled off the bed and took her in his arms.

'Come on, love. This isn't like you.'

'Let go!' Elbows pinioned—Stratton was a good eight inches taller, with a big chest and broad shoulders—Jenny thumped him ineffectually with the hairbrush.

'No. Not till you calm down.'

'They've got everything, Ted, everything we can't give them. A dog, and horses.'

'Well, Pete's always wanted a dog.'

'That's what I mean!'

Stratton rubbed her back for a moment, then tried a different tack. 'We've got horses.'

'No we haven't.'

'The coalman's horse.'

Jenny looked up at him, her laugh a cross between a sob and a yelp. 'Silly. I meant proper horses. Posh horses.'

'That's better. You know, love, if you're that worried, you could go and stay up there with them. I'm sure Mrs Chetwynd would know someone who'd take a paying guest.'

'And what would you do?' demanded Jenny. 'Starve?'

'I'd manage.'

'Of course you wouldn't. Not properly. I'm not leaving you, Ted.' She swatted him with the hairbrush, playfully this time. 'I don't want to hear any more about it.'

'All right then, you won't. Now, why don't you get back into bed, and I'll make us a cup of tea?'

Jenny's eyes widened. 'It's half-past five, Ted. We can't!'

'Why not?'

'What if somebody comes round?'

'We'll pretend we're not here.'

'What if it's Doris? Or Lilian?' Both Jenny's sisters had keys.

'They've only just left.'

'Two hours ago.'

'Come on...' Stratton kissed the top of her head. 'Stop arguing.'

Giggling, Jenny stood on tiptoe to kiss him back. 'You're a bad man, Ted Stratton.'

'Terrible,' Stratton agreed. 'Deplorable, in fact. A rotten ba—'

'Ted!' Jenny put a hand over his mouth. It was a game they often played in private. She liked to appear shocked by his language, and he dropped the milder swear words into his conversation to scandalise her. She'd be genuinely appalled, he knew, if she ever heard the sort of crudities that were par for the course in police work, and he was careful never to use those words around her.

'Honestly!' said Jenny. 'What with your language, and doing this in the middle of the afternoon, I don't—' She stiffened, and broke away from him. 'Someone's here. I can hear the key. One of them must have forgotten something. Let me get my things on. For heaven's sake...' She pulled off her dressing gown and scooped her blouse off the floor. 'Put your clothes on, you'll be quicker than me.'

Stratton groaned as the resonant boom of his least favourite brother-in-law issued from the hall. ''Ello, 'ello, 'ello! Anybody home?'

Reg Booth had a habit of reducing everyone to a single characteristic, as if they were merely supporting characters in the drama of his life. Stratton, being a policeman, was referred to as 'the long arm of the law', and his reluctant visits to Reg's house were always heralded with cries of 'Have you got a warrant?'

'What's he doing here?' Jenny whispered.

Stratton shoved his shirt into his trousers and his feet into his slippers. 'God knows. He must have borrowed Lilian's key. I'll go down, see if I can't get rid of him.'

Reg, a beefy man whose features seemed to have been slapped onto his face around a bulbous, pock-marked nose, always reminded Stratton of a music hall comedian. He secretly relished an image of Reg dressed in a loud suit and cowering under a proscenium arch while a furious crowd pelted him with eggs, rotten tomatoes and dead cats. His jokes, if they could be called jokes, deserved all that, and more.

Now, he was standing, legs wide apart, on the hall linoleum, brandishing an enormous and rusty sabre. 'Look at this beauty!'

'What is it?' asked Stratton.

'Arabic.' Reg gestured at the hilt with his free hand. 'Look at that workmanship. They used to ride into battle on camels with these.' He lunged forward with a warlike yell—Reg of the Desert—and narrowly missed the top of Stratton's ear.

'For God's sake, put it down. I don't want blood poisoning.'

Jenny clattered down the stairs looking flushed and patting her hair. Stratton noticed that her legs were bare, and wondered if Reg would pick up on it and put two and two together. He decided it was unlikely—Reg wasn't very observant at the best of times, and even if he did cotton to Jenny's dishevelled appearance, he probably wouldn't attribute it to what he leeringly referred to as (Stratton winced inwardly) 'conjugal doings'.

'What's happening?' asked Jenny.

'Reg has found an Arab sword,' said Stratton. 'Now all he needs is a camel to go with it.'

'What have you brought it round here for?' Jenny asked. 'It's filthy.'

Reg gave her a patronising smile. 'Never mind the whys and wherefores, my dear. Someone,'—he glanced meaningfully at Stratton—'has got to protect all you ladies from the Boche, even if it's only old Reg here. Experience counts for something, you know.' For the last nine months he had reminded them constantly of his service in the Great War, although, given the absence of medals or, indeed, corroborative evidence of any sort, Stratton very much doubted that his military career was as glorious as he made out.

Now he said, soothingly, 'I'm sure experience counts for a lot, Reg, but perhaps you should clean the sword up a bit before you go on parade with it. Where did you get it from, anyway?'

'Donald. Just been round to collect it. Belonged to one of his uncles, apparently—been stuck in the attic for years. He mentioned it when I asked him if he'd got anything we could use for the Defence Volunteers. Can't understand why he didn't tell me before. But that's why I'm here—you haven't got anything, I suppose?'

Stratton shook his head. Heaven help us, he thought, if the country's last line of defence is Reg with a camel sword. He'd heard one or two people—including Reg himself—say, 'If I go, I'll take one of them with me,' but he didn't know if it was truth or fashionable bravado. He also didn't know, he realised, what—if it came to it—he himself would do.

'Well, never mind. If you do think of anything,' Reg added, officiously, 'you'd better let me have it. We don't want valuable weapons getting into the wrong hands.'

As he turned to go, Jenny said, 'How's Johnny?' Stratton wondered why she'd asked. Reg's sullen nineteen-year-old son, recently turned down for the services because of flat feet, was not a comfortable subject at the moment. Even Lilian, who doted on the boy and could usually be relied upon to bring him into every conversation, hadn't mentioned him once over their midday meal.

'Fine! Couldn't be better.'

The heartiness wasn't convincing. 'Has he left his job at the garage?' Jenny asked.

Reg raised his eyebrows. 'Why should he want to do that? He's doing very well there. They think a lot of him, you know.'

'No, it was just...' Jenny shrugged. 'I saw him on Friday, out with a group of young lads. Hanging about. It was in the afternoon, and I just thought...Well, I was surprised he wasn't at work, that's all.'

'Probably out running an errand and saw some of his pals. They're like that at that age. High-spirited. Mark my words, your Pete'll be just the same.'

Listening to this, Stratton wondered if Reg, unable to cast Johnny as his brave soldier son, one of 'our boys' and all that went with it, had re-invented him as A Bit Of A Scamp. He felt a sudden prick of anxiety: if Johnny had got into bad company (and he was certainly capable of it) and his bloody idiot of a father couldn't, or wouldn't, admit that it was anything more than youthful high-jinks, the boy might easily go right off the rails and end up in prison. 'Do you want me to have a word with him?' he asked.

'Good Lord, no! Let the boy have his fun. God knows, we all need a bit of that, don't we? Especially in these troubled times.' He walloped Stratton between the shoulder blades in a manner that was hard enough to qualify as painful, rather than jovial, and continued, 'Too strait-laced, old boy, that's your problem. Never off duty. He'll mind his p's and q's all right, never you fear. Now, I must go forth. Duty calls, and all that. A fine repast, my dear, if I may say so,'—Jenny winced as he patted her cheek—'a veritable feast.'

He opened the front door, executed a couple of deep knee bends on the porch, and marched off down the garden path with the sword clasped to his shoulder. As they stood watching him go, Stratton thought, I should have realised there was no point offering to talk to Johnny. Even if Reg was worried about his son—and surely, for all his faults, the man had to have some feelings—Stratton was still a comedic policeman to him, not a real one. He'd often imagined Reg in the beery bonhomie of some saloon bar with his fellow commercial travellers, joking about having a copper in the family—'Have to watch your step with old Ted around, aye, aye!' All policemen were plodding, helmeted buffoons, just as all Scotsmen were mean and all land-ladies, termagants: life as a seaside postcard.

'You know,' said Jenny, shutting the door, 'I feel sorry for him.'

'Why?'

'Because he doesn't realise, does he? Do you know,' she continued, 'when Monica was six, she asked me, "Why does Uncle Reg keep telling jokes when nobody ever laughs?" I didn't know what to tell her. I could hardly say it's because he's so conceited he thinks we've all missed the point.'

Stratton glanced at his wife to make sure that mentioning Monica wasn't going to bring on more tears, but she seemed all right. Nevertheless, he decided it would be best to change the subject. 'Do you think Johnny's in some sort of trouble?'

'I'm not sure. It just seemed a bit odd. I mean, he should have been at work and he was just lounging about. I recognised one of the boys, the Dawsons' son. You know, the one who's been in trouble.'

'Why didn't you tell me?'

'Well,' Jenny busied herself with the kettle, 'when you came in from work yesterday, you went straight out to the allotment, so I haven't really had a chance.'

'You could have told me on Friday.'

'Yes, but...Well, you seemed a bit preoccupied.'

Mabel Morgan and those bloody teeth, thought Stratton. 'I was,' he admitted. 'Something at work. Do you think Reg'll talk to him?'

'No. And if he did, Johnny wouldn't listen. He despises Reg and now Reg has got something over him because he fought and Johnny can't. Honestly, Ted, I don't see it getting any better.'

Christ, thought Stratton, I hope me and Pete aren't going to be like that. 'Did you mention it to Lilian?' he asked.

'No point.' Jenny shrugged. 'You know what she's like, thinks he makes the sun shine.'

Stratton sighed. Jenny was right. Lilian had been finding excuses for Johnny ever since he could walk. 'There's something not right,' Jenny said, spooning tea into the pot. 'I know it.' Stratton wanted to say something reassuring, not just about Johnny, but the invasion, the children—all of it—but he couldn't think of anything. He suddenly felt the need to be by himself for a while, to potter, and perhaps turn things over a bit in his mind. When Jenny handed him his tea, he said, 'I think I'll take this out to the shed, love. God knows it needs tidying up, and I've been too busy down at the allotment.'

'You do that. I think I might put my feet up for ten minutes. Have a read of the paper.' Stratton knew this was Jenny's way of telling him that everything—for the time being—was all right. He wanted to kiss her, but, feeling that would be making too much of it, he contented himself with turning in the doorway to say, 'What about Reg with that old sword, eh?' and receiving a smile in return.

CHAPTER

5

Diana Calthrop emerged from the tube at South Kensington and stood on the pavement looking around her. She glanced at her watch—three minutes to four—then checked her appearance in a shop window. A tall, elegant blonde stared back with a slightly haughty expression; clearly, she did not look as tense as she felt. She tried to breathe slowly and deeply as, keeping her back to the street, she removed the glove from her left hand, slipped off her wedding ring, and dropped it into her handbag. 'It's just over there.' Diana jumped. Her colleague Lally Markham, equally tall and equally blonde, was standing behind her. She glanced in the direction Lally had indicated, and saw an innocuous-looking tea room.

'You're clear about what to do?'

Diana nodded.

'Ready?'

'As I'll ever be.'

'Remember, talk about normal things—the blackout, the weather—and if you can mention that you work at the War Office, so much the better. The thing is to get her to trust you.'

'I'll do my best.'

'Off we go, then.'

As they crossed the road, Diana prepared herself by making a mental inventory of what she knew about the Right Club: organisation of right-wing anti-Semites against the war, founded by Peverell Montague, Unionist MP since 1931, friends with Lord Redesdale, the Duke of Wellington, Lord Londonderry and Sir Barry Domvile, all members of the pro-Nazi Anglo-German Fellowship. Nothing much to connect him with Mosley—at least, not recently—but he was acquainted with William Joyce. Has accused the press of being Jew-ridden and distributed pamphlets with anti-Semitic verses, but since the arrest of Mosley the organisation has been under the control of Montague's wife...

The bell clanged as they entered the tea room. Diana was surprised by the interior; she'd expected something grander, or at least something less ordinary. The place was clean, but not in any way showy: polished wooden furniture, white napery, bowls of paper flowers, landscape prints on the walls, and a few people sitting, either singly or in pairs, at the tables. Diana and Lally arranged themselves at a table halfway down the room and ordered tea from the waitress.

After ten minutes sipping, smoking and chatting, the bell clanged again. Lally, who was facing the door, murmured, 'She's here.' Diana started involuntarily, and Lally said, 'It'll be fine. Don't be nervous. Just be yourself.' Her voice and expression—kind and slightly anxious—reminded Diana so much of her mother's just before Diana's coming-out ball that, for a moment, she wanted to laugh. She heard footsteps behind her and watched as Lally's face became animated, her eyebrows arching in an expression of delighted surprise. 'Mrs Montague!'

The real Mrs Montague looked somewhat heavier than her photographs had suggested, but her dark, liquid eyes and wide smile were turned on Lally just as brightly as they had been on the camera lens. Her light-grey suit, worn over a discreetly patterned blouse, was modishly severe, and a smart little hat completed the costume.

She could be my mother-in-law, or anyone I know, thought Diana, then wondered why she should be surprised by this.

'Do come and sit down!' cried Lally. 'That is,' she added, 'if you're not meeting anyone.'

'Thank you.' While Mrs Montague took off her gloves and drew up a chair beside Diana's, Lally continued to gush. Diana, watching her, was amused in spite of herself.

'It's marvellous you're here,' said Lally, 'I've so wanted you to meet my dear friend Diana Calthrop. We've known each other for years, haven't we, darling?'

Diana smiled. 'Oh yes. A very long time. How do you do?' She held out her hand.

The shake was perfunctory—a touch of the fingers—but the eyes still looked warm. Lally offered cigarettes, ordered more tea, and exclaimed several times about the serendipity of the meeting before saying, 'Diana and I were just saying how we miss our dogs, now that we're both in London so much.'

'Yes,' said Mrs Montague, 'It's dreadful, but what can one do? I must stay, for Peverell's sake—that's my husband, Miss Calthrop—and my little Dash would simply hate it here.'

Diana almost corrected the 'Miss' but remembered just in time that she was not, so far as the Right Club was concerned, supposed to be married. Instead she said, 'Dash? What a nice, old-fashioned name. Queen Victoria's dog was called Dash, wasn't it?'

'Was it?'

'I read it somewhere. A spaniel, I think.'

'Such nice little dogs...Are you interested in history, Miss Calthrop?'

'Oh, yes! I don't know much, of course, but I enjoy reading about it.'

'Diana's terribly clever,' said Lally. 'We used to have our lessons together and I was always stupid, but she was frightfully good at remembering things.'

'Only if I was interested in them,' said Diana hastily. 'I was always abysmal with figures. Not that it matters in my work, of course, but—'

'She's being modest, Mrs Montague,' said Lally. 'She's in the War Office.'

'That must be interesting.'

'Not really.' Diana grimaced. 'I'm in the filing department. Surrounded by pieces of paper.'

After a moment's pause, the conversation turned to the latest shortages in the shops, and a quarter of an hour's inconsequential chat followed before Diana glanced at her watch and said she didn't realise it was so late and she must leave at once, but she hoped that they'd meet again. Mrs Montague replied, blandly, that she hoped so, too, and five minutes later Diana found herself in the street, where she hailed a taxi.

'Dolphin Square, please.'

'Yes, miss.'

Once settled in the taxi, Diana took a deep breath, then fished out her compact and powdered her nose. She felt a lightness, an odd sort of internal buzzing, that she'd never experienced before—extreme exhilaration coupled with relief. Staring out of the window at the passing crowd leaving their offices and scurrying along the pavement, she thought, none of you know. I'm in this war—right in it—and none of you have any idea.

Since she'd left her mother-in-law's home in the country (she and Guy had shut up their house when his regiment had been sent abroad) she'd never had so much fun in her life. Staying with Guy's mother had been ghastly. They'd never got on and, unrestrained by Guy's presence, Evie had sniped continually about Diana failing to conceive and then, as she put it, 'managing to lose the baby'. When the war broke out, Diana, feeling both useless and a failure, had been desperate to get a job—any job—but had no idea of how this might be achieved. Even her London friends had found their attempts frustrated, and she had almost resigned herself to the suffocating monotony of a war spent in Hampshire when the miracle happened: Lally Markham, who really was an old school friend and who had managed to get work at the War Office, had offered to recommend her for a job. Evie, of course, had objected, but Diana had jumped at the chance, even though she didn't have a clue what Lally actually did. It wasn't just to escape, but to feel that she might, for the first time in her life, actually be doing something useful. Her references (and her social standing) being excellent, the woman in charge of female staff had sent her to work in the transport section at MI5.

Diana applied a fresh layer of lipstick, then sat back and closed her eyes. Right from the first day, when she'd reported to the Security Service's new offices in Wormwood Scrubs prison, she'd loved every minute, even though her work had only entailed sending out despatch riders and issuing petrol coupons.

The first time she'd met Colonel Forbes-James—with Lally, in the Scrubs canteen—she knew she'd made a good impression. 'He likes blondes,' Lally'd told her afterwards. 'Especially well-connected ones.' Diana knew that he was part of B Division—counter-espionage—but when she'd asked Lally about what it was that Forbes-James actually did, her friend had become vague and mysterious, hinting about special operations but refusing to provide any concrete information, other than that Forbes-James knew her father, Brigadier Markham, and had recruited her to work for him.

Diana had liked him immediately. His dark, round eyes, with their long lashes, and his button nose, gave him the slightly querulous charm of a pug. If she hadn't been so much in awe of his reputation in the department, she'd have been tempted to pat him.

He must have made some enquiries about her, because he'd invited her to lunch the following week and asked her about herself. When she told him she'd had a French governess, and had spent nine months in Bavaria learning German from an elderly countess who was desperate for foreign currency, he'd been impressed. To her astonishment, she'd found herself telling him everything: how her parents had died within three months of each other when she was nineteen; how she'd married Guy six months afterwards in a whirlwind romance and discovered, on her honeymoon, from his letters to Evie (*Dearest Darling, You will always have first place in my heart...*and signed, *Your infatuated* *boy*) how much he was in thrall to his mother. Then she'd told him about how, five years later, knowing full well her marriage had been a mistake and consumed by a sort of miserable wonder at her misjudgement, she'd found herself at Evie's house, lonely and unhappy, and how desperate she'd been to escape. When she got to know Forbes-James better, and understood more about his methods, she realised that her loquacity had been entirely due to his subtlety as an interrogator, but she never held it against him. She hadn't told him about the miscarriage, of course, nor that, instead of being sad about it, she'd felt first relief, and then a sense of guilt so extreme and remorseless that she had ended up resenting Guy for being the cause of it. It wasn't so much that she hadn't wanted a baby, but that she hadn't wanted Guy's baby, which was something she found hard to admit to herself, and certainly couldn't be mentioned to anyone else, ever.

The memory of what she'd told Forbes-James about Guy and Evie reminded Diana that her wedding ring was still in her handbag. She glanced down at her gloved hands and thought that, for the time being at least, it could stay there. She wasn't entirely sure what had prompted this decision, and she didn't want to examine it, either. Instead, she let her mind drift back to Forbes-James. A few days after that first conversation, he'd taken her out to dinner at the Savoy and asked her if she wanted to work for him. When he'd explained that his division, B5(b), was chiefly engaged in monitoring political subversion in Britain, she'd had to bite her lip to keep back a yelp of excitement. She'd imagined an immediate entrée to a world of intrigue and invisible ink, but, three days later, when she'd been transferred to his office, he'd merely handed her a stack of books and pamphlets and told her to learn as much as possible about fascism. Only when he was thoroughly satisfied with her knowledge did he explain that he wanted her to pass herself off as a sympathiser so that she could, with an introduction from Lally, infiltrate the Right Club. By that time she knew all about the organisation, but she'd been vaguely surprised that, after the arrest of Mosley, such things could still exist. 'Hydra's heads,' he'd told her. 'There are still a lot of very influential people who don't like the way things are going. Our job is to make sure they don't do any damage.'

Now, she'd established contact. The meeting seemed to have gone pretty well, although she needed to hear Lally's verdict in order to be certain. Surely Forbes-James would be pleased? That was the most important thing...The taxi pulled up outside Dolphin Square. Diana stepped out, paid the driver, and, just managing to restrain herself from breaking into a run, passed through the gateway and across the gardens towards Forbes-James's flat in Nelson House.

CHAPTER 6

T he air was hot and oppressive. Joe Vincent sat on the top step of the Tivoli Cinema's fire escape behind the Strand, lit a cigarette and glanced sideways through the iron railings at the alleyway below. A man in a long apron was prodding a broom at the debris on the cobblestones, and Italian waiters from the Villiers Street restaurants lounged, shirt-sleeved and smoking, at kitchen doors. A youth among them looked up and waved, then ducked as an older man—his father, perhaps, or an uncle—aimed a blow at his head. Joe couldn't hear the words that justified this action, but he could guess what they were.

He'd spent the morning as he spent every Monday morning, making up the week's programme, joining together reels of film with acetone cement that reeked of pear drops and made his head ache. When he'd started in the cinema as a re-wind boy Joe had been amazed that it took over 8,000 feet of film to show a 90-minute picture, and that was without the second feature, newsreel, adverts or trailers: now, nine years later and a chief projectionist, he could have completed the job in his sleep— which he might as well have done this morning. He felt numbed by grief. Without Mabel, his flat seemed miserably empty, more so as the hours of Sunday had stretched endlessly, and he'd drifted about her room, touching her possessions, not knowing what to do with himself. He didn't want to see anyone, to talk, to eat, even to get drunk, and the memories—everywhere he looked—were unbearable. In the end, he'd given himself up to misery, lain on Mabel's bed and sobbed until he fell asleep.

He saw the boy who'd waved being hustled inside by the other waiters, and half-heartedly flapped a hand at their retreating backs. What did it matter if they stormed up the fire escape and punched him in the face? Before, he would have re-created the incident for Mabel, embellishing the youth's hand-someness, and perhaps adding a kiss, blown from the palm of his hand. They would have savoured it together, given the boy a name and a history, and amused themselves devising a romance, but now...The memory wasn't worth saving, because Mabel wasn't there to share it.

'Mr Vincent?'

Joe twisted his head and saw the laced-up shoes of Jim Wilson, who was standing by the metal-clad fire door. Wilson, chubby, round-faced and twenty-two, had replaced Joe's previous assistant, who'd been called up in April. Projectionists were reserved until the age of twenty-five: Wilson had a dicky heart, which made him ineligible for the forces, but Joe, who had regis-tered a month previously, was expecting his call-up any day now.

'It's getting on,' said Wilson.

'OK.' Joe got to his feet and flicked his fag end over the side of the steps. 'Start the non-sync. I'll be there in a minute.'

'Righty-o. There's a cup of tea waiting inside.'

Joe lingered for a couple of minutes on the fire escape, thinking of Mabel, before following Wilson into the stifling projection box. A faint whirring noise from the non-synchronised sound machine's motor preceded an orchestral swell that flowed from speakers to the auditorium below. As a second-run cinema, showing films at least a month after the Odeons and Gaumonts had done with them, the Tivoli didn't have an organ and had to make do with records instead.

Joe checked the projector fan, and then, peering through the porthole at the arriving audience, spotted a few regulars: the pretty redhead who reminded him of his sister Beryl, the limping, respectable-looking elderly man who, sure enough, was joined a couple of minutes later in their usual seats by an equally respectable-looking elderly woman and, judging by what the pair of them got up to when they thought no-one could see, she was not his wife. This, supported by the fact that none of the usherettes had ever seen them arrive or leave together, had been the foundation for one of Mabel's favourite fictions: according to her, the woman had been a missionary in Africa who succumbed to the brutish blandishments of a tribal chief before being returned to England in disgrace, and the man had a wooden foot and a possessive wife. Joe made an automatic mental note to report their presence to her, then remembered. It's going to keep happening, he thought, dully. Things Mabel did, things she said, things she liked to hear about...He stared down at the auditorium, and wished he'd told her about his one and only sexual encounter in a cinema, three days after his fifteenth birthday, when he'd gone, alone, to watch Garbo in *Anna Christie*, and a stranger had touched him. Hot with shame and hard as a rock, wanting it to stop but desperate for it to continue, he'd been horrified and thrilled at the same time. That had been his first time, and for days afterwards, he'd thought of nothing else. Even when, later on, he'd met other men that he knew—without knowing how he knew—were the same as him, he'd never discussed it. Normal people, of course, would consider it repulsive, but not Mabel. She would have understood. Why hadn't he confided in her?

'Good house, Mr Vincent?'

Wilson's question cut across his train of thought. 'Not really. About the same as last week.'

'Mr Jackson says it's the same everywhere,' said Wilson. Mr Jackson, seedy grandeur and sly fumbles (usherettes only, thank God), was the manager. 'He says it's the war.'

'Must be. We'd better get going.' As the auditorium lights went down, Joe walked round to the back of the first projector and started the motor, which spluttered, then whined into life. This week's offering was a British picture, *Contraband*, with Conrad Veidt and Valerie Hobson. Normally, Joe would have been eager to see it, but today he was indifferent. 'Tabs, please.'

The music was silenced, the curtains parted, and the programme began. Joe remained behind the projector for a moment, staring into space, only recalled to himself when Wilson asked for the second—or possibly even third—time, judging by his tone, 'You all right, Mr Vincent?'

All right? Of course he wasn't bloody all right. How could he be? But neither Wilson, nor anyone else at the Tivoli, knew anything about Mabel. Cinema enthusiasts to a man—and woman—they'd have been fascinated to learn that he'd shared his home with a star from the silent era, but he'd never told them. His sister Beryl knew about her, of course—they had got on well—and she'd have to be told. Yesterday, he couldn't face it, which meant he'd have to telephone her at work. They wouldn't like that—Beryl was a dressmaker for a snooty Bond Street designer—but it couldn't be helped.

'I'm fine,' he said.

Wilson looked unconvinced. 'You look as if you could do with some air,' he said. 'I can do the changeovers.' He patted the second projector. 'She's all threaded up.'

Joe remembered that he hadn't thought to check. Best, he thought, to leave the change-over to Wilson, who in any case was perfectly competent. In Joe's current frame of mind the unforgivable might happen and the audience be left staring at a white screen. 'Thanks,' he said. 'I'll be right outside.'

Back on the fire escape, Joe contemplated another cigarette, but with only four left to last the day decided to wait. Instead, he sat with his elbows on his knees and his chin on his fists, wondering why he'd never told Mabel about the man in the cinema.

Mabel, as good a listener as she was a talker, had invited confidences, and he'd told her a great deal about himself, but not about that first initiation in the smoky, anonymous darkness. Mabel wouldn't have judged him for it. The idea of judgement made him wonder whether she, herself, wasn't now being weighed against some heavenly ideal. What would she say? Some things about her he knew: marriage to Cecil Duke, who'd directed her in *The Dancing Duchess* and *Let's All Be Gay!*, her dramatic escape from the house fire that had killed him, and the operations she'd had to try and re-build the lids on her ruined left eye. But there were other things that remained mysterious: the way she always looked out of the window before leaving the house, the sleepless nights when she got up and walked about the flat, the way she'd shut herself in her room for hours at a time ('thinking, dear, that's all'). He hadn't pried, just accepted. But her death? He couldn't accept that. No warning, no note, just, well, just that. Death. Gone. Finished. Not there anymore. And with no explanation. It didn't make sense.

He got through the rest of the day in a sort of self-protective trance and walked home to Conway Street after the cinema closed. The hall floor and stairwell were covered in newspaper and the house permeated by steam from his landlady's washing and the odour of her stew—added to, subtracted from, boiled and rehashed throughout the week—which smelled, according to Mabel, like a permanent fart. Joe's involuntary smile at the memory of this description made him wince as he tiptoed down the passage, not wanting to alert Mrs Cope, who lived on the ground floor. She was, on the whole, a kind woman, but he'd endured several hours of her barely concealed appetite for what she termed 'the tragedy' at the weekend, and couldn't stand any more of it. He placed his foot carefully on the bottom step to make sure it wouldn't creak, thinking how he just wanted the day to be over.

It wasn't. When he reached the top of the stairs, Joe saw that the door to his flat was slightly ajar. He stood on the landing wondering if he'd accidentally forgotten to lock up before he left for work, and then, hearing a noise from within, was about to retreat when the door was flung wide open by a large man. In a blink, Joe took in the thuggish frame that bulged inside the blue serge suit, the five o'clock shadow under the threatening, tilted hat, the badly sutured scar that bisected one cheek, and the meaty whiff of body odour. He spun round and made for the stairs, but the man reached forward, grabbed his arm, and held on to it. All Joe's attention was riveted on the face—cavernous nostrils choked with black hairs, cracked lips and stale breath—that was an inch away from his own.

'Well, well, well,' said the man, his voice loud with jovial menace. 'Home at last. Don't be shy, come on in.' As he gestured towards the door, Joe saw that there was another man, smaller, younger—a boy gangster—behind him. 'We want to talk to you. You see, Mister Vincent,'—the big man prodded him in the chest with a nicotine stained finger—'you've got something we want.'

Stratton stood at one of the urinals in the station's toilet, gazing at the white tiles in front of him and worrying about Mabel Morgan's missing teeth. The inquest would be held in a few hours' time. Ballard would give evidence, and assuming the verdict was suicide, which it undoubtedly would be, that would be the end of it. Jenny had remembered Mabel: 'She was one of Mum's favourites. Ever so beautiful—great big eyes, a bit like Greta Garbo. What a way to end up, though.' It didn't amount to anything, that was the problem—just speculation—and it wasn't as if he didn't have enough to do already: a passer by who'd tried to intervene in a robbery at a jeweller's was lying critically ill in hospital, and a fight between two gangs had resulted in a fatal stabbing, with all eight participants claiming they had no idea who did it because they were looking the other way at the time. In any case, it was well nigh impossible to think clearly with Arliss, who was spectacularly flatulent, parping away in the cubicle beside him.

Stratton finished, buttoned himself up, and was washing his hands when Arliss emerged looking pleased with himself, a clear victor in the battle with his bowels. Stratton nodded at him, and Arliss, smoothing the front of his tunic, ambled over to join him at the basin. 'That young chap,' he said, without preamble, 'the pansy who lived with the Morgan woman, got picked up on Monday night. Or Tuesday morning, I should say. Down in Soho, it was.'

'Oh? What for?'

'Not for anything, Sir. Right mess, he was. Weaving about all over the place. Someone did a real job on him.'

Stratton stood back from the basin to wipe his hands on the towel, and Arliss, who had, apparently, no intention of using it himself, carried on, 'Got himself beaten up for being a nancy, I'd say.'

'Is that what he told you?'

Arliss shook his head. 'Wouldn't tell me, would he? His sort never do. Lovely black eye,' he continued with a relish that made Stratton feel uncomfortable. 'And they'd clobbered his face something terrible, sir.' He chuckled. 'Not such a pretty boy now.'

'Was he pretty before?' asked Stratton, guilelessly.

Arliss flushed. 'You know what I mean, sir. For those that way inclined.'

'You said they'd clobbered him. Was there more than one?'

'Don't know, sir. He wouldn't tell us.'

I bet you didn't try too hard to find out, either, thought Stratton. 'Do you think it was something to do with Miss Morgan?' he asked.

Arliss looked surprised. 'Why should it be, sir? It's him being like that, isn't it?' He shrugged. 'What do they expect?'

Stratton spent a long, sticky day in the interview room, talking to various gang members who had mysteriously forgotten who they were with the previous night and who swore on their own lives, their mothers' and their kiddies' that they had seen nothing, honest to God, straight up, and by six o'clock he was more than ready to pack it in and get off home.

He found Ballard in the General Office, talking to one of the clerks. 'How did it go?'

'Suicide, sir.'

'As we thought.'

'Yes, sir.'

'Did you see the man she lived with?'

'Yes, sir. Joseph Vincent. Been in the wars a bit since I last saw him, though.'

'Got beaten up, Arliss says.'

'I suppose it's to be expected, sir.'

Stratton sighed. 'Yes,' he said. 'I suppose it is.' Having secured Vincent's address from Ballard, he left the station and walked towards Fitzrovia.

Vincent's landlady, Mrs Cope, answered the front door with such speed that Stratton wondered if she'd been waiting in a pre-sprinting position like the Olympic runners he'd seen on the newsreels.

When he introduced himself and explained that he was looking for Mr Vincent, she ushered him into her parlour. 'Gone away, sir. Staying with his sister. I expect you've come about Miss Morgan. Terrible business, if you don't mind my saying, sir. Quite an upset. Shook me entirely rigid.'

Sensing that she could have gone on in this vein for quite a while, and not wanting to linger, Stratton interrupted. 'Did you speak to him?'

Mrs Cope shook her head regretfully. 'Haven't seen him since Sunday. Left me a note—just for a few days, he said. He was ever so upset. Mind you, I could have said a few things—told me she was his aunt and it turned out she was nothing of the kind. I don't want to speak ill of the dead, sir, especially since she used to be in the pictures, but I believe in clean living.' The last two words were given extra weight by a series of emphatic nods that made her chins wobble. 'I've said it before, but I'll not have that sort of thing under this roof.'

Stratton didn't set her straight—she'd probably have the poor bastard out on the street in an instant if she knew the truth—but said, soothingly, that he quite understood, and did she have the sister's address?

'You won't catch him there now, sir. He'll be at work. The Tivoli cinema. Is something wrong, sir? Only I heard that the inquest—I wasn't there myself, of course, but one of my neighbours told me—'

'Just a routine visit, that's all,' Stratton cut her off with a reassuring smile. 'Nothing to worry about.'

'Well, as I say, I don't want to speak ill of the dead, but—'

As she clearly did want to speak ill of the dead, and was about to get into her stride, Stratton interrupted again. 'As you say, Mrs Cope. Now, if you'll just let me have the address, I've taken up quite enough of your time.'

Reluctantly, she dug out a piece of paper, which he copied into his notebook. At the door, after a bit more business about it being wicked and a shame, and in her house as well, Stratton escaped.

At the end of the street, he looked at his watch and decided to postpone the matter. He didn't want to set tongues wagging by calling on Vincent at work—his enquiry was, after all, unofficial. He stopped outside the Tivoli on his way home, and established that it was closed on Sundays. This Sunday, he remembered, it would be Doris's turn to make dinner (the sisters took the Sunday midday meal in strict rotation). He wouldn't be required to peel spuds, his sole domestic task aside from polishing shoes, and one he secretly rather enjoyed. That meant he'd be able to see Vincent in the morning at his sister's. He opened his notebook and flipped through the pages—Beryl, her name was, in Clerkenwell Road. Jenny wouldn't be too happy about it, but at least she'd be pleased this evening when he turned up in time for supper. Then he could spend a couple of hours at the allotment, as he often did on summer evenings, planting celery and Brussels sprouts, and mulling things over in his mind. It wasn't just his itchy feeling about Mabel Morgan, there was the sheer hopelessness of finding a witness for the gang fight, too. It was a fair bet that none of the club owners, bar staff, prostitutes or residents who might have seen something would volunteer any information—at least, not if they knew what was good for them. Stratton didn't blame them. He'd seen what could be done with a razor. Rumour had it there was one bloke who'd been held down while two men from a rival gang played noughts and crosses on his buttocks. Seventy-five stitches, he'd heard, but at least it wasn't visible—unlike your face. Stratton winced. Then there was his bloody nephew, Johnny, as if he didn't have enough to worry about, what with the invasion, and Jenny getting all het up about the kids...

Still, the first broad beans should be about ready. Perhaps he'd be able to take some back for Jenny. She'd like that.

Diana, seated at her dressing table, smoked a cigarette and contemplated her pots and brushes. The Tite Street flat, procured by Lally and just a walk away from Dolphin Square, was proving very satisfactory: bedroom, small kitchen, and a shared bathroom on the landing with a heater that gave off a rather ominous smell, but could usually be relied upon for hot water. It was cosy, and, with the help of a maid, fairly easy to maintain despite her lack of practice. So much nicer, she thought with satisfaction, than the cavernous, ecclesiastical gloom of Evie's vast manor house (re-built in 1859 in a style Diana privately thought of as Widow's Gothic).

Diana spat in her eye-black, dabbed it with the miniature brush provided, and applied it to her lashes. Evie actually seemed proud of the fact that the wretched place was uncomfortable; it was as if each draughty corridor, rotting tapestry and clanging pipe was a personal triumph. And then there was Guy's old room, a time-capsule of his adolescence, or maybe not. Her husband, Diana reflected, had never really managed to surmount that particular phase of life. The contents of his bedroom—coloured prints of battleships tacked to the panelled walls, stamp albums, toy soldiers, collections of birds' eggs and far too many tinted photographs of his mother—reflected him now, mentally stalled at the age of fifteen. Diana patted her face with powder and wondered if the army would succeed in 'making a man' of him. Judging by his infrequent letters (she'd bet her last penny that Evie received three for every one addressed to her), it wasn't likely; the war, for him, seemed to be merely a continuation of the Eton Corps. Of course, they weren't allowed to say much about what was actually happening, but all the same...

She was about to pick up her lipstick when a sudden memory of the incompetence—there was no other word for it—of their wedding night made her turn from the mirror in shame. She'd schooled herself never to think of it; even sitting here, alone, the humiliation was unbearable. It had been so unexpected. After all, Guy was eight years older than she, and his veneer of worldliness had led her to believe that he must know all about that sort of thing, that he would take the lead and...well, initiate her. She'd been so much in love with him, wanting to give herself—how revoltingly, coyly romantic it all seemed now! She'd lain there, waiting for it to happen, and...

Leaning forward, she massaged her temples hard, trying to squeeze the image out of her mind. The real problem, she thought, is that I've never understood about love. There hadn't been much of it in her childhood: her father's affections had been lavished on dogs and horses, but not people, and her mother, undemonstrative and distant, had never petted or praised. When her parents died, Diana felt that she'd never really known them at all. In childhood, she'd hankered after the sort of love one read about in books, the big, warm family, full of laughter and games and good counsel. Later, she'd yearned for the love she'd seen on the screen, the longing, the passion and the final kiss that made you good, made you whole, made you belong. When handsome, dashing, worldly Guy came along, she'd thought her feelings were real; it was only later that she realised, with horror, that he could have been almost anyone. Desperately clutching at what she lacked, she'd manu-factured the emotions by a process not unlike self-hypnosis, and fitted them to him. And Guy had needed a wife, hadn't he?

Evie, she'd later learned, had been urging him to marry, and Diana, the young, pliable orphan, was, in her eyes, perfect.

Not any more. Diana grimaced at herself in the mirror, then stuck out her tongue, but still the image of that first, terrible night refused to be jollied away, and anyway, it was a half-hearted effort. With her mother dead, a married aunt had taken it upon herself to give a vague sort of pep talk about male urges and wifely duties. She'd said it was bound to hurt a bit at first, but one soon got used to it and might actually come to find it not unpleasant and, if one was lucky enough to have a considerate husband, rather comforting. It would have been a lot more useful, thought Diana bitterly, if she'd simply told me how to—and here she deliberately framed the forbidden word with her lips as if launching it across the room.

Then at least she would have known what was supposed to happen. When it eventually had happened, on the last night of their honeymoon, after a week of avoiding each other's eyes and not mentioning it, she'd lain on her back, willing herself to relax but afraid to move in case it put Guy off. Watching his face, or what she could see of it in the dark, she'd decided that his grimace and the noises he made were less to do with passion and more with the sheer effort of getting the thing done.

Diana was about to finish her make-up when she noticed that her left hand was still unadorned. She got up and rummaged inside her handbag until she found her wedding ring. She contemplated it for a moment, then opened her jewellery box, dropped it in, and closed the lid. Then, in a series of swift, deliberate movements, she applied her lipstick, blotted it with a tissue, gave her nose a last dab of powder, and adjusted the neck of her evening dress. Gathering up her bag, gloves and coat, she locked the door of the flat behind her, and went out into the street.

The party was in Mayfair, at the home of Jock Anderson, an admirer of Lally's, for whom Diana had worked at Wormwood Scrubs. She asked the taxi to stop at Piccadilly Circus. It was a warm evening, her new shoes weren't pinching too much, and she wanted to compose herself a bit before entering a room full of people—somehow, the cab ride hadn't quite done the trick. She was gradually getting used to arriving at places unaccompanied, but she still felt diffident about it. The parties she'd attended with Guy were full of people of his age, not hers, and she'd usually found them pretty dull. The parties she went to now were much more lively. There was always someone to take you on to a night-club afterwards, and somehow the age of the guests no longer seemed to matter. She supposed that was because of the war: the feeling that one might as well have a bit of fun while there was still time. The thought of invasion frightened her, as it must, she thought, frighten most people, but it didn't do to talk about it.

She wondered who would be at Jock Anderson's party. Lally certainly, and, she hoped, Colonel Forbes-James. He'd been so pleased with her on Sunday when she'd gone to Dolphin Square to report on her introduction to Mrs Montague. She allowed herself to bask for a moment in the memory of how he'd nodded and smiled and pushed a wrapped present into her hand as she'd left his flat. It had turned out to be a jar of bath salts. She suddenly wondered how he'd come by it. It was impossible to think of him doing anything as frivolous as wandering about Selfridges selecting gifts, but how else would he have acquired such an item?

It was at this point, as she passed the entrance to the Royal Academy, that Diana became aware, although she couldn't have said quite how, that someone was following her, and that, judging by the footsteps, it was a man. She tried to persuade herself that this couldn't be the case, and when that failed, decided to put it to the test. She slowed down. He slowed down. She quickened her pace. He quickened his. When she turned right into Old Bond Street he turned, too. Putting all thoughts of the white slave trade, if it actually existed (people always knew someone who knew someone), out of her mind, she crossed the road and turned left into Stafford Street. He followed, and when she turned left again, into Albemarle Street, he stayed with her. With her destination now in sight, she was no longer worried. She marched confidently up the steps, rang the bell, and stood back to wait. Surely, she thought, he must give up now.

He didn't. In a matter of seconds, he was standing right behind her. She felt a prickle of fear. What the hell did he want? I'm not turning round, she thought. He can do whatever he likes, but I'm not going to pay any attention. In any case he'd look pretty stupid when Jock appeared—she just wished he'd hurry up—and gave him his marching orders.

She saw the door open, acknowledged Jock's smile, and then, before she could speak, he looked directly over her head and said 'Ventriss! Delighted you're here. Come on in.' Turning to Diana, he continued, 'I didn't know you two knew each other.'

'We don't,' said Diana, covering her embarrassment in the twin actions of handing her coat to Jock's elderly manservant and fussing, quite unnecessarily, with her evening bag. When she did look up—quite a long way up, because the man was very tall, even to her five feet seven plus high heels—she found herself staring into a pair of twinkling brown eyes. The man was older than her, about thirty, so ridiculously good-looking—and obviously aware of the fact—and so immaculate in his dress that she felt her chin lift automatically. 'This is Mrs Calthrop.' Jock sounded amused. 'Claude Ventriss.'

Diana drew off her glove, extended a deliberately limp hand, and murmuring, 'How d'you do?' swept down the hall without waiting for an answer. Spotting Lally in the crush of the front room, which was smoky, and, because of the blackouts, phenomenally hot, she secured a drink and, drawing the other woman aside, said, 'I've just been introduced to the most extraordinary man.'

'What's he called?'

'Ventriss. I didn't catch his first name.' This was a lie, but Diana felt entitled to it. After all, the man had followed her quite deliberately—he must have known jolly well where Jock's house was—and he was far too handsome for his own good. Lally laughed. 'His name's Claude. Works for us. I'm surprised you haven't come across him before, but now that you have...' she leant forward conspiratorially, 'Whatever you do, don't fall in love with him.'

'That's not very likely,' said Diana, with as much hauteur as she could muster.

'Isn't it?' asked Lally, innocently. 'Most women do. One sees it all the time.'

'Perhaps one does,' retorted Diana, 'But one's certainly not going to see it now.' As put-downs went, it wasn't exactly a trump, but it was the best she could manage in the circumstances.

Lally looked sceptical. 'Well, don't say I didn't warn you.' Before Diana could think of a response to this, they were joined by Forbes-James and several other people and the conversation, mercifully, took a different tack.

After a couple of hours, when she'd stopped feeling ruffled and was enjoying herself, Diana felt her arm being stroked. A deep voice said 'Excuse me,' and, as she was propelled around to face the speaker, a hint of conspiracy in the eyes of the man she'd been talking to—alarmingly similar to Jock's face in the hall earlier—told her exactly who the caresser was going to be. He said, 'I've been finding out all about you.'

'Have you really?'

Ventriss nodded. 'Really. I'm very impressed.'

'I'm so glad,' said Diana, sarcastically.

'You're quite the pin-up girl, aren't you?'

'Am I?'

'Oh, yes.'

Diana wasn't sure what to say next. She wished he wouldn't look at her with such a particular expression of dreamy greediness. She'd seen it on men's faces before, but they usually pretended to turn their attention elsewhere for a few seconds from time to time. Ventriss's gaze, continuous and unabashed, made her feel uncomfortable, and she knew that he wasn't going to be thrown off by mere *froideur*. 'Yes,' he repeated thoughtfully, glancing down at her naked left hand, 'Old F-J is very taken with you, Mrs Calthrop.' Remembering the sequence of events that had led her to consign her wedding ring to the jewellery box, Diana blushed. Hating herself for it, and trying to recover ground, she said, 'You know Colonel Forbes-James?'

'Of course,' he said absently, and carried on staring at her.

Diana pulled herself together. 'Why were you following me?' she challenged. 'You must have known I wasn't going the right way.'

'I liked the look of you.'

'You couldn't see me.'

'I couldn't see your face. But I promised myself that if you were a tart, I'd buy you, and if you weren't, I'd take you out to dinner.'

'You can't buy me that way, either.' Determined not to appear more rattled than she already was, Diana asked, 'Why did you think I might be a tart?'

Ventriss shrugged. 'It's not easy to tell from a woman's back. An expensive tart, of course,' he said, as an afterthought.

Diana tried to check herself—why was she even engaging in this ludicrous conversation?—but the words came out anyway. 'I might have been hideous.'

Ventriss shook his head. 'I knew you'd be lovely. Only beautiful women walk like that.'

'Like what?'

'With assurance. You know damn well people are looking at you.'

This, she thought, was a quite extraordinary thing to say; she'd been brought up to believe that it was wrong to think one was attractive or, indeed, noticeable in any way. 'Nobody will be looking at you, dear,' was how her Nanny had always put it. 'No I don't,' she said.

'Really?' Ventriss raised his eyebrows. 'I don't believe you.' After a moment's pause, he added, 'I'm going to leave you to your friends. I'll come and find you later, and we can have dinner.' He turned abruptly and disappeared into the throng.

Lally materialised at Diana's elbow. 'Fallen in love yet?' she asked.

'Certainly not.'

'Well, in that case, do you want to come on to the 400? Davey Tremaine's getting a party together. Unless you have other plans, of course.'

'No,' said Diana, firmly.
'You'll come, then?'
'Why not?'

Claude Ventriss appeared in the hall as Davey Tremaine was assisting Diana and Lally with their coats. 'You're ready,' he said. 'Good. We should be just in time for Sovrani's.'

'I thought you didn't have other plans,' Lally murmured.

'I don't.' Diana turned her back on Ventriss and mouthed, 'Help me.'

Lally shrugged. Diana glared at her, and turned to face Ventriss again. 'I don't want to have dinner with you,' she said.

'Yes you do,' said Ventriss calmly. 'You'll enjoy it.'

'I shan't.'

'Don't be childish. Of course you will.'

Diana glanced at Lally, who was patting her hair in front of a mirror and giving a very bad imitation of someone who wasn't listening. 'Escalope de Veau,' intoned Ventriss. 'Sûpreme de Volaille. Homard Thermidor. Sauté de Boeuf Stroganoff.'

'Do you know the entire menu by heart?' Diana snapped.

'Yes,' said Ventriss. 'And it's all delicious. Stop prevaricating and come with me.'

'No, I bloody well won't.'

'Huîtres Mornay. Coupe Jacques. Yes you bloody well will.'

'Have fun,' said Lally, sardonically.

Davey Tremaine winked. 'Pêche Melba,' he said. 'Crêpes au Citron.'

'Not you as well,' said Diana.

'You know you want to. Anyway, we're off. Enjoy yourselves!' Taking Lally's arm, Tremaine ushered her out of the front door and down the steps. Out-manoeuvred and cursing herself for being feeble, Diana decided it wasn't worth making a scene—she was pretty hungry, after all—and accompanied Ventriss into the street. 'Do you ever take no for an answer?' she asked.

Ventriss shook his head and stepped into the road to look for a taxi. Watching him, Diana thought, he probably doesn't get no for an answer—at least, not from women. Meekly, she allowed herself to be helped into the back of a cab, which had materialised as if by magic. (It would, she thought.)

'You'll have a lovely time,' said Ventriss, offering her a cigarette. 'Excellent food, and lots more people to admire you.'

'I told you, I don't want people to admire me.'

'No you didn't, you said you weren't aware of people looking at you. That wasn't true, either.' He smiled at her. 'No point in being beautiful if nobody's there to notice. It's wasteful.'

Diana was about to retort that she bet people noticed him all right when she realised that this would imply a compliment that she wasn't prepared to pay.

'No need to be coy about it,' he continued. 'You must know how lovely you are.'

'You sound like one of those stupid novels by men where the heroine looks in the glass and admires her beauty. It simply isn't like that. When a woman—any woman—looks at herself, all she sees are the things that need putting right. Now, can we please talk about something else?'

'Anything you like, Mrs Calthrop.' He glanced down at her (now gloved) left hand.

Feeling that it would be unbearable to go on like this for the rest of the evening, she said, 'Diana.'

After a slight pause, during which she prepared herself for something silly about goddesses or huntresses, Ventriss said, simply, 'Claude.'

'Are you French?'

'My mother. My father was English. Why don't you wear a wedding ring?'

She didn't answer immediately. She couldn't. Such a direct question was better than a lunge, she supposed, but not much. She looked at his handsome face and experienced, despite her best efforts to quell it, a sharp and disturbingly localised pang of excitement. For a split second she contemplated telling him that she was widowed, but refrained. However disappointing her marriage had turned out, to say that Guy was dead would be too much like wishing it, and she didn't. The other reason, much to her disgust, was a practical one: if he wished, Ventriss would easily be able to find out that Guy was still alive. She chose another lie. 'I'm afraid it was lost.'

'Oh?' Really, she thought, he might at least try to sound as if he believes me. Remembering Forbes-James's dictum about lying (tell a good one and above all stick to it), she looked Ventriss squarely in the eye. 'Yes,' she said, 'it went down a drain. I think my hands must have got thinner, because it just slipped off while I was washing them.'

'What a shame,' he murmured. 'Still, I daresay Mr Calthrop will buy a new one.'

'I'm sure he will,' said Diana, firmly.

'When he returns.'

'Returns?'

'I understand he's abroad, with his regiment.'

Diana laughed. 'You have been checking up on me, haven't you?'

'Yes. As I told you.'

'My turn to check up on you, then. Is there a Mrs Ventriss?'

'Not yet, no.'

They made desultory conversation for the rest of the journey. While they were talking, Diana mentally returned to the fact that he was unmarried several times, and felt—self-disgust rearing its head again, but more feebly each time—relieved. It had never been her habit to lie, or no more than anybody else did, anyway, but really, it was becoming surprisingly easy. Added to which, the knowledge that Ventriss didn't believe her story about the wedding ring was alarmingly enjoyable. She couldn't be tipsy, could she? She'd only had two drinks, although they had, admittedly, been pretty strong ones with a good deal of gin…all the same, she decided, she was quite sober enough to fend him off if he pounced. He'd already done the verbal equivalent, so a spot of mental preparation was definitely called for. Not that it wouldn't be nice, although, of course, quite inappropriate. And there would be the satisfaction of knocking him back when he thought she'd be his for the taking.

Having got this straight (or straight-ish) in her mind, Diana started to enjoy herself in earnest. The staff at Sovrani's clearly knew Ventriss well and made a great fuss of them both, and the dinner was as good as he'd promised. They talked about the war, but in a reassuringly off-hand way, and about Forbes-James. Diana knew she couldn't question Ventriss directly about what he did, any more than he could question her, but the fact that they both did it and knew they couldn't talk about it made it rather thrilling—to her, at least; she supposed it was nothing new for him. He must have taken any number of female agents far more experienced than she out to dinner and probably—the thought was at the back of her mind throughout the meal—bedded them afterwards.

While he settled the bill and chatted to the maitre d', she reflected that she hadn't laughed so much in months. It occurred to her that Guy, with whom she'd been—or thought she'd been— herself so terrifically in love, had never made her laugh much. Telling herself that the comparison was a dangerous one—she wasn't in love with Claude, and nor was she going to be—she snapped her compact shut and allowed herself to be helped into her coat with a full complement of bowing and general foreign flummery, before being escorted from the restaurant. The sudden fresh air made her aware of the effect of the wine she'd drunk with the meal, on top of the gin, and she allowed Claude to put a proprietorial arm round her as he ushered her towards another taxi. Like the first one, it seemed, despite the fact that it was now almost pitch dark, to appear out of nowhere as soon as they reached the kerb. Inside, after stating her address, she found that his hand was on hers (how had that happened?). It felt warm and nice, so she allowed it to remain there for the duration of the journey. She'd assumed that he would take the taxi on after seeing her to her door but he paid off the driver. She waited on the pavement while this was happening, feeling awkward. She must thank him—it would be unpardonably rude (as well as risky in the blackout) to rush off up the steps—but she wasn't at all sure of what might happen next.

As the cab drove off and Ventriss turned to face her, she was struck afresh, even in the near darkness, by his looks. She took a step back, felt her shoulders collide with the railings, and then, in short order, felt his hand on her neck, forcing her head up (not that it needed much help), his mouth on her mouth, his thigh between her thighs, and his other hand inside her coat, cupping her breast. After the initial surprise, Diana quickly found herself struggling between arousal—his mouth was lovely, and his thumb, expertly caressing her nipple with just the right amount of pressure, was giving her an alarmingly liquid feeling—and wondering how long she dared let it go on before slapping his face. Not that she wanted to, but he'd done the whole thing without so much as a preamble and that wasn't on, no matter how much she was enjoying it.

She was about to take action when he suddenly released her and, brushing her cheek with his lips, said, in a light, almost mocking tone, 'Goodnight, my dear. No doubt I'll see you soon.' Before she had time to do more than take a breath, the darkness had reduced him to mere footsteps on the pavement. Goodnight, my dear! As if she were a...a barmaid or something. Who the hell did he think he was? She peered after him, but the feeble circles of light from the veiled lamp-posts illuminated nothing but the ground beneath them. Serve him right if he falls over a dustbin, she thought, angrily, and listened for the satisfying sound of a clang and a curse. When none came, she turned, and, using the railings as a guide, groped her way up the steps and, after a furious scrabble in her bag for keys, through the front door. Flustered and thoroughly humiliated, she set about undressing and preparing for bed, attacking her face with cream and avoiding her eyes in the mirror.

Lying in bed, Diana found her anger giving way to self-recrimination. What the hell was she playing at? She'd been warned, hadn't she? Not that Lally or Jock, or anyone else for that matter, had been much help. Whatever she felt towards Guy, the man was fighting for his country, and she was carrying on like a...like what, exactly? She hadn't done anything—except allow herself to be kissed. And enjoy allowing herself to be kissed. And...For God's sake, she told herself irritably, it doesn't matter. In any case, she wasn't going to fall in love with him. She'd only be making the same mistake, and the consequences would be even worse. 'Oh, God!' She sprang out of bed, opened her jewellery box and, extracting her wedding ring, rammed it firmly back on her finger.

Stratton sat back and watched his brother-in-law Donald sipping his beer. They were in The Swan, which they frequented mainly because Reg was unequivocal in his preference for the pub in the next street. After another row with Jenny—actually, another abnormally loud conversation, which was as close as they ever got—about whether or not the children should come home, Stratton had decided to seek consolation in a quiet pint. The alacrity with which Donald had responded to his suggestion of a drink made Stratton wonder if he might not have spent his afternoon going over the same sort of ground with Doris. He determined to ask about this, but not until they'd exhausted the pleasurable subject of Reg's recent idiocies. 'They've been drilling at the football ground,' said Donald. 'Talk about the blind and the halt! There was one old chap staggering around with an assegai, for Christ's sake.' He took off his glasses and rubbed the top of his nose. 'I hope they frighten Hitler, because they certainly frighten me.'

'I saw that dirty great sword.'

'He insisted on taking it. I don't know what use he thinks it's going to be…I was in the toilet when he came round.' Donald shook his head. 'It's come to something when you can't even have a shit in peace.'

Stratton laughed.

'And when I said something about business being bad,'— Donald ran a camera shop—'he told me I'd be had up for spreading alarm and despondency! Said it was unpatriotic to complain. Mind you, I don't think he's doing too well, either, with the stationery orders...'

'Has he said anything to you about Johnny?'

'No, but he wouldn't, would he? I know Lilian's worried about him, though. She told Doris.'

'What did she say?'

'Bit of trouble at the garage. 'Course, Lilian says it's all their fault, says he's being bullied. Boot's more likely to be on the other foot, if you ask me.'

Stratton nodded. 'What did Doris say?'

'Not much she could say. You know Lilian.' Donald shrugged. 'I'm surprised she hasn't said anything to Jenny.'

'Not yet. But Jenny said she'd seen him loafing with some boys when he should have been at work, so...' After a few more shrugs, and oh wells, and some general stuff along the lines of don't-meet-trouble-halfway, they relapsed into a companionable silence. One of the things Stratton liked about Donald's company was that he knew when there wasn't anything more to be said. Unspoken between them was the knowledge that Johnny was a bad lot and Reg was a fool, and it was this, as well as marriage into a large and close-knit family, that had helped to cement their friendship. They'd never have criticised their wives to each other—not that Stratton had ever felt the need, and he suspected that Donald was the same—but they were both aware of their status as outsiders: Stratton, because he'd grown up in rural Devon (his accent, which had charmed Jenny when they first met, had been gradually eroded by years of contact with hard London vowels) and Donald because of his Scottish parents.

'Talking of children,' said Stratton, 'Jenny keeps saying we should have our two back home.'

'Yeah...' Donald sighed into his pint. 'Doris is the same about Madeleine. I keep telling her it's not safe, but...It's a funny thing. You get into the habit of not bothering each other, but all the time when we're not talking about it, I know she wants to and she's biting her tongue.'

'I know what you mean.' Stratton thought of Jenny that afternoon, staring through the taped window into the garden, her beautiful green eyes moist with unshed tears. She had claimed—in a tight voice that declared I-don't-want-to-discuss-it but meant exactly the opposite—to be watching the birds. 'God knows I miss them—even the squabbling and the racket. D'you know, I found myself in Pete's room the other night, reading one of his books? *Winnie the Pooh*. Bloody silly.'

Donald nodded. 'I've done a few things like that myself. Can't blame the women though—it's a lot harder on them, and—' His expression changed abruptly. 'Christ, what's he doing here?'

Stratton, who had his back to the door, said, 'It's not, is it?'

'It bloody is, and he's seen us.' Donald raised his hand in a halfhearted greeting. 'He's brought Farmer Giles with him. And the Major.' Stratton half turned in his seat to see Reg's porky buttocks pushing the tail of his jacket into divergent halves as he laid the camel sword, now clean and polished, reverentially on the floor before straightening up and patting his pockets for change. Next to him, bearing a pitchfork, prongs up, as if it were a standard, was Harry Comber, the grocer, etiolated and balding. Behind them was Major Lyons, a small septuagenarian, stiff and tweedy with bushy eyebrows, who always made Stratton think of a malevolent cairn terrier.

'I don't believe it!' Donald did a dramatic double-take. 'He's actually standing a round.'

Reg's meanness with money was legendary. He regularly subjected the rest of the family to unsolicited advice about house-hold savings, including—until he'd cut his arse on the remains of an acid-drop—the practice of using grocers' bags and torn up newspaper in the toilet.

'Shame you haven't got a camera with you,' said Stratton. 'We could capture the moment for posterity.'

Donald rolled his eyes. 'He's coming over.'

Reg, pint in hand and trailed by the others—at a respectful distance, because the sword, jammed underneath his arm, was weaving dangerously behind him—ambled over to greet them. 'Well met, indeed! Off duty, are we?' He winked, as though he'd caught Stratton doing something he shouldn't, made an expansive gesture, slopping beer on Donald's shoulder, and then, having ascertained that both their glasses were well over the halfway mark, said, 'Can I get you gents anything?'

'We're fine, thanks,' said Stratton.

'I can't think why you come in here,' said Reg, plonking himself on an empty chair. Donald opened his mouth, then shut it again, leaving the obvious answer—because you don't—hovering in the air. 'Don't mind if we join you?' Reg continued, pulling out the chairs next to him for Comber and Major Lyons.

'So why are you here?' asked Stratton.

'Bit of a crush at The King's Head. Just come off duty, you know.'

'We gathered,' said Donald.

'Got our armbands, you see.' Reg rotated his right arm towards them so that they could make out the letters LDV against the white cloth. Comber and the Major moved likewise, the latter letting out an affirmative yap as he did so. After a moment, Stratton, seeing that some response was called for, gave a hearty, 'Jolly good,' and raised his pint. 'Cheers!'

A moment's arm-raising, toasting and theatrical supping noises ensued, during which Stratton avoiding looking at Donald, and then Comber, lowering his glass, said, 'Candidly, I think this invasion stuff is all nonsense. It's Hitler's last throw. He wants to get the war finished before winter.' He lowered his voice. 'There's going to be famine in Europe.'

The Major looked disconcerted but contented himself with, 'Now we know where we are.' Stratton tried to remember exactly how many times he'd heard this remark in the last week, and felt a surge of irritation. 'I'm buggered if I do,' he said.

There was a short pause before Reg and Comber started to speak at once, Reg giving way with a small, fruity belch and applying himself once more to his pint as Comber launched into a long and obviously well-rehearsed spiel about how, candidly, there would be no food left in Germany by mid-October and how, candidly, dogs and cats were already being killed en masse because there was nothing for them to eat and how, candidly, the German people wouldn't put up with it for a second longer than they had to and then, candidly, Hitler would be done for. Stratton toyed with the enjoyable possibility of telling Comber, candidly, to fuck off, but a glance at Donald confirmed that this was impossible.

After ten more minutes of Comber's pontificating, a kick from Donald made Stratton gulp down the rest of his drink—waste of decent beer, but it couldn't be helped—remark, untruthfully, that Jenny would have his guts for garters if he stayed out too long, and depart, with Donald, amidst a barrage of jovial advice about not upsetting the little woman and injunctions from Comber and the Major to give our regards to your good ladies.

'We're fucking done for,' Donald remarked, as they walked back to Lansdowne Road.

'I know,' said Stratton. 'All that stuff about famine in Germany. He's conveniently forgotten about Dunkirk. Magnificent retreat, my arse! You can't win wars by evacuating people. It's just wishful thinking. Worst thing is when you find yourself doing it.'

'Yeah…Not like Comber, though.'

'God, no. I just keep thinking about how nice it'll be when we're together again as a family—what we were saying before.'

'If it happens.'

'Do you think it won't?'

'Don't know.' Donald didn't look at him. 'Best not to think at all, really. Mind you, having to listen to people like Comber talk a lot of piss doesn't help much.'

'They're enjoying it, though.'

'You'd enjoy it too if you were married to Joan Comber.'

'That's true.' Mrs Comber was a large, raw-boned woman, whose face bore an alarming resemblance to Stan Laurel's.

'You'd take any excuse to get out of the house.'

'Do you think they still...'

Donald grimaced. 'Would you?'

'No, but I wouldn't in the first place. Change the subject, for Christ's sake.'

'To what?' asked Donald. 'It's all pretty fucking gloomy, isn't it?'

'Yes,' said Stratton. 'It fucking well is.'

'Reg is a stupid old fart, isn't he?'

'He's a fucking stupid old fart.'

They grinned at each other. They'd always enjoyed the harmless, if juvenile pastime of swearing in each other's company. Normally, they were more inventive, even laboriously so, but at the moment, just being crude seemed to be enough to relieve their feelings. Stratton had always felt that the fucks, shits, and occasional cunts that oiled their conversation were like the visible tip of a vast sunken iceberg of things that he thought or felt, but that couldn't be spoken without revealing himself to be malicious, misanthropic, self-pitying, uncaring, arrogant, lecherous, cowardly, or some appalling combination of all of them. He'd occasionally wondered if Donald saw the swearing thing in the same way but that, again, was something quite impossible to put into words. When they parted in front of Donald and Doris's gate, two doors down from his own, Stratton felt oddly comforted. The conversation had provided confirmation that he did, as the Major had said, know where they were: in the shit, and without a shovel. There was, he thought, as he unlocked the front door, a sort of grim satisfaction to be taken from this.

CHAPTER 10

Jenny looked resigned when Stratton announced that he had to take the bus into London the following day, but, having secured several promises that he would be back in good time for lunch at Donald and Doris's, she kissed him and waved him off. The address Mrs Cope had given him for Joe's sister turned out to be a flat in the Peabody Buildings on Clerkenwell Road. Looking round the courtyard at the glazed brick entrances and rows of wash houses, Stratton wondered if Beryl Vincent had had the tenancy for long, and whether she was much older than Joe and would be over-protective of him. He checked the number—12—and found the right staircase. The concrete steps that smelled strongly of carbolic, and the two clean rag mats and row of potted geraniums at the top announced that Beryl, who, in Stratton's mind, had acquired the violent irascibility of a harridan, was house-proud.

He adjusted his hat, squared his shoulders, and knocked. After a bit of scuffling and soft murmuring, the door opened enough to show the red, curly head and saucy eyes of a pretty woman in her mid-twenties. 'Miss Vincent?'

The curls bobbed as she looked him up and down. 'Who's asking?'

'Detective Inspector Stratton, West End Central. Are you Miss Beryl Vincent?'

'Yes.' The girl's whole face, including her delightfully pert nose, crinkled in a frown. 'Is it Joe you want?'

'Yes, Miss Vincent. May I come in for a moment?'

'Of course. I'll go and wake him.' Beryl opened the door wider, revealing herself to be dressed in slacks and a sweater, and admitted him to a small room furnished with two easy chairs, a gas fire, a table heaped with slippery-looking fabric, a dressmaker's dummy and a sewing machine. 'I hope I'm not disturbing you,' he said.

'Oh, no. As a matter of fact, I was just about to make some tea,' said Beryl. 'Would you like a cup?'

'Please,' said Stratton.

She gestured towards a door behind her and said, in a lowered voice, 'Joe's in there. You won't be…He's quite upset about what happened, and we didn't expect…Well, what with the inquest and everything…I mean, I don't know what it is you want, but he's not very…'

Seeing her floundering—even if she knew about Joe, she was hardly going to say anything along the lines of, he's a pansy so he's got good reason not to trust the police—Stratton said carefully, 'I know that your brother was very…attached…to Miss Morgan. I just need to ask a few more questions, I shan't keep him long.'

Beryl smiled just long enough for Stratton to catch a glimpse of pretty, if rather squirrelly, teeth, invited him to sit down, and withdrew to Joe's bedroom. Listening to voices from within, he was sure that Joe had been awake before he arrived, and was now in a state of panic.

A shrill whistle brought Beryl racing from the bedroom— 'Joe's just getting dressed, tea ready in two shakes,'—before she disappeared into what had to be a very tiny kitchen and re-appeared with a tray, which she placed on the only clear corner of the table. 'Have to be careful,' she said, 'if I spill anything on this lot I'll never hear the last of it.'

'Are you a dressmaker?'

Beryl nodded. 'I work at Madame Sauvin's in Bond Street, but we've been so busy recently. You wouldn't think people would want evening dresses, would you, with things the way they are. Sugar?'

'No, thanks.'

Accepting the cup of tea, Stratton asked, 'Did you know Mabel Morgan, Miss Vincent?'

'Oh, yes. Not like Joe did, of course, but we got on ever so well. I couldn't believe it when I heard. Look...' Beryl leant over the back of the unoccupied armchair and pulled some complicated-looking pale pink knitting, strung on three needles, from behind the cushion. 'Bed socks. I was making them because she used to complain about her feet getting cold in the winter. I was sat here last night, right where you are now, listening to the wireless, and I must have been knitting away for ten minutes before I remembered...It wasn't right, her dying like that. I don't know what to do with this, now,' she added forlornly.

'What about someone in your family?'

'There's nobody. Mum died when we were small, and Aunt Edna—that's who brought us up—she passed away a couple of years ago.'

'What about your father?' asked Stratton, adding hastily, 'Not that you could give them to a man, of course.'

'He was killed in the last war. We didn't really know him—at least, Joe didn't, because he's younger than me. It's just the two of us now. You won't be too hard on Joe, will you?'

'I promise.' Stratton smiled. 'I haven't been hard on you, have I?'

'No, but...' Beryl looked confused again, and Stratton changed the subject by asking, 'What did you mean when you said Miss Morgan's death wasn't right?'

'Well, just that, really. It was rotten. Falling on those railings...I don't care what they said at that inquest, I don't believe it was suicide for a minute, and neither does Joe.'

'Why not?'

'She wasn't that sort.'

'What sort was she?'

'Brave. A fighter. I don't mean she went round clobbering people, although she certainly used to speak her mind. But she was game, never felt sorry for herself. And you'd have to, wouldn't you, to commit suicide?'

'What was it, then?' asked Stratton.

'An accident! She leant out too far, that's all. It could have happened to anyone. And,' she concluded triumphantly, 'Joe told me she hadn't got her teeth in, and I never saw her without them, never.'

'Was there anything troubling her?'

'Not that I know of. She'd have told Joe, wouldn't she?'

'Would she?'

'Course she would. They were as close as that.' She crossed the first and second fingers of her left hand and lifted it up in demonstration. 'Anyway,' she said abruptly, 'I'd better go and see what he's up to. Stuff this under your seat, will you? I don't want him to see it.' She dropped the jumble of knitting into his lap and left the room.

Stratton just had time to raise one leg and shove the wool under the cushion before she returned, pulling her brother along behind her. Stratton's first impression was that Joe was terrified— the man was actually shaking. He watched as Beryl pushed him into the armchair opposite his own, performed introductions, and handed over a cup of tea with instructions to drink it before it got cold. Despite the fear, the black eye and the bruised face, Stratton could see that, while his sister was pretty, Joe Vincent was actually (if this could be said of a man) beautiful. His head, with glossy hair, dark eyes, smooth skin, unsuitably generous mouth and perfect profile, reminded Stratton of the classical statues of athletes and young noblemen he'd seen on visits to the British Museum.

Beryl interrupted his reverie. 'I'll leave you to it, shall I?'

'Thank you,' said Stratton, and they both watched in silence as she gathered up various pieces of sewing equipment and retreated into what was, presumably, her bedroom. Alone with

Joe, Stratton continued to stare at him. He stared back with an expression that suggested Stratton was a wild animal about to attack at any moment, and eventually blurted out, 'What is it you want? I've told you people everything I know. I just want to be left alone.'

'I know you do, but there are one or two things I want to clear up.' Stratton paused. 'I understand you were in a bit of bother the other night.'

Joe fingered the bruise round his eye. 'It was just a misunderstanding...Nothing at all, really.'

'It doesn't look like nothing.'

'It's fine.'

'Doesn't look fine, either. What happened?'

'Chap I know,' Joe directed his comments to his teacup. 'Lent me some money, didn't he?'

'And?'

'Put it on a dog, didn't I?' Joe's voice was sullen.

'Did you?'

'Yes.'

'What was it called?'

'Bonny Beryl.'

'Beryl?'

'Yes, like my sister. That's why I put it on. I lost it, so I couldn't pay him, and he—'

'Which track?'

'White City.'

'When were you there?'

'Last...Monday.' Joe looked at Stratton for the first time since the start of the exchange, something like triumph in his face.

'Why weren't you at work?'

'Afternoon off.'

'So you were at the dog track at White City on Monday afternoon?'

'Yes, I was.'

'Sure about that, are you?'

'Yes!'

'I'm not.'

Joe's face turned a mottled pink. 'You calling me a liar?'

'Yes,' said Stratton, gently. 'But you're not a very good one. You see, I happen to know that dog-racing's been restricted to one afternoon a week, and the London meetings take place on Saturdays.' He wasn't absolutely positive about the day, but that didn't matter because he was willing to bet that Joe had never been to a dog track in his life, and the expression on the man's face confirmed that he was right. 'Now, why don't you start all over again, and tell me the truth?'

Joe fidgeted with his cup for a while, then said, 'It was an argument, that's all.'

'What about?'

'Money. Like I told you.'

'Tell me more.'

'Nothing to tell. I owed this chap some money, and I couldn't pay, so he cut up rough and...Well, you can see.'

'How much money?'

'Five quid.'

'He did that for five quid?'

'Well...' Joe hesitated. 'It might have been a bit more.'

'Really?' Stratton put his teacup down on the hearth. 'How much more?'

'About ten quid.'

'Ten quid more than five quid, or just ten quid?'

'Just ten.'

'I see. And what was this chap's name?'

'He's just a friend.'

Stratton raised his eyebrows. 'A friend?'

'Yes.' Joe looked defiant. 'Someone I know.'

'And what does someone look like?'

'Just...you know...ordinary.'

'So someone ordinary, who may or may not be your friend—although by the look of you, I'd say he was more of an enemy—lent you a sum of money which might have been five pounds or ten pounds, and then thumped you because you couldn't pay it back?'

'Yes.'

'Was he charging interest?'

'Interest?'

'Money on top of the loan. I believe it's about three per cent, but,' Stratton added, disingenuously, 'I should think a money-lender would ask for a bit more, wouldn't he?'

'He did ask for a few bob, yes.'

'A few bob? that would be, what, three bob? Four?'

'Five.'

'So your friend asked you to pay interest, did he? How long did you want to borrow the money for?'

'A week.'

'And what did you offer him?'

Joe turned pale. 'I don't understand,' he muttered.

'What security for the loan?'

'Oh. Nothing.'

'So, this friend who charges interest doesn't want security. Supposing you'd scarpered?'

'I didn't.'

'You said five bob, so...let's see...five bob on a tenner would be two and a half per cent, wouldn't it? Bit on the low side, I'd have thought. Not really worth his while. Perhaps,' said Stratton, thoughtfully, 'your friend ought to take a course in economics.'

'I don't know anything about that,' said Joe, sulkily.

'Evidently. Thought it was worth damaging his knuckles, though, didn't he?'

Joe shrugged.

'Where did you meet this man?'

'At the Wheatsheaf.'

'The Wheatsheaf in Rathbone Place?'

'Yes.'

'Not your local. Too far away.'

'Yes,' agreed Joe. 'But I go in there sometimes...Or I used to...' Joe stopped, his face whiter, if possible, than before.

'Used to...?'

'Mabel. Miss Morgan. It was her favourite pub. She liked the people in there—artists and all that. I used to pick her up from there on my way home from work.'

'Did Miss Morgan introduce you to the man who lent you the money?'

'She didn't know him.'

'So who did?'

'No-one. I mean, we just got talking, and...'

'When was this?'

'A few weeks ago.'

'What time? The Tivoli doesn't close until late. You'd have a job getting there before last orders.'

'I left early.'

'How early?'

'Half an hour or so.'

'So you met this man for, what, ten minutes, a few weeks ago, and he was prepared to lend you the money without any security?'

'I saw him again after that. He knew where I lived.'

'Did he visit you?'

'A few times.'

'Was Miss Morgan there?'

'I can't remember.'

'But she might have been?'

'I suppose so.'

'So she knew who he was?'

'No! I told you, she didn't know him. I must have given him my address, I can't remember.'

'So he never came to your flat?'

Joe lowered his head in defeat. 'I don't know,' he muttered.

'You've just told me he did, and now you're saying you don't know. Did he come to your flat or didn't he?'

'No.' Joe's voice was a whisper.

'This isn't getting us very far,' said Stratton. 'Let's say third time lucky, shall we? Now then,' he leant forward, 'this time, no dogs, no loans, and no strange men in pubs—or anywhere else, for that matter—unless, of course, they actually exist. And I'm guessing that this,'—he gestured at Joe's face, which had gone rigid—'wasn't the result of a lovers' tiff.'

'I don't know what you mean.'

'Oh, I think you do.' Stratton didn't enjoy threatening people, and, after all, the poor sod couldn't help what he was any more than he, Stratton, could help fancying women, but he was determined to get at the truth. He continued to stare at Joe, who was now looking intently at the unlit gas fire, as if searching for inspiration.

'You won't believe it,' he said, finally.

Stratton shifted back slightly, feeling the tension in the room break, knowing that Joe was close to telling the truth. 'Try me,' he said, mildly.

'I don't know why they came.'

Stratton remembered the conversation with Arliss. 'They?'

'There was two of them. Waiting for me when I got home.'

'When was this?'

'Monday. About half-past eleven.'

'At night?'

Joe nodded.

'So you'd been at the cinema in the morning, had the afternoon off, and gone back to work in the evening?'

Joe flushed and shook his head.

'So Monday isn't your afternoon off?'

'No. I don't have one.'

'Right.' Stratton reached into his pocket for his notebook. 'So, there were two of them, then?'

Joe nodded. 'At my flat.'

'How did they get in?'

'I don't know,' said Joe, miserably. 'I suppose Mrs Cope—that's my landlady—must have let them in.' Stratton scribbled a reminder to himself to ask Mrs Cope about this, although, given what he knew of the woman, he felt that she was unlikely, in view of the circumstances, to let such an event pass without remarking on it to all and sundry. 'Could anyone else have let them in?'

'There's two other lodgers, Mr Stockley and Mr Rogers.' Stratton noted the names. 'I suppose it might have been one of them, if Mrs Cope wasn't there. She goes out some evenings to see her daughter.'

'And Mr Cope?'

'She's a widow.'

'Do you know how they got into your flat?'

'They must have picked the lock. I shouldn't think it's that difficult...I mean, if you know what you're doing.'

'Have you any idea how long they'd been there?'

'Not really. I know they'd smoked a couple of cigarettes, because I saw them in the ashtray when I was clearing up afterwards.'

'Clearing up?'

'They'd made a real mess of the place. All her things...' Joe put his face in his hands. 'It was horrible.'

'All Miss Morgan's things?'

'Yes. Her clothes, and her pictures...newspapers with stuff from when she was in films, all over the floor. The mirror was broken, glass everywhere, and they'd pulled the mattress off the bed.'

'What about your things?'

'They'd gone through those, too, but...It was seeing her things like that, I couldn't...' Joe gulped and began to cry. 'I couldn't bear it...'

'It's all right,' said Stratton, softly. 'Here,' he fished in his pocket again, and pulled out his cigarettes. 'Have one of these.' Joe took one, cautiously, as if touching the packet might cause an explosion. 'I think,' Stratton leant across to give him a light, 'we might ask your sister if she'd be kind enough to freshen the pot, don't you? And then you can tell me the rest.' He got up and knocked on Beryl's door.

'Hello?'

Stratton stuck his head round. Beryl was sitting on her bed, sewing something intricate that looked as if it might be a neckline. 'Would you mind boiling a spot more water? I think Joe could do with another cup. A handkerchief might not go amiss, either.'

Beryl rose, skewering the material with a final jab of her needle. 'What have you been saying to him?' Without waiting for a reply, she barged straight past Stratton and, after taking one look at Joe, wheeled round and said, fiercely, 'You promised.'

Joe raised his head and regarded her through sodden eyes. 'It's all right, Beryl,' he said, softly.

Beryl continued to glare at Stratton. 'All right,' she said finally. She pulled a handkerchief from her sleeve and handed it to Joe before picking up the teapot and retreating to the kitchen. Stratton waited in silence while Joe mopped his face and blew his nose, and when more tea was brought and poured and Beryl had returned to her work, he said, 'Now then, these men. What do you think they were looking for?'

'I don't know, but that's what they said when they saw me—"You've got something we want." I didn't know what they were talking about, and I told them, but they wouldn't listen. They just kept on and on hitting me...I thought they were going to kill me.'

'And you can't think of anything it might be?'

Joe shook his head. 'I haven't got anything.'

'What about Miss Morgan? You said they went through her things, too.'

'Yes, but that was just clothes and trinkets and stuff. I told you.'

'Nothing hidden, nothing she wanted to keep secret?'

'No. She used to get a bit funny about people coming into the house, but...'

'How do you mean?'

'Well, she'd look out of the window a lot. Seeing who was in the street. If she had visitors, she'd throw her keys down, but I don't think that was very often...I mean, I was at the cinema most of the time, so...She didn't like the blackout much, but most people don't, do they?'

'Do you think she was frightened about something?'

'I wouldn't say frightened, just that she liked to know what was happening. I think it was more...well, she didn't have a lot of money, and she used to get a bit lonely, up there on her own.'

'But she went to the Wheatsheaf in the evenings?'

'Yes. She was quite well known there. If somebody bought her a drink, then she'd talk to them. She used to like that.'

'And she never went anywhere else?'

'I don't think so. At least, she was always at the Wheatsheaf when I came to fetch her, and when it started getting dark early, in the winter, I used to nip out of work and take her down there at opening time.'

'I see. So these two men said you had something they wanted, and you said you hadn't, and they hit you, and then what? Did they say anything else?'

'Not really. Just kept on about how they knew I'd got whatever it was.'

'Do you know how they got into the house?'

'No. We all have our own keys, so I suppose someone must have let them in.'

'Did they threaten you before they left?'

'Not…Well, they said something about how they knew I wouldn't go to the police. And I wouldn't have if I hadn't met that copper.'

'Don't worry, Joe. They don't know where you are, do they?'

'Not here, but they know where I work, and—'

'Did they say that?'

'No, but they can ask around, can't they?'

'I might be able to do something about that,' said Stratton, 'if you tell me a bit more about them.' Joe looked as if he doubted this, but didn't say anything. 'Did you find anything missing after they'd gone?'

'Not directly. I went out afterwards, when they'd gone. I didn't want to stay there, I thought they might come back…I didn't really know what I was doing. I had the idea I'd come over here, but I was pretty groggy.'

'That was when you met PC Arliss, was it?'

'Yes. I don't honestly remember much about it.'

'He said you were in a bad way,' said Stratton. 'What happened after that?'

'After I left the station, you mean?'

Stratton nodded.

'Then I came here.'

'So when did you go back to your flat?'

'Tuesday. After work.'

'They must have been a bit surprised at work when they saw your appearance.'

'The manager wasn't very happy, but I'm not on show to the public, so...' Joe shrugged. 'I was worried about going to the flat—I didn't really think they'd be there, but all the same...I just tidied up a bit, and packed a few things, and then I came here.'

'So, was anything missing?'

'There was one thing—it seemed a bit odd, and at first I thought maybe I'd just missed it, you know, it had gone under the bed or something, but I looked everywhere, and I couldn't find it. A photograph of Mabel when she was a star. She had it in a frame, on the mantelpiece.'

'Perhaps they were film fans. But that wasn't what they came for, was it?'

'No. I don't know what they wanted. I swear it.'

'I believe you,' said Stratton. 'Now then, suppose you tell me what this pair looked like?'

'One of them was tall, with a big scar on his face, here,' he ran one finger down his right cheek, 'He was wearing a hat, so I couldn't see his hair, but he was quite dark, and big. Bulky. He had a dark blue suit, and a dark tie, black shoes, gloves—both of them had gloves.'

'How old would you say he was?'

'About thirty. The other one was younger—more like a boy. Seventeen or eighteen, maybe. He was wearing a suit, too, similar sort of colour...brown hair, quite a pale face with freckles. I saw them when he was bending over me.'

'What did they sound like?'

'Ordinary. Londoners. Bit Cockney—like me, I suppose. They didn't shout or anything, just hit me. That was mainly the big one. The other one was watching.'

'The big one you told me about, with the scar. What did he smell like?'

'Well...' Joe hesitated. 'Not very good.'

'Needed a spot of Lifebuoy soap, did he?'

Joe's face broke into a grin. 'You can say that again. Why, do you know him?'

'Yes.' Stratton returned his notebook to his pocket. 'I do.'

CHAPTER 11

George Wallace. Great gorilla of a man with a razor scar down one side of his face, and he ponged, all right. None of the tarts in Soho would touch him, even for extra money, and Stratton didn't blame them. But what did a man like Wallace want with Joe? Wallace did most of his work for Abie Marks, the Yiddisher gang boss, but there was no reason why Abie...All right, he could get a bit sentimental when he'd had a few, everyone knew that, but Stratton honestly couldn't picture him as the sort who'd go to such lengths just to steal an old photograph of a forgotten screen star, however beautiful she'd been. He was pretty sure Joe wasn't lying when he said he didn't know why he'd been beaten up, and it obviously wasn't to do with being queer, or his attackers would have said so. Stratton had occasionally wondered if Abie wasn't a bit that way himself. True, he was never seen without a well-dressed girl on his arm, but there were a lot of boys around him, too: cocky young toughs from the ring or the gym, and pretty, feral slum boys who'd turn their hands to anything (or anyone) for a bit of cash. Joe didn't fit either of those types. And, Stratton thought, even if he had been excited by the apparent glamour of Marks's world, Beryl would certainly have had something to say about such undesirable company. Remembering how the brother and sister stood together at the head of the stairs, waving him off, Beryl's arm round Joe's waist, Stratton thought: she'll see he's all right...

Funny, neither of them had commented on the unusual timing of his visit—almost as if they'd been expecting it. Or expecting something, anyway. Can't blame the poor bloke for not wanting to talk to the police, thought Stratton. Given that advancement usually depended on the number of convictions a young officer could get, and that it was, on the whole, far easier to arrest a homosexual than a burglar, men like Joe knew jolly well that both their freedom and their reputation depended on keeping as low a profile as possible. Walking back up Theobald's Road, Stratton checked his watch and decided that there was just time to look in on Mrs Cope before he caught a bus back to Tottenham. If she was no help, maybe he could speak to the other lodgers, but he'd have to make it quick...

Stratton stopped outside Goodge Street station to consult his notebook—Stockley and Rogers—before turning down Howland Street and then right, into the tangle of narrower streets that surrounded Fitzroy Square. Being Sunday morning, it was quiet—no businessmen, civil servants, flannelled men from the BBC, or posturing Bohemians—just a few elderly locals. Despite the June sunlight, the tall brick houses, closed shops and shuttered pubs looked drab and neglected. There was a faint odour of piss and fried food in the air; newspapers, spent cigarettes and broken bottles littered the pavement, and a couple of torn ARP posters stirred in the light breeze. On one corner, a black beret hung from a spike, as if its owner had, in a moment of drunken confusion, mistaken the railings for a hat stand. The whole thing gave Stratton the eerie feeling of a revel suddenly abandoned in the face of some approaching cataclysm, and he had a vision of the inhabitants of the slovenly houses slumped, lifeless, over their pots and dinner plates and basins, death having taken them on the instant, leaving them blue-faced, with wide open eyes and mouths and vomit on their chins…Would it be like that? Stratton glanced at his gas mask case. As a police officer, he carried it to set an example, but a lot of people didn't bother. God help us all, he thought.

It soon became clear that Mrs Cope hadn't let the two men in. 'No, I wouldn't, not unless Mr Vincent told me they was coming, which he didn't, but even then you don't know who it is, do you? Might be anyone. Might be a fifth column, you know,'— she lowered her voice, 'spying for the Germans. What did these people want with Mr Vincent?' she asked. 'Is he all right? I'd never forgive myself if anything had happened to him.'

After Stratton had reassured her that nothing had happened to Joe, and that she could, indeed, forgive herself—which she seemed to do remarkably quickly—Mrs Cope responded to his suggestion that they start at the top and escorted him two flights up the dingy stairwell to Mr Rogers' rooms. Stratton was surprised that she waddled back down the stairs the moment his knock was answered, but soon wished he'd been able to follow her. Rogers was a small, plump and self-important man who said he had been out on Monday evening, but proceeded to give full vent to his theories about crime and delinquency, interspersing them with phrases like 'It's not for me to tell you how to do your job' (too fucking right, thought Stratton).

After about five minutes of this, Stratton decided he'd put up with quite enough fanny for one morning, and he didn't want to annoy Jenny by being late for lunch. He terminated the conversation and went down to the next landing in search of Mr Stockley, who was, in exaggerated contrast to his neighbour, tall, thin, and lugubrious. He came to the door in his shirtsleeves, and answered Stratton's questions in monosyllables. No, he hadn't seen any men on Monday, or let anyone into the house, and no, he hadn't heard anything. 'What were you doing?' asked Stratton.

'Playing my gramophone records.' He glanced over the banisters before adding, sotto voce, with the air of one confessing a guilty secret, 'Mahler.'

'Oh.' Stockley stared at him expectantly, and, feeling that some additional response was called for, Stratton tapped the side of his nose. 'I shan't tell anyone.'

On his way to the bus stop, Stratton reflected that, although both men had answered his questions, neither had shown any interest in why he was asking them in the first place. Clearly, they didn't know Joe well. Stratton felt positive that if Rogers had been aware of his fellow lodger's inclinations there would have been a lot more metaphorical digs in the ribs, but he supposed that the man was far too wrapped up in his own opinions to be pricked by curiosity. Stockley, on the other hand, was just relieved to get Mahler—who was, presumably, German, or at least Austrian—off his chest.

Fingerprints were pretty unlikely—Joe had said that Wallace and his chum were wearing gloves. And in any case, what with the gang murder and the jewel thieves taking up most of his time, his guv'nor DCI Lamb would bollock him from here to kingdom come if he discovered that precious working hours were being spent on something else. Especially if that something was—and Stratton could almost hear him say it—a confirmed suicide and a roughed-up bum-boy. All the same, he'd have a word with George Wallace tomorrow. The billiard hall in Wardour Street, or maybe the boozer up by the corner…Wallace wouldn't have gone far.

Stratton just made it back in time for lunch. Donald, opening the door, grimaced and muttered, 'Thank God you're here. He hasn't stopped.' Stratton arrived in the kitchen to find Reg in the middle of a typical Sunday lunch performance, getting in the women's way and hamming it up at every opportunity, before finally, when the baked apples appeared, breaking into song in what he imagined was the accent of Stratton's childhood, accompanying himself by banging his spoon and fork on the table:

'Puddin'! Puddin'! Puddin'!
Gi' me plenty o'puddin',
So pass me plate,
And don't be late,
And pile it up wi' puddin'!'

As usual, everyone ignored this and concentrated on handing round bowls and scraping the last of the rather watery custard from the jug. Up to that point, Stratton had felt too distracted by what Joe Vincent had told him to want to punch Reg more than about three times—which was several times fewer than average. Now, he glanced across at Johnny and saw, on the boy's face, a snarl of undisguised hatred directed towards his father.

It had occurred to Stratton more than once that Reg had acted the buffoon so much and so often that his real self was now hopelessly submerged beneath a heap of comic songs, yarn-telling and lofty pronouncements. When he looked at Johnny, it struck him that, although someone as fundamentally ridiculous as Reg could never be called tragic, the consequences for his son might well be exactly that. While this thought was hardly comforting, it did serve to take his mind off talking to George Wallace, which he wasn't looking forward to in the least.

CHAPTER

I t was only the third time Diana had been inside Forbes-James's flat. Apart from the functional and phenomenally untidy office in which they were sitting, it was a perfect example of Edwardian masculinity. There were sturdy objects in ivory, brass and wood, pigskin coverings, gold stampings and crests on every surface, yet it wasn't quite a typical bachelor flat. Its hearty manliness was relieved by a painting of flowers and another—rather surprising, this—of boy bathers, as well as toile de Jouy, petit point, and a small collection of Sevres porcelain. Diana supposed that these items must be contributions from his wife, a lady of almost mythical status who was thought to reside in the country. Forbes-James never spoke of her, displayed no photographs, and no-one Diana knew had ever seen her.

She was jerked out of her reverie when F-J asked, 'What do you know about Lord Redesdale?' He took a cigarette out of his case and tapped it, waiting for her answer.

Diana collected her thoughts, thankful that she had done her homework thoroughly before meeting Mrs Montague. 'Lord Redesdale's acquainted with Montague. He's a member of the Anglo-German fellowship with Domvile, the Duke of Wellington and Lord Londonderry. His daughter, Unity Mitford, was friends with Hitler, and Redesdale and his wife met him on several occasions. Unity tried to commit suicide when war broke out and the family brought her home.'

'Good, good,' said Forbes-James distractedly, shuffling things on his desk.

'It's here, sir.' Diana pulled the silver table lighter from beneath a sheaf of papers and handed it over.

'Thank you. Don't know why she has to keep moving it about.' He lit the cigarette and glared in the direction of the wall behind which Margot Mentmore, the telephonist, was sitting in her cubbyhole. 'And?'

'Well, I wouldn't have thought he was dangerous, just misguided, like a lot of those people, but surely Montague is dangerous, and I don't understand why he's not in prison, Sir.'

'The usual reasons.'

'But Mosley—'

'I know. We wanted the lot of them, but there you are. The people's elected representatives...' He sighed. 'Can't keep packing them off to Brixton. Looks bad.'

'But surely it doesn't matter what it looks like! I mean, now that they've changed the law, surely—'

Forbes-James held up a hand to stop her. 'Defence Regulation 18B (1A),' he quoted, wearily, 'states that members of hostile organisations may now be arrested if they are likely to endanger public safety, the prosecution of the war and the defence of the realm, yes. However, as I believe I told you, there was a great deal of fuss when they tried bringing it in at the beginning of the war, which is why it was modified so that we were only able to detain those of hostile origin or associations and those involved in acts prejudicial to public safety, etcetera. It's taken a lot of time and effort on our part to convince the Cabinet that wider powers are necessary. Rounding up Mosley and a bunch of pro-fascist East Enders is one thing, but we can't keep frog-marching people off to gaol if we don't like the look of them.'

'Especially people in high places.'

'Exactly. Makes a bad impression. Alarm, despondency and all the rest of it. People have to be able to trust, especially now... Anyway, what about this afternoon? How did it go?'

'I think I'm making some progress. I saw Mrs Montague again—Lally thinks she's taken a shine to me, she insisted on paying for our tea—and we've made an arrangement to meet on Friday evening at her flat. She's going to introduce me to some of her friends.'

'Good. What did you talk about?'

'Well, she wanted to know where I grew up, and that sort of thing, so that was easy enough, and she told me about her house in Fakenham and we talked about the country for a while, walks and things, and I said I was missing it, and how dreary it was to work in an office when one was used to being outdoors. And then I thought I might go a bit further, so I said I thought the war was spoiling everything. She was very sympathetic, so then I said something about it being a mistake not to have gone on appeasing Germany, because it would lead to disaster, and that it was all right if one felt that war was morally defensible, because then one could put up with things better, but I didn't—you know the sort of thing...Lally was marvellous, saying I had common sense about politics, but keeping it all quite general, as you said.'

'Excellent. What else?'

'She mentioned Sir Neville Apse.'

'Apse?' Forbes-James looked surprised. 'Miss Markham did?'

'Not Lally, sir. Mrs Montague.'

'Why?'

'Well, I was talking about how dull it was at the War Office, and she suggested I ought to apply for a transfer to something a bit more interesting, so I pretended I didn't know much about it, and said I thought it would just be more of the same—filing and so on—and that's when his name came up.'

'Does Montague know him?'

'She didn't say, sir. It was all pretty vague, and I thought I'd better not ask too many questions, but she said she'd heard he was in the thick of it—those were the words she used.'

'What else did she say?'

'Not much, sir. Just that as we were at war, we should all do our bit. You know, the usual.'

'Yes...' Forbes-James shuffled more papers.

'May I ask what Sir Neville does, sir?'

'That's the odd thing. He's part of this section, but he's responsible for looking into reports of Fifth Columnists. Enemy agents and so on. Poppycock, mostly, but we have to check. Old ladies with spies under their beds, parachutists dressed as nuns...'

'Why nuns?' asked Diana.

'God knows. Sinister, I suppose...' He waved a hand at her. 'You know...flapping. I can't imagine why the woman thinks you'll be any use to them there, but as she's mentioned it, I'd better see if I can arrange a transfer. Come to think of it, might be quite useful for Apse to have a woman about the place...You'll carry on reporting to me, of course, that shouldn't present any problems. Apse has a flat across the garden in Frobisher House. Works there, and stays there during the week. I'll have a word with him tonight, say I'm overstaffed.'

'What's he like?'

'Not bad. Bit of a cold fish.'

'You don't think he's pro-fascist, do you?'

'Heavens, no. But if that's where she wants you...When you see her on Friday, tell her you've been thinking about it and decided to apply for the transfer. You can come here afterwards and tell me how it went.'

'Yes, sir.'

'Good. Splendid. Scotch?'

'Thank you, sir.'

Forbes-James rose, brushing cigarette ash from his suit as he did so, and went over to the filing cabinet, where there was a tray with glasses and a decanter. 'Soda?'

'No thank you.'

'Sensible girl. Come and sit on the sofa.'

'I think I'd better tidy it first, sir.'

'Good idea. You can put all those'—he indicated a slew of bulging files, the partially disgorged contents of which were papering the cushions—'on the desk.'

'I don't think there's room, sir.'

'On the floor, then.' He sighed as Diana picked up the bundles of paper and dumped them by the fireplace. 'She's supposed to tidy up, but she never does.' Diana took this to refer to Margot the telephonist and said, 'Do you ever give her the chance, sir?'

'I suppose not. Oh, well...' He settled himself on the sofa and handed over her glass. Diana took it, and sat down on the other end. 'No, no,' he said, irritably, patting the cushion next to his own. 'I shan't bite.'

'No, sir.' Diana moved nearer.

'That's better.' She jumped as Forbes-James put a hand on her knee.

'No need to behave like a virgin in a troop ship,' he said crossly, taking it off again. 'You're quite safe with me.'

'Yes, sir.' Diana smoothed her skirt. 'Of course. I'm sorry.'

'However,' Forbes-James continued, 'I understand you met Claude Ventriss at Jock's party.' He stared at her.

'Yes, I did.' Diana hoped her voice sounded neutral.

'Took you out to dinner, didn't he?'

'Yes, sir.'

'Enjoy yourself?'

'I...' For an insane moment, Diana thought of telling him the story of the evening, but, realising how it might sound, said merely that it had been very pleasant.

'Pleasant, was it?'

'Yes, sir.'

'What do you know about him?'

'He works for you, sir.'

'That's right. But be careful. He isn't safe.'

'Sir?'

'You're a beautiful woman, my dear,' Forbes-James said, rather gruffly, 'Don't need me to tell you that. Ventriss has something of a reputation.' He sounded disapproving.

'So I understand, sir.'

'Your business, of course, what goes on…things happen, and so forth…Don't want you getting hurt, that's all.' He looked into his glass. 'Had any more letters from that husband of yours?'

'Not recently, no. I expect I shall soon.'

'And the flat? That's all right, is it? Happy there?'

'Yes,' said Diana. 'I love it.'

'Excellent.' He stared at his glass again, and said, 'I seem to have finished this rather quickly. Fancy another?'

Diana, taking this as her cue to leave, declined. 'I should say goodnight, sir.'

'Of course.' Forbes-James stood up, and, to her surprise, pecked her on the cheek. 'Mind how you go.'

'Yes, sir. Have a nice evening.'

In the hall, Margot turned from her bank of telephones, stretched her long legs, and said, 'Finished?'

'Yes.'

'Like a drink?' She reached into her handbag for her compact, and inspected her face. 'We're going round to Leo's.'

'Who's Leo?'

'Leo Birkin. You know,' she added, impatiently, 'from A section. Jock's going, and Lally.'

'No thanks. Think I need an early night, for a change.'

'Jock said Claude might drop by later on.'

'Claude?'

'Ventriss,' Margot gave Diana a knowing smile over her mirror. 'Your dining companion.'

'Oh, him.'

'Yes, him.'

'I don't think so, Margot. He's very charming, of course, and great fun, but I really have got to catch up on some sleep.' Diana thought that she had, on the whole, managed to say this in a normal, down-to-earth sort of way. Margot, who'd been paying close attention while powdering her nose, grinned. 'Well, if you're absolutely sure...'

'I am. But thanks, anyway.' Diana walked back to Tite Street in the twilight with the uncomfortable feeling that Margot, as well as Forbes-James, had understood a great deal more than she'd actually said. Why did everyone persist in behaving as if the thing was a fait accompli? She'd had dinner with the man, that was all—she hadn't committed herself to anything—and next time, if there were a next time, she'd just...Just what? Well, she wouldn't fall into his arms, anyway. 'I can look after myself,' she muttered, angrily. 'I'm not a complete fool.' Aware that the words didn't quite match what she was thinking, and that the irritation was, to an extent, manufactured, she felt suddenly foolish and ashamed, glad to be alone. She might deny it until she was blue in the face, but the attraction was there, all right. Determined to nip all thoughts of Ventriss in the bud, she walked faster, as if, by increasing her speed, they might be outpaced.

Opening the outer door, she saw there was a letter from Guy on the hall stand. This is more like it, she thought, sliding a nail under the flap immediately so she could start reading as she went up the stairs, knowing as she did so that it was less the action of a woman in love with her husband than a simple defence mechanism.

Dearest, We are still waiting for orders, very tedious. We have drunk all the wine, smoked all the cigars, and eaten most of the food. The troops are fed up with attending lectures, but on the whole behaving tolerably well, although last night there was the most fearful rumpus because some rowdy—

Reaching the landing, Diana saw, propped against her door, an enormous bunch of red roses. Shoving the letter into her handbag, she bent down to read the card:

Thank you for a wonderful evening. With love, Claude.

It was much later, just as she was about to drop off to sleep, that Diana remembered she hadn't finished reading Guy's letter.

CHAPTER 13

Stratton entered the billiard hall and stood inside the door for a moment, adjusting to the gloom. It was a large rectangular room with peeling paint, kitted out with half a dozen green baize tables at one end and a scattering of small copper-covered tables by the door, each with its own Players ashtray, and flanked by an assortment of battered wooden chairs. There was a hush as he'd entered, and beneath the false ceiling of smoke, all heads turned to stare at him, stiff and alert as dogs that sense a threat—Alfie Swan, Danny Distleman, Mickey Horsfall, Johnny Mount. Stratton knew them all. Knew what was in their pockets, too—pieces of cork embedded with razor blades that could be strapped to the palm, the victim to be lulled into security by a friendly clap on the shoulder before a swipe with the other hand laid open half his kisser. Vitriol, too—one of them, Tommy White, had thrown that in his girl's face and done five years for it. He was there, watching along with the others, holding a billiard cue by his side. Stratton wondered how many deals he'd interrupted. The place was far more crowded than usual—but then, if the villains could no longer make as much money at the races, it made sense that they'd turn to thieving to supply the growing black market. Food, booze, cigarettes, false ID cards—you name it—and there'd be a lot more to look forward to, as well.

The crowd parted, silently, as Abie Marks stepped out of a door at the back and walked towards him. He reminded Stratton of a film star playing a gangster: big, and handsome in a no-good way, with his smart suit and glace shoes, his blue-black hair shining like wet prunes, and his bright, white smile. 'Care for a drink, Inspector?'

'You don't have a licence.'

'Only keep it for friends, Inspector, such as your good self.'

'No, thank you.'

'Cigar?'

'No, thank you.'

'Something to eat, then? Anything you fancy—I'll get one of the boys to fetch it in from next door.'

Stratton shook his head. 'I've come for a word with George Wallace.'

'Wallace?' Abie's smile vanished, leaving his eyes cold and vigilant. Without taking them from Stratton's face, he said, 'Fetch him.' The young lad beside him—tough little face with a tight, closed expression—turned and melted into the crowd.

'Like to step into my office, Inspector?'

Stratton considered for a moment. He'd never accepted anything from Abie, nor would he, but a bit of privacy might make things easier. 'Thank you,' he said.

'This way.' The crowd parted again, drawing further back this time, as if in fear of contamination, as he followed Abie across the room. Abie ushered him into the office with a flourish, and closed the door. 'Make yourself at home.' Stratton glanced round the small room, which was an odd mixture of scruffy and plush with lino and a boarded up fireplace, and a large desk with a big leather swivel chair behind it. The only other chair, in contrast, was a rickety wooden affair, doubtless intended to underline the inferiority of the sitter. A glittering phalanx of bottles stood on top of an elderly filing cabinet, and behind them, a large doll with golden curls and glassy blue eyes. Seeing the direction of his gaze, Abie asked, 'Sure you won't have anything?'

'No, thanks,' Stratton repeated, and settled himself on the swivel chair. 'Present?' he said, nodding at the doll.

'My little girl—birthday tomorrow. It's all above board, you know,' Abie smiled—or rather, showed his teeth. 'I got nothing to hide.'

'I'm sure you haven't,' said Stratton, adding to himself, not here, anyway. There was a knock on the door and the boy stuck his head round. 'He's here, Mr Marks.'

'Bring him in, then. Don't keep the Inspector waiting.'

George Wallace, framed by the doorway, looked larger than Stratton remembered. Smelled worse, too—Stratton caught a pungent whiff as the man advanced into the room and seated himself in front of the desk. 'What can I do for you, Inspector?' he asked. His voice was carefully neutral, but his eyes were as cold as Abie's.

'Just some questions,' said Stratton, blandly. Turning to Abie, he said, 'If we could have a few moments...?'

Abie bowed his head. 'Of course, Inspector. Just give me a shout if you need anything.'

'Thank you.'

Marks closed the door behind him. Stratton, leaning forward, elbows on the desktop, said, 'Take your hat off.'

Wallace's impassive stare mirrored the innocent gaze of the doll behind him. 'You're indoors,' said Stratton. 'Might as well make yourself comfortable.' Reluctantly, Wallace removed his trilby and balanced it on his knees, revealing a brilliantined slick of black hair.

'That's better,' said Stratton, deliberately avuncular. 'I hear you're fond of the pictures, George.'

'What?'

'The pictures. Films.'

'What about them?'

'I was hoping you'd tell me. Where were you on Monday night, George?'

'I was here.' He nodded in the direction of the door. 'They'll tell you.'

'I don't doubt it. But you weren't here all evening, were you?'

'Who says I wasn't?'

'You paid a visit, didn't you?'

'I don't know what you're talking about.'

'I think you do,' said Stratton mildly. 'You and your pal went to see a man called Vincent.'

'No,' said Wallace flatly. 'We was here.'

'Who's "we"?'

'The boys. Mickey, Danny, Johnny...Why don't you ask them?'

'And your pal? Shall I ask him?'

Wallace shrugged. Stratton, knowing that he was a far more accomplished liar than Joe, and knowing, also, that the men in the next room would swear blind that Wallace and the boy, whoever he was, had been in their company all night, if necessary, said, 'You were seen.'

'Who saw me?'

'Mr Vincent, for one, and a couple of others noticed you in the street. Described you very well, as it happens. Both of you.'

'They're lying.'

'Why would they do that?'

'We wasn't there. We was here.'

'By "we", I take it you mean you and your new chum. Why don't you tell me his name, George? Or is he a very special friend?'

'I haven't got no special friend.' Stratton saw that, under the impassive toughness of his exterior, Wallace was angered by the implication that he was queer.

'So you keep telling me. Want to keep him under wraps, do you? Is that it?'

'No. I don't know what you're talking about, and I've told you I was here. Can I go now?'

'Not yet. These people I mentioned, witnesses, they saw you in the street with your best boy, outside Vincent's house.'

'There wasn't anybody—' Wallace stopped. Damn, thought Stratton. It had been an obvious trap—clumsy—but although the man was angry, he wasn't angry enough. He stared at Stratton and shook his head slowly from side to side, a you-won't-catch-me-that-way expression on his face.

'I know that you and your friend went to see Mr Vincent on Monday night, and you threatened him and messed up his flat. What were you looking for?'

'Nothing. I wasn't there.'

'You pinched a photograph.'

'I never. I told you,' Aware that he was on the home straight, Wallace sounded almost bored. 'I wasn't there.'

'A silent film actress called Mabel Morgan. Favourite of yours, was she?'

'Never heard of her.' Wallace clapped his hat back on his head and stared defiantly at Stratton, his arms crossed. 'That all?'

'No.' Stratton stood up, walked round the desk, leant against it, and lit a cigarette. He threw the spent match at Wallace's feet and blew the smoke directly into his face. 'Listen,' he said, softly, 'If you lot want to carve each other up, that's fine with me. I don't care what you do to each other. But when you start hurting decent people, that's a different matter. If you, or any of that scum out there, lays one finger on Vincent, I will cripple you so badly you'll think this,'—Wallace jerked backwards as Stratton jabbed his cigarette at his scarred cheek—'was a birthday present. By the time I've finished with you, you won't know which end to shit out of. Understand?'

Wallace nodded. Stratton leant forward and snatched the hat off his head. 'I said, do you understand?'

'Yes.' He stared at Stratton with hot, furious eyes.

'Good.' Stratton threw the hat into his lap. 'Now piss off.'

CHAPTER 14

It wasn't exactly a balls-up, thought Stratton, as he straightened, rubbed his back and looked down at the neat rows of little seeds, but it hadn't been a roaring success, either. He'd gone to his allotment to try and forget his feeling of irritation at his failure to make headway with Wallace. Abie Marks, who had reappeared in the office a few moments after the man had left, had known better than to gloat, but the bastard had been unable to resist a reprise of his mine host routine, and that, compounded by his failure to make any sort of progress with his other cases, had left him in a thoroughly bad mood. He'd decided on the way home that a bit of sun and sowing the last of the spinach might improve matters, but so far it hadn't helped much.

Picking up his trowel to cover the seeds with earth, he found himself thinking of his father, tending vegetables in the garden of the small, damp farmhouse where he and his brothers had grown up. He'd often wondered what the old man would have made of his life, and the people he dealt with on a daily basis. Working on the allotment, which was the closest he ever came to the country-side nowadays, always seemed to conjure him up—a carthorse of a man whose three sons had inherited his massive build; a man with warm, leathery hands, who wore a cap, black-rimmed with dirt and sweat, and had endless patience.

He'd always considered his life to be an improvement on his father's with its familiar, instinctive pattern of work, relentless as the seasons—lifting, tugging, toting, trudging through day after day before dropping off to sleep by the fire after supper and waking just long enough to haul himself up the stairs to bed. His surviving brother, Dick, had returned to Devon in 1919, glad to be home, and had eventually taken over the running of the small farm, but for as long as he could remember Stratton had dreamt of uprooting himself from the grey, gluey mud and finding another sort of life. It wasn't that he'd been unhappy. There were many things that he'd loved about the place—his family, the farm cats, the smell of hot horses, the warmth of the cows as they came in from the fields to be milked, dusty rectangles of light in the barn, excitement when a pig was killed—but he hadn't wanted to stay there. He hadn't grown up wanting to be a policeman. That suggestion, oddly enough, had come from Dick, who'd pointed out that it was an outdoor life with a pension at the end of it. At the time, it had seemed as good as anything. The decision to come to London had been a deliberate one, and, once he'd got over the initial shock of the crowded buildings, the roaring, grinding traffic and the teeming humanity, he'd discovered that he liked it.

Stratton pushed markers into the earth at the ends of the rows, pulled up a couple of onions to take home, then bent down to examine the marrows. The first one looked about ready. He grimaced. Bloody tasteless things, and the kids weren't around to help eat them—not that they'd ever liked them, either, and now that they weren't here to be set an example…Stratton shook his head at the direction his thoughts were taking. The cooking was Jenny's business, and she thought marrows were good for you, kept you regular, or something. It wasn't his job to interfere.

He harvested the marrow, tucked it under his arm, and headed for home. It was a great pity, he thought, that Pete and Monica hadn't been able to go and stay with Dick in Devon, but with his sister-in-law being poorly it wouldn't have been fair to expect her to look after two extra kids. Shame, because until a couple of years ago they'd all gone down there for holidays—loved it, too, helping out on the farm...

Thinking of Monica's tears when it was time to come home, Stratton recalled how his father had wept unashamedly on their stepmother's shoulder after they'd had the telegram about his eldest brother Tom, in 1917. He remembered standing in the kitchen doorway, watching as Auntie Nellie wrapped her arms around him and he sank against her, sobbing. That was the only time he'd seen them touch. Stratton's mother had died when he was six, and Nellie, her spinster sister, had moved in as housekeeper, marrying his father—to the disapproval of the vicar, who refused a church wedding—a couple of years later. Now that he was older, Stratton occasionally found himself wondering about the nature of their union. They'd shared a bed, of course, a big, lumpy, sagging thing that rolled like the sea when you sat on it, but compared to himself and Jenny, the relationship had seemed...What? Functional. Workmanlike. But then his father had always been taciturn, using speech only when all other forms of communication—grunts, shrugs, lifts of the chin—had been exhausted. He smiled at the memory, then frowned as a half-glimpsed advert for Coca-Cola in a café window reminded him once more of the afternoon's conversation with George Wallace.

Finding Lilian seated in the kitchen when he got home didn't help matters. He deposited the marrow and onions next to her impressively large breasts—the best thing about her, in Stratton's opinion—which were resting proprietorially on the table, then stumped upstairs to wash for supper, but not before he'd caught a glimpse of a particular expression on both women's faces. It was a sort of determined serenity which meant that they had discussed the fact that both Reg and himself were, in their different ways, being 'difficult' about the children, and that the thing to do was to respond with an impenetrable front of wifely forbearance. This would mean that everything they said would act as a sort of reverse camouflage for everything they weren't saying; except, of course, that neither, unless pushed beyond an acceptable point (thus making Stratton a swine and a bully and putting him thoroughly in the wrong), would admit it.

He dried his hands with unnecessary violence and decided he might as well go and lie down for ten minutes. Lilian would surely leave soon and Jenny, once alone, might be prevailed upon to drop it. He really didn't think he could face another argument about the kids, not tonight. He stared out of the bedroom window across the gardens, and saw, in the alleyway that separated their row from the one beyond, the slim figure of a boy, bobbing up and down on the balls of his feet like a boxer warming up for a fight. A second glance told him that it was Reg and Lilian's son, Johnny, ducking and weaving, outsmarting an imaginary opponent in a series of complicated sidesteps, before a volley of sharp jabs to the chin drove his adversary backwards and the boy administered the killer punch. Stratton, who'd done a fair bit of boxing when he was younger, decided that the invisible man must have had a glass jaw. He watched as Johnny raised his clenched fists in a salute of triumph, and danced out of sight behind an overgrown buddleia, then turned away from the window to take off his shoes and lie down, hands clasped behind his head. After a few minutes listening to the murmurs of conversation from the kitchen and wearily re-marshalling his arguments about why Pete and Monica should stay exactly where they were, his eyelids began to droop; a short time later, he turned over and fell asleep.

CHAPTER 15

As she followed Mrs Montague down the hall, Diana, despite her thumping heart, noticed that her hostess had thick ankles. For some trivial and despicably feminine reason, this made her feel better about the task in hand. Another glance at the ankles— they really were rather awful—calmed her to the point where she felt, if not exactly confident, then at least able to put up a decent show in front of the coven of Right Club ladies who were waiting in the sitting room. This sense of self-possession was reinforced by her first, very uncharitable thought upon entering, which was that she had rarely encountered such a monotony of ugliness. Steered around by Mrs Montague to shake hands, she reminded herself that being ill-favoured did not mean you were stupid. This thought, by some devious reverse process, brought with it a sharp reminder of Claude Ventriss. Diana forced herself to concentrate: Lady Calne, Mrs Mountstewart, Mrs Chapman, Miss Taylor, Miss Blackett. How would she ever remember all the names?

There were no men present—presumably, thought Diana, because most of them had already been rounded up under Regulation 18B (1A), and quite right too—and all the women were considerably older than she was. Their expressions were kindly but curious. Diana smiled and nodded, careful not to appear too enthusiastic or fulsome, and, having been introduced to everyone, accepted a drink and subsided onto a plush sofa between sturdy Mrs Chapman and angular Miss Blackett, who gave off a strong impression, almost an odour, of genteel but hard-boiled virginity. Mrs Chapman engaged her, briskly, on the subject of gardening, followed by skirt lengths, vitamins, and tennis parties. Miss Blackett nodded emphatic agreement with all Mrs Chapman's pronouncements and, to Diana's relief, most of her own. They were joined for a short time by Miss Taylor, a small woman with worried eyes, who fidgeted a great deal and kept repeating 'Dreadful, dreadful,' before scuttling away to help Mrs Montague's maid hand round more drinks.

At this point, Mrs Chapman was summoned by Mrs Montague. Miss Blacken rose with her, and their places were immediately taken by Mrs Mountstewart and Lady Calne. The conversation this time was petrol rationing, spiritualism and Lord Calne's priceless jade collection, and Diana felt that she'd acquitted herself reasonably well. In the closing stages of this, Lady Caine said, 'Mrs Montague tells me you're finding the War Office a bit of a bore, my dear.'

'I am rather,' admitted Diana, hoping she looked suitably shamefaced. 'I know one shouldn't say so, of course.'

'Well,' said Mrs Mountstewart, 'It's always good to feel one's making a contribution, especially at a time like this.' Diana, feeling that this was a way of getting her to commit herself without having to commit anything in return, decided she'd better keep things as neutral as possible for the time being. 'It's possible,' she said, in a lowered voice, 'that I may get something a little more interesting.'

'Really?'

'It's not certain, but I'm supposed to be having an interview with Sir Neville Apse. I don't know him, of course, and actually, I ought to thank Mrs Montague for giving me the idea. She spoke very highly of him so when this chance came up, I jumped at it.'

'Naturally,' said Lady Caine, blandly. 'Sir Neville is very well thought of. I'm sure that working for him would be a far better use for your talents.' Diana thought she detected a trace of sarcasm, but Lady Caine gave her a winning smile, patted her arm, and said,

'Mrs Montague speaks very highly of you, Miss Calthrop. She tells me you have a great deal of sense about political matters.'

Diana decided to take the plunge. 'Well,' she said, 'I must admit, I'm not too keen on the war.'

'Why's that, my dear?' asked Mrs Mountstewart.

Here we go, thought Diana.

'Well,' she said, 'I can't help thinking that the government didn't handle it very well. Chamberlain could simply have dissolved Parliament and held an election on the issue of whether we should go to war. No-one would have voted for it, would they?' She smiled. 'Everyone with a grain of sense prefers peace to war, don't they?' There were nods of encouragement and sympathetic murmurs. 'They could have solved the Jewish problem by re-settling them somewhere else. And as for saying that we are fighting against evil things in Germany, what about Soviet Russia? The Communists are far worse, and we're not fighting them, are we? It's just my opinion, of course,' she added modestly, 'but I think it was a terrible mistake to divide Germany as we did at Versailles, putting millions of Germans inside the Polish frontiers. It was bound to cause trouble, and then saying we would help Poland was practically telling the Germans that war was inevitable because we wanted to fight them sooner or later. And now...' Diana sighed. 'It's dreadful. British men are getting killed, and one feels so futile...' She tailed off, fearing she might be overdoing it.

'I know.' Lady Calne patted Diana's arm again. 'One does. But perhaps there will be a way you can help.'

'Do you think so?'

'Oh yes, dear,' said Mrs Mountstewart. 'It would be a pity to waste a mind like yours. I think it would be an excellent idea if you were to get this job you were telling us about.'

Diana stood in the doorway of Nelson House, pulling on her gloves. Forbes-James had been delighted with her progress, and had organised a meeting with Sir Neville Apse at lunch the

following day. Telling herself firmly that she'd done a good afternoon's work, and quashing any feelings of trepidation about what
was to happen next, she set off through Dolphin Square garden
towards the Embankment. Halfway along the path, she spotted a
tall figure standing by the gateway, and stopped: it couldn't be...
could it? A second glance told her that it was. Claude Ventriss.
Afterwards, she told herself that he'd hailed her before she'd had
a chance to turn and walk in the other direction, but that wasn't
true because she'd been rooted to the spot, heart thudding helplessly, waiting for him to approach. As he'd dashed towards her,
hat in hand, she'd been unable to take her eyes off him. 'I hoped
I might find you here,' he said. 'Will you have dinner with me
this evening? I can pick you up at eight.'

She'd agreed immediately, without even the presence of
mind to make a token show of thinking it over. She floated back
to Tite Street, light-headed with joy. Even the sight of Guy's letter
on the dressing table didn't diminish the feeling. After all, why
shouldn't she enjoy herself? She'd earned it, hadn't she? And one
evening's fun wouldn't hurt...She folded the letter and tucked
it into the jewellery box next to her wedding ring. This had, of
necessity, been taken off as F-J thought it better that the Right
Club didn't know she had a husband in the forces and had over-
ridden her objections that this could easily be checked if anyone
cared to. She couldn't put the ring on again—Ventriss thought
she'd lost it. Pushing away the thought that she could just as well
have told him she wasn't wearing it because of work, she collected
her washing things and went out to the bathroom. Lying back
in the ancient, claw-footed bath, she abandoned herself to happy
anticipation of the evening ahead, and managed, by and large, to
ignore the draught on her neck from the ill-fitting window.

Ventriss collected her in a taxi and took her to dine at the Café
Royal, where he ate oysters and beef stroganoff and Diana,
who was too excited to be hungry, opted, to his disgust, for an

ómelette. They finished the meal with Crêpes au Citron, coffee, and liqueurs. She wasn't having nearly as much fun as she'd thought because he spent a great deal of the dinner leaning on the balustrade and waving to people he knew, several of whom came up to the table to chat. Their determined jollity—a jostling, good-natured insistence on having a good time—reminded Diana of the impending invasion. The way that the men and, more particularly, the women, persisted in looking her over was annoying. Despite telling herself that this was in the line of work, the fear that one of them might know Evie or F-J and report back grew on her until it became almost paralysing. Also—although she knew it was entirely contradictory, because Ventriss was nothing more than a colleague, after all—her irritation that he wasn't paying her more attention eventually spilled over to the point where she pushed away her coffee cup and snapped, 'I'm not on approval, you know.'

There was a hint of hurt, as well as mockery, in his brown eyes. 'I know you're not.'

'Well, I feel as if I am. All these people...Perhaps you should hand out particulars.'

'You're being silly, darling. In any case, they do approve of you—and so do I. Why don't we go somewhere else?'

Diana had expected him to make a crack about her liking to be admired, and found herself thrown off guard. 'Where?' she asked.

'Nightclub? Or what about a walk? It's quite warm, and there's a full moon tonight.' He glanced under the table at her high heels. 'If your feet can stand it.'

'Yes,' said Diana. 'Fresh air. I'd like that.'

They crossed Piccadilly, passing the boards around Eros and the large buildings fortified by sandbags, and headed down the Haymarket towards Trafalgar Square, where they stood, side by side, in front of the National Gallery. They were close, but not touching, and she could feel warmth coming off Ventriss, almost like a faint vibration, or…a wave, she thought. Like being tuned into a wireless set. The buildings, with their huge columns, were pale and clean in the moonlight, and everything seemed sharper, heightened. She was seeing it all, experiencing it, and yet, at the same time, she was conscious of nothing but the man next to her, as if it was his presence alone that made it real and important. 'Nelson looks out of place now all the other statues are boarded up,' she said.

'Yes,' said Ventriss. 'He needs a tin hat.'

'Poor Nelson.'

'Not at all. He's had his victory.'

'Will we have ours?'

'Who knows? Too early to say.'

'Yes, it is…' She turned to look at him. 'I never thanked you for the flowers. They were lovely.'

'You're lovely.' Ventriss put his hands on her upper arms and pulled her to him. Thinking that he was going to kiss her, she readied herself, closing her eyes, but after a moment she felt herself released, and, when she looked, she saw that he was staring down at her with a solemn expression. Feeling idiotic, and hoping she hadn't looked too swoony, because she had wanted him to kiss her, very much, she asked, 'What's the matter?'

'Why did you marry Guy Calthrop?'

'I was in love with him.'

'Was? What about now?'

'I don't know.' Diana shook her head. She really didn't want to talk about it—Ventriss confused her enough as it was. 'I was very young, and it happened so quickly. Perhaps I just thought I was in love with him, but it seemed real, and then…'

'And then what?'

'I'm not sure. I suppose I must have thought—no, I did think—that marriage would be wonderful, but…'

'It wasn't?'

'No. It's hard to explain. I wasn't deliriously happy, but I thought we could make a go of it. It was only when the war came and Guy went away, and I was living with my beastly mother-in-law that I realised perhaps I didn't have to do that after all, and...' Diana stopped, feeling disloyal. However she felt, it wasn't fair to turn Guy—Guy who wasn't there to defend himself, and with whom there had been some good times, and for whom she still felt affection—into an excuse for bad behaviour. 'I shouldn't be telling you all this,' she said, crisply. 'I think I had better go home.'

'If you like,' said Ventriss, calmly. 'I'll walk you to the station—unless you'd prefer a taxi.' That was it! No protest, no anything.

'A taxi,' she said, peering in the direction of Whitehall. 'I think there's one coming.'

'I'll get it.' Ventriss descended the steps. 'Come on!'

She was still smarting when the cab pulled up in Tite Street. How could he just...relinquish her like that? And all those questions about Guy—sheer impertinence, not to mention bad taste. And pretending he was about to kiss her...The worst thing about it all was, she had no-one to blame for any of it except herself. Everyone had warned her, hadn't they? But oh no, Diana Calthrop always had to think she knew better.

Her bad mood continued while she got ready for bed, until, lying on her back in the dark, the mixture of anger at Ventriss and self-loathing got the better of her, and she began to cry. Groping under the pillow for her handkerchief, she sat bolt upright and blew her nose loudly. This couldn't be allowed—it was all moonlight, and liqueurs, and...and nonsense.

She snapped on the bedside lamp and went over to the dressing table for a cigarette. Seeing her reflection in the glass, she thought, what if Claude were to see me like this, but hastily revised the thought to what if Guy were to see me—or people generally—because weeping women were bad for morale, and so forth. 'Ridiculous,' she muttered. 'There's no-one to see.'

That was better. She couldn't afford to let things get on top of her like that. She took a cigarette out of the box, and, muttering to herself that she'd better find an ashtray, went to fetch one from the kitchen. Mustn't upset the maid by making a mess, or the woman might give notice. She lit her cigarette. Then, deciding that some tea might help, she filled the kettle and lit the gas. Cooking simple things for herself was still a novelty and rather hit and miss, but at least she had managed to master a pot of tea. Absurd, she thought, to have to learn at the age of twenty-four. Why hadn't they been taught such things? Any sort of culinary procedure was a sharp reminder that she'd been trained for nothing but a life of relentless frivolity like her mother's: fittings at the dressmakers, luncheons, the hairdresser, shopping and parties...And it would have been her life, if the war hadn't intervened. As she watched the blue flames licking the base of the kettle, she suddenly remembered how Guy, in the first month of their marriage, had taught her to make scrambled eggs on the cook's night off. He'd learnt as a fag at Eton, and she remembered him standing behind her, holding her round the waist and directing her as she stirred the mixture. She'd burnt the first lot, because he'd kept kissing her. She'd loved him, then, despite her misgivings about his closeness to Evie. That evening, they'd laughed and been happy...

The noise of the boiling kettle caught her attention. As she switched off the gas and warmed the teapot, she thought, with a sudden flush of shame, Guy is my husband and I am seeing another man behind his back. She shouldn't be fuming about Claude's behaviour but examining her own. It has to stop, she thought, rinsing the pot. Whatever happens, I must not see him again. Vigorous with resolution, she spooned in tea leaves, added water, and stirred. I shall drink this, she told herself, then I shall go to bed and sleep and be at my best for Sir Neville Apse tomorrow. And, whatever else happens, I shall not permit myself to think about Claude.

Diana, regarding Sir Neville Apse over the remains of a very good lunch in Claridges dining room, decided that he must be about the same age as F-J—fifty-ish—but she'd been entirely caught off guard by how handsome he was. He had fine, chiselled features, thick black hair with a white stripe down the middle—an aristocratic badger—and a tall, elegant frame. Although—unlike, say, Claude—he didn't give the impression of being conscious of the power of his looks, Diana felt that he probably was, all the same. There was a hint of self-awareness about his graceful movements, and a suggestion of arrogance in his manner that was just a touch more than the usual endowment of breeding, a public school education, and all the right connections. It was, she thought, part of a general air of amusement with being amused by the world, including, on this occasion, herself. Was it because of her sex? Perhaps he was different with F-J...She wondered, fleetingly, what it would take to shake his composure.

'The problem is,' he was saying, 'that wars tend to be regarded in terms of black and white, when, in reality, the...moral palette, if you like, is better viewed as different shades of grey: compromise, difficult choices, and so forth. Unavoidable, I'm afraid; and at times like this, one has to deal with all sorts of unsavoury people. Doesn't mean one trusts them, of course. But that's the bigger picture—we needn't concern ourselves too much with that.'

Diana, who had the impression that he'd given this little speech several times before—even the hesitation seemed rehearsed—nodded to show that she was paying attention.

'As far as the spy network is concerned—theirs, I mean— the truth is that we simply don't know the extent of it. We believe that the Abwehr will try to recruit IRA sympathisers, resentful Welshmen, deserters from the forces, criminals and so forth, but we have no idea of either the success or the efficiency of their operation.' He paused, and stared at her for a moment, before continuing. 'The interests of the spy and the thief aren't so very different, you know. Both trade in stolen goods.' He smiled, and Diana smiled back. 'But at least half the people you'll encounter,' he continued, 'will be cranks or fantasists, and at least half of those will be elderly ladies imagining Germans under their beds, but every report, however lunatic, has to be investigated. You'll find that in most cases, what passes for patriotism is actually a healthy instinct for self-dramatisation. So…' His fingers touched the base of his empty glass and pushed it half an inch towards her, as if it were a chess piece. 'Do you think you're up to the job?'

'I'll do my best, sir.'

'I'm sure you will.'

Diana held his gaze for a moment—again, that look of thinly-veiled amusement—then, lowering her eyes, noticed that her fingers were on the stem of her own glass, and that she had, unconsciously, mimicked his chess-playing action with a push of her own. I don't believe he's pro-fascist, either, she thought. Or—as F-J had said, a 'cold fish'. In fact, she rather liked him.

'What the bloody hell is going on?' Stratton shoved his way through the throng of shouting, gesticulating bodies in the police station foyer towards PC Ballard, who was standing, helmet askew, in the middle of the melee, vainly trying to calm a group of four swarthy men with moustaches and long aprons. One had a split lip, another a bloody towel wrapped round his hand, and all of them were yelling foreign imprecations at the tops of their voices. A tiny, black-shawled crone was howling in the arms of a policewoman who was patting her ineffectually on the shoulder, and a red-faced PC Arliss was yelling for quiet. Old Cudlipp, the desk sergeant who should have been on duty, was nowhere to be seen, but Stratton thought he detected the sound of groaning from behind the wooden partition.

He turned round just in time to see two of the men break away from Ballard and make a lunge for Arliss, who disappeared immediately beneath a welter of milling arms and legs. Stratton dived after them, grabbed their collars and jerked them upright. 'Break it up, now, gents. We don't want a free-for-all.' Arliss beat a hasty retreat behind the desk, and a sudden hush fell on the room as both men, now held at arm's length—Stratton was almost a foot taller than either of them—glared at him, panting.

'Let's try and sort this out, shall we?' He let go of the men, who shook themselves angrily. The oldest of the men who had been haranguing Ballard spat on the floor.

'None of that,' said Stratton. 'This is a police station, not a prizefight. What's the problem?'

'I think,' said Ballard, looking uncomfortable, 'that it might be better if I explained in private.'

'Fair enough. Are they all together?'

'Yes, sir. Same family.'

'Right.' Stratton turned to the policewoman. 'Miss Harris, I suggest you take this lady through to the back and give her a cup of tea. See if you can make some sense of what's happened.'

'I don't think she speaks English, sir.'

'Never mind. Just do the best you can.'

Policewoman Harris put her arm round the elderly woman's shoulders, and was about to escort her from the foyer when the man who had spat leapt forward. 'Stop!' he roared. 'You no arrest my mother!'

'I'm not arresting anyone,' said Stratton, mildly. 'But I will if you don't pipe down. Now, PC Arliss here will take you through to a nice, quiet room where you will wait nice and quietly until I have had a word with PC Ballard.'

When Arliss had ushered the four men out, Stratton turned to Ballard. 'Well?'

'Thank you, sir,' said Ballard. 'I know it's not your—'

'Never mind that. Are they aliens?'

'No, sir. Greek.'

'So what are they doing here? You'd better start from the beginning.'

'We were on Frith Street, sir, patrolling, and there was a disturbance at the barber's shop, so we went to investigate, and there was a fight in progress—the old lady was belting one of the customers with a hairbrush, and calling him...Well, I don't know what she was calling him, sir, because it wasn't English, but it sounded pretty nasty to me. He was trying to fend her off, and then the others got involved, and a mirror got broken, and the gentleman got cut, and one of them gave him a black eye. He wants to bring charges, sir, and Arliss thought they were Eyeties, you see, so he wanted to bring them in anyway, and he sent for the Black Maria. We managed to get them here, but they were all shouting at once...' Ballard shook his head. 'Quite a to-do, sir.'

'Did you make any sense of it?' asked Stratton.

'Well, sir, I think the gentleman was having his hair cut, and he said he was polishing his spectacles under the sheet, sir,' Ballard indicated his crotch, 'and the lady seems to have thought he was doing something else, because of the...' he made a graphic gesture with one hand, 'the...movement, sir, and of course she couldn't see what he was doing, so she fetched him a whack with the hairbrush, on his...' Ballard winced, '...you know, sir, and broke the spectacles, and then, well, all hell broke loose.'

'Is that what he told you?'

Ballard shook his head. 'He just said he was polishing the spectacles and she attacked him, sir, without warning. The others—they're her sons—obviously they could understand what she was shouting, but they didn't want to tell me, because... well...'

'Because they didn't want you to know that their mother knew about such things.'

Ballard nodded. 'Family honour, sir. One of the other customers told me. He saw the whole thing.'

'And where is he now?'

'I took his details, sir. In case we need a witness.'

'I see. And the man was polishing his spectacles, was he? According to your witness?'

'Yes, sir. They were in his lap when they got broken, under the sheet. But he said, sir, that it looked very like...Well, what the lady thought, sir. The barber wants to bring charges against the gentleman for breaking up the shop. And they're furious with Arliss because he called them Eyeties, sir.'

'Terrific. Where's the chap with the glasses?'

'With Cudlipp, sir. I thought I'd better get him out of the way before they did him any more damage.'

'Well, I'll go and see him—see if we can't straighten this out. In the meantime, you go back to our barbershop quartet and tell them we're sorting it out and that if I hear a peep out of any of them, they'll find themselves in the cells.'

'Very good, sir. Thank you.'

'And straighten your tunic. You look as if you've been through a hedge backwards. What's their name, by the way?'

'Polychronopolos, sir.'

'Bloody hell.'

'Yes, sir. That's what I thought.'

Stratton found Cudlipp in a cubbyhole next to the Information Room. Sitting next to him, with partially cut hair and a swelling eye, was Joe Vincent's fellow lodger, Mr Rogers. When he saw Stratton, he leapt to his feet. 'Are you in charge here? That woman attacked me, and I want to know what you're going to do about it!' He produced the mangled glasses. 'Look!' he said, thrusting them in Stratton's face. 'Just look at that! Something's got to be done.'

'In the circumstances,' said Stratton, 'that might not be such a good idea.'

'What do you mean? What circumstances?'

'Why don't you sit down,' suggested Stratton, 'and we can discuss it.'

Mr Rogers cast wildly about him as if all the chairs had suddenly been removed by magic. 'I was assaulted,' he said. 'Quite unprovoked—woman's obviously deranged, a danger to the public, and if you...if you...' He tailed off and stared at Stratton, who thought he detected a hastily disguised flicker of fear.

'We've met before,' said Stratton.

The man hesitated. 'Yes. At my rooms, I think.' Stratton thought that "rooms" was going it a bit for Mrs Cope's dingy lodging house, but merely said, 'That's right. DI Stratton.'

'Rogers.' The man tucked the glasses into his pocket and stuck out his hand. 'What did you mean about the circumstances?'

Seeing that the man had no idea that he might have offended, Stratton said, 'It's rather delicate, sir.'

'Delicate? Look at me!' Rogers, his indignation re-surfacing, held a shaking finger up to his eye.

'As you say, sir, the lady attacked you. May I suggest you sit down, and I'll explain.'

'Nothing to explain. Woman's off her head.' Clearly feeling that he had driven the point home, Rogers sat.

'Do you need me, sir?' asked Cudlipp. 'I ought to get back to the desk.'

'Of course.' When he'd left the room, Stratton asked, 'Have you any idea why Mrs Polychronopolos attacked you?'

'There was no reason at all! I was sitting quietly, minding my own business, having a haircut.'

'You were polishing your spectacles, weren't you, sir?'

'Yes, and that bloody woman smashed them to pieces. They'll have to be paid for.'

'I'm afraid Mrs Polychronopolos was upset. She thought you were committing an indecent act. Your hands were under the sheet, sir. In your lap. She witnessed a jerking movement, and came to the unfortunate conclusion that you were masturbating.'

'What!'

'Masturbating, sir.' Stratton managed to keep a straight face, but it was a near thing.

'You mean, she thought that I was doing—that in the...' Rogers gestured wordlessly.

'Yes,' said Stratton, adding, smoothly, 'Not the best place for it, you'll agree, sir.'

'No...but look here...I mean...' Rogers spluttered, then shouted, 'That's defamation! I could sue her for that, in fact, I've got a good mind to—'

'Do I take it,' Stratton interrupted, 'that you were polishing your glasses, sir, and not engaging in the other activity?'

'Of course I was! The whole thing's disgusting! What I want to know is, what are you going to do about it?'

'If I were you, sir, I'd let the matter drop.'

'Drop? I've been assaulted!'

'I'm just thinking of how it might appear in court.'

Rogers was silent for a while. Judging by the expressions passing across his face, Stratton could almost see the man's thoughts: visions of a magistrate peering at him over half-moon spectacles, giggles and nudges from the gallery as euphemistically worded accusations were made—engaging in a lewd practice, self-abuse, manipulating his person. He would be made a laughing stock or, supposing he was not believed, a pathetic disgrace, and his elderly mother's shame and sorrow would be unbearable...At last Rogers spoke: 'Ah,' he said.

'I'll leave you to think it over,' said Stratton.

Exiting as fast as he could, he ran down the corridor to the Gents', where he could laugh without being heard. Ballard came in while he was splashing his face with water. 'Sir?'

'He's not going to press charges. Have your lot calmed down a bit?'

'They're still arguing, but at least they're keeping the noise down.'

'Good. And the old lady?'

'Fine, sir. Sitting there as if she's in church.'

'I think you'd better get them all together and explain that we can quite understand how the misunderstanding happened, but that it was only a misunderstanding, and the best thing would be to go home and forget all about it. Oh, and make it clear that we know they're not aliens and they've got every right to go about their lawful business and so forth, won't you?'

Ballard nodded. 'Thank you very much, sir.'

'You're welcome. Best laugh I've had all week. I'll tell Rogers he's free to go, and then I think I'd better have a word with Arliss about geography.'

Ballard's mouth twitched slightly. 'Yes, sir. But I think you'll be lucky, sir, if you don't mind my saying. Wogs begin at Calais, and all that.'

'I know,' said Stratton, wryly. 'I can but try.'

Rogers stood up, white faced, when Stratton re-entered the room. He'd taken care, on the return journey down the corridor, to arrange his features into what he hoped was a solemn but kindly expression, and to expunge all thoughts of wanking and magistrates from his mind. Rogers, it seemed, hadn't succeeded in this. Still shaken by the spectre of police charges and public humiliation, he was a cowed man, desperate to re-establish himself as a law-abiding, conscientious citizen, for whom anything beneath the trousers was strictly off limits.

'Well?' said Stratton. The top of Rogers' head barely reached his chin, and when he looked up, Stratton's impression was of a small boy caught with an apple up his jumper. 'I see what you mean, Inspector,' Rogers said, easing his collar with a nervous finger. 'It could have been very embarrassing. But really, I had no idea at all...'

'I understand,' said Stratton, paternally. 'Perhaps it's best to say no more about it.'

'I quite agree.' Rogers nodded enthusiastically. 'You're absolutely right.'

'PC Ballard is just having a word with the gentlemen from the shop, and I'm sure that once he's explained matters it'll all be plain sailing, and you'll be free to go about your business.'

'Well, that is good news. I'm very grateful to you, sir, for sorting it out.'

Noting the 'sir', Stratton thought he might as well take a flyer.

'There's nothing else you'd like to tell me, is there, while we're waiting? Of course,' he added, 'I'm sure the gentlemen from the shop will be understanding, but there's always a risk that they'll decide to press charges, and it may not be possible to dissuade them.' He stared intently at Rogers, who swallowed several times.

'Well,' he said, 'Now that you mention it, I did remember something, after you came to see me.'

'What was that?'

'Those chaps you were asking about, the ones who came to see Joe Vincent. I did see someone. I was,'—he cleared his throat—'mistaken, when I said I was out. That was a different evening entirely. It only came back to me after you'd gone.'

Stratton raised his eyebrows.

'I thought of it a couple of days later,' said Rogers, 'Funny thing, memory.'

'Yes, isn't it? Did you let them in?'

Rogers nodded. 'There were two of them. I can't say I got a good look, but one was a tall man, wearing a suit if I remember rightly, and there was a younger one with him.'

'Can you remember anything else?'

'The younger one was shorter, medium height, I'd say. Dark hair, brown I think, not black. No hat—the older man had one. I'm pretty sure the young one was wearing a suit as well, but I can't really recall. Something dark, anyway.'

'What time was that?'

'About nine o'clock, I think.'

So the men had been there for over two hours. 'Did you hear any noise coming from upstairs after that?' Stratton asked.

'I don't remember anything. A couple of bumps, perhaps. I must have thought it was the men coming back downstairs. I could have told them Joe wouldn't be there.'

'Why didn't you?'

Rogers looked nonplussed. 'I don't know. I suppose I thought they might want to leave a note or something.' Or you didn't like the look of them, thought Stratton.

'Had you seen them before?' he asked.

'No, never.'

'Well,' said Stratton, 'it's better than nothing. But,' he continued, severely, 'it would have been a lot more help if you'd remembered all this when I asked you.'

Rogers looked crestfallen. 'I'm sorry,' he said, 'it slipped my mind. I mean, it didn't seem very important, and I didn't think. I suppose I just thought they were friends of Joe's, and I forgot about it.'

Like hell you did, thought Stratton. 'Never mind,' he said reassuringly, 'I know now. But these little things...We do rely on the public to help us in our investigations, you know.'

Rogers beamed—he was back on the right side of the fence, helping the police, status restored. 'Of course,' he said, and then, emboldened, 'Might they have had something to do with Miss Morgan?'

Stratton countered this question with one of his own: 'Did you know Miss Morgan?'

Rogers, having been helped back on to the moral high ground once more, consolidated his position with a disapproving sniff. 'I knew what she looked like, of course,' he said. 'And I'd heard her often enough. Singing, banging about...Joe's a quiet lad, Inspector, considerate, but, to be honest, I've been on the point of complaining to Mrs Cope a few times, about the noise she made. Of course, she spent most of her evenings in the pub.' The last word was invested with enormous disapproval.

'Are you quite sure you didn't hear anything?' asked Stratton.

'No. I was listening to the wireless.'

'So you heard nothing?' Rogers shook his head.

'Did you hear Mr Stockley's gramophone?'

'I don't think so. I don't remember hearing it. Mr Vincent is all right, isn't he? I haven't seen him since...Not that I keep a look out but...nothing's happened to him, has it?'

'No,' said Stratton, adding, in a voice that precluded further questions, 'He's gone away for a few days.'

'Oh,' said Rogers, with the air of one who'd just received privileged information. 'To be honest,' he added, 'I never thought Miss Morgan was a good influence on him. Not that it wasn't most regrettable...I was most surprised when I found out she'd been in films, but then I'm not a picturegoer myself.'

Stratton, feeling that nothing more was to be gained from Rogers, managed to get rid of him after repeated handshakes and assurances of gratitude and a lot of guff about nasty misunderstandings and distressing unpleasantness. He went off to find Arliss, reflecting as he did so that the morning hadn't been entirely wasted, after all.

CHAPTER

18

Diana gazed at the empty birdcage behind Mrs Wright's head and hoped she wouldn't actually nod off before the old lady started to unburden herself. She'd been out late the night before, dining with members of the Right Club, and the low-ceilinged cottage parlour was stuffy and cramped. Photographs of Mrs Wright's dead husband and her only son, killed in the Great War, covered every surface.

Diana sipped her tea, and waited. She'd come down on the train to investigate a rumour that the church tower was being used to house an enemy transmitter. Having inspected the tower and ascertained from the vicar that this couldn't possibly be the case, she'd come to assure the source of the complaint that she had nothing to fear. This sort of thing was, as Apse had foretold, becoming pretty routine: in her first week's work she'd travelled to Barnet, Woking and Aylesbury to convince fearful (or, in one case, simply dotty) elderly ladies that their neighbours weren't consulting maps with evil intent or signalling to the Germans with lighted cigarettes, and that their foreign servants (a bewildered Portuguese couple) were not hatching plots to overthrow the country.

'It's the old church tower,' said Mrs Wright. 'It isn't used any more, and nobody goes there, you see.'

'I've spoken to the vicar, Mrs Wright, and he assures me that no-one has been up there. It isn't safe.'

'But I saw someone. He had a ladder.'

'It was the verger, Mrs Wright. He was making some repairs. The tower is empty. We do appreciate your concern, but there's really nothing to worry about.'

Mrs Wright leant forward and grasped Diana's hand. 'But there is, my dear. It's not surprising you didn't find anything—they can make these transmitters the size of a cigarette packet, and then they hide them between the bricks. I have proof.'

'What sort of proof?'

'Topsy.'

'Topsy?'

Mrs Wright turned her head to look at the empty cage. 'My canary. He died.'

'I'm sorry. But I don't see...'

The old lady patted her hand. 'Of course you don't, dear. I'll show you.' She rose from her chair, opened a drawer in the dresser, and produced a small bundle wrapped in a table napkin, which she placed in Diana's lap. Realising what it must be, she tried not to flinch. 'They killed him.'

'Who killed him, Mrs Wright?'

'With the transmitter.' The old lady looked impatient. 'The rays. They come over the cottage, from the machine in the tower. Canaries are sensitive to that sort of thing—that's why they use them in coal mines, poor lambs.'

'But they use them to detect gas. Carbon monoxide and methane and things like that.'

'Exactly!' Mrs Wright beamed as if she were a teacher and Diana a clever pupil. 'That's why Topsy died. Look!'

Diana, who'd been trying to avoid the sight of the package on her knees, gave a discreet sniff. It didn't smell too bad...hoping that Topsy hadn't been dead for very long, she took one corner of the material between a thumb and finger and tugged, gingerly. The material unrolled enough for her to see a stiff bundle of yellow feathers with pathetically extended claws. 'You see?' said Mrs Wright. 'The rays killed him.'

'I don't think so,' said Diana, gently. 'Was he very old?'

Mrs Wright shook her head. 'He was in the best of health. And then last week, he stopped singing, and I could see he wasn't well at all. He was listless, and his eyes were dull, and he wouldn't eat…and then he died.'

'Perhaps it was a disease?' suggested Diana.

Mrs Wright shook her head again. 'He was fine.'

'This room is quite hot, isn't it? Perhaps he didn't like it.'

'Canaries need warmth. They come from hot places, you know.'

'Yes, but…' Diana was starting to feel desperate. 'Topsy was an English canary, wasn't he? I mean, he was born here. Perhaps…' she tailed off.

'I'm afraid there is only one explanation,' said Mrs Wright, firmly.

'What about the birdseed?' asked Diana. 'If the shortages have made it hard for the seed merchants to get hold of the right things—for the mixture—that might have affected him.'

Mrs Wright stopped shaking her head and looked thoughtful. 'I suppose that is possible,' she admitted. 'The man in the shop did tell me they'd had some difficulties.'

'I expect that's it, then,' said Diana, trying not to sound as relieved as she felt. 'I really do think it's the most likely explanation. Have you told him about Topsy?'

'No. Perhaps I ought to have a word with him.'

'I think that's an excellent idea,' said Diana.

Having succeeded in persuading Mrs Wright that it wasn't necessary for her to take the canary's corpse back with her for a post-mortem, Diana walked back to the station. After only a scratch breakfast and no lunch, she felt quite feeble with hunger and fortified herself as best she could on grey tea and an awful pie in the station buffet while waiting for the London train.

She secured a seat in a second-class carriage full of young WREN couriers talking about their boyfriends. It made her think of Claude—dangerous territory, this, like walking across a mined beach—but she gave herself up to it all the same, and thoroughly enjoyed it. Despite her good intentions, she'd been frantic when he hadn't contacted her for three whole days after the debacle in Trafalgar Square, and then pathetically relieved (although careful not to show it), when he'd telephoned her at Apse's office—which obviously meant that he'd been keeping tabs on her movements—and asked her out to dinner. Afterwards, they'd gone to dance at the Kit-Kat Club in Regent Street. It had been Diana's first visit, and she'd thought it rather louche, but great fun. Their goodnight kiss had made her tingle all over, and she'd gone home feeling light-headed with happiness, although the delirium was somewhat spoiled by a horrible sense of guilt about Guy. How is it possible, she asked herself, to feel elated and miserable at the same time? No one could hope to make sense of such a confusing conflict of emotions.

The sound of the WRENs' giggles brought Diana out of her reverie. Admiring their uniforms, so much more flattering than those of the ATS, she listened to their chat, reflecting that none of them were married, yet they seemed to know far more about men than she did. This struck her as unfair, but then again, she had it all to discover—if she chose to, of course. Otherwise, the thought of staying married—and faithful to—Guy, and sharing only his bed was depressing. It wasn't his fault—after all, he wasn't a bad man—but the monotony of it, the sheer boredom, year after year, of having to school herself to be numb, not to want, not to have feelings…Someone should have warned me, she thought. Stopped me from getting married. Told me I was too young. But who? Her aunt had thought it a good match, which, seen at a distance, it was, and lots of her friends had been married at nineteen. That was the purpose of the season: the launch into society, the suitable husband. And anyway, she'd been so sure of her love for Guy that even if someone had told her, she wouldn't have listened…A sudden and very intense physical memory of

Claude's thumb rubbing her nipple through the fabric of her dress made her turn towards the window, fearful that one of the girls might catch her blushing. There's no point dwelling on any of this, she thought. I have a job to do. I must, must, must—she closed her eyes tight and willed the imaginary Claude to remove his hand—concentrate on the important things.

She entered Dolphin Square from the Embankment and turned right for Apse's flat in Frobisher House, opposite Forbes-James's block. Like F-J, Apse worked partly from his home, but his flat was on the top floor, in the shape of an E minus its middle stroke. The front door opened onto a large office-cum-sitting room, and all the other rooms—the kitchen with its outside fire escape; the bedroom, the dressing room and so on—came off a dark, narrow L-shaped corridor. Privately, Diana thought that F-J's flat, with its balcony onto the river, was much nicer and airier. Apse's flat was a bit like the man himself, dark, with rooms concealed around corners. Not that F-J was open, exactly—that business about his wife, for instance—but Apse was...Diana frowned, searching for the right word.

'Distant', that was it. As if you were speaking to someone who was standing on the other side of a wall. Not because he wouldn't meet your eye, and he certainly wasn't furtive, but he didn't seem to be wholly there. But he appeared decent enough, so perhaps she was exaggerating this impression of distance because she was supposed to be suspicious of him. If he were pro-fascist, then it made sense that he would be guarded in his speech—and Mrs Montague and her friends certainly seemed to think that he was, or might be, sympathetic to their cause. She'd brought up his name several times in their company, but received very little response, beyond vague murmurings about reliability and usefulness, which she didn't feel she could query without drawing attention to herself. But he must be up to something, surely, or why would they have wanted her to work for him?

Lady Apse, who was at the flat when Diana arrived, proved something of a surprise. She wasn't sure what she'd expected, but it wasn't the slender woman with the shy, almost girlish manner who greeted her. The slim figure, pale blue kitten eyes and soft, light brown hair belied her age, which must have been at least forty, and Diana's overriding impression was of someone unworldly, whose idea of the best lark in the world would be a midnight feast in the dorm.

After about five minutes' chit-chat, during which Apse smiled at his wife with the slightly superior air of one who finds a mild enjoyment in the sound, if not the substance, of feminine prattle, Lady Apse said that she really must go or she'd miss her train. 'I'll leave you to Miss Calthrop, darling,' she added, and then gave a sort of terrified giggle as if she'd uttered something outrageously risqué.

'Of course,' said Apse. 'You mustn't miss your train. I'll ring for the driver.' Turning to Diana, he said, 'I've managed to get my hands on a FANY.'

'Fanny, dear?' Lady Apse looked puzzled.

Diana, who had a mouthful of sherry, just managed to avoid choking.

'First Aid Nursing Yeomenary. They're mostly drivers nowadays. We'll be sharing her with F-J,' Apse added, to Diana. 'Had to pull a few strings, of course.'

'Perhaps you should change your brand, Miss Calthrop,' said Lady Apse solicitously, proffering her cigarette case. 'Try one of these.'

'Thank you,' said Diana, just as the driver announced herself.

'Victoria Station,' Apse told the young woman, who looked as if she were about to burst with excitement. She saluted smartly, and withdrew. Apse kissed his wife, and said, 'Give my love to Pammy and Pimmy, won't you?' Turning away to give them some privacy, Diana just caught a glimpse of Apse's hand

touching Lady Apse's cheek. 'It's been lovely seeing you, darling.
I hope the journey isn't too awful.'

Diana was struck by the softness in his voice as he said his
children's names—unless Pammy and Pimmy were dogs, of
course...

'Good day?' said Apse, when his wife had departed.

'Rather odd. In fact, I narrowly avoided bringing you back a
dead canary. The owner thought it had been killed by rays from
an enemy transmitter.'

'Dear God,' said Apse faintly, sitting down behind his desk.
'Pour some more sherry, will you?'

As Diana refilled their glasses, he said, 'I'm afraid I've got
another crank for you tomorrow—a man in Epsom who thinks
the racecourse is going to be used as a landing ground for enemy
aircraft. I've got the letter here somewhere.' He sifted through a
pile of documents and handed her a letter written on flimsy paper
in small, spidery writing, with several words heavily underlined.
'I'm sure you can sort it out. There's another beauty here. Listen:

*Dear Sir, I am writing because I have been very worried
for some time about the effect of the water on my husband.
Over the last year I have noticed a decline in his manly
nature which I believe is caused by chemical contamination from enemy agents. The trouble started last year
after the supply was interrupted and the pipes dug up and
tampered with by foreign workmen. I am careful always
to boil water drunk by myself and my husband but we
have noticed a change in the taste and it is my considered
opinion that the men in this area are looking seedy and
not as they should. I would not write of such an intimate
matter but it seems to me that the good of the country is at
stake if this continues, because women will not have children and as a consequence will become selfish and spend
money on cosmetics and in frivolous pursuits, which will
weaken the fabric of the nation so there will be no chance
of holding firm against the enemy...*

'There's a lot more in the same vein. She says they've been married for thirty years, so she must be fifty if she's a day.'

Diana, controlling her laughter with an effort, asked, 'Where does she live?'

Apse consulted the letter. 'Fulham. You could go tomorrow, after Epsom. Transport willing, of course.' He sniffed the paper and grimaced. 'Devonshire violets. Perhaps she should change her perfume. Here, take it with you.'

Three hours later, Diana, seated with Jock and Lally at La Coquille, finished her sabayon and, taking advantage of a lull in the conversation, turned the stem of her glass in her hand as if considering something and said, 'Do you know, I feel awfully futile.'

Jock put down his spoon. 'How do you mean?'

'Well, I know we have to follow things up, letters about spies and so on, and of course, it's important to reassure the public, but what about the real subversives?'

'Real?' Lally raised an elegant eyebrow.

'I mean the high up people,' said Diana 'Well, not Mosley and co, obviously, but those sympathisers who haven't come out of the woodwork yet, who'd be in a position to help the Germans if there were an invasion.'

'But that's what we are doing,' said Lally. 'Or trying to.'

'Most of them are behind bars,' said Jock, easily. 'And the others, well...' he shrugged. 'Everyone knows everyone, so it shouldn't be too difficult, at least in theory.'

'You mean because one was at school with them, or university?'

'Of course. Or with their brothers or uncles or cousins.'

'But that doesn't mean you know them, does it?'

'It means you know their background, and their...pedigree, if you like. It's dangerous to get into the state of mind where one sees enemy agents around every corner. One knows that people are respectable—of course, that respectability may be a camouflage for absolutely anything, but most of it will be harmless.'

'Hitler isn't harmless,' said Diana.

'No, darling,' said Lally. 'But he isn't respectable, either.'

'But, just because somebody isn't…well bred, it doesn't mean they're no good.'

'Of course not,' said Jock. 'For heaven's sake, Diana, there are procedures for that sort of thing, checking on people, and so forth.'

'Yes,' said Diana, 'but a lot of it does seem to depend on the old school tie.'

'That's true,' said Jock. 'It does. And it doesn't take account of the hidden self.'

'Hidden?'

'The secret self, the innermost being.' He stared at her, thoughtfully. 'The part we do not—in some cases, dare not—reveal.'

Diana thought of Ventriss and felt uncomfortable: this wasn't the way she'd intended the conversation to go at all. Jock's eyes were boring into her like a pair of gimlets. She forced a laugh. 'That can't be true. It would mean that everyone was harbouring some frightfully interesting secret or a scandal or something.'

'I didn't say it was interesting. Except to the people themselves, of course. But then, some people enjoy playing detective. Supposition, conjecture, hypothesis…or prying, to call it by another name. It's in their nature. You'll find it's common amongst agents. Claude Ventriss, for example.'

Diana, aware that Jock and Lally were exchanging meaningful glances, lowered her eyes and toyed with her glass. After a moment's uncomfortable silence, Jock continued, 'It's a certain cast of mind. Digging about, looking behind the mask, and so forth. Of course, the safest thing is to be exactly what one seems to be, and I daresay most people are exactly that, so really it isn't a mask at all.'

'But Claude Ventriss isn't what he appears to be, is he?' said Lally. 'He's a double agent. Or so rumour has it.'

'Claude?' Diana blurted, astonished. 'Is that right?' she asked Jock.

'I have absolutely no idea,' he said, blandly. 'And it's best not to speculate. The less one knows...'

'You don't allow for female curiosity,' said Lally.

'Curiosity,' said Jock, solemnly, 'can be a very bad thing.'

'Even for an agent?' asked Diana, desperate to hear more. 'You've just told us it's common to play detective.'

'It may sound contradictory, but yes: especially for an agent. There are times when one must close one's eyes. It's a question of self-preservation. What you don't know is just as important as what you do know. You might,' he continued, 'think that knowledge is power, but if you know something about somebody that they don't want you to know, it can make you very vulnerable. And,' he added, turning to look straight at Diana, 'you should also remember that some people enjoy danger. They don't feel alive without it. Claude lived in Germany before the war, and France. As far as I can gather, he was a playboy. He's not doing it for the money, because he doesn't need to—which, by the way, is fairly unusual—but because he enjoys walking on a tightrope.'

'So he is a double agent,' said Lally, triumphantly.

'I didn't say that,' said Jock.

'But,' Diana said, trying not to sound too eager, 'if he is, then—'

'You should remember,' Jock interrupted, wagging a finger at her, 'what happened when Pandora opened the box. And I think,' he added, 'that it's high time we changed the subject.'

As she walked home, Diana thought, miserably: I'm no good at this. She'd thought herself so clever, chatting to Mrs Montague and her cronies from the Right Club, but Apse was a different thing altogether, and as for Claude, if he was a double agent...I ought to resign, she told herself. I should go to F-J and tell him I can't split my brain into two parts. After a few minutes imagining the scene, it occurred to her that she might not be allowed to resign—that the little she knew might be deemed too much for security—and that she might have to spend the rest of the war, even the rest of her life, in some dingy MI5 basement, filing papers. She imagined herself as an old woman, bent double over a filing cabinet...

Diana shook her head, baffled. Both my conspicuous self and my secret one are thoroughly confused, she thought, then smiled as she remembered the letter from the woman in Fulham about the water supply. A decline in his manly nature...What must her secret self be like? It didn't bear thinking about. She grinned to herself, rolled her eyes, and increased her pace towards Tite Street.

CHAPTER

19

'"Hitler's 100-minute speech to the Reichstag, in which he talked vaguely of wanting peace, and at the same time admitted that if the war goes on either Britain or Germany will be annihilated, was received with cold scepticism throughout the world last night…"'

Stratton paused in his reading aloud of the *Daily Express*, and looked across at Jenny, who was sitting in the armchair opposite, knitting energetically. The light from the table lamp beside her fell across her cheek and lit up her bright brown hair. Stratton had a comfortable, after-supper feeling; Jenny had cleared away their evening meal of ham and salad, followed by rice pudding with a blob of jam in the middle, and, at his request, had brought him a cup of tea in the sitting room. She had smoked her customary cigarette (he knew she didn't really like them but she'd read somewhere else that it was the smart thing to do after meals), and was now click-clacking her way through a ball of grey wool. Stratton, who found her small affectations endearing, gazed at her and thought how lovely she looked.

Jenny glanced up, enquiringly. 'Why have you stopped?'

'I was just admiring you.'

'Oh…' She looked faintly embarrassed. 'Get on with you.'

'What are you knitting?'

'A balaclava for Pete.'

'In the middle of summer?'

'He'll need it in the winter. And I won't have Mrs Chetwynd say I don't look after them.'

Stratton thought that last remark was rather more to the point as Pete had already got a perfectly good balaclava, but he refused to be drawn. 'Shall I carry on?' he asked.

Jenny gave him a mutinous look, but conceded temporary defeat and said, meekly, 'Yes, dear.'

'Hitler says, "Mr Churchill thinks Germany will be annihilated. I know it will be Britain."'

'Oh, he does, does he?'

'He does. "I am not the vanquished begging for mercy. I speak as a victor. I see no reason why this war must go on."'

'He makes me tired. What else is there?'

'The RAF's still doing well. And we've bombed Krupps.'

'Perhaps that's why Hitler wants peace.'

'Or he's running out of supplies. There's a headline here: "Hitler boasts: We can face blockade for ever—even in food." Sounds like hot air to me—and Harry Comber says there's going to be famine in Europe. Mind you, I don't know how he knows.'

'I worry about how we're going to manage.'

Stratton raised his eyebrows. 'You've got the place stocked like a grocer's shop. I've never seen so much food.'

'Yes, well...' Jenny looked uncomfortable.

'You haven't been buying under the counter, have you?'

'No! Well, not much. Everyone's doing it, Ted.'

'You mustn't. I know it's tempting, but—'

'Tempting! It's not new gloves, it's food!'

'I know, love. But all the same—' He shook his head. 'How can we expect the kids to grow up honest if we're breaking the rules?'

Jenny stopped knitting and glared at him. 'Pete and Monica aren't here,' she said. 'In case you hadn't noticed.'

Here we go, thought Stratton. What had Donald said in the pub? All the time we're not talking about it, I know she wants to and she's biting her tongue…And now it was out in the open. He wondered what he should say next, then thought of the other thing Donald had said before that stupid fucker Reg had lumbered over and interrupted them: Can't blame the women, it's a lot harder on them.

'I don't like it any more than you do,' he said, gently, 'but there's nothing we can do about it, you know that.' He paused for a moment, to see how this was being received—not too badly, judging from the fact that the glare had been replaced by a sort of all-purpose scowl—then turned back to the paper.

'There's good news about Roosevelt. He's going to give us all the help he can, according to this. "Franklin Roosevelt, the only man in the history of the United States to be nominated as presidential candidate for a third term, said in his historic broadcast: "I do not regret my persistent endeavour to awaken this country of ours to the menace for us. So long as I am President I will do all I can to ensure that that remains our foreign policy…We face one of the great choices of history. It is not alone a choice of government, government by the people versus dictatorship. It is not alone the choice of freedom versus slavery. It is not alone the choice between moving forward or falling back. It is all of these rolled into one." Blimey.'

Jenny nodded approvingly. 'He's a good man.'

'So we're not all no-hopers, then.'

Jenny rolled her eyes, then said, 'Do you think that means America's going to enter the war?'

'I don't know. It sounds as if Roosevelt wants to, but there's a lot of Americans who oppose him. They don't want to get involved.'

'I suppose you can't blame them,' said Jenny. 'I mean, we didn't want to get involved, did we? Not at the beginning, at least.'

'Well, we'll be in trouble if they don't,' Stratton said, gloomily. 'I wish they'd get on with it.'

Jenny put down her knitting, rose from her chair and gave him a kiss on the cheek before taking the cups through to the kitchen. Stratton wasn't sure if it was meant as an apology for snapping at him or an attempt to cheer him up or a bit of both, but whatever it was, he thought, it was nice.

Being bollocked, Stratton decided, would be a lot easier to cope with if DCI Lamb didn't look so much like George Formby. How were you supposed to take someone seriously if they looked like a human being reflected in a tap? At least, being a Londoner, he didn't sound like George Formby as well, but the facial resemblance—jug ears, weak chin, protruding teeth and tiny bull-terrier eyes—was quite enough to be going on with.

It was 9.30 on Monday morning, and he was standing in front of Lamb's desk, trying to concentrate while his superior tore a strip off him, but his attention was riveted by Lamb's blunt, square forefinger jabbing his desk for emphasis. For some reason, he kept finding himself wondering where else the finger had been that morning—up his nose? Up his wife's—Stop it, Stratton told himself, for God's sake. What's wrong with you?

'What's wrong with you?' Lamb shouted. 'I thought you were a good copper, Stratton, but this' (pock!) 'isn't' (pock!) 'good enough!' (Pock, pock!) 'We need results, and fast.' He stopped bashing the desk long enough to pick up a piece of paper and wave it in Stratton's direction. 'Mr Fuller died on Friday!' It took several seconds before Stratton remembered that Mr Fuller was the chap who'd been injured in the jewel robbery and Lamb, seeing his momentary puzzlement, said, 'For God's sake, man! The jeweller's shop.'

'I'm sorry, sir. I wasn't notified.'

Lamb snorted. 'You should have been keeping tabs on it.'

'Yes, sir.'

'I don't suppose you've come up with anything, have you?'

'Not yet, sir.'

'Well, get on with it!'

'Yes, sir.'

'And that business with the gangs...What was the man's name?'

Mercifully, Stratton didn't have to think about that one. 'Kelland, sir.'

'Any further forward with that?'

'No, sir. We've interviewed everyone concerned, but none of them are prepared to admit they saw anything.'

Lamb sighed. 'No surprise there, just keep trying. And stop wasting your time with that dead actress, or whatever she was.'

'Sir?'

'You know what I'm talking about—Miss...What was it?'

'Miss Morgan, sir.'

'Yes, her. Suicide, pure and simple. No more to be said.'

Stratton very much wanted to ask Lamb how he knew about the enquiries he'd been making into Mabel Morgan's death and—possibly—the subsequent happenings at Joe Vincent's flat, but he kept quiet. Dr Byrne, the pathologist, perhaps? Maybe they'd met at some dinner or other and Byrne had complained about him. Joe himself was out of the question, as was Wallace, and Abie Marks was hardly more likely.

'Well,' said Lamb, 'Make sure you get onto the Fuller business straight away.'

'Yes, sir.' Before Stratton had the chance to say anything else, Lamb had swept out from behind his desk and was removing his hat and coat from the stand. 'By the way,' he said, 'there's another one just come in—found dead in Ham Yard, sometime this morning. Strangled, apparently. Don't waste too much time on it—concentrate on the other matter. Think you can do that?'

'Yes, sir.'

'Good. Now, I must leave. I've got a meeting with the Sub-Divisional Inspector.' Stratton held the door open for him, muttering, when Lamb was a safe distance down the corridor, 'And you can stick your ukulele up your jacksie while you're at it, sir.'

Back in his office, Stratton felt the beginnings of a headache. He wondered if Fuller's widow had made a complaint. Even taking into account the fact that she would be very upset, it was a bit soon for that sort of thing...It couldn't be anyone at the station—apart from the other DIs, he out-ranked everyone except Lamb, so...Was Lamb in line for a promotion, or something? He hadn't heard any rumours, but that didn't mean it was impossible. And now there was this woman killed in Ham Yard. Stratton picked up the paperwork that had been left on his desk. At least he'd be able to do the poor cow the courtesy of setting a few things in motion before he got stuck into the Fuller business. He began to read: Half past three this morning—PC 14—Victim identified as Maureen Mary O'Dowd, common prostitute, 28, known as Big Rita...

Stratton rubbed his hands over his face. Something was, very definitely, going on.

It was half-past ten when he left the station. He'd managed to make quite a lot of headway on Maureen O'Dowd, which was good—except, of course, that it wasn't the case Lamb wanted solved. The man had never given a toss about dead tarts, unless they appeared in the newspaper headlines. Fuller was going to be altogether more difficult to solve—the absence of witnesses, for one thing, and no fingerprints on anything because the bastards had worn gloves. However, the lateness of the hour meant that he'd be able to catch Joe Vincent as he was leaving the Tivoli without arousing the suspicion of the cinema's manager. He'd telephoned Doris at half past six and asked her to give a message to Jenny that he'd be late, so he wasn't worried about that, although Jenny—and you couldn't blame her—would undoubtedly have something to say about it when he finally did get home. It was a relief, he thought, that someone in the family had a telephone. He wished he'd got one before the war—there was no chance of it now.

He exchanged greetings with the Indian doorman as he went past Veeraswamy's, and made his way up Regent Street towards Piccadilly Circus. Reaching the cinema, he estimated that Joe wouldn't finish work for at least ten minutes, so he had a smoke and hung about peering at the dimly-lit display outside the building. The week's offering was *Strange Cargo*, starring Clark Gable and Joan Crawford, along with *Arouse and Beware* with Wallace Beery, John Howard and Dolores Del Rio. He admired the poster—well, the Dolores Del Rio part of it, anyway—and ignored the photograph of Joan Crawford, who didn't appeal to him. It was a shame he never had time to go to the pictures any more. He used to enjoy them when he and Jenny were courting.

Preoccupied with these thoughts, he almost missed Joe, who'd left the Tivoli by a side entrance, and he had to run to catch up with him. Joe jumped as he felt Stratton's hand on his shoulder. 'It's all right, Joe, it's me—DI Stratton.'

Joe turned and peered at him. 'Sorry, Mr Stratton. It's the blackout. Makes you jumpy.'

'I know,' said Stratton. Even in the dim light, he could see that, even after two weeks, Joe's bruises were still in evidence. 'All right, are you? Not had any more trouble?'

'No.'

'Still at your sister's?'

'Yes. I'll be called up any day, and I didn't want to go back to Conway Street. Beryl doesn't mind—she says it's company, and we rub along. Besides, I'll be going for basic training in a week or so.'

'Army?'

Joe nodded. 'Did you find him, Mr Stratton? The man. You said you knew him.'

'I found him. He won't be bothering you again.'

Joe grinned. 'That's a real weight off my mind. I'm ever so grateful to you, Mr Stratton. I can't tell you how much. It scared me silly, what they did.'

'Well, they won't be back. I wanted to ask you again about Miss Morgan, Joe, if you noticed anything odd about her manner on the day she died.'

'You don't think Mabel killed herself, do you, Mr Stratton?' Joe's voice was eager. 'Beryl doesn't. Nor do I.'

'I don't know. It could have been an accident.'

'I don't believe that, either. It was a normal day, Mr Stratton. I looked in to say goodbye—she liked to stop in bed, so I just used to put my head round the door and give her a cup of tea—and she was fine.'

'Did she say anything to you?'

'Nothing particular. Just said "Good morning", and she asked me to get her a quarter of acid drops. I remember that... Last thing she ever said to me. Acid drops. But,' he added, 'that doesn't sound like someone who's going to do themselves in, does it?'

Stratton had to admit that it didn't, but then again, perhaps Miss Morgan had been keen to preserve an illusion of normality. 'Did she often ask you to get things for her?'

'Sometimes. I mean, it wasn't odd or anything. She liked acid drops.'

'I see. Thank you, Joe. And good luck.' Stratton clapped him on the shoulder. It felt awkward, and he wondered whether Joe was aware of it. 'You'll be all right. Look after yourself—and mind you give my regards to your sister.'

'I will, Mr Stratton. And thanks again. I appreciate it, you taking all this trouble.'

'My job, lad,' said Stratton, sounding, even to his own ears, a shade too hearty. 'You get along home.'

What a stupid thing to say, Stratton thought, as he made his way to the station. Good luck. The poor bastard would probably get his head blown off. And what did he, Stratton, know about it, anyway. He'd never been a soldier. But we have to say these things, he thought. Just as we can't admit that we're scared—because there's nothing more frightening than fear itself.

It was a pity, Stratton thought, that Rogers hadn't told him about letting in Wallace and the boy when he'd asked the first time, but there it was. And as for DCI Lamb...Lamb stew. Monday was washday, and they always had lamb stew—one of his favourites, the smell forever linked in his mind with damp clothes and Jenny, pink-cheeked, her face framed in tendrils of hair that had escaped from their pins...Stratton smiled. Lamb could wait. His cooked—and much nicer—namesake was a far happier subject altogether.

CHAPTER 20

'All beak and feet.' Lady Caine prodded the game pie with her fork.

'I know,' murmured Diana, 'but what is one to do?' They were lunching at the tearoom in South Kensington, with Mrs Montague and Lady Calne's twenty-year-old daughter, Helen Pender, who worked at the Red Cross Headquarters in Knightsbridge.

'Of course,' said Mrs Montague, 'for some people, nothing has changed. One hears of Jews everywhere, buying up supplies and boasting about how they've evaded the call-up. And now that the bombing's started, able-bodied Jewish men are pushing their way into the shelters in front of women and children.'

'Dreadful,' said Lady Caine. 'They're absolutely taking over London. How long do you think the bombing will continue?'

'It might be three or four months,' said Mrs Montague. 'At least until Christmas. The Luftwaffe is very well equipped. Of course, we've only got ourselves to blame.'

Diana joined in the general murmur of agreement, and, while toying with her pie in the vain hope of finding an edible morsel, allowed her mind to drift. The talk everywhere was the same—the raids, and people's experiences, and the experiences of

people they knew, or had heard of—and besides, she was tired. Since the bombing started had begun on 7 September she didn't seem to have slept much at all and she felt listless and weary. How long could you go without proper rest, she wondered. A week was bad enough, but what if Mrs Montague was right about it lasting for months? How on earth would she feel then?

The anti-Jew talk was only the sort of thing one would hear anywhere—she obviously wasn't going to learn anything new today. What she really didn't understand was how, if all Jews were supposed to be capitalists and financiers and so forth, they could be Reds at the same time: the two things just didn't fit. The only time she'd ventured a remark of this sort was to one of the rare men one saw at Right Club gatherings. She'd prefaced it with a lot of self-deprecatory flim-flam about being a mere woman and therefore liable not to understand things very well, and she'd been told that it was all part of the conspiracy and it didn't do to forget, even for a moment, that all Jews were very cunning. Diana dabbed her lips with her napkin, drank some water, and tried, vaguely, to remember the name of the person who'd said this. Quite a handsome man—American, which was unusual—tall, and...Watson? No, that wasn't it...

She jumped slightly as Helen Pender, who was seated next to her, dropped her cutlery onto her plate with a clatter and pushed back her chair. 'Would you excuse me for a moment?' Helen's voice was abrupt, and, as she edged behind the chairs to get out into the main body of the restaurant, Diana felt a hand brush her shoulder—deliberately. Taking this as an invitation to follow, she also excused herself from the table.

In the cloakroom, she busied herself repairing her lipstick until Helen emerged from the cubicle. Her eyes and nose had a slightly pinched, pink look, as if she'd been trying, unsuccessfully, not to cry. 'Is something the matter?' Diana asked.

'I'm sorry,' said Helen. 'I know I don't know you well, but I couldn't bear to sit there for another moment. It's Mummy, you see. We had the most fearful row last night. About Walter.'

'Oh?' Diana, who was clearly supposed to know who Walter was and why Lady Calne was having rows about him, nodded encouragingly.

'It's ghastly. I know he's not our sort of person—well, he couldn't be, could he, being American, but all the same... Honestly, it's quite unbearable, you really can't imagine...Mrs Montague thinks he's splendid. She's told Mummy he's a terrific asset to the cause. Mrs Montague doesn't know about us, of course, and Mummy's so horridly suspicious she just won't listen.' She started to cry again. Diana, comforting her, tried to make sense of the jumble of information. 'She simply can't see,' gulped Helen, 'that none of it matters any more.'

'Of course not,' said Diana soothingly, patting Helen's shoulder abstractedly while the penny dropped: Walter, American, an asset to the cause...The man at the Right Club who'd talked about the Jewish conspiracy. Not Watson, but...Wymark. That was it, Walter Wymark. What exactly had he been doing, she wondered, that Mrs Montague thought so splendid? Gathering information, perhaps—not the sort of out-of-date stuff that she'd been passing over on F-J's instructions, but important things. She'd got no idea what he did—a journalist, perhaps, or maybe the Embassy...? Diana tried to concentrate on what Helen was saying and make the right soothing noises. As an older and married woman, she felt she ought to be able to offer some tremendously wise statement about human relationships and matters of that kind—clearly that's what was needed—but she couldn't think of anything to say beyond the fact that these things were difficult and took time, and that Lady Calne was bound to come round when she saw how committed Walter was. 'Oh, he is,' said Helen eagerly. 'He sees things so clearly, far more than—' She broke off as the cloakroom door opened and, to Diana's annoyance, Mrs Montague appeared.

'Good heavens, is anything wrong?'

'Just nerves,' said Diana quickly. 'It's the raids. I've been feeling pretty much on edge myself.'

'Of course,' said Mrs Montague. 'Everyone's the same. People are suffering dreadfully, and it's all so unnecessary.'

It took quite a few minutes, and a great deal of face powder, to make Helen calm and presentable enough to return to the table. Diana, who had been hoping to find out more about Walter Wymark, found herself thwarted when Mrs Montague insisted on staying to supervise the proceedings. Still, there were bound to be other opportunities, and now she had established a bond with Helen, it shouldn't be too difficult to bring the subject up on a future occasion.

There was no stop opposite the Ritz Hotel, but it didn't matter because the Piccadilly buses always pulled up to let girls off. 'Have a good time, darling,' called the conductor, as Diana stepped off the platform. 'Mind how you go!' It was early evening, and she was meeting Claude in the hotel bar. On the way, she'd read Evie's latest letter, which was full of complaints about disappearing servants. 'How is one supposed to manage with a staff of five?' What does she expect? thought Diana, and then, I bet they couldn't wait to see the back of her. 'I don't mind so much for myself, but when dear Guy comes home...' The subject of Guy's leave, which surely couldn't be long away, was one she'd deliberately avoided. She'd have to ask for leave at the same time, and if it were granted...Of course, the more she and Claude were seen in public together, dancing and so on, the greater the chances of some friend of Evie's spotting them and reporting back; but even without this worry, the idea of a week with Guy at Evie's house filled her with dread. Of course, she'd pretend to be pleased, and act the part of the dutiful wife...

Sitting on the bus, she'd suddenly remembered what F-J had said about the qualities of a good spy: 'The person must be honest, loyal, and trustworthy, but only to us.' Well, thought Diana, she was honest and loyal to F-J—she was firmly convinced about the rightness of that—but she certainly wasn't being loyal to her husband. She'd wondered if betrayal did not, perhaps, bring its own, rather nasty reward, even if you were doing it for the good

of your country—the memory of the exalted feeling and sense of power in the taxi after her first meeting with Mrs Montague made her uneasy. It was, when you came down to it, the satisfaction of having one up on somebody else. She remembered Jock's words, back in June, about danger making one feel more alive, and shivered. Was she turning into a different sort of person? These things never seemed to bother Lally, but then Lally wasn't married, and was obviously having the time of her life. Diana felt envious: so far, she'd resisted Claude's advances, but the idea of being his mistress was undeniably thrilling; as thrilling as the thought of Guy's touch was dreadful. His fumbling attempts at carnality were quite bad enough, but the knowledge that her husband's real desire was to please his mother by fathering a son and heir was repulsive to her.

What can I do? she thought. The answer, of course, was nothing. Better to enjoy herself while she could than to dwell on what couldn't be changed. In any case—and this thought hadn't been far from her mind since the first night of the raids, when she'd stood on the roof of Nelson House with F-J and watched the East End go up in flames—it might be her last chance. It might be the last chance to see Guy, too, if he was killed…How would she feel then? For a moment, the tangled shipwreck of her emotions, never far submerged these days, threatened to surface in its horrible entirety, but she managed—only just, because it was becoming more and more difficult—to suppress it.

The Ritz bar was crowded with officers, and women in uniform—FANYs, mainly, and Diana looked round quickly to check whether Sir Neville Apse's driver, Rosemary Legge-Brock, was amongst them, but couldn't see her. She was in the process of being accosted by an enormous and ferocious-looking man with a monstrous moustache and a very thick accent when Claude appeared and rescued her. 'Who on earth was that?' she asked, when he'd gone.

'One of King Zog's bodyguards, probably. They're all over the place. Anyway, don't let's worry about him. How are you? Apart from being utterly beautiful, that is.' Claude ordered drinks and proposed dinner and dancing at the 400 Club afterwards. 'Take your mind off it,' he said, reaching for her hand under the table.

Diana, who hadn't been aware that she was showing any sign of her anxieties, was surprised. 'I'm fine.'

'I know you are, darling, but you've got that bomb look. Lovely, in your case, but slightly stunned.'

Diana laughed. 'I'm probably better that way. It's just that one doesn't get much sleep.'

'Don't I know it,' said Claude, ruefully. 'It's all right for F-J, having that luxurious shelter at Dolphin Square and outside fire escapes in case it gets too lively when one's upstairs. I've had to fix myself up with a mattress underneath my bed—borrowed four enormous tins of polish from the porter, jacked the legs up on that, and put a board across the top. I reckon it'll protect me if the ceiling comes down, and at least'—he looked at her mean-ingfully—'it's private.'

Diana decided to ignore the last bit. 'We've got a shelter of sorts at Tite Street,' she said. 'The basement. You wouldn't believe how some people snore. The girl from the flat below mine—only about five feet tall, and terribly delicate—but she sounds like a hippopotamus.'

After dinner, they made their way down Piccadilly to Leicester Square, accompanied by distant bangs and flashes of light that seemed to tear the sky open. The 400 Club, with its red silk walls, deep, plush banquettes, and floor length velvet curtains, was glamorous and intimate, softly lit by standard lamps and single candles on the tables. Claude ordered cham-pagne, which was delivered by Mr Rossi himself, and then they joined the other dancers. The small floor was packed so tightly with officers and their girlfriends that it was difficult to do more than sway in time to the music, but Claude was a good dancer, easy to follow and skilful at avoiding other couples, so Diana shut her eyes, let him hold her close, and lost herself in the music.

A sudden dull, but very loud, explosion made the room lurch. Lamps shook, candles guttered, and drinks slopped from glasses. The music faltered slightly, then continued as if nothing had happened, with new timpani provided by small chunks of plaster falling from the ceiling and the crash of bottles falling off tables. The dancers carried on, mechanically, but it was harder now, like trying to make your way across a ship's deck in a storm. Diana was aware of Claude's breath in her ear—he was saying something, but she couldn't hear the words—and then he took her hand and led her back to their table, now ringed by smashed glass and sprinkled with plaster dust. Claude took out his handkerchief and flicked the mess from her seat. His mouth moved again, and Diana cupped her hand to her ear in an I-can't-hear-you gesture. 'I said,' Claude's voice popped at her, suddenly, like a balloon bursting, 'Let's sit this one out.'

Diana smiled and nodded—she didn't feel up to talking quite yet—and sat down. Another thud, closer this time, made the chair buck beneath her like a horse so that she had to hold on to the edge of the table to stop herself falling, and then Claude was beside her, helping her to her feet, and, in the chaos of noise and plaster dust, a man was shouting, 'Everybody out! Building's on fire!'

Claude put his arm round her and they joined the crowd of people filing up the stairs and onto the street—patrons, waiters, and musicians clutching their instruments.

Outside, the pavement was so hot that it scorched through the thin soles of her shoes, making her hop. Every surface was frosted with broken glass that shone in the glare from the flames, and purposeful figures—wardens, firemen, a nurse—crunched as they moved through it. Every so often, a face passed before her, lit up, strained and grimy, and then darkened again when a shadow fell on it, as if she were watching riders on a carousel. She looked upwards, and saw the black London roofscape silhouetted against a sky turned copper-coloured by fire as Claude urged her forward through the throng in the road. Diana had the impression that no-one was speaking, but perhaps, she thought, it was because their voices were swallowed up in the roar and crackle of the flames. They went over Charing Cross Road and into Leicester Square station. Lally was there, with Davey Tremaine. Both their faces were grimy, and, looking at Claude, Diana noticed that his was, too, and supposed that she must look equally dishevelled. 'Have you come from the 400?' asked Lally. Diana nodded, still too shaken to speak. 'We didn't see you. Not surprising—it was a bit of a crush. Let's get down to the platforms.'

Davey bought four one-penny tickets, and they managed, after stepping over a mass of supine bodies, to find a quiet corner at the bottom of the steps to the Piccadilly line, where they sat down. The air was warm and fetid, and the platforms crammed as far as the eye could see with squalid nests of ragged blankets on which people sat or reclined, drinking tea, playing cards, knitting, chatting, and sleeping. 'I'm jolly glad I don't have to come down here every night,' said Lally.

'They're not supposed to,' said Claude. 'The *Daily Worker*'s been kicking up a hell of a fuss about it—ruling classes in their luxury shelters denying protection to the proles and so on.'

'Well, they're right, aren't they?' said Diana. 'It isn't fair. Especially when the East End gets it worse than anywhere else.'

'No, it isn't. But we're fortunate,' said Claude. 'Doubly fortunate, in fact.' With a conjuror's flourish, he produced a bottle of champagne from inside his jacket.

Diana gaped at him. 'Where did you get that?'

'I picked it up on the way out. Sleight of hand.' He pulled a glass from each pocket. Davey Tremaine clapped him on the back. 'Well done, old chap.'

'It isn't ours,' said Diana.

Claude shrugged, and started pouring. 'Don't want the rescue squad getting drunk on the job. Here,'—he handed a glass to Lally—'you and Davey can share.'

Lally took the glass and raised her arm in a toast. 'Boyfriends, not bombs!'

'Absolutely,' said Claude. 'We'll drink to that, won't we, Diana?'

Diana felt herself blushing, and hoped that the dirt on her face would camouflage it. She fished her compact out of her handbag, and set about repairing the ravages as best she could. Lally, turning away from Claude and Davey, winked at her.

An ARP warden, picking his way down the stairs, stopped in front of them. 'You ought to get that seen to, miss,' he said, looking down at Diana's feet. When she followed his gaze, she saw that the front of her long evening dress was hemmed in blood.

'Let me have a look,' said Lally, lifting Diana's skirt a modest few inches. There was a long, vicious-looking gash just above her right ankle. 'Must have been all that glass,' said Claude.

'There's a first aid post at Tottenham Court Road,' said the warden. 'Could you get there, miss?'

'I'm fine,' said Diana. 'Honestly. I hadn't even noticed it.'

'That'll be the shock,' said the warden. Spotting the champagne, he added, 'Cup of tea, that's what you need.'

'I'll look after her,' said Claude. 'They must have done their worst by now,' he said to Diana. 'Think you can walk to Jermyn Street? We'll never find you a taxi, and it ought to be bandaged.'

'It doesn't hurt,' said Diana, avoiding Lally's eyes.

'Maybe not now,' said Claude, 'but it will. Not afraid, are you?' His eyes were wide, challenging her to admit fear.

'Of course not,' she said, briskly.

'Come on, then.' He handed the bottle to Davey, and helped her stand up, saying, 'You two enjoy yourselves.' Davey grinned, and Lally looked up at Diana and mouthed, 'Look out.'

By the time they'd crossed Lower Regent Street, Diana was limping. Claude carried her up the stairs in his arms, deposited her on the sofa in his sitting room, and went to boil the kettle. Looking round, Diana decided that the place looked like a warehouse. Most of the pieces—solid, worthy and Victorian—were too large for the space, and she found herself wondering how on earth they'd been got up the stairs. The furniture seemed to encroach on the room, and the blackout screens and dark wallpaper, which was covered in a series of murky landscapes, did nothing to lift the spirits. The only modern objects were the wireless and an electric cocktail shaker.

'Hideous, isn't it?' Claude reappeared, carrying a tray with tea and brandy. 'It was my father's.' Glancing round, he said, 'I suppose I don't notice it much. Would Modom care for tea with a spot of brandy?'

'Modom would.'

'Good. Then we'll have a closer look at that ankle, if Modom would kindly remove her stocking.'

He left her to drink her tea, which seemed to contain rather more than the spot of brandy he'd suggested, and returned a few moments later with a bowl of water and a small first-aid kit. Kneeling on the rug at her feet, he lifted her skirt and bathed the wound with warm water—'I'll try not to hurt you, darling'— bestowed a kiss on it, and then bandaged it with a deftness that surprised her.

'Where did you learn to do that?'

'Oh, here and there,' he said, airily.

'Have you had much practice bandaging girls' legs?'

'Heaps. But none of them were as nice as yours.'

'I'll bet you said that to all of them.'

'No, I didn't. What do you take me for?'

'What you are.'

'Which is what, exactly?'

'A seducer and a shameless philanderer.'

'Well, now you're here, would you like to be seduced and shamelessly philandered?'

'You can't philander someone. It isn't a verb.'

'It is now.' Claude slid his hands under her skirt and lifted it up to her knees. 'Your legs really are quite lovely, you know.'

'So I've been told,' said Diana, pushing her skirt down again.

'Have you? By whom?'

'Oh, thousands of people.'

'Really? Did they all...do this?' Still kneeling, he pushed back her skirt again, brushing her fingers aside, and stroked the insides of her thighs, making her skin tingle. I ought to stop him, she thought. How tiresome, when it's so nice...'Certainly not,' she said, wriggling away from him. 'They were very polite.'

'So they didn't do...this?' His fingers were actually inside the leg of her knickers now. Diana stiffened involuntarily, but it was no good. The warm, dangerously liquid feeling she'd had that first evening when he'd touched her breast came flooding back, only further down her body, and hugely intensified. The pressure of his fingers, and what he was doing to her, was just...she bit her lip to stop the sigh that was rising in her throat. They'd never got this far before—but then, she'd never been to Claude's flat before, had she?

'Come on, Diana...'

'I haven't...' her voice was shaky. 'We can't...'

'Diana...' Claude got up and, putting his hands on her shoulders, pushed her backwards so that her shoulders thudded against the hard arm of the sofa. 'Come on,' he coaxed, leaning over her. 'Just relax. Enjoy yourself ' His hand was under her skirt again, and his fingers...'That's it. That's better, isn't it? Good girl...'

'No!' Diana writhed beneath him, trying to bring herself back to a sitting position, and, when this failed, grabbed at his hair.

'Hey!' Claude withdrew his hand and sat up straight, wincing.

'Claude, we mustn't. Let me sit up properly.'

'Do you know,' Claude grinned and pushed her firmly backwards, 'I don't think I will. I don't think you deserve it, after that.'

She felt him pulling up her skirt. 'Please, Claude. You're squashing me.'

He wasn't listening. 'You're beautiful,' he murmured into her ear. 'So...beautiful...'

'Claude!'

'You'll love it, darling, you know you will...'

'No, Claude, we can't.'

'Don't worry, angel, I'll look after you.'

'What do you mean, look after me?'

'It's like a bus ride,' he said, stroking her neck with his free hand. 'You know the stop where you want to get off, but you actually get off at the one before.' He kissed the tip of her nose.

'You mean you don't actually...'

'No darling, not inside you. Now are you going to be a good girl, or...' Before she had a chance to free herself, he grabbed both her arms, and, pinning them behind her head, held her wrists together in one hand with humiliating ease. 'Well...?' Without waiting for a reply, he kissed her again, this time on the mouth.

'Don't tell me,' he said a few moments later, 'that you didn't enjoy that, because I know you did. You look so lovely like that, with your hair coming loose...And you want to, Diana. You know you do.'

'Yes, but...' Of course she wanted to. Badly. Why was it always the woman who had to put the brakes on, she thought. It wasn't fair. Even Guy had expected that, before they were married, although, with hindsight, that had been more in the manner of a man who wants to make a show of fighting but is relieved when his friends hold him back. He'd have been horrified if she'd actually lain back and let him do what he supposedly wanted...

'I'm married, Claude.'

'Never mind, darling. We shan't let it spoil our fun.'

'It's not fair to Guy,' said Diana. A sudden resolve made her begin to struggle in earnest, wriggling from side to side and bucking her hips against his. His response, apart from the erection she could feel pressing on her lap, was to increase his pressure on her wrists, bending her arms backwards, sending a sharp jag of pain across her shoulders and making made her wince. 'You're hurting me!'

'I know, darling. But if you behave yourself, we can replace the pain with a far more pleasant sensation...'

'I'm not a child, Claude.'

'Then stop behaving like one.' He jerked her arms again, so that she cried out. 'After all, it's not as if you're a virgin.'

'That's not the point.'

'Quite a little hypocrite, aren't you? I'm here, and you're here, and that—' relaxing his grip on her wrists, he ground his crotch against hers—'is the point. In any case,' he continued, 'you're far too lovely not to be enjoyed, and we're not supposed to waste things—it's against regulations.'

His expression was so earnest that Diana started to laugh. 'What rubbish!'

'Not at all. As servants of His Majesty's Government, it's our duty to set an example.'

'But there's no-one here to see.'

'Would you prefer an audience?'

'No!'

'Just as well.' Expertly, Claude undid the back of her dress and began sliding it off her shoulders, taking her underwear with it. 'I'd much rather keep this—' She groaned as he nuzzled her breast, 'all for myself. You see, pleasure is so much nicer...'

'Claude!'

'Stop making excuses.'

'But—'

'Enough!' He pulled her upright. 'You're not going back out there, Diana. They could start again at any moment—it isn't safe.'

Diana fumbled clutched awkwardly at her dress, trying to cover herself. 'It isn't very safe in here, either.'

Claude took hold of her hands and kissed them. 'Yes it is, darling. Quite safe. And much more comfortable. You've made all your excuses.' He took her chin in his hand and pressed his forehead against hers. 'You've put up a jolly good show, darling,' he murmured. 'Full marks. Now let's have some fun.'

Diana lay on her back and stared up at the underside of Claude's bed. 'My goodness,' she said, with a little laugh, 'How strange. I didn't know...That was...that...'

'Ssh...' Claude leant over and caressed her cheek, then took her hand under the bedclothes. 'I love you,' he said.

'I love you, too.'

Later, as she fell asleep in his arms, her last, drowsy thought was that she'd burnt her boats, but oddly, she found that she didn't much care. Perhaps she would in the morning, but not now...

CHAPTER 21

'Sir?'

Stratton looked up from his desk to see Ballard standing in the doorway of the office, covered in brick dust and holding a battered iron deed box in his hands. 'Blimey. Where have you been?'

'Conway Street, sir.' Ballard put the box down on the floor and mopped his face with his handkerchief, looking in distaste at the muck that came off on it. 'It's bad, sir—three houses down. Hell of a mess. The lodgers were in the shelter, but the land-lady...' Ballard shook his head, slowly.

'Bad, eh?'

''Fraid so, sir. Not much left at all. Direct hit. High explosive.'

'Oh, dear. Miss Morgan, the one who jumped, she lived in Conway Street, didn't she?'

'That's why I'm here, sir. That was one of the houses. The ARP man gave me this.' He prodded the box with his foot. 'Thought it looked important. When I saw the name I remem-bered you asking me about her, sir, and I thought you might like to see it.' He squatted down and blew on the top of the box. As the last of the dust lifted, Stratton could see the word 'Morgan' painted in white. 'There's a label on this handle,' said Ballard, showing him a brown paper tag tied on with a piece of string.

'Let's see.' Stratton peered down at it. 'Initials. W. B. & C. Whatever that means. Have you looked inside?'

'No, sir. It's padlocked, see?'

A hammer and chisel'll soon see to that, thought Stratton, but all he said was, 'Thanks. You've brought it to the right place.'

'I thought so, sir.' Ballard's face was impassive, and Stratton wondered what he was thinking, but didn't ask.

'Best get yourself cleaned up,' he said. 'I think Cudlipp's got a clothes brush somewhere.'

'Yes, sir.'

Left alone, Stratton walked around the box. Was this what Wallace had been looking for? It was a pretty big thing to hide—under the bed was the obvious place, but Joe had said they'd pulled the mattress off, so it couldn't have been there. And surely Joe would have removed all his things before he left, and Mabel's too if he'd wanted to keep them, so where had it been? Not under the floorboards—it was too large for that, or for a cistern...He lifted it up—not too heavy—and stowed it under his desk. He'd have to take it home with him; if DCI Lamb were to find him messing about with Mabel Morgan's possessions, there'd be hell to pay. And he'd have to get it out of the station without exciting the curiosity of Cudlipp...Stratton looked at his watch. One o'clock: time for lunch. Or rather, time for a walk—one that would take him to Conway Street.

He crossed Oxford Street and walked up towards Fitzrovia. A newspaper seller on the corner of Newman Street had chalked OUR SCORE 44 AT HALF TIME on his board. 'Don't worry,' he called out as Stratton passed, 'It'll take them a hell of a time to knock it all down!'

In Conway Street, three houses at the end of a row of five-storey dwellings, mostly rooming and boarding, were down, and several more had had their fronts blown off. Tasting the dust in his mouth, Stratton ran his tongue round his teeth and grimaced. The road was covered in a mixture of bricks, slates, shattered glass, and wooden beams and joists, and where one house had been sliced in two he could see, high up on the fourth floor, a man's coat still hanging from the back of a door. Above that, balanced precariously on ragged boards, was a child's cot. Stratton thought of Pete and Monica, safe in the country, and wondered what had happened to its occupant.

Ten or fifteen oldish men and women were standing about, red-eyed and haggard. Had these been their homes? One woman was holding a china basin—the remains of her life, perhaps—in shaking hands. Next to her, an elderly man in a Homburg hat was staring at the debris. The brick dust on the group's clothes made them look as if they were wearing shrouds. As he passed, Stratton heard Homburg hat say, 'It's happening right across London.' He pronounced it 'acrawss' in the Edwardian way.

The old woman said, 'Will they find us somewhere to go before tonight?'

'Everywhere,' said the man. 'The whole of London.' The woman ignored him, and kept repeating, in a quavering voice, 'We haven't anywhere to go. Will they find us somewhere?'

Stratton skirted the rubble and made his way towards the ARP warden, who was standing at the end of the road talking to one of the demolition crew. 'DI Stratton,' he said. 'Are you the one who found the deed box?'

'That's right.' The warden looked exhausted. 'Down there.' He gestured vaguely towards the shattered houses.

'Was there anything else?'

'Just the usual. Nothing like that.'

'Many casualties?'

'Old lady dead from number thirty-five, and we had to send three to the hospital.'

'Everyone out?'

The warden nodded wearily, and was about to turn away when a tall, raw-boned man appeared at his elbow, carrying a tatty-looking piece of carpet. 'I need to get the geyser out,' he said, urgently. 'I've got two more payments to make on it.' The warden stared at him. 'Only two more payments,' the man repeated.

'I'm afraid you'll have to wait until the demolition squad have finished,' said the warden. 'I'm sure it's in there somewhere.'

'You'll tell me, won't you?' asked the man. 'When I've got the geyser,' he explained to Stratton, 'I'll be satisfied.' He tipped his hat and went to join the other onlookers. Stratton turned to the warden, bewildered.

'Can't blame him,' said the warden. 'Looting. You wouldn't believe the trouble we've had, and it's getting worse.'

'They're not likely to make off with a geyser, are they?'

'Those bastards'd take anything. Ought to be ashamed of themselves.'

Stratton pointed out the distressed woman he'd seen further down the street, then walked back to West End Central, thinking how extraordinary it was how quickly you got used to the raids—the bombing itself, the fear and the din, the changes it made to the landscape...New views seen through gaps in rows of houses, and on moonlit nights the place looked almost fragile—the thought that you might be looking your last on some familiar piece of architecture made you more aware of it. It was the effect on people, like that poor old duck in Conway Street, which shocked and angered him. Tottenham hadn't had it too bad so far, thank God. After the first few raids, when she'd clung to him, shaky and crying, Jenny seemed to have got used to it. Stratton had been worried about her being alone in the Anderson shelter if the warning went when he was at work, but as Doris and Donald had volunteered to join her if this happened, it was no longer a problem. Since the bombing started, she'd stopped agitating for Pete and Monica to come back, and had even gone so far as to tell him he'd been right all along, but he knew better than to make a song and dance about that. What will be left when they do come back, he wondered. Would everything be flattened? The newspaper seller had said it would take a hell of a time, which was true, but the Nazis had all of Europe's resources at their disposal. With the civil defences worked to exhaustion—not to mention the police, he thought, yawning—how long could one little island stand it?

He stopped to indulge these reflections, but after a moment, his melancholy feelings struck him as unsuitable and repugnant. He remembered reading somewhere that sentimentality was the exact measure of a person's inability to experience genuine feeling. He reflected that he couldn't have put it better, or even half as well, himself, and, in any case, standing about feeling sorry for himself wasn't going to help. DCI Lamb may have been mollified, back in July, by his solving the business at the jeweller's shop and the murder of the prostitute Maureen O'Dowd, but he hadn't yet managed to discover who'd stabbed Kelland in the gang fight and nor, frankly, was he ever likely to. Besides which, there had been four more thefts from jewellers' shops in the last month, plus a spate of robberies from high-class furriers, and two nights ago an eighteen-year-old 'hostess' had been assaulted in a night-club in Rupert Street.

Thinking about these cases reminded Stratton of what the warden had said about looting from bombed buildings. Just the sort of stupid thing, he thought, that his nephew Johnny might find himself involved in. He hadn't seen the boy for a while, and neither Reg nor Lilian had mentioned him. The problem was, Stratton thought, that boys like Johnny knew everything in theory but nothing in practice. They learnt—or thought they learnt—about 'real' men from James Cagney and George Raft, and about women from strangers who scrawled their desires and conquests on the walls of public lavatories. He made a mental note to take Johnny aside for a chat, then rejected this idea on the grounds that this would be interfering. It was Reg's job, after all, not his. And in any case, the boy wouldn't have listened.

Smuggling the deed box out of the station after work was less of a problem than Stratton had anticipated. He carried it home and stowed it under the bench in the garden shed before going in to kiss Jenny and wash for tea. He went upstairs, wondering what the box would contain, when a sudden image of the cot, high up in the ruined house, compelled him to open the door of his daughter's room. Looking round, he saw, on the shelf in front of her two least favoured dolls, a small piece of pale pink knitting. He remembered Jenny teaching Monica to knit the previous summer, their heads, one chestnut and one dark, bent over tangles of wool, and Monica's proud announcement, once she'd got the knack of it: 'I'm going to knit my doll a scarf, and knickers to match!' They'd laughed about it; Jenny had worried Monica by pointing out that knitted knickers were both uncomfortable and unhygienic, and he'd had to assure her that the doll wouldn't mind. He picked up the little scarf and examined it. It was very neatly done; Monica, like her mother, was careful and deft. Good at drawing, too, Stratton thought proudly, though heaven knew where she got that from, because neither of them were particularly artistic.

Hoping that Jenny wouldn't walk in on him, he lifted the dolls' skirts in turn to see if either of them was wearing the matching knickers. Neither was, and, feeling a little foolish, he stuffed the miniature scarf into his pocket and left the bedroom.

After tea, he left Jenny listening to Hippodrome Memories on the wireless, and went out to the shed. Clearing a space on the work bench, he lifted the box onto it and took a hammer and chisel from his rack of tools. The padlock gave at the first blow and Stratton, with deliberate slowness, removed it, returned the tools to their place, and lifted the lid.

CHAPTER 22

'I love you.' Claude had said it. Not before, or during—neither of which counted—but afterwards. And he hadn't just gone to sleep, as Guy did. Instead, they'd smoked cigarettes and laughed and told each other secrets, and when the AA guns woke them at half-past four and Diana sat up suddenly and banged her head on the underside of the bed frame, he'd held her in his arms and stroked her hair.

She had crossed the Rubicon. She knew now what it was really like. Returning home on an early tube, tired but happy, she replayed the events of the night over and over in her head. 'I love you.' He'd said it. He had actually said it. Each time she thought of it, the memory of his words seemed to renew her energy, and by the time she got to Tite Street, she bounded up the stairs in a mood of sheer elation.

Seeing Lally waiting outside her flat, Diana stopped abruptly on the landing and caught her breath. 'What are you doing here?'

'I came to see if you were—'

'At home?'

'Still in one piece.'

'What do you mean?' asked Diana, opening the door. Lally didn't answer, but followed her in and stood watching her as she began to remove her evening clothes and unpin her hair. 'If you're not going to answer,' said Diana, donning a short slip and shrugging on her silk dressing gown, 'I shall ignore you.' She went into the kitchen. Lally leant against the doorframe, arms folded, and watched her making tea. 'The thing is,' she said, as they waited for the kettle to boil, 'that the last time Claude pursued someone like this, it ended rather badly, and I thought you ought to know.'

'For heaven's sake, Lally,' said Diana, brusquely, 'I'm not a complete innocent.'

'I know that. Listen to me, Diana. I know we make jokes about Claude, but—'

'Did F-J put you up to this?'

Lally looked puzzled. 'No. Why should he? He doesn't know where you were last night, does he?'

'No, but—'

'He's warned you off too, hasn't he?'

'Not really,' Diana hedged. 'He just said...well, what you said, really. Ladies' man, heartbreaker, that old stuff,' she added.

'Because it's true,' said Lally. 'This other woman worked for F-J, and she was married, too.'

'Oh?' Diana, feeling a flicker of apprehension, bent over the teapot in order not to have to look at her.

'It was over a year ago,' said Lally, 'and Claude wanted her to leave her husband—divorce him. She was absolutely mad about him, and eventually she agreed and told her husband about the affair and that she was going to marry Claude. Then Claude said he hadn't meant it and they'd had their fun and she ought to go back to her husband, but of course it was too late by then. She couldn't go back. She had a complete breakdown, and...Well, she committed suicide.'

'Good heavens,' said Diana, lightly. 'She must have been unbalanced.'

'Stop being so brittle, Diana. That's what Claude does to people. He unbalances them.'

'Well, I'm absolutely fine.'

'Are you?'

'Yes! You don't understand.'

'Darling, I understand exactly. That's why I'm worried about you—I've seen this before.'

'How well did you know this person?'

'Not very well, but that isn't—'

'Well then, you can't really know why she did it.'

'I know that Claude doesn't take women seriously, Diana. You've got to be careful.'

'If you're so concerned, why didn't you tell me all this before?'

'I should have done. I just didn't realise how far...you know...And last night, when you went off with him, I suppose I ought to have said something then, but I didn't want to—'

'Say anything in front of him? In case it wasn't true?'

'I know it's true, Diana. I suppose...Well, Claude frightens me. There's something about him. That probably sounds silly, but all the same...'

'It does, rather.' Diana poured the tea. 'Why don't you drink this? Consider me warned, and then I can get dressed and go to work.'

Lally took the cup. 'You're not warned, though, are you? You're in love with him.'

'Who says so?' Diana asked, settling herself in front of the dressing table mirror.

'The look on your face says so.' Lally turned and caught her eye in the mirror. Flushing, Diana lowered her gaze. 'And the way you've been behaving, and the fact that you haven't really listened to a word I've said.'

'Yes I have.'

'Well, I hope so. I am your friend, Diana. To be honest, I rather guessed that things weren't altogether blissful with Guy, or you wouldn't have been so eager for a job.'

Diana, startled, jerked her head up. 'How did you guess?'

'Well,' Lally shrugged. 'For one thing, you'd have started a family, wouldn't you?'

'We...' Diana bit her lip. She couldn't bring herself to tell Lally about losing the baby. 'It's fine for you,' she said, defensively. 'Boyfriends, not bombs, and all that.'

Lally, looking hurt, countered, 'It is rather hard cheese on Guy.'

'Guy's having a whale of a time.'

'If you say so. I don't want to quarrel with you, Diana.' She deposited her cup and saucer on the mantelpiece. 'I have to go. I'm glad you seem...' She tailed off, frowning. 'I just hope you know what you're doing, that's all.'

Left alone, Diana sighed. 'Why can't anything be simple?' she muttered, as she re-pinned her hair. Why did Lally have to come and spoil everything? Close on the heels of that thought came the annoying reflection that Lally, far from trying to spoil things, was being helpful, and ought to be heeded. Pulling on her skirt, Diana wondered about the young woman who'd committed suicide. She hadn't asked her name—hadn't wanted to know. In any case—she glanced at her wristwatch—she didn't have time to think about any of it now. She was going to be late for work if she wasn't careful. She finished dressing, scooped up her handbag and gas mask and rushed out of the flat.

Diana arrived at Apse's just in time to see him ripping up a letter and dropping it into the wastepaper basket. Something about the haste with which this was done made her suspicious. So far, she hadn't managed to come up with a single incriminating fact about the man, and she was beginning to believe it was hopeless, but the look on his face when he saw her was definitely furtive. A less controlled person, Diana thought, would have jumped.

'Sorry I'm late, sir,' she said. 'Got caught in a raid last night. Bit slow off the mark this morning.'

'Never mind.' Apse recovered himself quickly. 'You look…' he frowned, searching for the right word, '…tired but happy.' He gazed at her curiously, in a way that made her think of a zoologist studying a new and interesting specimen.

'Do I?' Diana feigned surprise and hoped she wasn't blushing. 'I suppose I am.' Damn, she thought, he's got me on the wrong foot again. 'Relieved to be here, sir. It was pretty lively last night.'

'Yes,' said Apse, thoughtfully. 'So I gather.' It was hard to tell from his tone whether he was referring to the raid or to some intelligence he'd received about Diana's behaviour.

'Heavens,' she said, as breezily as she could manage. 'Did you sleep through the whole thing?'

'Chloral,' said Apse. 'And bromide. Perhaps,' he said, looking her squarely in the eye, 'you ought to try it.'

'Perhaps,' said Diana. Unable to look at him for one more second, she busied herself in removing her hat. When she returned from the cloakroom, she noticed that the letter Apse had torn up was no longer at the top of the pile in the wastepaper basket, and decided she must rescue the pieces as soon as he had left the room.

At half-past eleven Apse announced that he had a meeting with F-J, and departed. Diana, who was about to catch a train for Aldershot where she was investigating rumours of spying, hastily upended the wastepaper basket, gathered up all the likely-looking scraps of paper and shoved them into her handbag.

The train was packed, all seats taken, and the corridors were full of soldiers sitting on their kit-bags, playing cards and complaining loudly of being buggered about. Diana stumbled over their legs, looking for a lavatory, and found herself in the middle of a gang of boisterous young men. One, his pack stuffed inside the top of his uniform, bellowed, 'I'm in the family way!'

'You're in every bastard's way,' grumbled the sergeant, then, seeing Diana, added, 'Beg your pardon, miss.' She looked at the floor, embarrassed, and aware of the men's eyes. Do they know that I am someone's mistress, she thought. Can they tell? She certainly felt different, so perhaps it showed. After what seemed a long time, but was probably only a few seconds, she said, 'Excuse me.'

As the men moved aside to let her through, she caught sight of the letters WC on a door and fought her way towards them. Once inside, she shook the scraps of paper out of her handbag and set about piecing them together. The handwriting looked feminine, and her excitement increased when she caught sight of the words 'German' and 'secret'. Perhaps it was from Mrs Montague, but why risk disposing of it in the wastepaper basket? She turned over another piece of paper and saw the words 'a field belonging to...' Invasion plans? Yes, there was something about penetration, defence...Apse must have been about to burn the letter when she'd disturbed him. Diana knelt down on the floor and began feverishly arranging the scraps on the closed lavatory seat. There was an address in Shropshire, a name—Lavinia Driffield—or was it Duffield? and the words 'Nazi sympathisers', and 'local farmer with access to'—and then something about a horse...a code of some sort? This was serious, and very likely urgent. She'd have to get off the train at the next stop and telephone F-J, or, if that proved impossible, send a telegram.

The pieces were still too jumbled for her to extract any coherent meaning from them—she'd have to fit them together properly, with names, dates and plans, so that she could read it to F-J if she managed to speak to him. As she shuffled the paper jigsaw, her eyes widened. It couldn't be...and yet, this was the only way the torn edges fitted together. But...'My God!' Diana clapped a hand over her mouth. She scanned the assemblage of phrases, scarcely able to believe her eyes:

Forced me to submit...congress with a stallion...satisfy his depraved Nazi lust...heaving flanks...immense above my...Prostrated as I was...thrusting his...prevent myself from being invaded...nearly senseless...so completely at his mercy that I existed only to receive...

After which, apparently, the woman's equine paramour was given hay and water, and she was escorted back to her cottage, presumably, Diana thought, by the depraved Nazi. She was horrified that anyone could imagine such things, much less write them down, and appalled at herself for reading about such filthy perversions, and—thank God she was alone—for feeling disturbed and excited by them. Not the horse thing—that was repulsive. Impossible, as well. Diana wondered what sort of horse the woman had imagined. A cart horse? An Arab steed? A Shetland pony?

That was absurd, but it was the words themselves that had stirred her, in a way that Elinor Glyn had never done. If that letter had been about a man...

No wonder Apse had torn it up. No wonder, too, that he'd looked uncomfortable. She'd misread his mood entirely; it hadn't been guilt she'd seen in his face, but embarrassment.

She gathered up the pieces of paper, crumpled them into a ball, and returned them to her bag. Part of her wanted to laugh at her mistake, but the other part...She sat down on the lavatory, her legs clamped tightly together, feeling a mixture of arousal and shame. That, and the memory of Lally's words about Claude and her response to them, produced such an appalling maelstrom of confused emotion that she felt almost sick. She wished she could spend the entire journey in the cubicle, but somebody was banging on the door, and she could hear the stamping of feet and the high, thin whine of a child.

For the rest of the afternoon, while Diana was sitting amidst the dusty clutter of a Victorian mausoleum—silk screens, cases of stuffed birds, brass candelabra and God knew how many bad oil paintings—and trying to placate an elderly tweed-clad gentleman who was almost entirely camouflaged against a sofa of some similarly hairy material, Lally's words...Claude said he hadn't meant it, they'd had their fun...committed suicide...and those of Lavinia What's-her-name's...dominated and utterly...

drove himself more deeply into…powerless to resist…alternated in her mind. Seeing Apse again was going to be sheer torture. I must find a way to forget about that letter, she told herself. She sighed, so that the tweedy man stopped speaking for a moment before resuming his complaint, his voice pitched a peevish semi-tone higher in response to her interruption.

It was already nine o'clock when the train pulled into Victoria station. As she stepped round the piles of kit-bags on the platform, Diana decided that the lateness of the hour excused her from returning to Dolphin Square. She caught a bus back to Tite Street where she found a letter from Evie informing her, rather curtly, that Guy would be coming home on leave in two weeks' time, and her presence would, therefore, be required—'if you can bear to tear yourself away from whatever it is you are doing in London'. She sighed. Her mother-in-law was clearly unshaken in her belief that her contribution to the war effort was wholly frivolous, and, as she could hardly disabuse her of this, it would have to stay that way. A sudden vision of telling Evie, over dinner, about the woman with the horse made her snort with laughter. She'd probably faint, thought Diana, face down in the soup, and it would serve her right for thinking she was just messing about with type-writers and going out a lot. Although, of course, the second part was absolutely true…She took out her writing case and sat down to compose a suitable reply, but realised that there was no point in writing anything until she'd spoken to Apse about some leave.

Guy might have told me himself, she thought crossly. The realisation that she wasn't as annoyed about this as she ought to have been made her feel almost as guilty as she had that morning, when Lally'd remarked that it was hard cheese on Guy. At least, she thought, I am doing useful work. It was true that she had not, as yet, had the opportunity to question Helen Pender about Walter Wymark's work for the Right Club, but there was bound to be an opportunity soon. And Mrs Montague was clearly pleased with her: at their last meeting, she'd given her a rather horrid silver brooch with an engraved emblem of an eagle and a snake and the letters PJ, for 'Perish Judah'. Her first inclination was to wrap it in tissue paper and put it in the bottom of her jewellery box with no intention of looking at it again, but she'd realised it would be politic to sport the beastly thing at subsequent meetings. So far, so good, except that she was no nearer to discovering the nature and extent of Apse's involvement with the Right Club.

She sat back and rumpled her hair and let her thoughts drift back through the day. On the whole, it had been a wasted afternoon—the tweedy man had proved to be a harmless crackpot like all the others, but that letter...

And Claude. Claude. Oh, dear...She crossed her legs. *Les plaisirs solitaires*, the French called it...She couldn't use the English word, even in thought. It was too crude and embarrassing. A foreign tongue placed it at a distance, gave it sophistication... What was happening to her? The intensity of feeling between her thighs was becoming actually painful.

This was dreadful: perversity, morbidity, self-indulgence. All wrong. You're Guy's wife, she told herself. Stop it. Then the excuse: it's probably because I'm tired; things are bound to seem different after a good night's sleep—if I can only get one. She decided she'd have a bath. The evil-smelling heater hadn't been very reliable of late, but she might be able to coax it into producing just enough hot water for a quick soak before the raids started.

Sprinkling F-J's bath salts into the tepid water, Diana remembered his warning—things happen, and so forth...Don't want you getting hurt...As she slipped off her dressing gown, she wondered, in a disinterested way, if she were heading for a smash. If I am, she thought, easing herself into the scented water, there seems to be nothing—despite F-J or Lally—that I can do about it, nothing at all. She lay back in the bath and closed her eyes.

CHAPTER 23

Stratton looked at the contents of the deed box. The top layer consisted of advertisements for films and cuttings from magazines with names like *Kinematograph Weekly*, and, staring up at him from the middle of the pile, a pair of enormous eyes in an ethereally beautiful face with delicate features and a small, pointed chin. So, that, he thought, was Miss Mabel Morgan, and she was, or had been, a knockout.

The magazine cuttings seemed to consist mostly of sugary titbits about her career, looks, and hobbies. Taking these out, Stratton saw a bundle of letters tied up in red ribbon and several piles of unmarked film canisters. He prised the lid off one of the top ones and found that it did, indeed, contain a reel of celluloid.

He paused, scratching his head. He'd have to come up with some way of watching the films. Perhaps Donald would know someone with projection equipment; owning a camera shop would surely put him in contact with such people. But that could be left until later. For now, he would concentrate on the letters. He untied the ribbon, settled himself on the rickety chair, and began to read.

The letters bore no addresses or dates, and were directed to someone called Bunny and signed only with the nickname

Binkie. And as if that wasn't bad enough, thought Stratton, they were full of the affected language of fashionable people in the twenties—everything was 'divine' or 'bogus' or 'shy-making'. It reminded him of an Evelyn Waugh novel he'd once attempted to read—he could see that the thing was well-written, and some of it had made him laugh, but the characters were such a shower that you wished you could knock their heads together.

Presumably, one of the writers was Mabel Morgan—why would she have kept the letters otherwise? Perhaps the other was her husband—the one Ballard said had died in a fire—or maybe a lover. Stratton reached for the pile of cuttings and discovered that she had been married to a film director called Cecil Duke. Perhaps that was how these people usually spoke—Stratton, who'd never met anyone like them, didn't know. But it was a bit much that they wrote with a lisp, as well as talking with one...Somehow, though, it didn't match Joe Vincent's description of a woman with a fondness for pubs and acid drops. Where had Mabel Morgan actually come from? He should have asked Joe more about her while he had the chance.

Stratton put the letters back in the box and went to find Jenny, who was busy with some darning. 'You remember I asked you about Mabel Morgan?'

'Yes...' Jenny looked up, abstractedly, then back at the sock in her hand.

'Do you remember anything else about her?'

'Only that Mum used to like her...There was another one, too, Lilian Hall-Davis. I was thinking about her back in the summer, after what you said—she committed suicide, too. Put her head in a gas oven. That was quite a few years ago, before Mum died. Dreadful, to think of someone being that unhappy.'

'Do you remember if Mabel Morgan made any talking pictures?'

'I don't think so. Maybe that was the trouble.'

He returned to the shed and re-applied himself to the letters:

Bunniest, Will you mind awfully if I don't come down for the weekend? We had a vile evening at Plumstead's. The décor is fantastically outré, with little gilt chairs all over the place, and orchids, and murals on the walls, but the rooms are frightful and the man absolutely refused to light the fire when I asked. Clement was a perfect beast. I can't bear him when he's not amusing. He would keep on talking about the war, some fearfully dull story of how he'd lost his platoon, and the whole thing was too ghastly for words. We all got tight. Constance was positively spifflicated and overflowing with mother-love and insisted on dragging her beastly children out of bed at two o'clock to sing madrigals. The result is, of course, that I feel quite frightful this morning and can't think of going anywhere, even to see you, my darling. My poor lamb, I know it's agony for you, but we'll find a way to make up the time...

Nauseated by the tone of this, Stratton stopped reading and lit a cigarette. The references to getting tight suggested that the writer was a man, but it clearly hadn't been an all-male gathering, because of the woman Constance, who obviously wasn't much of a mother. Poor kids, thought Stratton, being woken up in the middle of the night and made to perform like trained monkeys in front of a crowd of leering, drunken strangers...He looked at the next letter. The contents weren't much better: a lot of stuff about some old chap reminiscing about actresses who were the toast of his youth, a procession of women who were tipsy, or neurotic, or both, and somebody getting the pox, which was simply too shaming...Really, Stratton thought, it was astonishing that the pair of them had managed to make any films at all if all they ever did was get drunk and catch diseases.

He picked up a third letter, read the words '*My precious Pinkle-Wonk*,' and decided that was quite enough for one evening. Walking back to the house, he tried to imagine Jenny calling him a pinkle-wonk, but failed. Just as well, he thought—as far as he was concerned that, on its own, would be adequate grounds for divorce.

Jenny had put away her darning and was re-reading Pete's letter from the previous week. 'I don't like the sound of this school they're sharing with,' she said. 'It seems ever so stuck-up.'

'Bound to be.' Stratton shrugged. 'It's a public school.'

'You don't think they're being horrible to Pete and his friends, do you? Children can be very unkind.'

'I don't suppose they let them mix much,' said Stratton. 'Can't have the lower orders getting ideas.'

Jenny made a snorting noise. 'Well, they must have mixed a bit, because Pete told us about how they'd renamed the dormitories, remember? After people from Captain Scott's Expedition.'

'Not a very good omen, if you ask me—Scott, Evans, Wilson, Oates—they all snuffed it, didn't they?'

'Don't, Ted.' Jenny looked stricken. 'You know how much I worry.'

'Sorry, love.' Stratton patted her on the knee. 'I'm sure they're fine,' he added, with more confidence than he felt. 'We'll be able to see for ourselves in a couple of weeks, won't we?'

'Yes. I don't know what the journey's going to be like, though. Pete says here, "You will have to change and take the local train because there is no petrol and Jack has gone to the farm."'

'Is Jack the chauffeur?'

'The pony. The chauffeur's been called up. It was in Mrs Chetwynd's last letter. I must say, it is kind of her to write to us so often.'

When the siren hadn't sounded by half-past ten, they decided to risk sleeping in their bedroom. Enjoying the comfort after the cramped and rather damp conditions in the Anderson shelter, Stratton decided that it would be the best thing all round if Pete and his chums weren't allowed to spend much time with the public-school boys. He definitely did not want his children growing up to be the sort of people who were likely to call each other pinkle-wonks.

Jenny prodded him in the ribs. 'What are you laughing at?'

'Oh, nothing.' He turned his head and looked at her, pretty and buxom in her nightgown. 'Come here.'

In the last few minutes before sleep, Stratton remembered what Jenny had said about Lilian Wotsit putting her head in a gas oven. 'Before Mum died...' So that would make it before...what? 1934. There'd been talkies for a few years by then, and if Mabel Morgan had committed suicide because she couldn't get speaking roles, she must have been out of work for quite some time. But why couldn't she get speaking parts? If Mabel had been refused the roles because she didn't sound right, that would mean, surely, that there was something wrong with her accent, that she didn't sound smart enough. And if that was the case, those letters... People who wrote things like that, however revolting they were, would be educated, wouldn't they? It's no good, he thought, it's all just speculation. He'd have to find out more about her.

CHAPTER

24

Stratton took a long swallow of PC Cudlipp's filthy tea, and surveyed the mess on his desk. It had been a terrible day. He and Jenny had been woken by raiders at three, stumbled out to the Anderson, and lain awake listening to the bombs until around five, when he'd dozed off only to be woken by the warble of the 'Raiders Passed' signal at six. He'd given up after that, and, still in his dressing gown and pyjamas, trudged across to the garden shed and read some more of Mabel Morgan's letters.

By the time he'd reached the police station he felt exhausted, and discovering that the girl who'd been assaulted at the nightclub was fifteen, not eighteen, and on the run from an approved school, hadn't improved matters. The club owner's claims of innocence were risible, and his attempts at bribery had been insultingly clumsy—in comparison, Stratton thought, gangsters like Abie Marks were positively subtle.

After an hour and a half spent sifting papers and getting nowhere, Stratton glanced at his watch, saw that it was almost six o'clock, and, remembering that he wanted to call on Beryl Vincent on the way home, hurried from the station.

Beryl, however, wasn't at her flat in Clerkenwell Road. Stratton debated putting a note through her letterbox, but decided against it. The visit wasn't an official one, and he didn't want her trying to contact him at Savile Row.

Jenny greeted him at the door with a serious face and, assuming it was because he was late, he hastened to apologise, but she shook her head abstractedly and disappeared back to the kitchen.

He knew better than to question Jenny while they were eating—she'd tell him when she was ready—so they talked about her new job at the Rest Centre, helping families made homeless by the bombing, and about the possibility of buying some wax ear-plugs to deaden the noise of the raids. When Jenny had cleared the plates and made the tea, Stratton asked 'What's the matter, love?'

Jenny fiddled with the knitted tea-cosy for a moment, then said, simply, 'Johnny.'

'Ah.' At least it wasn't the children.

'He's in real trouble, Ted. He's been dismissed from the garage for fiddling petrol coupons. Weeks ago. Mr Hartree told me.'

'Did he now?' Stratton frowned. Mr Hartree, who owned the garage, was wire-thin, lecherous as a monkey, and about as shameless.

'Don't look like that, Ted. He wasn't being...you know... silly.' A slight redness appeared in Jenny's cheeks as she said this. 'He's worried about the boy, that's all. Says he's in with a bad crowd. I don't think Lilian and Reg have any idea.'

'They must know he's been sacked.'

Jenny shook her head. 'Lilian would have told me. You've got to talk to him, Ted.'

'That's Reg's job.'

Jenny rolled her eyes. 'Fat lot of good he'll do.'

'I probably won't do much better, love, but I suppose I could have a go,' said Stratton resignedly, adding, 'when I get the chance.'

'For heaven's sake don't say anything in front of Reg. Get him on his own.'

'I'm not daft, you know.'

Stratton finished his tea and walked round to Donald and Doris's to ask about borrowing a projector. Donald thought a bit, then said he knew someone who knew someone but that it might take a few days, and with that, Stratton had to be content. He refused the offer of a cup of tea and returned home, where he sat down in his favourite armchair and slept. The sirens woke him at half-past nine, and he went out with Jenny to the Anderson. Making his large frame as comfortable as he could on one of the narrow, iron-hard mattresses, he went back to sleep without bothering to remove any of his clothes.

The following morning, gas leaks and burst water mains, casualties of the previous night's bombing, caused most of the buses from north-east London to be diverted miles away from their usual routes. When Stratton asked the ticket collector where they were going, the man replied, cheerfully, 'No idea, guv.'

He decided it would be quicker to walk. Clouds of acrid smoke drifting down Regent Street alerted him to a possible catastrophe, and, hurrying round the corner of Vigo Street, out of breath and three-quarters of an hour late, he found a scene of devastation. West End Central police station was more or less gutted: the ferroconcrete structure was still standing, but everything else—fittings, partitions, and furniture—had been reduced to piles of smouldering wreckage. The ceiling of the Communications Room hung in festoons over sodden mounds of plaster and brick dust, in the midst of which Arliss and Ballard, looking dishevelled with field telephones on their laps, were trying to deal with urgent messages. Several other PCs were combing through the remains of the CID office for exhibits, watched by a large crowd who were chatting, pointing, and, in most cases, scarcely bothering to conceal their glee. A crew of demolition men who were supposed to be clearing the rubble sat on the ground, engrossed in the charred remains of police files and pointing out the more interesting and confidential details to a group of auxiliary firemen.

Stratton caught sight of Cudlipp, who was holding a dented kettle and poking disconsolately through the mess, and went over to join him. 'What the hell happened?'

'Parachute mine, Sir. Right on the steps.'

'Any casualties?'

'No-one killed, Sir. Policewoman Harris got a broken leg— they've taken her to hospital—and DCI Lamb got a nasty knock on the head from a sheet of plywood. Just as well those windows had already gone, or he'd have been decapitated. He's gone to hospital, too. I shouldn't think we'll be seeing him any time soon.'

'Oh, dear.' Stratton, feeling acutely guilty, tried to sound sorrier about this than he actually was. All the same, it sounded as if Lamb would be out of his hair for quite a while, and that had to be a good thing. 'Emergency procedures working all right?' he asked.

'Such as they are, sir. They're sending us to Great Marlborough Street. I don't know when we'll be back to normal,' he added glumly. Looking around, Stratton seriously doubted if anything would ever be back to normal, but decided to say nothing.

An Indian waiter from Veeraswamy's appeared at Stratton's elbow. 'Excuse me, sir. Very bad business all together. Boss saying using kitchen if wishing, sir. Making tea for men, sir.'

'That's very kind of him,' said Stratton. 'Thank you.' Turning to Cudlipp, who was looking mutinous, he said, 'You heard. Go with this gentlemen and make some tea.'

'But sir...'

'But nothing,' said Stratton, firmly. 'In the absence of DCI Lamb'—he looked round quickly to make sure that no other senior officers were present—'I'm in charge of this station, or what's left of it, and I'm giving you an order.'

Cudlipp looked at him resentfully and started muttering something about darkies and dirty habits. 'For God's sake,' said Stratton, exasperated, 'they're offering to help. Off you go.'

Making a mental note to thank the restaurant manager in person for the use of his kitchen, Stratton started towards the demolition squad, intending to confiscate the files, but Ballard intercepted him, waving his notebook. 'Urgent call, sir. Church on Eastcastle Street caught a packet last night, and they've found a body.'

'That's hardly surprising,' said Stratton, mildly.

'Not a bomb casualty, sir. This one was buried.'

'They usually are.'

'Not in the normal way, sir. The body's not supposed to be there and the warden says it looks funny.'

'Funny?'

'He says the head's been smashed in, sir.'

'I see. What's the name of the church?'

'Our Lady and St. Peter, sir. Left-footers.' Seeing Stratton's puzzled expression, he added, 'Papists, sir.'

'Oh. Yes. Well, I suppose it would be, with a name like that.'

Stratton could picture the church—he'd walked past it hundreds of times, but never been inside. It was Victorian, gloomy and forbidding. He thought that it might be made of multi-coloured brick, but years of London smog had given it such a thick coating of soot that he couldn't be certain about this. 'I don't suppose,' he said, 'that you've unearthed the Murder Bag?'

''Fraid not, sir.'

'Never mind. You might let them know I'm on my way—if you can get through, that is—and see if you can get hold of the photographer and send him over. Send a messenger if you can't do it by telephone, and tell Bainbridge and Ricketts to stop those men reading the files. Then get this place cordoned off before it turns into a complete circus. Have we heard anything from HQ?'

'No, sir.'

It wasn't entirely surprising, Stratton reflected as he walked up Regent Street. Scotland Yard probably had troubles of their own. In any case, they'd be better off without a lot of top brass hanging about and getting in the way.

The last time Stratton had been inside a church was for Jenny's mother's funeral. He didn't remember very much about the service, except that there'd been a storm. They'd trooped outside and gathered round the grave in the sort of lashing rain against which umbrellas were useless while the vicar gabbled through 'Man that is born of woman hath but a short time to live...' like a horse-racing commentator.

There was something terrible about destroying a place of worship, he thought, as he stared at the giant mounds of bricks, pillars and smashed stained glass that had been the Church of Our Lady and St. Peter. With the awkward reverence of the non-churchgoer, he negotiated his way past a jumble of broken pews, brass fittings and shattered pictures of lachrymose saints martyred for a second time, towards the back of what was left of the building. An ARP warden, accompanied by an elderly priest, his cassock incorrectly buttoned over his pyjamas and an oversize tin hat jammed firmly on his head, came to greet him. He put out a hand. 'DI Stratton, West End Central.'

'George Crosbie,' said the warden. 'And this is Father Lampton.' The priest, who was staring down at his slippered feet, seemed disinclined either to speak or shake hands. After a moment, he wandered away, bending down every so often to peer into the rubble. The warden watched him go, then turned to Stratton.

'Not Catholic are you, Inspector?'

Stratton shook his head.

'He's fretting about his reliquary.'

'His what?'

'The box where they keep the holy bits and pieces. They've got the foreskin of St. Giles or the left tit of St. Gertrude or something, and he's determined to find it. I've told him not to go poking about—for all we know, there could be a time bomb in this lot—but he won't listen.'

'Is there a St. Gertrude?' asked Stratton.

'Buggered if I know. Honestly, you'd think he'd have better things to worry about, wouldn't you?' Not waiting for an answer,

Crosbie continued, 'Anyway, this body. If you'd care to follow me, Inspector, I'll show you.'

With a last glance at the forlorn figure of Father Lampton, who was now blowing dust off a piece of splintered board, Stratton accompanied the warden, taking as much care as he could not to step on anything that looked as if it might be sacred. Passing the stone font, which, though chipped and gouged, was still standing, he noticed, sticking out of the pile of debris that filled the receptacle, another piece of board like a wafer on top of an ice cream. Pulling it out, he read the words '—st falls' and wondered, briefly, what they meant.

The warden led him down some rickety stairs to what must have been the crypt, which was now partially open to the sky. Nine or ten tombs, their stone tops smashed in and their wrought iron railings scattered about like spillikins, stood along the right side of the room. The resurrection of the body, thought Stratton. He didn't know what the last trump would sound like, but the angels who blew it would certainly need a hell of a lot of puff if they wanted to compete with a fleet of Dorniers. He followed the warden to the end of the row of tombs, where a large hole in the floor, made by falling masonry, had revealed a makeshift earth grave beneath the stone slabs. Inside, Stratton could see a tangle of dusty limbs that culminated in a dented buff-coloured ball that looked, at first glance, as if it belonged on top of a newel post. Bending down, he saw that the features—the head was in profile—had been smashed flat.

'That wasn't caused by the bombing,' said Crosbie. 'He was like that when we found him.'

'He?'

'The—' Crosbie checked himself. 'Oh, I see what you mean. Figure of speech. It's not likely to be a woman, is it?'

'No idea,' said Stratton. 'Have you moved anything?'

'No. Thought we ought to leave it.'

Stratton squatted down and picked up a handful of the soil, noting the yellowish deposits. It would have to be checked, but he'd bet it was lime, and builder's lime at that. Builder's lime would delay putrefaction, whereas quicklime would destroy the corpse. He wondered if whoever buried the dead person knew this. He looked up at the warden, who was staring impassively at the body. 'Do you know if there's been any building work done here recently?' he asked.

'Couldn't say.' Crosbie shook his head. 'I could ask Father Lampton, if you like, but I've not been able to get much sense out of him so far.'

'I'll ask him later. Right now, we need the pathologist, then the body can be moved. Where's the nearest telephone?'

'There's one in the pub down the road, but I don't know if it's working.'

'In that case, we'd better send someone round.'

'No-one here. They're all in Berners Street. Whole row came down—hell of a mess.'

'In that case, can you take a message to the Middlesex?'

Stratton accompanied Crosbie to the foot of the steps, then found a place to sit that was as far away from the body as possible without being directly underneath any dodgy looking bits of wall. He hoped that someone other than Dr Byrne was on duty, and then stared up at what was left of the vaulted ceiling, wondering if this part of the building was older than the rest. All he knew about church architecture was that there were a lot of strange bits and pieces, like squinches and quoins, which did not, as far as he knew, form part of any other type of building. He remembered the piece of wood in the font: '—st falls'. Must be the end of 'Christ falls'. A vague memory came back to him of reading this, once, on the wall of a Catholic church...when? Why had he been there? A funeral, perhaps, or a wedding? The Stations of the Cross, that's what it was. He lit a cigarette, glad to have pieced it together, but his satisfaction was quickly quashed by the thought that the missing persons files at West End Central had probably been wholly or partly destroyed, which meant that identifying chummy was going to be even more difficult...Not to mention the way people were moving around nowadays because of the war, and it might be a foreigner, in which case...Stratton groaned. As if life wasn't complicated enough already.

Hearing shuffling noises from above, he put out his cigarette and stood up, brushing dust off his clothes. It wasn't the pathologist, as he'd hoped, but Father Lampton, who made his way unsteadily down the steps, a tin cup in his hand. Ignoring Stratton's greeting, the priest began to sprinkle water in the direction of the tombs, muttering incantations under his breath. Stratton caught up with him and placed a hand on his arm. 'Excuse me.'

The priest shook his head and flicked some of the water in Stratton's direction. Several drops fell on his sleeve and Stratton, unthinking, brushed them off. The movement caught Father Lampton's eye, and he looked at Stratton for the first time.

'What?' he said in a querulous voice. 'What is it?'

'DI Stratton, Father, from West End Central. I'm afraid I need to ask you some questions.'

'Questions?' repeated Father Lampton, vaguely. 'Now? I'm busy.'

'I know, Father, but it won't take long. It's about the body.' The priest eyed Stratton with distaste. 'There will be further questions once we have more information, but at the moment I'd like to know if any of your congregation have gone missing—anyone who attends church regularly, but hasn't been coming recently.'

'Well,' said Father Lampton, 'there are the evacuees, of course, and one or two of the mothers, and the men who've been called up...One of my older parishioners died recently, and one poor soul was killed in the bombing, but apart from that, I don't know of anyone.'

'I see. Has there been any building work carried out here in the past year? Repairs, and so forth.'

'Yes.' Father Lampton nodded. 'Strengthening the roof.' Gazing at the ruins around him, he added, sadly, 'Man proposes...'

'When was the work carried out?'

'February or March. Does it have a bearing on the matter?'

'It might. Do you remember the name of the company who did the work?'

'McIntosh, McInnes...' Father Lampton shook his head. 'No, that's not right...McIntyre. That was it. McIntyre.'

'Thank you.'

'Is that all?'

'Yes, Father. For the time being.'

The priest gave Stratton a curt nod and shuffled away in the direction of the stairs. Left alone, Stratton sat down again. The man's reaction was probably due to shock—it was his church after all—and he supposed that dousing the place in holy water was probably as good a response as any.

After half an hour, during which time Stratton smoked two more cigarettes, scribbled 'McIntyre—Builders' in his notebook, and hoped that Cudlipp was managing not to give mortal offence to the staff at Veeraswamy's, the photographer arrived. He was in the process of setting up his equipment when Crosbie returned, accompanied by Dr Byrne. Bollocks, thought Stratton; it would be.

'Well, where is it?' said Byrne, as if he'd been the one kept waiting.

'Over here.' Stratton led the way past the tombs. Byrne gave the corpse a curt nod—which was more, Stratton thought, than he'd got by way of greeting—then stood back to allow the photographer to finish. 'Moved anything?' he asked Stratton.

'I'm not a complete idiot, you know.' Byrne gave him a look that suggested he very much doubted this, but didn't reply.

Stratton sent Crosbie to the station to fetch a reservist to guard the place until such time as the mortuary van could be spared to collect the body, and settled down to watch Byrne at work. The man was efficient, he thought, admiring the neat way he took measurements and made sketches, you had to give him that.

Twenty minutes later, Byrne straightened up, and Stratton felt it was safe to venture a question. 'How long do you think it's been here?'

'A few months...' The pathologist unrolled his sleeves. 'Can't say until I've examined it properly. I must say,' he added, 'I feel rather like an archaeologist.' Stratton was surprised to see that the man's features had arranged themselves into a sort of rictus, and, realising several seconds too late that it was meant to be a smile, responded with a hearty chuckle. 'Short hair,' Byrne continued, 'and men's clothes, as far as I can tell, but you never know.' This, judging by the expectant look on his face, was meant as another sally, and Stratton guffawed obligingly. Christ, he thought, any minute now we'll be slapping our thighs and clapping each other on the back.

'He was murdered, was he?' he asked.

'Looks like it.'

'Was it the blow to the head?'

'Several blows. There's a depressed fracture to the skull, which can't have done him much good.'

'What about the earth? Those yellow deposits—I wondered if they might be lime.'

'Might explain the lack of insect activity. We'll have to have them analysed, of course.' It was clear from Byrne's tone that he felt he'd unbent quite enough, and Stratton knew better than to press him. 'Right,' said the pathologist, stowing the last of his things in his bag, 'I'll be off. I'll let you know when I've completed the examination. In normal circumstances, I'd say Friday, but...'

'Of course,' said Stratton, hurriedly—the mounting evidence that Byrne was actually human was beginning to unnerve him. 'I'll be in touch.'

Having instructed the reservist who'd arrived, Stratton returned to the station to find Cudlipp standing on the corner of Vigo Street having a blazing row with one of the cooks from

Veeraswamy's. The man was brandishing a heavy ladle, but Cudlipp, arms akimbo and with a familiar expression of stubbornness on his face, held his ground. 'You are thinking I know bugger nothing,' screamed the cook in a fury, 'but I know bugger all!' Clearly feeling that this was an unanswerable riposte he turned and stamped back to the restaurant.

Stratton managed to turn his laughter into a cough. He wasn't going to bother to ascertain the facts—Cudlipp, he thought, was bound to have started it—but Cudlipp, it seemed, was determined to give them to him whether he liked it or not.

'Tried to pinch my kettle, sir. Thieving wog.'

'Where is it now?'

'Here.' Cudlipp indicated the battered object, which was on the ground behind him. 'Safe and sound.'

'Good.' He shooed Cudlipp back in the direction of what was left of the station and went to have a word with the restaurant's manager.

When he emerged half an hour later, the first thing he saw was the rotund form of Sub-Divisional Inspector Roper, who'd arrived from Scotland Yard and was being given a tour of the damage by Constable Ballard. Laboriously, Stratton made his way over to them and stood waiting for Roper to finish whatever it was he was saying. Several minutes passed, during which Stratton's eyes were glued to the thread of saliva that linked Roper's pipe, which he'd removed from his mouth to wave in the air for emphasis, and his bottom lip. As Roper moved his hand, this glittering connection grew longer and longer until finally, it broke, leaving a shiny residue on his chin. Eventually, Roper stopped talking and turned towards him. 'Were you looking for me?'

No, thought Stratton, I'm just standing here for a bet. Aloud, he said, 'Yes, sir. DI Stratton, sir.'

Ah, good.' Roper jammed the pipe back into his mouth and talked round it. 'Bit of a mess.'

'Yes, sir.'

'Any news on DCI Lamb?'

'None yet, sir,' said Stratton, hoping this was correct.

'Well, keep up the good work. Come up with anything on that stabbing yet?'

'The gang fight? No, sir. It's difficult to get the witnesses to talk.' As you damn well know, he added to himself.

'Well, keep at it. Things are bound to be a bit tricky for a few days, but we'll muddle through it somehow. Been up to Eastcastle Street, have you? The church?'

'Yes, sir.' Feeling that something more was called for, Stratton added, 'The body's been there for a while, sir. We'll know more when Dr Byrne's had a look at it.'

'Good. The thing is to keep going. You'll be at Great Marlborough Street in a day or two.'

'So I understand, sir.'

'It's bound to be rather hugger-mugger at first, but I'm sure you'll bed down pretty quickly.' After several more platitudes of this type, accompanied by a spot of pipe-jabbing, Roper departed.

After a suitable pause, Ballard asked, 'How did it go at the church, sir?'

'Dr Byrne's turned into a comedian.'

'Must be that Blitz spirit we've heard so much about,' said Ballard, sardonically.

Stratton grinned. 'Anything come in while I've been away?'

'A couple of things, Sir. If you'll follow me...'

After sorting out a few minor matters, Stratton went to find Constable Ricketts, who was standing guard over several tatty heaps of police files. 'What's left of Missing Persons?'

'Here they are, Sir.' Ricketts gestured at a small stack of papers, which were variously burnt, saturated, or ripped.

'Is this it?'

'I'm afraid so, sir. I was about to take them round to Great Marlborough Street. SDI Roper told us to use the hand ambulance, sir.' As if on cue, Arliss appeared from behind a mound of rubble, pushing a glorified wheelbarrow in front of him.

'Where did you find that?'

'It was stored in the basement, sir.'

'Good grief,' said Stratton. 'Well, you'd better get on with it, then,' he added, gloomily. 'Just try and put the Missing Persons stuff somewhere where I can find it, will you?'

'Yes, sir.'

Stratton watched as Ricketts trundled off, Arliss walking beside him trying to hold the files steady and stopping every few yards to grab at torn, gritty pages that had loosed themselves from the pile and fluttered into the road. 'Christ Almighty,' he muttered, and went in search of the remains of his office.

Constable Bainbridge, aided by a policewoman, had managed to gather a few of the unspoilt bits and pieces in a desk drawer. Looking through them, Stratton was pleased to see that the photograph of Jenny and the kids which he kept tucked out of sight, was, miraculously, intact. A good omen, he thought—not so much as a crack in the glass. His notes on the girl who'd been assaulted at the nightclub were also unharmed. Thank heavens for small mercies, Stratton thought, as he shook them to get rid of the dust.

Seating himself on a couple of the wooden food boxes provided by Veeraswamy's, he began making out a list of the nightclubbers he needed to interview. Halfway through, he stopped to light a cigarette and gazed at the chaos around him. It was all very well, he thought, for SDI Roper to make fatuous remarks about keeping going and muddling through, but he wasn't the one who had to do it. And as for the corpse in the church…Stratton drew in a soothing lungful of smoke, and sighed deeply. I know bugger nothing, he thought. Bugger nothing, bugger all.

CHAPTER 25

Three days later, Stratton was settled—if you could call it that—in the DI's office at Great Marlborough Street. DI Jones, who was a good sort, had been resigned, if not happy, about the fact that the room wasn't really big enough for two desks, and that he had to perform a sort of hula dance in order to get to his chair. Stratton, who was at the end with the door, had just enough room to sit down, and, provided he didn't want to push his chair back to relax, was reasonably comfortable. DCI Lamb had been sent home from hospital to convalesce, so there was no problem from that quarter, but Cudlipp had thoroughly upset the Marlborough Street desk sergeant by commandeering the tea-making facilities, and both men had a tendency to barge into the room unbidden to air their grievances.

The tea was worse than ever and the decreased sugar ration meant that there was no way to disguise the taste. Added to which, the window, shaken out of alignment by nearby explosions, was refusing to open, so that Stratton and Jones peered at their work, and sometimes each other, through a dense haze of cigarette smoke. The Maintenance Department, which consisted of two depressed-looking individuals, was currently occupied in poking rods down the blocked basement lavatory. So far, their efforts had resulted in a malodorous brownish lake about the pedestal, but nothing else. It had taken them three weeks, Jones told Stratton, to get even that far, so neither man was expecting fresh air any time soon.

Still, at least he was making some progress on the nightclub business. As he was leafing through his notes, comparing statements from various witnesses, the telephone rang. Snatching up the receiver, he felt a sense of amazement that, in spite of the chaos, the mechanism still worked. 'Stratton.'

'Byrne here.'

'Good morning, Doctor.'

'I'm sorry it's taken me so long to get back to you. We've had a lot to do, with the bomb fatalities. Most of the work is done by the attendants, of course, but it's pretty complicated—human jigsaw puzzles.' Byrne chuckled. Blimey, thought Stratton, another joke. Wonders will never cease.

'Anyway,' said the pathologist, 'I've got some information for you. The body's male, five feet ten inches, around fifty years old, well nourished, had a dental plate—not there now but you can see the marks—some fillings...Oh, and you were right about the lime, by the way. It's builders' lime, which is why the body's in a relatively good condition.'

'How long had it been there?'

'It's difficult to estimate, but I'd say between four and six months. The cause of death was a severe blow to the head. Triangular wounds to the top and the back...let's see...seven pieces of bone, varying in size from half an inch to three inches, driven inwards, and there's another triangular wound above the left eyebrow, bones of the nose broken...Quite a mess. Looks as if it's been done with some sort of blunt instrument.'

'A cosh?'

'No. The marks suggest something broader, with a hard edge, straight—a spade, perhaps...what else?' There was a pause while Byrne looked through his notes again. 'Oh, yes. Nothing to say who he was, and no identifying marks on the remains of the clothes, I'm afraid. Hair's brown—what's left of it.'

'What were they like?'

'The clothes? Well, I'm no expert, but, judging from the bits we've got, I'd say they were poor stuff. Shoddy. There was no wristwatch, but we did find a scrap of handkerchief with a laundry mark on it.'

'That's better than nothing,' said Stratton. 'What is it?'

'Wait a minute...here we are. CV89.'

'CV—Charlie Victor?'

'That's it.'

'Well, at least we can make a start.'

Stratton asked DI Jones if he could borrow someone for a couple of days to get cracking on the local laundries. Policewoman Gaines was a strapping girl with a pink-and-white complexion and a sensible manner. 'Go back eight months,' Stratton told her. 'It shouldn't take you very long.'

He found an address and telephone number for the building firm of McIntyre Brothers in the directory, and the manager, Mr Patterson, confirmed that yes, they had been responsible for some repair work at the premises of Our Lady and St. Peter in Eastcastle Street. Stratton explained that the church had been bombed, and blathered a bit about making routine checks before asking for more details. His questions elicited the fact that the work had been carried out at the beginning of March, which tallied with what Father Lampton had said, and information from the company's time-sheets showed that a carpenter, Peter Eddowes, had been on the premises from the fourth of March until the twelfth, not including the tenth, which was a Sunday. Labourers Thomas Curran, Paddy Connelly and Jock McPherson had also been there, until the fourteenth, and the plasterer, Albert Drake, and his mate Jim Phillips had joined them on the eleventh and worked until the job was finished on the fifteenth.

'Are these men still working for you?'

'Yes, except for McPherson and Phillips. They left in June. Called up.'

'Would they have kept their tools on the premises overnight while they were working?'

'That's the usual practice, yes. Provided there's somewhere to leave them, of course.'

'I see. I will need to speak to all of these men, Mr Patterson, in the next couple of days.'

'There's nothing wrong, is there?' The manager sounded worried.

'Oh, no,' said Stratton. 'As I said, it's purely routine.'

He made an arrangement to visit McIntyre Brothers' offices, which were in Cleveland Street near the Euston Road, at five o'clock, and thanked Mr Patterson for his help. He stared into space for a moment, thinking, then asked DI Jones if he knew anything about whitewash.

'Not apart from sloshing it on the wall of the outside lav when I was a kid. What do you want to know?'

'What it's made of.'

'Quicklime.'

'Thanks.'

'Glad to be of assistance.' Jones grinned and went back to his work.

That couldn't be it, then, thought Stratton. Funny, there'd been enough whitewashed buildings on the farm when he was growing up, but he never remembered anyone actually painting them...But builders' lime, he thought, would be used in mortar, for laying bricks, so perhaps the labourers had used it. Maybe whoever buried the body had thought it was quicklime and hoped it would destroy the evidence. Stratton wondered why the man had been in the church in the first place—assuming, of course, that that was where he had died. The fact that the killer—or killers—had bashed his face in suggested that they didn't want him identified. It had to be more than just a robbery, otherwise why kill him? Even if they hadn't meant to kill, why go to all that trouble to bury him afterwards? It must have taken quite some doing to prise up those slabs from the floor—tough work for a man on his own, and time consuming, too. Stratton didn't think a woman could have done it, even a big, healthy one like Policewoman Gaines. Here, he became momentarily diverted by the image of Gaines thundering down a hockey-pitch in a gym slip, sturdy legs pounding the grass and breasts bouncing...

Collecting his thoughts before they ran amok, Stratton returned to his notes about the assault in the nightclub. Policewoman Gaines made an appearance in person at quarter past four, looking pleased with herself. 'Good news about the laundry mark, sir, I've managed to track it down.'

'Well done.'

'It's from Venner's Steam Laundry, sir, in Mayfair. The mark belongs to a man named Sir Neville Apse.'

'Does it indeed?'

'Yes, sir. I've got an address for him here.' Gaines handed him a piece of paper.

Dolphin Square. Stratton wondered whether Apse was a Member of Parliament, and, if so, why his disappearance hadn't been reported in the newspapers. 'Thank you, Miss Gaines.'

'Anything else, sir?'

'Not at the moment. But I may need you again in the next couple of days—provided DI Jones doesn't object, of course.'

Sir Neville Apse, Stratton thought. That was a name to conjure with...and if it were the name of the corpse, then he'd bet his bottom dollar that things were about to get very complicated indeed. They always did when people in high places were involved. But then again, Byrne had described the clothes as poor stuff, not smart tailoring. Still, he thought, at least DCI Lamb wasn't around to stick his oar in—not yet, anyway.

The visit to McIntyre Brothers didn't prove helpful beyond confirming that the men's tools, including two spades, had been stored at the church overnight, and that builder's lime had been used in the preparation of mortar. One of the labourers, Curran, second generation Irish with a spuddy face and sprouts of ginger hair, had seemed a bit shifty and uncomfortable, but there could be all sorts of reasons for that—selling off building materials on the side, or a previous run-in with the police…Anything, really. Bugger anything, in fact. He must remember to tell that one to Donald, and find out if there'd been any progress on the film projector at the same time. Quickening his pace, and hoping that the buses had got back to normal—or were at least travelling in something approaching the right direction—he headed for home.

CHAPTER 26

Stratton sat on the sofa in Sir Neville Apse's flat-cum-office at Frobisher House in Dolphin Square, waiting until such time as the owner of the place would deign to see him. After a brisk telephone conversation, Sir Neville, who was clearly very much alive, had agreed to spare him ten minutes, but it hadn't been easy. Their short conversation had left Stratton with the impression that Sir Neville was the kind of aristocratic Englishman who believed that he had a particular knack for endearing himself to the lower orders—in this case, Stratton—by patronising them in a hearty voice. Stratton twiddled his thumbs and hoped that the meeting wasn't going to be as tiresome and unhelpful as the circumstances seemed to indicate. He'd gathered, without actually being told, that Sir Neville was something to do with the War Office, and the signs (the FANY driver he'd seen outside, and the glacial beauty with the clipped, upper-class tones who had let him in) were of someone pretty important. Perhaps, Stratton thought, he was one of those well-connected types who'd been recruited in White's, or some other gentlemen's club, for hush-hush work by a chap who was at school with him, but whatever it was, he was sure it would be far too important for the ears of a common copper.

Hearing the murmur of men's voices in the corridor, he pricked up his ears. 'Letter from the wine merchants…stock destroyed by enemy action so they can't fulfil specific orders.'

'Better hope it's not the Barolo.'

'Making them up from whatever's available, apparently. Nuisance…Still, one shouldn't complain.'

No, thought Stratton, one bloody well shouldn't. As privations went, it wasn't worth mentioning, but this was a different world. It wouldn't have surprised him much to find that things didn't even taste the same in places like this—apples like bananas, for instance, or water like wine. Barolo, perhaps, whatever that was like.

When Sir Neville appeared after twenty minutes, without even the offer of a cup of tea, Stratton stood up and held out his hand. Sir Neville ignored it and flapped a languid wrist at him. 'Ver' good, sit dine.' Christ, thought Stratton, not even an apology for keeping him hanging about, despite the fact that he had turned up at precisely the time requested. Probably shows how terrifically common I am, he thought, as he subsided once more onto the sofa. Stop it, he told himself. The snarl of the underdog was just as bad as rolling over because of someone's rank—both would influence his judgement. He considered Sir Neville's handsome, patrician face, well-cut suit, and long-limbed frame, and found himself wondering if his wife ever called him Pinkle-Wonk in intimate moments.

Seeing Sir Neville's frown, and realising that he must be grinning, Stratton hastily composed his features. 'I am conducting a murder enquiry,' he said, firmly, before Sir Neville had a chance to say any more about how busy, and, by extension, how much more important than Stratton, he was.

Sir Neville raised his eyebrows. 'And how may I help?'

'Do you know the Church of Our Lady and St. Peter in Eastcastle Street, WI?'

'I am an Anglican.'

'Have you ever visited that church?'

'No. To the best of my recollection the only Roman service I have ever attended was a wedding, at The Church of the Immaculate Conception at Farm Street in Mayfair.'

'Your laundry is done in Mayfair, isn't it?'

'I have no idea. I'm not responsible for the laundry. The housekeeper may know, or possibly my wife, Lady Violet.'

'Nevertheless, we have a handkerchief bearing your laundry mark.'

Sir Neville's eyebrows went up again. 'Have you indeed?'

'Yes, we do. It was found on a corpse discovered at Our Lady and St. Peter. The provenance of the mark was confirmed by Venner's Steam Laundry. Do you have any idea how it might have got there?'

'None at all. I suppose I must have dropped it, and this... individual...picked it up.'

'Do you remember losing a handkerchief?'

Smiling, Sir Neville shook his head. 'No, but it's hardly of great importance, is it?'

'It is now.'

'Yes, I suppose it must be, but I'm afraid I can't see how I can be of assistance, Inspector.'

'I see.' Stratton stared at Sir Neville's bland expression and thought just how satisfying it would be to punch him. As he was standing up to leave, the door opened and a younger, almost offensively handsome man appeared, the glacial beauty in tow. 'Hope you don't mind, old chap,' he said, 'but I'm taking your Girl Friday out for a spot of lunch.'

'Not at all,' said Sir Neville, smoothly, 'as long as she's back by half-past two.' Looking at the girl, he said, 'Enjoy yourself, Diana.'

'Yes, sir. Thank you.' With that, the pair of them departed, not having cast so much as a glance in Stratton's direction. The woman was beautiful all right, in a haughty way, and very slender, with lovely legs. Stratton guessed that the pair either were, or soon would be, lovers. Good luck to Handsome, he thought—the girl might be good-looking, but she was chilly enough to freeze your cock off.

Taking his leave soon afterwards, Stratton walked down the Embankment, reflecting that the man had shown no curiosity about the identity of the corpse—he hadn't even asked whether it was a man or a woman. But then, Stratton thought, he hadn't surmised either—most people would assume it must be male. He wondered if this was significant, or if it was more a case of Sir Neville being uninterested in things that did not concern him directly.

He returned to Great Marlborough Street and asked Policewoman Gaines to look through the remains of West End Central's Missing Persons files and see if she could find anyone who matched the description of the body. Most of the rest of the day was spent embroiled in the details of the nightclub business— there were several glaring contradictions in the statements, but as most of the witnesses had, by their own admission, been roaring drunk, this wasn't exactly surprising. By the time Stratton had checked on most of the points, it was looking horribly as if the chap who'd tried to rape the young hostess was the son of a bishop—more people in high places.

By half-past five, he'd had managed to track down the girl's mother and had high hopes of effecting a reunion, which, he thought, would be something, at least. He was considering his next step when Gaines knocked on the door. 'May I come in, sir?'

'If you can. Why don't you sit down here, in fact? I can perch on the corner of the desk.'

'Thank you, sir. I'm afraid quite a lot of the records were destroyed, but I do have two names for you.'

'Excellent. Fire away.'

'Gannon and Vaisey. Both in their late forties or early fifties, and reported missing in the last six months.'

'Both before the raids started?'

'Yes, sir, but that's not conclusive, is it? I mean,' she added, hastily, 'they might have been killed since, mightn't they, sir?'

'Absolutely.'

'Well, sir, the first one, Peter Gannon, is forty-eight. Five foot ten, brown hair, blue eyes, cast in one eye. Dairyman, worked in Rathbone Place—wife reported him missing on the ninth of March, hadn't seen him for a week...Last person to see him was his employer, Mr Smithson. That was on the fifth. He was wearing his uniform. There was some trouble at home, so that could be the reason he left.'

'Have you checked with the hospitals?'

'Yes, sir, for both of them. Nothing at all.'

'Who's the other?'

'Emmanuel Vaisey. Forty-six years old. Reported by his wife on the eighth of March. He's had mental problems since the last war, apparently, so that might have had something to do with it. Address in Lexington Street. Wife keeps a tobacconist there; Vaisey didn't work.'

'Right. Well done. I'll need a copy of all that on my desk by tomorrow morning.'

Gaines beamed at him. 'Right you are, sir.'

He struggled home on four different buses, crammed with people who'd been prevented from travelling by tube because floods caused by bomb damage had put a large section of the Northern line out of action. When he finally managed to secure a seat, five stops away from home, he closed his eyes and let his thoughts drift first to Policewoman Gaines and then, by way of contrast, to Sir Neville's Girl Friday.

Diana, he'd called her. Diana...Stratton spent the rest of the journey wondering what she'd look like naked.

CHAPTER
27

Diana let herself into Forbes-James's flat. Margot Mentmore wasn't at her post, so she crossed straight to the door of the office, knocked, and was pushing open the door when F-J's voice called out sharply, 'A moment, please!' and she hastily closed it again. Odd, she thought, that he wasn't behind his desk, where he usually sat when he interviewed people. Must be something less formal...Or perhaps Mrs Forbes-James was in there. Diana hoped she was—she was dying to see what F-J's wife looked like. But surely he'd have invited her in and introduced them? But of course he hadn't known it was her on the other side of the door. Her visit wasn't scheduled—Guy's leave meant that F-J wasn't expecting to see her for at least a week. Guy's leave. Diana sank into Margot's chair and groaned. She'd been trying to avoid thinking about it ever since Evie's letter arrived.

Diana could hear the murmur of voices, but couldn't make out what was being said. She rose as the office door opened and F-J appeared, doing up his cuff, in the company of a distinguished, grey-haired man. 'This is Dr Pyke...Mrs Calthrop.' As they shook hands, he added, 'Dr Pyke is a neighbour, Diana. He's been kind enough to check my blood pressure.'

'I didn't realise you were unwell, Sir,' said Diana. 'I wouldn't have bothered you, only...'

'I'm fine,' said F-J. 'Merely a precaution.'

Dr Pyke nodded. 'Can't be too careful. Your boss is a busy man, Mrs Calthrop.'

When he'd gone, Diana said, 'I'm very sorry I disturbed you.'

'It doesn't matter in the least,' said F-J. 'Please don't apologise. Now...' he ushered her into the office. 'What have you got to tell me?'

Forbes-James frowned. 'A policeman?'

'Yes, sir. This morning. Detective Inspector Stratton.' As she said this, Diana noticed that two of his shirt buttons, hitherto camouflaged by his tie, were undone.

'And you've no idea what it was about?'

'No, sir. But I thought you should know.'

'I see. You heard nothing?'

'No, sir.' Diana averted her eyes from F-J's. 'I had to go out, sir.'

'I happened to bump into Ventriss on my way out at lunchtime,' said F-J. 'He appeared to be heading in the direction of Frobisher House.'

'Yes, sir. We had lunch together.' Diana thought she'd managed to say this without any particular inflection at all, but F-J shook his head with a sorrowful expression that made her want to squirm. It hadn't only been lunch—they'd gone back to Tite Street afterwards—and it seemed to her that F-J somehow knew or guessed this. 'Apse seemed very preoccupied this afternoon, sir,' she said hurriedly. 'I had a lot of paperwork to finish, but he told me I could go—I had the impression he didn't want me there.'

'Probably thought he'd let you off early—you've got a week's leave, haven't you?'

'Yes, sir. I'm going to Hampshire to stay with my mother-in-law, but he'd forgotten about it—I had to remind him.'

'Well,' F-J pushed his chair back, signalling that their interview was at an end. 'I imagine it was purely a routine matter—someone they've picked up—but thank you for letting me know.'

'Yes, sir…Your buttons, sir.'

'Buttons…?' F-J looked disconcerted and glanced down.

Diana blushed. 'Not there, sir. Your shirt.'

'Oh, yes. Yes, of course. Dear me…' Tidying himself, F-J accompanied her to the door. 'All things considered,' he said, 'I think it's as well you're going away for a few days. Your husband has leave as well, doesn't he?'

'Yes, sir.'

'It'll be good for you to spend some time together.' He smiled and patted her on the arm. 'Get to know each other again. You're off now, are you?'

'I'm having supper with Mrs Mountstewart first, sir.'

'Mrs—?'

'From the Right Club, sir.'

'Excellent. Goodnight, then.'

'Goodnight, sir.'

Diana rushed down the stairs, relieved to be away from F-J's scrutiny. How awful! For F-J, as well. He must have been horribly embarrassed, she thought, or he'd never have forgotten who Mrs Mountstewart was. She'd never known him to forget anyone's name, ever.

The policeman's visit was clearly quite unimportant, and she'd obviously turned up at completely the wrong time. She must learn to tell the difference between things that needed reporting and things that didn't matter. But, she thought angrily, how am I supposed to know what's normal? Nothing was normal any more, especially in her life…Get to know each other again… Remembering F-J's words, Diana groaned inwardly. I never really knew Guy in the first place, she thought. And I don't know myself, either, not anymore: that's the problem. How could she look Guy in the face after what had happened with Claude? And as for Evie…Sheer hell. And she had no-one to blame but herself.

CHAPTER 28

Diana watched her mother-in-law surreptitiously, using her book as cover. Evie, she noted with a twinge of remorse, had aged in the past few months. Her skin was dry and weather-beaten, knotted veins stood out on the backs of her hands, her neck was crêpey and her face set into hard, permanent lines. Not that you could see any of this very well in the gloom of the vast drawing room, with its stained glass windows covered by blackout shutters and the solitary gasolier that hung under the vaulted ceiling at the centre of four pillars of polished granite. Perhaps, thought Diana, it was better that one couldn't see too clearly—the October weather, which was desiccating Evie, seemed to be having the opposite effect on the house: there were warped boards and strange patches of damp all over the place.

She looked across at Guy, who was absorbed in squinting at some sort of manual about tanks. He'd gained some weight since he'd been away, which had surprised her. His face, as well as being quite a lot pinker, was definitely plumper, and there was a fleshy little roll of neck above the back of his collar. In an effort to tilt the balance away from the slight—in truth, considerably more than slight—revulsion she felt about these things, Diana made herself remember how well he'd looked in his uniform when he'd arrived. Looked at objectively, with his thick corn-coloured hair and blue eyes, he was still handsome, and although his uniform fitted rather snugly, it suited him well...Sensing that Evie was watching her watching Guy (or, rather, looking in Guy's direction, since he had now, unaccountably, turned into Claude), she switched her gaze and stared into the enormous stone fireplace.

Remembering, despite her best efforts, herself and Claude on the bed at her flat after their last lunch together, Diana hoped that Evie, whose eyes were now boring into her, couldn't read her thoughts. She'd wanted so much to ask Claude about the woman who'd committed suicide, but she hadn't. It's because I'm afraid, she thought. Frightened of what the answer might be. I know he's dangerous, yet I can't help comparing Guy with him, and that isn't fair. She wondered how soon she could decently make an excuse to go up to bed, but the problem was that Guy, directed by an almost indiscernible nod from Evie, would immediately follow her. She'd got out of it the previous night by pleading a headache, but since the excuse had undoubtedly been reported to Evie, and, judging by their expressions when she came down to breakfast, thoroughly discussed, it wouldn't be prudent to use it again. She consoled herself with the thought that at least she wasn't in danger of becoming pregnant. Overheard whisperings between two ATS girls at a hostel where she'd stayed the night after visiting a dotty old woman in Bournemouth had alerted her to the existence of something called Volpar paste, which she'd obtained from the doctor. One had to use it with a nasty rubber thing called a cap, which took ages to get into the right position. As long as they do the trick, she thought, because if Guy did succeed in making her pregnant, she'd have to come back to Hampshire for the baby, and spend the rest of the war cooped up with Evie...She couldn't bear to think about it. Only five more days, she told herself. Four more days and four more nights to be got through before she was free again.

She wondered if Guy was hating it all as much as she was. Not seeing his mother, of course—he was obviously enjoying that—but being with her. He had seemed genuinely pleased to see her, and she'd been glad too, of course—although that was more from knowing that he was safe and well, than from any desire to spend time with him...That was merely awkward, as if they'd just been introduced at a dinner party and quickly run out of things to say to one another. Once, she thought sadly, I could have sat and chattered to him for hours...Evie had invited people—friends of hers, mostly—for lunch and dinner, which would help, but Diana was painfully conscious of the fact that she was avoiding being alone with Guy as much as possible.

She wondered if he'd noticed this. So far, she'd managed to have several long, solitary walks, using the excuse that she needed the fresh air, when really she just wanted to get out of the house so that she could indulge herself in thoughts of Claude. Four more days and nights...Diana glanced at her watch. It was only quarter past nine, but she felt that if she had to sit under Evie's gaze for another second, she'd go mad. She got up and reached for her evening bag. Murmuring, 'Do excuse me', she began the long walk to the door, heels echoing on the parquet, knowing that Evie was watching her every step.

Closing the door, she let out a sigh of relief and ran down the main staircase, across the hall, through the dark morning room and the boarded-up conservatory, and out on to the terrace, where she fumbled in her bag for a cigarette.

Staring into the darkness of the garden, she reflected that Guy didn't seem to be enjoying the bed part of things any more than he had before he went away. He'd made a half-hearted attempt to make love to her before dinner, and when she'd rebuffed him, saying that there wasn't time, he hadn't insisted. Perhaps, she thought, he expects me not to be interested, or he's been having an affair, too, or slept with lots of foreign tarts or something. She marvelled for a moment at how worldly she'd become, then wondered if Guy had ever thought about somebody else while he was doing it to her. This idea wasn't a pleasant one, but then, when the time came, would she be able to stop herself thinking about Claude? That would be dreadful. Surely, she thought, other people's marriages can't be like this? Maybe they were. Perhaps her parents' marriage was like it. She shook her head, bewildered.

The door opened behind her, and there was Guy. 'You don't mind, do you?' he asked, diffidently.

'Of course not.' Her reply was automatic. For a second, she wondered what he would have done if she'd said yes, she did mind rather a lot and would he please go away. This made her feel ashamed, and she was trying to think of something friendly to say to make up for the meanness of her thought when he said, 'Jolly dark out here.'

'Yes.'

Guy took out his cigarette case and they smoked together in silence, while she racked her brains for a neutral topic of conversation.

'We haven't had much chance to chat, have we?'

'No, I suppose not.'

'It sounds as if you've been having fun in London.' There was a short pause, during which Diana's mind filled with horrible thoughts: had Evie heard something? Had she told him? What was he going to say next?

'Judging from your letters.'

'Ohh...' Thank God it was too dark for him to see her face. 'My letters. Yes, I have been having fun.'

'Wouldn't have thought it was much fun filing papers all day.'

'I'm enjoying it.'

'Are you really?'

'Yes.' What's wrong with him, Diana wondered irritably. She'd just said she was enjoying it, hadn't she?

'I wish you'd think about coming back here. Mummy gets awfully lonely, you know.'

'She's got plenty of friends.'

'I know, but it's not the same as if you were here, darling. And it isn't safe in London.'

'I'm used to it. Anyway, I can't just walk out of my job.'

'I've no doubt you're very good at it, darling, but I'm sure they'll be able to find another office girl.'

I can't tell him about it, Diana thought miserably. I can't tell him anything. 'I want to be part of it, Guy. If I was here...' She nearly said 'stuck here', but managed to stop herself in time. 'I wouldn't feel I was doing my bit.'

'But there are lots of things to do here: the evacuees, for instance.'

'They've gone home.'

'There'll be another lot now the raids have started. And there's the WVS, and the Nursing Home. Mummy never complains, but I know she's finding it terribly difficult managing on her own.'

'She isn't on her own. She's got Mrs Birkett, and Ellen, and Reynolds, and—'

'You know what I mean. Anyway,' he added, slyly, 'if you have a baby, you'll have to come back.'

'I don't want a baby, Guy.'

'Of course you do,' he said, breezily.

His dismissive tone made her angry. 'No, I don't.'

'Don't be silly, darling.'

'I'm not being silly. I don't want a baby.'

'Why not?'

'Because I don't. Not now, not yet.'

'Oh, darling. I know everything's a bit upside down because of the war, but if you had one, you'd love it.'

'How do you know?'

'Don't be childish, Diana. Of course you would. And Mummy would be delighted.'

'I'm sure she would.' Diana dropped her cigarette and ground it out with her foot. 'But I'm not going to have one.'

'I know you had a bad time before, darling, but I'm sure you'd manage better this time, and—'

'Manage to keep the baby, you mean? I didn't lose it deliberately, you know.'

Guy looked embarrassed. 'Of course not. You're tired, darling.' He patted her shoulder, clumsily, in the dark. 'I'm sure that once you've had a good rest, you'll see it differently.'

'I shan't. But I am going up to bed. You can go and report back to Evie if you like. I'm sure you'll have plenty to talk about.' She ran back indoors, slamming the conservatory door behind her so that the glass panes rattled behind their blackout blinds.

Lying in bed, staring at the imitation coffering on the ceiling, Diana thought, now I've really blotted my copybook. Open rebellion—they'd be discussing it now, downstairs. She could picture Evie on the sofa beside Guy, stroking his head and telling him not to worry, she'd have a quiet word and put things right...Oh, God, why hadn't she just kept her mouth shut?

She turned off the lamp and curled up on her side. The guilt she'd felt, both about Claude, and about the poor unwanted baby she hadn't been sorry to lose, that had made her so sharp with Guy, was suddenly overtaken by misery. The thought that this bloody house was the closest thing she had to a home filled her with a sense of hopeless despair. Tite Street was lovely, of course, but it didn't really count, and besides, she couldn't stay there for ever...She longed for the release of sleep, but it wouldn't come. The thought of the morning, when Evie would take her aside for a 'little talk', filled her with dread.

A couple of hours later, she heard footsteps in the corridor: Guy. She stared into the darkness, her body rigid beneath the bedclothes. Surely not tonight...? The steps grew closer, and seemed to stop just outside the door. No, please, no...Diana held her breath. The steps started up again, and the sound faded as he went down the passage. Thank God...He must have decided to sleep on the daybed in his dressing room. She turned over and closed her eyes.

She didn't go down to breakfast, which meant nothing until lunch because Evie did not approve of eating in bed, and in any case the bell didn't work. She stayed in her room until half-past eleven, when Guy put his head around the door to announce that he and his mother were lunching with some people in the village—and he was sure she'd rather stay in her room and be quiet until she was feeling better.

She watched from her window until the trap had taken them out of sight, then dressed and crept down the staircase, keeping an ear out for Mrs Birkett and Ellen, and fled into the garden. After a couple of hours' aimless walking, she found herself standing beside the lake where, two years ago, her beloved dachshund had drowned. She wept, knowing that the tears were for herself rather than poor little Clarence, and disliking herself for it.

Trudging back to the house, she told herself not to be ridiculous. Far worse things happened to people, especially at the moment—husbands killed overseas, wives killed at home, people and their children being wounded and crippled, their homes and possessions destroyed. What did she have to cry about?

Lunch had been left for her in the dining room—ham, a few pieces of tired lettuce, half a tomato and a slice of beetroot which had bled over everything else on the plate. Even Mrs Birkett, the cook, seemed to hate her, she thought. She forced some of it down and secreted the bits she hadn't managed to eat inside her hand-kerchief. It would be ruined, but that couldn't be helped. Angry that she was being treated like a schoolgirl—and aware that she was behaving like one—she went up to her bedroom and stayed there, lying on her bed and trying to read, but mostly staring up at the ceiling, until four o'clock.

During tea, which was taken in the drawing room, Guy and Evie maintained an exaggerated politeness towards her but talked mainly to each other, discussing the people they'd lunched with, whom she'd never met. After about half an hour of this, Guy, at a nod from Evie, stood up and said he hoped they'd excuse him, but he needed to speak to Reynolds about the garden. Diana rose from the sofa to follow him, saying, 'I think I'll just go and— Ouch!' Evie's hand shot out and caught hold of her wrist. She tried to jerk away, but Evie, still seated in her armchair, had a surprisingly strong grip. 'I think it's time we had a chat, don't you?' Behind her, Diana heard a quiet click as the door closed. 'Please let go, Evie. You're hurting me.'

Her mother-in-law stared at her for a moment before releasing her. 'Sit down.' Defeated, Diana did so, rubbing her arm.

'I have a lot of friends in London,' Evie said, 'And I have heard certain rumours. I didn't give them much credence—people will talk about anything, especially nowadays, and you know that I have always tried to see the best in you.' She gave Diana a small, poisonous smile. 'I thought it was probably some stupid infatuation—after all, you're still young, and you haven't had a mother to advise you, but I had hoped that by now, as a married woman of twenty-four, you would be mature enough to know better. I was sure it would blow over in time—these things always do—and as the man in question has a reputation as a philanderer, I comforted myself with the thought that you could not possibly be so idiotic as to fall in love with him. I was determined to say nothing, but what Guy told me last night about your coldness towards him puts the matter in a rather different light. I have not, of course, mentioned this sordid business to him—after all, he has quite enough to do with fighting this war, and it's hardly the time to start worrying him over trifles. Especially when...' Evie lowered her eyes. When he might not come back, Diana thought, with such an uprush of guilt that she felt as if she were about to be sick. 'However,' Evie continued, 'I see that it has gone further than I thought. Surely, Diana, you want to make Guy happy?'

Unable to speak, Diana stared at her shoes.

'Perhaps you don't think he deserves happiness?'

There was only one answer to this, and Diana gave it. 'Of course I do.'

'A child would make him happy, Diana. A son. And that is your duty, just as Guy's duty is to fight for his country. You know that, don't you?'

Diana nodded.

'Do you? I want an answer.'

'Yes.'

'Well then, let's have no more of this nonsense. If you give me your promise—your solemn promise—that you won't see this man again, we will say no more about it. Otherwise I will have to tell Guy, and that would hurt him more than anything, to know that while he has been risking his life for his country, his wife has been making a fool of herself over some…some roué. Do you understand me?'

'Yes,' said Diana. 'I understand.'

'Good. I know that what happened before—losing the baby—must have been upsetting for you, but that's no reason not to try again. I take it you haven't compromised yourself with this man.' Evie stopped, waiting for a response. When none came, she said, 'You know what I am talking about.'

'No,' lied Diana, 'I haven't.'

'I love my son,' said Evie. 'I cannot protect him in battle, but I will do everything in my power to protect him at home. Do you understand that?' Diana stared at her—the mouth was smiling, but the eyes were alight with a terrifying fervour that made her heart thump painfully in her chest.

'Do I have your word that you won't see this man again?'

'Yes.' It came out in a whisper.

'In that case, we'll say no more about it. Now, I imagine you'd like some time by yourself. Perhaps you should go for a walk. Mr Reynolds has taken Guy to see the greenhouses, so you might prefer to avoid that part of the garden.'

Once outside, Diana leant against the conservatory wall and lit a cigarette with shaking hands. By the time she'd finished it, the memory of the fanaticism in Evie's eyes had receded a bit, and she began to berate herself for being feeble and not standing up to her instead of meekly agreeing not to see Claude again. What else could she have done, though? That look on Evie's face…Diana shivered. She hadn't been imagining it: Evie would do anything to protect Guy, she thought, deliberately shying away from considering what 'anything' might involve. Fancy a grown man allowing his mother to fight his battles for him! But, she thought, that wasn't entirely fair, because Guy didn't know anything about Claude. And of course she didn't want to hurt him, but…

Guy did want a child, she knew, but he undoubtedly wanted one more because Evie desired a grandson. Supposing it was a girl, anyway? Then she'd have to have another, and if that wasn't a boy, either…Except that she hadn't actually agreed to have a baby, had she? Evie had simply taken that as read. But the thought of never seeing Claude again, never kissing him, never…

It was the only thing, she admitted to herself, that had kept her going this week, imagining herself reunited with him in London, and now that had been taken away, there was nothing… In a few short weeks, Claude seemed to have become the foundation stone of her life; now she'd have to learn to manage without him. Resign herself. Life could—and would—go on, and there was her work. Well, she'd keep her promise, but that was all. Pregnancy was unthinkable.

For an insane moment, she imagined herself asking Guy for a divorce, but that was unthinkable, too. In four days' time he'd be back with his regiment, bound for God knows where. She couldn't do it. In any case, he'd undoubtedly refuse, and if by some miracle he agreed, what would F-J think? He might be forced to dismiss her, or, failing that, demote her. And how would Claude react? He'd said he loved her, but there was Lally's story about the woman who'd killed herself—*she* had thought Claude was in love with her, hadn't she? And as for Evie…*I will do everything in my power to protect him at home.*

Flinging away her cigarette, she ran down the terrace steps and across the lawn, scrambling down and then up the steep sides of the ha-ha, her breath coming in tearful gasps as she stumbled over the tussocky grass of the field beyond, watched by a dozen pairs of melancholy bovine eyes. Once in the woods, she sat down at the base of a big tree and pulled out her handkerchief to blow her nose, only to discover that it was full of leftover bits of ham from lunch and blotched pink from the beetroot. For some reason, the sight of this made her cry even harder than before, and, engulfed by a tide of self-pity and unconstrained by thoughts of other people's problems, she howled with misery.

At quarter to seven, she realised she ought to go back to the house and dress for dinner. Leaning against the rough bark, surrounded by the earthy, comforting smell of leaf mould, she suddenly wondered why she should. She wanted to stay put and fall asleep like one of the babes in the wood, but people didn't do things like that in real life. Besides, there was bound to be a Home Guard Patrol later, and she'd probably be mistaken for a German parachutist and shot. I wouldn't care, she thought. At least, if she were dead, she'd be released from this pretence, from Guy and Evie's wishes, from her longing for Claude. She struggled wearily to her feet and walked back to the edge of the trees. The cows had gone for milking, and the house, standing at the top of its slope of lawn, its gables and turrets dark against the weak evening sun, looked forbidding and hostile, like a prison. 'What am I going to do?' she said, aloud.

Diana stared at her reflection in the bathroom mirror. Somehow, she'd managed to get earth all down the front of her dress, under her fingernails, and in her hair. She looked as if she'd been rolling in it. Her eyes were pink-rimmed and swollen, and her nose red. Splashing her face, she wondered if there might be enough hot water for a bath. For the sake of her dignity—what was left of it—she did not want to go down to dinner looking like a ragamuffin.

A great deal of banging and groaning from the plumbing produced three inches of warm water and a lot of condensation. Diana bathed quickly and returned to her bedroom to change her clothes. She put on her favourite evening dress, re-did her hair and covered her face with a thick layer of powder. It occurred to her, as she was blotting her lipstick, that she would need to replace her ruined handkerchief. Opening the drawer where the maid, Ellen, had unpacked her underwear, she took a clean one from the embroidered case her mother had given her for her seventeenth birthday. As she was about to close the drawer, it struck her that its contents did not look quite as she had left them. There'd been no reason for Ellen to go through her things—there was no laundry to come back, and no mending to be done, so...

Kneeling in front of the chest of drawers, she scooped out brassieres, stockings and knickers and threw them onto the floor. Petticoats and camisoles followed until the drawer was empty. Diana stared at the lining. The tube of Volpar paste and the round box containing her cap, which she'd carefully hidden beneath her underclothes, had disappeared.

CHAPTER

29

Policewoman Gaines was waiting for Stratton when he arrived at Great Marlborough Street at half-past eight. 'Good morning, sir. I've been asked to tell you that DCI Machin wants a word, sir.'

'Machin?' Stratton was momentarily confused.

'Our governor, sir.'

'Yes, of course. Now?'

'Yes, sir. He said immediately.'

'Right-o. Lead the way.'

Following Gaines down the corridor, Stratton wondered at the sudden urgency. He hadn't seen anything of DCI Machin, beyond a quick welcome-to-the-station and we're-rather-tight-for-space conversation, and had assumed, or, rather, hoped, that he'd be left alone to get on with his job.

'DI Stratton, sir.' Gaines withdrew, and DCI Machin, who had been seated behind his desk, half rose, looking uncomfortable. 'Stratton. Take a seat.'

'Thank you, sir.'

Machin sat down again, cleared his throat several times, and said, 'Settling in all right?'

'Yes thank you, sir.' For God's sake, thought Stratton, get on with it, man. You didn't summon me here for that. Machin hummed and ha'd a bit, in the manner of someone who wasn't sure how to break bad news. Stratton's mind leapt immediately to the obvious, and he said, urgently, 'It's not my wife, is it, sir? She hasn't been...'

'No, no. Nothing like that.'

Thank Christ for that, thought Stratton. Relief made him miss the first part of what Machin said next.

'...from Scotland Yard. I understand you went to see...' he glanced at his notes, 'Sir Neville Apse, yesterday morning.'

'Yes, sir.'

'Well...' Machin looked even more uncomfortable. 'He's not very happy about it.'

'Sir Neville isn't?'

'No. And neither was SDI Roper, when Sir Neville made his complaint.'

'I don't understand, sir. His handkerchief was found on a murder victim. The body hasn't been identified yet, and...'

Machin held up a hand. 'Be that as it may...' Be that as it may? I don't believe I'm hearing this, thought Stratton. 'I have strict instructions that he is not to be troubled again.'

Troubled? 'This is a murder investigation, sir. I have to—'

'SDI Roper was very clear. You are not to approach Sir Neville again unless you have permission to do so.'

'May I ask why, sir?'

Machin looked at Stratton with an I'm-finding-this-hard-enough-so-don't-make-it-any-worse expression on his face. 'Sir Neville is engaged in work of national importance.' He pronounced the last two words with audible capital letters.

You mean he's MI5, thought Stratton. A spy, and a well-connected one at that. 'I'll request permission next time, sir.'

'It would be better if there wasn't a next time,' said Machin, pointedly, adding, 'but I'm sure there won't be any need.'

Christ Almighty, thought Stratton. 'Yes, sir,' he said, in as neutral a tone as he could manage. 'I'll see to it.'

Stratton was relieved to find his office empty; he needed a few minutes by himself. He supposed he ought to thank his lucky stars that DCI Lamb hadn't been on the receiving end of the telephone call, or he'd never have heard the last of it. SDI Roper being 'very clear' meant that Machin had been given a rocket, which, given that Stratton didn't even work for him, was bloody unfair. And really, Machin had been pretty decent about it, considering...All the same, life was quite difficult enough without the two of them going on as if he'd just farted in church.

Policewoman Gaines put her head round the door. 'I thought you might like a cup of tea, sir.'

'Thank you.' Stratton took a sip of the grey liquid, and grimaced.

'Sorry, sir. It's the best we can do.'

'It's warm and wet, anyway.'

'Yes, sir. I've got a message for you, from the hospital.'

'Which one?'

'The Middlesex, sir. It's about Emmanuel Vaisey. Brought in dead last night, Sir. Heart attack. Wife identified him. They think he'd been living on the streets.'

'He was the one with mental trouble, wasn't he?'

'Yes, sir. I suppose that must account for it.'

'I should think so. Well, it's one we don't have to worry about.'

Arriving at the Express Dairy in Rathbone Place, which had been the workplace of the missing Peter Gannon, Stratton noted that the building was next door to the Wheatsheaf pub where Mabel Morgan had spent many, if not most, of her evenings. Stratton determined to enquire about her after he'd talked to Gannon's employer Mr Smithson. At least, he thought, the barman wouldn't be likely to telephone Scotland Yard with complaints about him.

Mr Smithson's face darkened at the mention of Gannon. 'Ran out on me, didn't he? Did his rounds in the morning, and that was the last I saw of him. Letter five weeks later, giving notice—no forwarding address.'

'Have you any idea where he's gone?'

'No. His wife might know, but...' He shook his head. 'Poor woman.'

'And you received this letter when?'

'April sometime.'

'Do you remember seeing a postmark?'

'Can't say I do. Something happened to him, has it?'

'I hope not,' said Stratton. 'Unreliable, was he?'

'No, his work was satisfactory—till he took off, that is.'

'Why do you think he went?'

'Don't know. Might be a woman involved, I suppose, but I shouldn't have thought he was much of a one for the ladies, not with that funny eye.'

'Funny?' Stratton looked at his notes again. 'Oh, the cast.'

'That's right. Made him a bit odd looking.'

On the way out, Stratton caught sight of the machine for putting cream on pastries, which now stood unused, and wondered when he'd be able to have a rhum baba again. Not that they were ever as good as they looked, but all the same... The memory of tea-time treats made him think of Monica and Pete. He'd be seeing them in less than a week...He thanked Mr Smithson, and went next door to the Wheatsheaf.

The barman was busy polishing glasses in the Saloon Bar. 'We're closed, sir.'

'DI Stratton, Great Marlborough Street.'

'Oh, sorry, sir. What can I get you?'

'Nothing, thanks. I've come for a spot of information about one of your regulars—or former regulars. Have you worked here long?'

'Past two years, sir.'

'Right. What's your name?'

'Trewitt, sir.' The barman sounded wary. 'Shall I call the governor?'

'That won't be necessary. It's about Miss Morgan.'

'We heard about that. A real tragedy, that was.'

'I understand she was often here.'

'Oh, yes. Most evenings.'

'What was she like? I mean, her behaviour.'

'Well, she was friendly...I don't really know what to say, just a nice woman.'

Stratton, noting that Prewitt had said woman, not lady, asked, 'What did she sound like?'

'Oh, you know...London.'

'What sort of voice?'

'Cockney, really. When she first told me she'd been in films I didn't believe it, because she didn't sound like they do, but then she told me it was before they brought out the talkies...She showed me a magazine with a photograph of her, before she had the accident—beautiful. You'd never have thought it, but it was all true. People used to buy her drinks, and she'd tell them about it and show the picture. You know the sort of thing, sir.'

Stratton, who did know the sort of thing, thought how sad it was to be reduced to cadging drinks in return for anecdotes.

'Did she drink a lot?'

Prewitt thought about this for a moment, then said, 'A fair bit, sir. We get a lot like that in here—writers and theatrical types. And like I said, a lot of people bought her drinks.'

'Did she use any strange expressions? Old-fashioned slang, that sort of thing.'

'Oh, no, nothing like that.'

'Would you say she was an educated person?'

'Well, she wasn't stupid, but I wouldn't say she'd had a lot of schooling, no.' None of which, Stratton thought, as he headed off in the direction of the Gannons' flat in Scala Street, made Mabel Morgan sound anything like the writers of the letters in the deed box. Surely nobody who spoke normally would write in such an affected way? But if she wasn't either Binkie or Bunny, why keep the letters?

Stratton turned this over in his mind as he waited for someone to answer the door. Mrs Gannon was a small woman, with bitter eyes and a sort of flattened quality, which—together with the faded floral pattern on her apron—made him think of a badly pressed flower.

When Stratton explained who he was and why he was there, she invited him in. The Gannon home was two rooms at the top of a dark staircase, and the whole house, as far as he could see, had a dilapidated air, inside and out. The main room, which contained a gas range and some threadbare washing drying on a clothes-horse in a corner, looked out onto a grimy school building and a yard, now empty of children.

'Gone off, hasn't he?' Mrs Gannon said. 'A woman.'

'Do you know where he's gone?' asked Stratton.

'Wrote me a letter, didn't he? Wanted me to send his clothes, but I popped them, didn't I? Needed the money. Said he'd send me something, but he never did.'

'When did you receive the letter?'

Mrs Gannon shrugged. 'Dunno. Spring, sometime. April, I think it was.'

'Have you kept it?'

'In there somewhere.' She jerked her head in the direction of the second room.

'Could I have a look at it, please?'

'What d'you want to see it for?'

'It's just a routine enquiry, Mrs Gannon. Checking up on people who've gone missing.'

'He's not missing, is he? He's with a woman.'

'You didn't tell them at the police station.'

'Never thought, did I?' she said, belligerently. 'Got enough on my plate.'

'May I see it?'

'I suppose so.' She disappeared into the other room and emerged a couple of minutes later, with a much-folded piece of paper, which she thrust at him. 'Go on, then.'

He glanced through the letter: *...and that is all I can say dear and I hope you will forgive me for it. If you would send my clothes on because I have not anything at present can you send them to this address which is where we are stopping at present.* The address, written at the top, was in Belmore Lane, Holloway, N. Stratton noted it down and returned the letter to its owner. 'I've not seen him since he went,' said Mrs Gannon, adding, defiantly, 'I don't know if he's alive or dead, and I don't care, do I?'

Clattering down the stairs, Stratton decided that Mrs Gannon couldn't have murdered her husband—not without help, anyway. She certainly didn't look as if she could move a body or lift a paving stone on her own. Still, he'd need to speak to someone at the station in Holloway to check that Gannon was living at the address on the letter. He had a friend up there, Ralph Maynard, who'd been at Vine Street with him in the early days. A telephone call ought to do the trick. He could do that back at Marlborough Street.

When he got home that evening, Jenny handed him a message from Donald: *Will have projector by tomorrow. When's the film show?*

CHAPTER

30

Diana dumped her suitcase onto the bed at Tite Street and collapsed, flat on her back, beside it. The train journey back from Hampshire had been hellish—slow and cramped in a stuffy carriage with the blackout blinds drawn—and she'd returned home to an overpowering smell of sewage from a ruptured waste-pipe in the next street. She was exhausted and she ached all over. What the hell was she going to do? The last four days, and a good part of the last three nights, had been spent thinking about it, but she could find no solution. She couldn't ask Guy for a divorce—that was out of the question. She must have been mad even to consider it. Even if it were possible, and even if—in the best case—Guy was a gentleman and allowed her to divorce him, it would mean a lot of sordid business involving private detectives and hotel rooms, and social taint, if not actual disgrace. And supposing she had a baby? Unable to say anything about the confiscation of her contraceptives, which had to be Evie's doing since Guy, she was sure, knew next to nothing about such things, she'd lain rigid, fingers crossed behind Guy's back as he...he... You could hardly call it 'making love', it was more like...what? Gardening, that's what it was like. Planting a seed. And she might as well have been a flowerbed for all the attention he'd paid her.

He hadn't even stayed afterwards, just gone sheepishly back to the bed in his dressing-room, leaving her to cry herself to sleep.

It had been his diffident, apologetic quality afterwards, coupled with her mounting anger at being treated like a mere thing, which had caused her to erupt in fury on the last night of their stay, fighting him off, hitting and scratching, and calling him the filthiest names she could think of. But instead of turning away from her in disgust, he'd been excited by it; more aroused, in fact, than she'd ever seen him.

'Going to fight me, are you?' he'd said, pushing her down on the bed. He'd held her there with one hand and unbuttoned his trousers with the other, and the look on his face was...Diana shut her eyes and tried to blot out the image. She didn't want to remember.

'Leave me alone, you bastard!' She'd struggled to sit up, and even attempted to scratch his face, but it hadn't made any difference. She wouldn't have been much of a match for him anyway, but months of army training had made him strong and very fit.

'That's your game, is it?'

'What are you talking about? It's not a game—Guy, I don't want—' He'd put a hand over her mouth. True, he'd removed it quickly enough when she'd bitten him, but even that hadn't made him stop. 'You little bitch.' His voice was thick, coarser, different. Ignoring her protests, he'd pinned her to the bed, yanked her silk nightdress up so viciously that it tore, rammed his knee between her legs hard enough to bruise, and pushed himself inside her.

'Please, Guy, don't.'

He'd grinned at her, then, but a sudden flicker of grim purpose across the stupid, lustful expression on his face had made her realise that he knew damn well she wasn't playing a game and he didn't care. The really odd thing about it—the thing she didn't want think about—was that she could see that if she had wanted him to do it, it would have been quite enjoyable, certainly more than usual because...

Diana sat up and shook her head violently, trying to erase the memory. Despite what had happened, she couldn't entirely blame Guy for being angry with her. After all, she could hardly explain to him about Claude, or about not wanting his child. Perhaps there was something wrong with her. Perhaps she wasn't normal. After all, women—if married—were supposed to want children, weren't they? That was the natural course of things. Or at least her duty, as Evie had said. After all, she didn't have to fight, did she? She didn't even have to remain in London and risk being bombed if she didn't want to. Guy only wanted what any man might reasonably want from his wife...

She'd just have to wait—not long, a week, at most—to find out whether or not she was pregnant, but if the answer was yes...? 'Oh, God!' She clenched her fists and dug her nails into her palms, as if by inflicting pain on herself she could drive away the possibility.

Supposing Guy were to be killed? Then, if she were pregnant, she'd be left with his child, and Evie. But if she weren't... For a few minutes, Diana gave herself up to the fantasy of marrying Claude, conveniently forgetting both Guy's existence and that of the woman Claude had abandoned, before returning to miserable reality.

Sighing, she opened her suitcase and began to unpack. She could have left it to the maid, but it was something to do.

'It's all nonsense,' she said aloud. 'Pie in the sky.' She dumped a pile of clothes on the bed, looked at them for a moment, and suddenly felt that she didn't even have the energy to work out what she ought to do with them. She sat down again and lit a cigarette. It occurred to her that if Evie were to see her now, sitting on her bed smoking—she'd be horrified. 'Oh, who cares?' she said aloud. 'Who bloody well cares?'

CHAPTER

31

$\mathcal{S}$tratton had a telephone call from Maynard at the Holloway police station the following afternoon. 'Your man Gannon's there, all right. Nasty piece of work—ugly, too. Living with a woman called Beatrice Dench. Frankly, it's a wonder that one woman could fancy him, never mind two.'

Well, that was that. He spent most of the rest of the day trying to get some sense out of the bishop's son who had assaulted the girl in the nightclub. He was terrified, contrite, and hysterically over-cooperative. After two hours, during which he'd confessed everything he'd ever done, from scrumping apples to nocturnal fumblings in the dorm, Stratton was beginning to despair of ever getting a straight story when Ballard put his head round the door. 'If I could have a word, sir?'

Stratton followed him outside. 'What is it?'

'The guv'nor, sir. Theirs, I mean. Wants a word, sir.'

'Right.'

DCI Machin was looking uncomfortable again. 'This young chap you've got…Cockcroft. He can go.'

'Go?' echoed Stratton, adding a belated 'Sir?'

'We're not taking this any further. I've been speaking to the bishop, and I'm assured that his son is a young man of good character who has never done anything like this before, so…'

'That doesn't mean he won't do it again, sir, if he thinks he can get away with it.' Privately, Stratton didn't believe this—he doubted if Cockcroft, who was scared shitless, would do so much as ask a girl to dance, at least for a while—but that wasn't the point.

Machin cleared his throat. 'We have received assurances.'

'From the bishop, sir?'

'Yes. I'm told he's a young man of great promise, so it wouldn't be right to wreck his career because of a single boyish indiscretion.'

'Rape, sir. It's not exactly an indiscretion.'

'The bishop would like to speak to the girl's mother.'

That, thought Stratton, meant an offer of money. How much, he wondered. £25? £50? 'She was fifteen, sir.'

'I know that,' said Machin, irritably, 'but we,'—him and his new chum the bishop, thought Stratton—'think that is the best course of action, so I want you to tell Cockcroft that he is free to leave.'

'But—'

'Now, DI Stratton.'

Stratton left Cockcroft to sweat for as long as he reasonably could without actually being insubordinate, then let him go. On his way home he reflected that the bishop of wherever it was probably knew the Commissioner. Serve him bloody well right if the woman didn't accept his offer—but that, he knew, was unlikely.

After supper, he went round to see Donald about the projector. He'd read the rest of the letters in the deed box—a lot more Pinkle-Wonkery but nothing useful—and although he was interested in seeing the films, he wasn't convinced that they would yield anything, either.

'I've been looking at the instruction book,' said Donald, showing him the projector, 'and I'm pretty sure I can get it running. We can look at some of them now, if you like.'

Stratton helped Donald to move some of the sitting room furniture out of the way, then went back to collect the films from the shed while his brother-in-law set up the projector and screen. Jenny had said she'd go with him because she wanted to talk to Doris. There was something about the way she announced this that made him wonder if the chat mightn't be something to do with Johnny. She hadn't repeated her suggestion about him talking to the boy, but Stratton knew it had been on her mind. He felt bad about not having done it, but there hadn't really been an opportunity. Jenny had always been closer to Doris than Lilian. There was barely a year in age between the two of them, while Lilian was four years older, and they were similar in temperament as well as looks—Doris was a taller, darker version of Jenny.

Looking at the canisters under his arm, eleven in all, Jenny said, 'You're not meant to have these at home, are you?'

'No,' said Stratton, 'so keep your lip buttoned.'

Jenny looked at him curiously. 'You don't normally bring things home.'

'I don't think this is normal,' said Stratton.

'Oh...' Jenny looked as if she was about to ask him what he meant, then thought better of it. 'It's something to do with Mabel Morgan, isn't it?'

'Yes. Films.'

'In those boxes?'

'That's how they store them.'

'I never knew that.' Jenny tapped one of the canisters. 'Do you know which ones they are?'

'No idea. There aren't any labels.'

'Won't you get into trouble?' she asked, as they walked down the road.

'Nobody knows I've got them.'

'But that's...' Jenny sounded worried. 'That's bad.'

'It isn't good,' Stratton admitted, 'and it's certainly not the way we're supposed to do things, but I've got a...a...sort of a feeling about it. What the Americans call a hunch.'

'But you said she killed herself.'

'I know, but I think there's a bit more to it than that.'

'I see,' said Jenny, carefully, and again, Stratton had the impression that she wanted to say more.

'Ooh,' said Jenny, when she saw the sitting room. 'It's just like being at the pictures. The blackout curtains are just the thing. You could charge people for admission. I've always fancied being an usherette.'

'Not likely,' said Stratton. 'All those men in the dark, they wouldn't be able to keep their hands off you. Still,' he sent her towards the kitchen with a pat on the bottom, 'you can fetch us some tea, if you like.'

Donald prised the lid off the first canister and began to thread up the projector. 'Where have you been keeping them?' he asked.

'In the garden shed.'

'Fair enough. But I shouldn't bring them into the house. This stuff is pretty flammable, and if you got an incendiary— kaboom! Right, here we go.'

Stratton settled himself on the sofa as the screen flickered into life, and a title—*The Bat*—appeared across it, followed by Mabel Morgan's face, mouthing silently, and, seated beside her on a sofa in a well-appointed room, a handsome man who kissed her hand and then got down on one knee. *Will you marry me, my darling?* read the caption. Mabel's face alight with pleasure—*Yes! I will be your wife.* The man returned to the sofa with an elegant flick of his coat-tails and took her in his arms, and immediately a winged shadow fell on the wall behind them. They turned, and Mabel's face appeared in close-up with an expression of exaggerated horror, fingertips on cheekbones—*The bat!* The man held up his arms as if to ward something off. There was more face-pulling from the pair, and then Mabel turned away from the camera, her hand to her forehead—*Our love is doomed*—while the man gazed at her with an expression of romantic agony, and then—then the image went from positive to negative and back again, and dissolved into a frothing patchwork of blotches, through which Stratton made out the words *I can never*—before the screen turned black.

'It's perished,' said Donald. 'Like seeing ghosts,' he added thoughtfully. Stratton looked at him in surprise. His brother-in-law wasn't given to flights of fancy, but Stratton knew exactly what he meant, and seeing the dead woman disappear like that gave him the creeps. 'Funny, isn't it?' he said. 'That picture can't be more than about twenty years old, but it seems like...'

'History,' said Donald. 'A different time.'

'Odd seeing it like that, without any music,' said Stratton. 'I never really used to notice it much—didn't realise what a difference it made.'

Giggles from the kitchen heralded the entrance of Jenny, with one of Doris's trays suspended rather precariously from her neck by a spare length of washing line.

'Here we are. Ice cream's off, cigarettes are off. Even sugar's off.' She caught sight of the blank screen. 'Oh dear. Has it broken down?'

'It's not the equipment,' said Donald, 'it's the film. Celluloid isn't stable.'

'Does that mean,' Jenny handed him a cup of tea, 'that in twenty years' time people won't be able to see the pictures from today?'

'It's all improved now. Modern stuff lasts longer.'

'I shouldn't think they'll want to,' said Stratton, accepting his cup. 'They'll want new ones, in colour...I wonder what the world will be like in 1960?'

There was a short pause as they contemplated this, until Donald sighed and said, 'God knows.'

When Jenny had returned to the kitchen, he asked, 'Want to try another one?'

'Fire away.' Stratton sat back on the sofa and drank his tea while Donald set to work. The next picture was a one-reel comedy—*Gertie and Bertie's Day Out*. Mabel played a nursemaid who, distracted in the park by the attentions of a soldier, let the terrible twins out of her sight to make mischief. The film was in better condition than the previous one, and ended with the soldier lying in a horse-trough and Mabel covered in flour. After that, they watched a melodrama called *His Finest Hour*, and then Stratton suggested that Donald try the last canister in the stack.

The title, *The Waltz*, was followed by a film of two men, dancing together in an empty ballroom. Clean shaven, immaculate in tails, with glacé shoes and dark, slicked-back hair parted in the middle in the fashion of the Twenties—young sophisticates, enjoying themselves—they stared solemnly at each other through eyes ringed with kohl.

'Practising, do you think?' said Donald sardonically.

'They don't need to,' said Stratton. 'They know the score already.'

Donald snorted. 'This wasn't shown at a cinema.'

'No. Strictly private, this one.'

They watched in silence for a couple of minutes, Stratton trying to think where he'd seen the taller man before. He looked somehow familiar, but Stratton couldn't remember when or where he'd seen him. When the dance ended, the men embraced in a parody of a screen kiss, the shorter man's head thrown back with abandon, to receive the mouth of the other.

'Bloody hell!' said Donald. On the screen, the men parted, and, holding hands, bowed to the audience. It was at that moment, when he saw the taller man full face, that Stratton remembered where he'd seen him, and something about the way in which the head was inclined confirmed it. 'That's it!' he said.

'Someone you know?' asked Donald.

'Mmm,' said Stratton, trying to sound non-committal.

'Don't worry, I shan't ask awkward questions.'

Stratton and Jenny walked home in silence, lost in their own thoughts. The first sirens went just as Stratton opened the front door, and they rushed upstairs to change into trousers and jumpers and gather up eiderdowns, the torch and the bucket.

As they lay side by side on their wooden bunks in the darkness of the Anderson shelter, listening to the raids in the distance, Stratton reached across the narrow gap and took Jenny's hand. She gave it an answering squeeze, and said, 'Did you enjoy the show?'

'What?'

'Those old films. Did you find what you wanted?'

'I found something,' said Stratton, 'but I liked the usherette best. She's a knockout. I'll be going back to that cinema—see if she'll come out for a date.'

'Silly,' said Jenny. She raised Stratton's hand to her lips and kissed it. 'We'd best try and get some sleep before they come any closer.'

Stratton lay back and thought about what he'd seen. He was positive he knew the identity of the tall man. It wasn't good, and what was more, he'd need to keep it to himself, at least until he'd considered what to do. But what could he do? I can't change anything, he thought, least of all the fact that the man in the film is—younger but, quite unmistakably—Sir Neville Apse. Rubbing a weary hand over his face, he closed his eyes.

A week later, violent stomach cramps woke Diana at quarter past three, and she sat up, confused for a moment. Then she realised, with an immense surge of relief that made her want to laugh out loud, what the pain meant. Pushing back the bedclothes, she saw the smudge of blood and thanked her lucky stars she hadn't been in the shelter—the all-clear had sounded just after two, and she'd come back upstairs, changed her trousers and jersey for a nightdress, and gone to bed.

She got up and looked in the bottom drawer of the chest for a sanitary towel. Thank God, she thought. Three days late, but she wasn't pregnant. She found the discreet velvet bag where she kept her things, donned her dressing gown, and tiptoed out to the bathroom.

Feeling almost light-headed with happiness, Diana set about removing the stain from her nightdress—it wouldn't be prudent to leave it for the maid. The girl had become difficult in recent weeks because of the bombs, and it might be impossible to find a replacement. She'd read somewhere that cold water was the thing for blood, and a vigorous rub with a piece of soap had got most of it out surprisingly quickly. Back in bed and wide awake, she sat up with her arms around her knees, listening to the muffled thuds of distant bombs.

Perhaps she ought to write to Evie and tell her: *Sorry, not having baby despite your best efforts, hope this finds you as it leaves me*...Stifling a giggle, she reached for her cigarettes, lit one, then picked up a letter, received from Guy that morning. He'd been expecting to rejoin his regiment abroad, but there had been a change of plan and they were now somewhere in Scotland, *so I may be able to see you again sooner than expected*...Diana sighed. There was no mention of what had happened between them on the last night at Evie's, but she hadn't really expected it—Guy hadn't said anything before he left, and it wasn't a suitable topic for writing. Dropping the letter on the counterpane, she closed her eyes and allowed her thoughts to drift to Claude.

He'd written to her, and even telephoned her at Apse's office, but so far she'd managed to avoid seeing him. But she couldn't avoid thinking about him, and as the days went by, she did so more and more...A jeering voice in her head told her, for about the thousandth time, that she was weak and pathetic, that she should have defied Evie and walked out there and then, but she knew it wouldn't have been right. Over the last ten days she'd picked up her pen to write to Claude at least twenty times, but the memory of her mother-in-law's words and the fierce intensity of her gaze had prevented her. Of course, it was only a matter of time before she bumped into him, and in any case, she did owe him some sort of explanation, however perfunctory...

Gingerly, she rubbed her aching stomach. A hot water bottle would be the best thing, but she'd lent it to the girl downstairs and forgotten to ask for it back...She crushed her cigarette in the ashtray, then got up again to rummage in her handbag for aspirin. She took two with a mouthful of water, then put out the bedside light and curled up, hoping for sleep.

The following day, feeling better for a few hours' rest, she arrived at Nelson House to find Apse's flat empty. A note on the table read, *Urgent appointment, back after 11.* Diana looked at her wristwatch. She didn't have to go anywhere until the afternoon, so that meant over two hours to search the place. She started with the desk, pulling open drawers and sifting through their contents, careful to put everything back exactly as she'd found it. By half-past ten, she was running out of places to look, and turned to the small, poky kitchen, where she began examining the contents of the cupboards. She was thinking of giving up—after all, she'd never known Apse to set foot in the kitchen—but decided to check the cutlery drawer first. Removing the knives and forks, she passed a cursory hand over the lining paper and found that it seemed to be thicker in one corner. When she turned it back, she saw a sheet of paper, folded in two. Easing it out, she found that she was staring at a page of typewriting, with columns of letters arranged in groups of four that made no sense whatsoever. Not a foreign language, Diana thought, but a code. She couldn't just take it—Apse might check—so she'd have to copy it, and because it was gibberish that would take time. The kitchen clock said twenty to eleven: too risky to do anything now, and besides, there was the post to be sorted through before he returned. Diana slid the paper back where she'd found it, and, heart pounding, went to her desk and began opening the day's letters.

CHAPTER 33

'The heifers don't have very good manners, Dad,' said Monica, slipping her hand into Stratton's as a group of cows lumbered past the fence on the way to be milked, barging and rolling their eyes. 'They always push like that. The old ones wait for their turn.'

'I wish you'd stand back, dear,' said Jenny nervously from somewhere behind them.

'It's all right, Mum,' said Monica. 'They won't hurt us. That one's my favourite,' she added, pointing out a passing Friesian to Stratton. 'Her name's Matilda. It's Daisy really, but I think that's quite boring.'

'Come on, Dad.' Pete tugged at his other arm. 'I want you to see Jack.'

'Who's Jack?'

'The pony. We told you, Dad, remember? Come on!'

Stratton grinned at his rosy-cheeked, excited children, pleased that they seemed enthusiastic about the workings of Mrs Chetwynd's farm. 'Off you go, then. We'll be right behind you.' As Monica and Pete raced off down the lane, he turned to Jenny. 'All right, love?'

She gave him a slightly worried smile. 'All these big animals...But it's nice to see they're enjoying themselves.'

'Must be in the blood,' said Stratton.

'Your blood. They certainly don't get it from my side. But they do look well, don't they?'

Stratton, thinking that he detected a slightly wistful note to this question, said, 'Just as good as if you'd been looking after them yourself. I told you they'd be all right, didn't I?'

Jenny smiled and took his arm. 'Come on,' she said, 'Let's go and see this blessed horse.'

At least, Stratton thought, she seemed to have relaxed a bit. She'd spent most of the train journey unable to keep still, patting her hair and leaning over to brush imaginary specks off his jacket, until he'd told her sharply that it wasn't a fashion parade and the kids wouldn't mind how they looked. He'd wished the words back as soon as they were out of his mouth—after all, he was just as nervous about meeting Mrs Chetwynd as she was. But from the moment when Pete and Monica had charged down the station platform towards them, yelling, and Jenny, delighted and embarrassed at the same time, had hugged and shushed and tried to inspect both of them at once, it had been fine, and he couldn't remember feeling happier. It was so different from the last time they'd seen them, when they'd been wan and miserable, taken in by a woman who hadn't cared for them, so that he and Jenny had refused to leave until the billeting officer had assured them that a decent place would be found. As they hadn't had the opportunity to see it, they'd never laid eyes on Mrs Chetwynd, and still hadn't—it was her afternoon for the WVS Committee, and she'd instructed the children to take their parents down to the farm for tea and a walk round before coming up to the house. However, the farmer and his wife had been hospitable and friendly and the kids seemed to be thoroughly at home.

Pete insisted on lugging their suitcase as they trudged up the drive to the big house, puffing and panting behind Monica, who held Stratton's hand and skipped. 'It's just round this corner,' she said, when they reached a curve in the road. 'You'll see it in a minute.'

As they rounded the bend Jenny stopped suddenly, causing Pete to bump into her and drop the suitcase. 'Gracious!'

It was far larger and grander than any house Stratton had ever seen—unless you counted paying thruppence for touring some great mansion full of paintings and taxidermy—and he felt lost for words. 'Your face, Dad!' said Monica. 'Mrs Chetwynd doesn't live in all of it. Lots of the rooms are closed up.'

'Closed up,' repeated Jenny, faintly. 'I should think they would be.'

Stratton relieved Pete—who was now very pink in the face—of the suitcase, and took Jenny's arm. 'Try not to say hello to any suits of armour by mistake.'

'Ooh, creepy,' said Jenny. 'Mrs Chetwynd hasn't got any of those, has she? I always think they're going to start walking around by themselves.'

'Da-ad,' said Monica. 'There aren't any suits of armour.'

'Gone to the Home Guard, have they?' asked Stratton. 'I'm sure your Uncle Reg could do with one. Might even keep him quiet for five minutes.'

This made Pete and Monica giggle. Jenny pursed her lips at Stratton and shook her head, then asked, 'Hadn't we better go round to the kitchen? We don't want to disturb anyone.'

Before Stratton could reply to this, Monica, looking very grown up and sensible, said, 'It's all right, Mum. We're allowed to use the front door.'

Jenny stared at the enormous portico. 'But...'

'Honestly,' said Monica, gently. 'It's fine. We thought like that at first, going round the back and everything, but Mrs Chetwynd's very nice. Isn't she, Pete?'

Pete nodded. 'Everyone's nice, except Mrs Lavvy-brick.'

'Mrs Who?' asked Jenny.

Both children began giggling, Pete with exaggerated hilarity.

'Mrs Laverick, Mum,' said Monica. 'She's the daily woman.'

'I hope you don't call her that.'

'Mrs Lavvy-brick,' repeated Pete.

'Stop it!' hissed Jenny.

'Mis-us Lav-vy-brick!'

'Pete! They'll hear you. Honestly, I thought we'd taught you better man—'

She froze as the front door opened and there, standing on the threshold, clad in a tweed suit, was a thin woman with a long, gentle face, like a friendly old horse. 'Mrs Stratton!' she said.

Stratton, who was conscious that Pete and Monica were still sniggering behind their hands, watched as Jenny, who was pink with embarrassment, stepped forward to greet her. 'How do you do, Mrs Chetwynd? It's so kind of you to invite us.'

'Not at all. I know how much the children miss you. Mr Stratton, how do you do?'

Following her down the hall to a small and surprisingly cosy sitting room—'Always use this, the other's much too big to be comfortable,'—Stratton thought Mrs Chetwynd had a sort of rawboned appearance, all knuckles and wrists and ankles. There was no bosom at all, and even the hair seemed angular, made so by a number of pins which stuck out from the small, hard knot at the base of her neck.

They had more tea, brought in by the housekeeper, which embarrassed Jenny all over again, and then a chat, and Mrs Chetwynd proved to be every bit as nice as her letters, and the children's, had suggested. Pete and Monica took them on a guided tour of the house, and then the garden, where they looked round the ruins of the Norman keep and were introduced to the three dogs. They had a very good dinner—Stratton couldn't remember the last meal he'd had where there was no talk of shortages—and after brandy, and even a cigar (which he hadn't much wanted but Mrs Chetwynd insisted that she missed the smell), they went up to bed.

They had great fun examining the room, Jenny exclaiming in awed whispers over the half-tester bed, the good furniture and the vases ('Don't touch, Ted, you might break something'), and later, they'd lain with their arms round each other, repeating the things Pete and Monica had told them.

'What about Mrs Lavvy-brick?'

'Oh, Ted, that was awful.'

'You turned bright red.'

'I didn't, did I?'

'Scarlet.'

Jenny gave him a little shove. 'Oh, stop it.'

'All right.' Stratton took hold of her hand and started to nibble her fingers.

'Ted, we can't. Not here.'

'Why not? They do it too, you know.'

'Ted!'

'Well, they do. Upper class people don't lay eggs, you know.' Jenny laughed so much that she had to stuff a corner of the pillow into her mouth.

Lying awake afterwards, Stratton wondered if it might not be worth investing in a few chickens. He decided to discuss it with Jenny when they got home. With winter coming on, she might not be too keen to surrender her egg coupons in exchange for meal, but perhaps in the spring...If we're still here, he thought, grimly. He returned, then, to the subject that had been bothering him all week: what to do about Mabel Morgan's film. Jenny, who'd been far too excited about seeing the children, hadn't pressed him for any more details, and neither had Donald. Which was just as well, because he couldn't tell either of them anything. Just thinking about the reaction he'd get from DCI Machin, and from Lamb, (who must be due back some time soon), when he told them about Sir Neville Apse and his male dancing partner, was quite hair-raising enough.

CHAPTER

33

Diana wondered afterwards how she'd managed to get through the day—which had included an interminable and badly-cooked lunch with several ladies from the Right Club—without giving anything away. Fortunately, she had plenty to do sorting out paperwork, which Apse, like F-J, seemed to think would somehow manage itself if left long enough in the in-tray. She excused herself several times to go and sit in the tiny bathroom where, heart thumping and brain pounding with a mixture of jubilation and terror, she held on to the rim of the basin with white-knuckled hands and stared at her face in the mirror, feeling that the taut countenance that glared back could not really belong to her at all. 'This is me,' she whispered to it. 'This is now. Pull yourself together.'

At half-past six, Apse gave her the perfect opportunity to talk to F-J by asking her to drop off some documents at his flat on her way home. She raced across the garden clutching the papers and almost fell up the stairs in her haste to reach him. Margot Mentmore opened the door. 'Woooh! The cavalry's arrived! Are you all right, Diana? You look awfully hot and bothered.'

'Fine, thanks,' Diana panted. 'Is F-J here?'

'Of course, I'll tell him you're here. How's the delightful Claude? We haven't seen him for a while.'

'I don't know,' said Diana, irritated. 'I haven't seen him, either.'

'Really?' Margot raised her eyebrows. 'Have you two love-birds quarrelled?'

'We're not lovebirds,' snapped Diana.

'Oh, no, of course not.' Margot rolled her eyes. 'Perish the thought.'

F-J, an unlit cigarette in his mouth, was peering under the piles of paper on his desk when Diana entered his office. 'She's hidden it again,' he said.

'Here.' Diana extracted a box of matches from her handbag.

'Thank you. What have you got for me?'

'These, sir.' Diana deposited Apse's documents on top of a stack of books. 'And I've got something to report.'

'Oh? You'd better sit down, then. Drink?'

'Thank you, sir.' Diana removed several folders from a spare chair while F-J splashed Scotch into a couple of tumblers.

'Fire away.'

'Well, sir…' When Diana had finished explaining about the coded message she'd found at the bottom of the cutlery drawer at Apse's flat, F-J stared out of the window for a moment, and then, turning back to her, said, 'I see. You're sure about this, are you?'

'It was there, sir. I saw it. Some sort of code, I thought, arranged in groups of four letters.'

'I see,' he repeated, his voice heavy with disappointment.

'I'm sorry to be the bearer of bad news, sir.'

'Yes.' F-J sighed, and turned to look out of the window. After a few minutes staring across the garden in the direction of Frobisher House, during which Diana kept quiet and sipped her drink, he turned back and said abruptly, 'You'll have to search his flat.'

'But sir, I—'

'Thoroughly. And we'll need a copy of that document. Apse tells me he'll be spending the weekend with his family, so you can do it on Friday night when there's no-one there. Go through everything—and I do mean everything, Diana.'

'You mean his bedroom, sir? His private things?'

'Yes,' said F-J. 'I know it's distasteful, but it's got to be done.'

Walking back to Tite Street, it crossed Diana's mind that perhaps F-J would rather not have known about Apse. But I had to tell him, she thought, even if he doesn't like me for discovering it. He'd certainly treated her with less warmth than usual—no enquiry about Guy, or her week down at Evie's, although, on reflection, that was probably just as well.

The thought of never seeing Claude again, or kissing him, or feeling his arms around her, gave her an actual, physical ache in the chest. Heartache. The word came to her with a sort of dull surprise. I suppose that's something else I've learnt, she thought. The jeering, worldly voice in her head, which had been growing more intrusive each day, said, 'My, aren't we growing up?'

'Yes,' muttered Diana, 'We bloody well are.'

On Friday at five o'clock, after three days that seemed to pass in a flash, Apse left Frobisher House, valise in hand, to catch the train to the country. Diana went home, changed into slacks and a jersey, then drew the blackout curtains and sat in her room, smoking and counting the hours until it was dark enough to return to Dolphin Square. The worst of it was having no-one to talk to about Apse or Claude or any of it. She couldn't tell Lally about Apse, and if she mentioned Claude she would—deservedly, it had to be said—get another flea in her ear. We'd only end up rowing, she thought, remembering how angry and defensive she'd been with Margot earlier in the day. Lally and Margot were good friends, she knew. Some people have a gift for that sort of thing, she reflected wistfully, but I don't seem to be one of them.

She stared at the photograph of her parents that she kept on the dressing table, but it wasn't reassuring. All it did was to remind her that, without it, she would hardly have been able to remember their faces at all. When she thought of her mother, she pictured a face in a sort of mist, vague and wispy, with blurred features, and the thing she most clearly recalled about her father was his smell, which had been a mixture of pipe, dog, and leather. Perhaps they hadn't been good at friendship either, and she'd somehow inherited their lack of warmth. Her very childhood seemed long ago and not properly connected to her, as if it had happened to a different person.

At half-past nine she poured herself a small Scotch—Dutch courage, why not?—and lay down on her bed, scouring her memory for something comforting to latch on to. Eventually, she came up with a ludicrous infant mistake over the Lord's Prayer, which she'd heard as 'Our Father, Which art in Heaven, Harold be Thy name...' It hadn't seemed odd to her at the time—after all, God's son was called Jesus, so why shouldn't God have a name, too? It had struck her as strange that people could be called Harold, when, as far as she knew, no-one was called Jesus, but she accepted it, just as she accepted everything else, because it was all she knew. It just goes to show, she thought, that nothing is ever what it seems...I am not what I seem, even to myself. As one got older and life got more complicated, the mental acrobatics grew more difficult—and never more so than now.

Shrugging off her mood of self-pity, she downed the rest of her drink, checked that her torch was in her handbag, and put on her shoes and fur coat, the fine September weather having yielded to bitter cold in October. The sirens were starting up as she left the house. For a second, it crossed her mind that she could, reasonably, use this as an excuse not to go—but only for a second. Thoughts of Evie's reaction if she were killed, combined with her sense of duty to F-J, only served to harden her resolve. Clutching her torch and muttering prayers through gritted teeth, she made her way as quickly as she could down to the Embankment. By the time she got there, the noise of the raid and the boom of guns was continuous, and the sky, criss-crossed by searchlight beams, was rose coloured from a dozen fires burning on the other side of the river, the light of which turned the water a dirty yellow. She saw a man and a girl coming towards her, and just had time to hear her say, 'I told you we should have gone to the pictures, we'd be better off there,' when a swishing, rushing noise, which seemed to be coming right at her, shook the pavement. She had a moment of utter blankness and then, as the very air seemed to disintegrate around her, felt herself pushed flat on the ground.

In the calm that followed the explosion, she lay on the gritty, dirty flagstone, enveloped in a cloud of dust and smoke that made her choke, and felt nothing but numbness. A small voice in the middle of the silence asked, 'Where did it go?'

'I don't know,' answered the man. 'Over there somewhere.' Diana felt a tug on her sleeve. 'You all right, miss?'

'I think so.' She struggled into a sitting position, and saw the man and the girl beside her. 'Here,' said the man, offering his hand. 'Thank you.'

'Well, it can't have gone in the river,' said the girl. 'We'd have heard the splash.'

'Not with all that racket,' said the man.

Diana looked round. 'Over there,' she said. A few hundred yards down the road was the silhouette of a vast jumble of debris that had once been a house but looked, in the dim and flickering light, like nothing more than a huge heap of coal that had slewed out onto the pavement.

'That'll be it,' said the man. 'Told you it wasn't the river.'

'Well, it might have been,' said the girl. They continued on their way, still arguing. Diana took a few steps after them, with the vague intention of going to help, but her feet didn't seem to want to take her. She stood, dazed, trying to will herself forwards, but her legs were shaking too much to obey any signals, and, fearing that she might simply fall over like a ninepin, she tottered across the pavement and leant against the nearest wall. After a moment, she was aware of an odd, insistent noise, and realised that her teeth were chattering. There is nothing I can do here, she thought. This is someone else's work. Slowly, using the wall for support, she began to move forward, stumbling on the debris and glass that littered the pavement, willing herself to concentrate only on the next step.

By the time she reached Dolphin Square, fire engines, tenders, and ambulances were hurrying past towards Chelsea Bridge, and her strength had returned, together with a feeling of elation, almost hilarity, at something conquered. She ran up the stairs of Frobisher House with renewed energy, opened Apse's front door, and shone her torch into the office. Apse had pulled the blackout curtains before he'd left, so the beam would not be seen from outside. She took off her shoes and carried them into the kitchen, where she deposited them on the floor, washed the grime off her hands and set about copying down the coded message. Somehow, the near-miss had sharpened her brain; seldom had she known such clarity of thought. Leaning on the wooden draining board, writing down the meaningless sequence of letters, she felt as if she were wired up to an electrical circuit that made her bright and sharp and instant, like light itself. The noise of the raid and the answering ack-ack was all around her, and several times, when the bombs seemed almost on top of her, she stopped and folded herself in the space under the draining board. Her rational mind knew it would make no difference if the place was hit, but somehow sheltering underneath some-thing, even if it was only a thin plank of wood, made her feel safer while the building shook and a thin rain of plaster dust fell from the ceiling. She caught herself praying, 'Our Father Which art in Heaven, Harold be Thy name...' and laughed. Surely, she thought, as she scrambled to her feet, God would not mind?

She was determined to complete her task: if Apse's flat were hit before she'd finished, then any evidence she might gather would be lost. She checked and re-checked her copy of the message, put it in her bag, returned the original to the drawer, then went down the corridor to the bedroom to set about searching the wardrobe. There seemed nothing out of place—shirts, suits, shoes and all the usual accoutrements—and the only thing that struck her as peculiar was a framed photograph of a young boy and girl (Pammy and Pimmy, perhaps?) hidden beneath a pile of underclothes in the chest of drawers. Maybe, she thought, Apse had put it there to stop it being damaged if the building was hit. It seemed a vain hope, but people did strange things out of a kind of superstition...perhaps, by protecting this image of his children (assuming they were his children) Apse felt that he was protecting them. This thought gave her such a feeling of warmth towards him that she felt instantly shamed by what she was doing, closed the drawer, and left the room in confusion. As she was about to return and set to once more, she heard, through the noise of the raid, another sound—quiet, closer—a click, and then a creak. Someone had opened the door of the flat.

Diana froze. Another second, and whoever it was would turn on the light and see her standing there. Behind her, in the corridor, was a full-height cupboard, built into the wall. Almost without thinking, she opened the door and, seeing a space beneath the lower shelf, dropped onto all fours and crawled into it, pulling the door closed a second before the light was switched on. After a moment, a lull in the bombing allowed her to hear the scuffling of feet on the mat, the sound of someone depositing a bag on the floor, and then a voice—Apse, but why had he come back?—said, 'Here we are.' A male voice—a London accent, not Cockney, but not far off it—said, 'Nice place.' Diana's heart thudded in her chest, almost as loud to her ears as the guns. More murmurings, from the direction of the office; she strained to listen. She heard the sound of drinks being poured. Thank God she'd replenished the water in the jug on the tray that afternoon. If Apse went into the kitchen, he'd see her things on the floor...What on earth was he doing? Why wasn't he in the country with his family? Perhaps the railway station had been bombed, and he'd had to come back, or...what? And who was the other? She didn't recognise the voice—it sounded young, but it couldn't be the son of one of his friends...a servant from home, perhaps, who'd gone into the services? 'When you followed me,' the man was saying, 'I thought you was a policeman.' The man must be from the Right Club, Diana thought, or one of Mosley's followers who'd managed to stay out of gaol. She remembered

Apse's words about dealing with unsavoury people—but this, clearly, was someone he trusted enough to bring into his home. She heard laughter, and then Apse's voice, 'A friend told me to look out for you.' He sounded different, almost—to Diana's disbelief—coquettish.

'A good friend?' asked the man.

'A very good friend. Let's drink to friends, shall we?'

Diana heard the clink of glasses, and more bombs, this time duller and further away. The raiders must be leaving, or at least moving further down the river. Then more clinking of glasses, and whispering, and feet, moving towards her down the corridor...Two sets of footsteps. The strip of light at the bottom of the cupboard door darkened momentarily as they passed. They must be heading for the bedroom, she thought. There wasn't anywhere else for them to go. She hadn't finished her search, so perhaps he was going to give the boy something to take with him—an incriminating document—something that she hadn't been able to find, under the floorboards, or...Oh, God. She'd switched on the bedside lamp. Apse would be bound to notice, and then...

She waited for the exclamation, but it didn't come. Instead, there was a sudden giggle, high and girlish, from the bedroom behind her, and low noises—movement, shuffling about, and a creak as if someone had sat down on the bed. Diana heard a long sigh, then a groan, and then the boy said, 'Let me do that.'

Apse spoke. 'You haven't shaved today.'

'You like that, don't you?' said the man, and then, after a pause, 'I don't kiss.'

Diana clapped a hand over her mouth. Claude had pointed out a male tart to her once, in Piccadilly. He'd been walking with an elderly gentleman who had appeared, in the dim light afforded by the shaded headlamps of a passing car, to be wearing rouge. Claude had laughed at her for being shocked and said that the boys at his school had practised kissing on each other for lack of girls, and that some of them never grew out of it. But Apse had—he was married, with children, so he must have...

Remembering the photograph of the children she'd found in the drawer, a thought struck her: he'd put it there not for the reasons she'd supposed, but because he'd planned to bring someone back for an assignation, and his desire was so strong that even the heavy raids hadn't deterred him.

There were grunting noises now, heavier than before. Recognising the rhythm of sex, Diana, appalled, put her hands over her ears and shut her eyes tight. What if Apse were to come out of the bedroom and find her? She could pretend ignorance—saying that she hadn't overheard anything wasn't going to work, the place was too small for that—but could she make him believe that she hadn't understood what she'd heard? If he didn't...Supposing he thought she was trying to blackmail him? Possibilities raced through her mind, each more horrible than the last. He might even try to kill her—she knew he knew people, just as F-J did, who would do unofficial jobs, and she'd heard rumours about unreliable double-agents being 'got rid of' in various ways, one in the middle of the North Sea...Diana's stomach heaved, and for a terrible moment she thought she was going to be sick. I've got to get out of here, she thought. *Now.* While they're still in the bedroom.

She pushed open the door and crawled out on her hands and knees. The light was still on in the hallway—the carpeted distance to the door, in reality about twenty feet, stretched out in front of her like miles, and her shoes were still in the kitchen. Diana got to her feet and, holding her breath, tiptoed towards it. As she scooped up her things in shaking hands, she heard, through the wall, the sound, half-sigh, half-moan, of release. She hurried to the front door, and, after a few seconds fumbling with the catch, managed to open it. Closing it silently behind her, she ran along the passage and down the stairs in her stocking feet. She pulled open the outside door, and rushed into the garden, where there was still light enough from the fires to send her tottering in the direction of the nearest flower-bed, where she vomited between the rose bushes. She stood on the path, stomach heaving and throat aching from the bitter mixture of bile and the Scotch she'd drunk earlier, and looked up at the dark façade of Frobisher House. She could hear nothing beyond the distant trump-trump of artillery and the odd rumble of passing traffic from Grosvenor Road—no outraged shouts, no running feet.

She put on her shoes and, turning, looked in the direction of F-J's flat. Then she remembered that he wouldn't be back until Monday.

Standing in the telephone box at the end of Chelsea Bridge Road, Diana wasn't entirely sure how she'd arrived there, or what she was going to do. She only knew she needed to talk to someone, needed help, needed...What? Praying that the line was still working, she put a coin into the slot and dialled. Hearing the operator's voice, she pressed Button A and said, without thinking, 'Gerrard 73468, please.'

After a moment, a male voice on the line repeated the number. 'Claude?'

'Diana? Is that you?'

'Yes, it's me. Claude, I...'

'What is it? Are you crying?'

'Yes...I can't...'

'What's happened?'

'I can't...I...it's awful, I can't...'

'Calm down. Take deep breaths...Better?'

'Ye-yes.'

'That's my girl. Now then, what's going on?'

'I can't tell you now. Claude, please...'

'Where are you?'

'Chelsea Bridge Road. Claude, I can't bear it.'

'Don't say any more. Just go home, and stay there. Can you do that?'

'Yes.'

'Good girl. Go now. I'll be there as soon as I can.'

'Oh, God.' Diana hung up the receiver and leant against the side of the phone box. I must be mad, she thought. What have I *done*?

Diana stumbled home as quickly as she could in the blackout, and was sitting shivering on the end of her bed, huddled in her coat and wishing that she hadn't telephoned Claude, when her bell rang. She went downstairs and found him standing on the step, bearing half a bottle of brandy.

'Come on,' he said, taking her by the elbow. 'Let's sort you out.'

They went up to Diana's flat where he pushed her into an armchair, put a blanket over her legs, and thrust a large drink into her hands. 'Get that down you,' he instructed. 'Don't speak until you've finished it.'

Diana nodded obediently and took a big gulp of brandy, which burned her throat and almost choked her. Claude, perched on the arm of the chair, rubbed her back until she stopped coughing.

Diana looked at him through watering eyes. 'Sorry,' she said.

'Don't be stupid.' Claude handed her his handkerchief. 'Mop yourself up.' He watched her apply the handkerchief, then put a hand on her chin and twisted her head towards him. 'That'll do for now, anyway,' he said, critically. 'Your colour seems to be coming back. I must say, it's nice to see you again, even like this. I thought you'd stopped talking to me.'

'I had,' said Diana, 'but it wasn't—'

'Later,' said Claude. 'Finish your drink.' He slithered off the arm of the chair to the floor, where he took off her shoes and started rubbing her feet.

'What are you—'

'Not another word until you've had your drink.'

'Now then,' he said, a few minutes later, stroking her right foot, which was in his lap. 'You've obviously had a shock. Tell me what happened.'

Diana started to tell him, haltingly at first, and then in a great rush of words. 'This man,' she finished, 'It was obvious he was a...you know...like a prostitute, and Apse had brought him there for...for...I heard them, Claude. It was horrible. How could he?'

Claude shrugged. 'People do. I must say, I'd never have guessed about Apse.'

'Of course not. He's married.'

'So are you, darling.'

'That's a horrible thing to say. It isn't the same at all!'

'It's not so different.'

'Yes it is, it's...it's...' Outraged and lost for words, Diana twitched her foot away from him.

'For heaven's sake, Diana.' Claude leant back and looked at her. 'It's high time you realised that what people say, and the... forms, for want of a better word, that they observe, are quite a different thing to how they actually are. It's only a question of degree, after all.'

'It's much more than that! It's disgusting.'

'To you, perhaps. Not to everyone.'

'It's illegal!'

'That,' said Claude, 'is the problem. But it only matters if you get caught.' He shook his head. 'Poor old Apse. I had no idea you were watching him, you know. I'm surprised that F-J didn't realise he was a...Unless...'

'Unless what?'

'Nothing. Just thinking aloud. It does make things rather messy, all this.'

'Messy?'

'That's the thing about buggers, darling. Blackmail. Very simple, and very effective.'

'You mean the Right Club?'

'People like the Right Club...That's what you've been up to, is it? I did wonder.'

'Yes,' Diana admitted, cursing herself. Thinking that now it made no difference, she asked, 'You mean, that Apse could be passing them information because they've threatened him?'

'It's possible. Probable, in fact. You'll have to tell F-J first thing tomorrow.'

'I don't know how.'

'Oh...' Claude waved a hand in dismissal. 'Don't worry about that. He'll understand.'

'Will he?'

'He's a man of the world, Diana. It's not the first time something like this has happened, and it won't be the last.'

'Yes, but—'

'Telling F-J is the least of your worries. Are you sure Apse didn't hear you?'

'No. At least, he didn't run after me.'

'Hardly surprising, given the circumstances.' Claude grinned. 'I can't imagine him charging out of the door without his trousers.'

'It's not funny, Claude.'

'I know it isn't, darling. But if he did hear something—it's not a particularly large flat, after all...Obviously the door wasn't forced, so he'd know that whoever was there had a key. Do you know who else has one?'

'Lady Violet, I suppose, but...'

'But she's hardly likely to be sneaking around in the middle of an air raid. In any case, she'd have turned the lights on. You said he'd done the blackouts.'

'Yes.'

'Apse might think it was F-J, of course. Or me.'

'You?'

'Possibly. But the point is—if he did hear anything—that he doesn't know it was you. You're sure you didn't leave anything behind?'

'I don't think so.'

'You put the paper back, did you? After you copied it.'

'Definitely. I remember doing it.'

'That's good.' Claude patted her ankle. 'Now tell me why you weren't speaking to me.'

'Guy's mother,' said Diana. 'She knows about us. She made me promise.'

'How did she find out?'

'Rumours. People in London.'

'It sounds as if she ought to be in Intelligence. She's obviously wasted in Hampshire.'

'It's serious!'

'I know. We'll just have to be extra careful, won't we?'

'Claude, I promised her. And there's something else.'

'Oh?'

'Something Lally told me. Stop stroking my leg.'

'Sorry.' Claude removed his hand. 'I was under the impression you liked it. Tell me what you heard.'

'It was about a girl who killed herself because of you. She was married, and—'

'Julia Vigo.' Claude sighed. 'I can guess what she said. However—' Seeing that Diana was about to interrupt, he held up a hand. 'What Lally doesn't know is that Julia was addicted to drugs.'

'That's ridiculous! She worked for F-J. Lally told me.'

'Yes, she did. But F-J didn't know. Not at the time.'

'He must have. It would have been obvious.'

'Why? Do you know how a drug addict behaves?'

'Well...' Diana thought for a minute, then realised she didn't. 'Raving, I suppose. Confused. Mad.'

'Not at all. I didn't know, either.'

'Then how...?'

'I found the stuff afterwards. Somebody had to tidy up her flat.'

'But her husband—'

'Wanted nothing more to do with her. She'd left him.'

'Yes, for you.'

'No. She'd left him before that happened. I had nothing to do with it.'

'Then why did Lally say you had?'

'That was the story that got about. F-J wanted to keep the part about drugs out of it because of her people, and because it wouldn't do the reputation of the service any good. There had to be some sort of explanation, and that was the obvious one.'

'What about your reputation? Don't you mind?'

Claude shrugged.

'How can you be so blasé about it? Let go of my leg!'

'Sorry. You shouldn't be so hard to resist.'

'Be serious, Claude.'

'Oh, stop saying that.' Claude got to his feet and patted his pockets for his cigarette case. 'The fact is, Diana, that people always talk, and I don't suppose it's the worst that's been said about me, by a long chalk.'

'Well, I think it's awful. I'm going to tell Lally that it wasn't anything to do with you.'

'No, you're not.'

'But—'

'No!' Claude stood over her, his hands on her shoulders. 'I mean it, Diana. You're going to keep your mouth shut.'

'But if it's the truth...'

'It is. Which is why you're not going to discuss it with anyone. In fact, you're going to forget all about it.'

Diana, remembering Jock's words, said, 'What you don't know can't hurt you.'

'Exactly.' Claude kissed her on the forehead. 'Now,' he said, running the backs of his fingers down her cheek, 'I suggest we make ourselves comfortable.'

'Wait.' Diana pushed his hand away, and Claude retreated to the bed.

'What now?' he said, irritably.

'When you tidied up her flat, did you…I mean, surely whoever examined her would have known…?'

'For heaven's sake! Pyke dealt with all that.'

'Dr Pyke?' asked Diana, surprised.

'Yes. Now can we please—'

'F-J's Dr Pyke? But I thought he was just…' A sudden, and horribly clear, image of F-J glancing down at his fly made her tail off.

'I believe that F-J finds him very useful on certain occasions,' said Claude, cryptically. 'Look, darling, I did have an affair with the woman, and I didn't exactly cover myself in glory, but it wasn't my fault that she died. That would have happened anyway, sooner or later. Now, why don't you come here,' he patted the bed, 'and we won't say any more about it.'

'You won't say anything about Apse, will you? About what I told you.'

'That entirely depends,' said Claude, 'on whether you're prepared to be nice to me or not.'

'Claude!' Close to tears, Diana threw the blanket off her legs and leapt out of the chair. 'For God's sake, you can't—'

'Stop it.' Claude got off the bed and took her in his arms. 'I was joking.' He rubbed her back while she cried, and made soothing noises, and plied his handkerchief. After a while, her resolve was swallowed up by tears, an overwhelming mixture of relief and anxiety, and a desperate need to be comforted, and she allowed herself to be undressed and taken to bed.

CHAPTER
36

Stratton negotiated the three steps from his chair to the office door with difficulty. Space for storage, even for the small number of documents salvaged from West End Central, was limited at Great Marlborough Street, and most of the files that remained—waterlogged, torn, and reeking of smoke—were now stacked around his desk.

The woman was waiting for him outside. Stratton didn't hold out much hope, since the information they'd had to circulate about the unidentified body was pretty meagre, but at least someone had come forward. According to Policewoman Gaines, this woman, a Mrs Symmonds, thought that the missing man might be her husband.

She was a scrawny little thing with a thin, drawn face—forty, perhaps, but almost certainly younger than her looks suggested—scruffy and unkempt in a mangy-looking grey coat. Maybe, thought Stratton, giving her the benefit of the doubt although it was nearly eleven o'clock, she'd spent the night in the underground and hadn't been home. In any case, she looked as though she could do with a cup of tea. Stratton arranged this, then escorted her to one of the interview rooms. 'Arthur Symmonds,' she said, without preamble. 'My husband.' She didn't sound upset or angry, just tired and fed up.

'When did you last see him?'

'February sometime. Been gone ever since.'

'Did you report him missing?'

'Oh, no...' Mrs Symmonds looked surprised. 'He does go off sometimes. Business.'

'What business is that?'

'Oh...' She looked intently at the wall behind Stratton's head, as if expecting the answer to be written there. 'Just business. Dealings,' she added, nodding as if this clarified the matter. 'He had to go away sometimes, you see.'

'Away where?'

'Round and about. I don't know, really. It's been over six months now, so I thought perhaps...' She looked at Stratton expectantly.

'Where do you live, Mrs Symmonds?'

'Poland Street. Number fourteen. Above the grocer's.'

'How old is your husband?'

'Forty-five. Forty-six, now.'

'What date is his birthday?'

'The sixteenth of April.'

'How long have you been married?'

'Oh, a long time...' Mrs Symmonds screwed up her face in thought. Unusual, noted Stratton. In his experience, it was men who had difficulty remembering, not women.

'Eighteen years, now.'

'The date?'

'Nineteen twenty-two. Fifth of May.'

She'd remembered that fast enough. Perhaps it was just the way he'd phrased the question. 'Can you describe him for me?'

'Well, like it said, really. Quite ordinary. Brown hair, you know...'

'Straight, wavy?'

'Oh, straight.' She said this as though wavy hair was a particularly revolting aberration.

'Eyes?'

'A browny colour.'

'Hazel?'

'No, browny, like I said.'

'What about his teeth? Had he been to a dentist, that you know of?'

'Oh no, nothing like that.' After a moment she added, with obvious pride, 'He had his own teeth.' Leaning forward, as if about to make a confession, she said, 'I've been worried about his feet.'

'His feet?' echoed Stratton, disconcerted by the sudden transfer from one end of the body to the other.

'Yes. They were hurting him. Terrible corns, he had. I kept telling him he should see a foot doctor.'

'Did he?'

'I don't know. He wasn't keen on doctors. The money, you see…I got some stuff from the chemist. Green plaster. I've been keeping it for him.' She stared at the wall again, and then finished, pathetically, 'I told him I was going to get something. I thought he might come back for it.'

Stratton said gently, 'Was there anyone else?'

'Another woman, you mean?'

'Yes.'

Mrs Symmonds shook her head, firmly. 'Nothing like that. I'm sure of it.'

'But he did go away from time to time?'

'For business.' she said, sharply. 'I told you.'

Stratton made some notes, wondering if there might be another Mrs Symmonds tucked away somewhere, also with a corn plaster, waiting patiently for her husband to return. Assuming Symmonds was the man's real name, of course…

'Did your husband,' he asked, 'know anyone by the name of Apse?'

'Apse? I don't think so. Funny sort of name—I'd remember.'

'You're sure?'

'Oh, yes. He never mentioned anyone of that name.' She hesitated for a moment, then said, 'Can I have a look at him?'

'The thing is, Mrs Symmonds, that...'

'If I could see him, I'd know, and then...Well, I'd be easier in my mind if I knew.'

'I understand that, Mrs Symmonds, but unfortunately the body is not...not suitable for viewing.' For Christ's sake, Stratton told himself, we're talking about a human being, not a house for sale. 'It's been buried, you see, for several months, so it's not... well, not recognisable.'

'Oh.' Mrs Symmonds turned pale. 'I didn't know.'

'Of course not. Now, why don't you finish your tea, and I'll send in a policewoman to take a statement.'

'Statement?' Mrs Symmonds rose from her chair in alarm. 'But I haven't done anything wrong. I only—'

'Of course you haven't,' said Stratton, soothingly. No-one's saying you've done wrong. It's just so that we can have an official record. It'll help us find your husband.' Or, he added mentally, tell us if he's now our mouldy old corpse.

❀ ❀ ❀

When Mrs Symmonds left, half an hour later, Stratton told Policewoman Gaines to check the Records Office for an Arthur Symmonds, born on April the sixteenth, 1894. 'Start there,' he said, 'and if necessary, follow it up. And find out if Symmonds attended a local chiropodist.'

'A what, sir?'

'Foot doctor.'

'Oh. Yes, sir.'

Gaines departed, and Stratton sat at his desk, smoking and worrying, as he'd worried on and off every day that week, about how he was going to tell DCI Machin about Sir Neville Apse's film appearance. Perhaps the man could be persuaded to look past his deference to SDI Roper and decide that the thing needed looking into. On the other hand, perhaps he'd get another slapped wrist and be told that he was not, under any circumstances, to frighten the horses. It had to be done, he knew that—now it was merely a question of working out the best way to do it, and it would be a lot easier before DCI Lamb came back and started planting his great feet on everything.

'I think there might be a link between an apparent suicide we had at West End Central back in June and the body that was found in the church, sir, but it's rather delicate, so I thought I ought to have a word.'

DCI Machin looked at him warily, and shifted about in his chair. 'You'd better go on, then.' Stratton, who already had a feeling that it was going to be the bishop's son all over again, outlined his discovery of Mabel Morgan's box and its contents. Machin listened, looking more miserable by the minute. When Stratton mentioned the film, he actually groaned.

'There's always the risk of blackmail, sir, and I wondered if Miss Morgan's death might not be connected in some way. She might have been after him for money—there were several things about her death that struck me as odd at the time, and we know she'd had a visit from a couple of thugs just before she died. When we found Sir Neville's handkerchief on the corpse in the church, I did think there might be more to it, and—'

The DCI raised a hand to stop him. 'All right. You've made your point.'

'If I might question Sir Neville again, sir, it would help.'

'Yes, yes,' Machin said, testily. 'I understand that. But you are not to approach Sir Neville until I give you permission.'

'When do you think that might be, sir?' Stratton knew he was sailing close to the wind, but he couldn't help himself.

'I don't know. But you are not—and I mean not—to do anything until I tell you.'

'Yes, sir.'

'And what were you doing removing evidence from the station and taking it home?'

'It wasn't at the station, sir, it was given to me when—'

'That's not the point. It's the principle of the thing. I want that box—with everything in it—on my desk by tomorrow morning.'

With a sinking heart, although he hadn't really expected anything else, Stratton said, 'Yes, sir.'

'And for God's sake, stop charging about like a bull in a bloody china shop.'

The following morning, after Stratton had surrendered the deed box and received another lecture in which upset apple carts and rocked boats featured heavily, he entered his office to find Policewoman Gaines already there, proffering a cup of tea with one hand and clutching a sheaf of paper in the other. 'Anything on Symmonds?' he asked, wearily.

'No-one of that name in the records, sir, with that birthday. I found an Arthur Daniel Symmonds, born on the fourteenth of April 1894, but he's at RAF Waddington in Lincolnshire. We checked, and he was posted there in May this year—he's an instructor—and he's been there ever since.'

'We?'

Policewoman Gaines flushed slightly. 'Constable Ballard has been giving me a hand, Sir. Not on duty,' she added, hastily. 'In his own time, sir.'

I don't blame him, thought Stratton. 'Very commendable,' he said, 'as long as it doesn't interfere with his work.'

'No, sir. Of course not, sir.' Gaines's face was now a very pretty shade of rose. Stratton studied it for a moment, then said, 'Any others?'

'No, sir. Well, there were, but they're either too young, or too old...' Gaines looked down at her notes, more, Stratton thought, from embarrassment than because she needed to refresh her memory, '...and there are two serving overseas. That's been confirmed.'

'What about chiropodists?'

'Nothing so far, sir.'

'Well, keep looking.' Feeling he'd been rather churlish, he added, 'You're doing a good job.'

Which is a damn sight more than I am, he thought, as Gaines left the room. Perhaps his first theory was right and Symmonds really was a bigamist using a false name. After all, it was possible to obtain forged identity cards and ration books. Presumably, Symmonds had taken his with him when he'd disappeared, and whoever'd killed him—if he was killed—had removed them. It was certainly worth checking. Gaines could do that, too, with or without the help of Ballard. Really, Stratton thought, I ought to issue a warning; after all, it was against the rules, but what the hell. He'd probably have done the same if he were in Ballard's position. Actually, there was no 'probably' about it—he'd have had a pop at her, all right, and bugger the consequences.

He wondered what would happen to the deed box. Would Machin, after consulting SDI Roper, conveniently 'lose' it? Christ, talk about one law for the rich…Bollocks to that, thought Stratton. There had to be some connection between Mabel Morgan, Sir Neville and the corpse in the church, not to mention Marks and Wallace—and the sooner he discovered who the dead man actually was, the clearer it would be.

CHAPTER

37

As the car turned the corner, Diana, sitting in the back with Forbes-James, saw Bletchley Park for the first time. It was a late Victorian mish-mash of different styles—a rotunda, Dutch gabling with pineapple-shaped finials, black-and-white mock Tudor timber and crenellations. The architect, whoever he was, had obviously been told to lay it on with a trowel. On the right side of the house was a stableyard with a clock-tower, and on the left, a green painted, prefabricated wooden hut. There seemed to be an awful lot of building work going on—men in overalls and flat caps were everywhere, sawing planks on the lawn in front of the house before carting them off to a messy-looking site of half-erected structures on the far side of the brick outbuildings.

Diana had expected the car to be met by a soldier, and blinked in astonishment when she caught sight of Phyllis Garton-Smith, with whom she'd done the season, hurrying towards them. Phyllis was clad in civilian clothes—blouse, skirt and pearls—and behaved as if the pair of them had simply motored down for a weekend house party. 'Wonderful to see you, darling! Admiral Candless is expecting you, sir,' she told F-J. 'I've been asked to show you around—or rather, not, because one isn't allowed to see anything. I've no idea what's going on over there,' she waved an arm in the direction of the building work, 'except that they keep demolishing perfectly nice flower beds and putting up these wretched huts.'

'What are you doing here?' asked Diana, when F-J had been escorted away by a WREN.

'Filing clerk. It's priceless. Uncle Tony got me the job. I haven't the first clue what it's all about. No-one has, really—at least, no-one I know. Isn't it a hideous house?' Linking her arm in Diana's as they went into the entrance hall, she continued, 'Jeanie's here, too—Sally Monkton's sister, you remember—and Merope Wright, and...' Diana listened with half an ear as she took in the decoration and the Italian marble pillars, and caught sight of elaborate panelling and ornate ceilings as they passed various once grand rooms, most of which were now partitioned at odd angles with boards. It wasn't so much a house party, she decided, more like an Oxford College she'd once visited—if you ignored the teleprinter and the various women rushing about the place. Besides these, the house seemed to be full of slovenly middle-aged schoolboys, clad in tweeds and baggy flannels.

'They're all geniuses, or so I'm told,' Phyllis murmured. 'They seem quite mad to me, but one gets used to it. I saw one chap take his tea down there,' she gestured out of the window towards a large duck pond, 'and when he'd finished, he looked at the cup in amazement, as if he'd absolutely no idea how it got into his hand, and threw it into the water. Quite extraordinary. Anyway, how are you, darling? I hear you've been having a high old time in London, you lucky thing...Is that lovely man your boss?'

'Yes,' said Diana.

'It's all right, darling, I know I'm not supposed to ask questions. Even if I did, I don't suppose I'd understand the answers, but they're terrifically fierce about it. When I arrived, they told me I'd get sent to the tower if I ever breathed so much as a word. Anyway, it's all frightfully important. I expect you're gasping for a cup of tea, aren't you?'

'I am, rather.'

'We can get one in the mess room. They don't really like us in there, but they don't ask too many questions.' She led Diana into a room full of armchairs, where two men, one wearing a mackintosh, were playing ping-pong. Both were leaping about, scarlet in the face, and each time they hit the ball—which didn't seem to be very often—they would shout a number ('317,811!' '514,229—Prime!' '832,040!') that bore no relation whatsoever to the score. 'Genius at play,' whispered Phyllis, settling her in an armchair by the window. 'Or they could be working, one can never really tell. Anyway, they're quite harmless. Shan't be long.'

Left alone, Diana tilted her face to the thin October sunshine. Listening to the faint chattering of the teleprinter and the clatter of the ping-pong ball on the table, she wondered how long F-J would be closeted with Admiral Candless, and whether it would be one of the boffins now prancing in front of her who would be given the job of translating their coded message into something intelligible.

I should never have told Claude, thought Diana. She'd cursed herself afterwards for her weakness, but at the time... He'd been so kind, coming round to the flat with brandy, and calming her down. All the same, she thought, I should never have let him take me to bed. It must never, ever happen again. So far, she'd managed to avoid him, but they were bound to run into each other sooner or later, and then...Diana massaged her temples. It was all very well to make such a resolution while sitting here in a comfortable armchair and feeling reasonably at peace, but what would happen when she saw him again?

Reporting back to F-J, which she'd done first thing on the Saturday morning, had helped to improve matters, and so had his assurance that he'd arrange for her to be transferred to another department. Telling him about Apse, though, had been just as excruciating as she'd feared. He'd asked several times if she were sure about what she'd overheard, but hadn't—thank goodness—pressed her for any details. As Claude had predicted, his attitude had been one of resignation. 'The whole thing's a bloody nuisance,' was what he'd said. 'Does anyone else know?'

'No,' Diana had replied. 'At least, not to my knowledge.' Fortunately, F-J had taken her obvious discomfort for embarrassment (which it was, partly), and not as evidence of lying. 'You didn't hear any mention of it at the Right Club? Anything that didn't make sense at the time?'

'No, sir.'

'Unfortunately, it remains a possibility. The first thing to do is get some sense out of that message. You're coming with me. Don't worry, I'll deal with Apse—I shall tell him I'm borrowing you to cope with a backlog of paperwork. That'll solve the immediate problem.'

'Here you are.' Phyllis presented her with a cup of tea, ducking to avoid a wide shot from the ping-pong table. 'Look out!' Both men started violently, as if they'd just noticed that there were other people in the room, and the one in the mackintosh came over to retrieve the ball from behind Diana's chair.

'Your lovely boss should be out in a minute,' Phyllis said. 'The Admiral's terribly brisk. He's so used to bellowing orders at people on great big ships that he's forgotten how to talk normally. The billeting officer's found your Colonel a room at The Bull in Stony Stratford—he'll be dining with the Admiral first, of course—and you're coming with me. It's just outside the gates—a hostel—but you meet the most wonderful people. There's a girl in my corridor from the East End, and you'll never guess...'

Diana drifted off again, staring out of the window and thinking about Apse. Perhaps his air of self-satisfaction wasn't merely to do with who he was, but also because—thus far, at least—he'd successfully concealed not one, but two secrets from everybody. Although surely the strain of not being what you appeared to be would make you worried, not smug? It would me, she thought. I'd be terrified all the time. Unless, of course, one actually relished the danger, as she suspected Claude would if he really was a double-agent.

Phyllis nudged her arm, and she looked round and saw a WREN standing beside them. 'Follow me, please.'

F-J and the Admiral were standing on the lawn, admiring the duck pond. After a few moments conversation, F-J told Diana to meet him at quarter to nine the following morning, and they departed. 'You poor darling,' said Phyllis, 'you must be shattered. Come on. There'll be time for you to lie down before dinner if you like. We're going to the Hartleys'—old friends of Ma and Pa—terribly sweet. I go there for baths.'

The following morning Diana, feeling exhausted, presented herself at Bletchley Park. The Hartleys had indeed been terribly sweet, and the hot bath had been lovely, but they seemed to regard her as an authority on everything that was going on in London and wouldn't stop asking questions, and then Phyllis had wanted to stay up half the night chattering.

She was taken to a large room filled with long tables covered in grey, army-issue blankets, where F-J was sitting with three others, one of whom was the mackintoshed table-tennis player from the previous day. Beside him was a little chap with a flat face that made her think of a barn owl, who blinked at her in surprise, and a younger man with protruding teeth. F-J made introductions. 'Professor Upjohn' (mac), 'Professor Ingersoll' (owl-man), 'and Mr Matthews' (teeth). 'This is Mrs Calthrop.'

All three men leant forward as Diana put her copy of the coded document on the table in front of them. After studying it for a moment, Professor Upjohn said, 'You're not sure of the language of the plaintext?'

'Plaintext?' Diana looked at F-J for enlightenment.

'The language of the concealed message.'

'Oh, I see. English or German, I should think.' Diana realised she didn't actually know whether Apse spoke German, but had simply assumed it.

'Those are the most likely,' said F-J.

'Can you be fairly sure it comes from this particular organisation?' asked Upjohn, as the other two pored over the paper.

'I believe so,' said F-J, who must, Diana thought, have explained about the Right Club before she arrived. 'But not necessarily. It might have been obtained from another source.'

'And you don't know what that source might be?'

'An embassy, perhaps. I've spoken to our chaps in London about it, and it doesn't appear to be anything official. Not from us, anyway.'

'Is there,' Professor Upjohn asked Diana, 'any particular key you think this Right Club lot might have used?'

'Key?'

'A word or phrase.'

'Well...' Diana remembered the horrible silver brooch Mrs Montague had given her. 'PJ, perhaps. It stands for Perish Judah.'

'That's J—U—D—A—H?'

'I suppose so. I've never seen it written down.' Beside him, Professor Ingersoll began writing rapidly in a notebook.

'Nothing else?' said Upjohn. 'Names, that sort of thing? Books? Poems?'

'The founder, Peverell Montague, or Protocols of the Elders of Zion or something like that, you mean?'

'Yes.'

'Well...' Diana considered. 'There's a rather nasty little verse that Montague wrote. I could write it down for you, if you like.'

'Please.' Upjohn pushed a piece of paper towards her, and Diana began writing: *Land of dope and Jewry, Land that once was free, All the Jewboys praise thee, While they plunder thee.*

She finished and handed it to Upjohn, who raised his eyebrows. 'Sorry,' she said, awkwardly. 'It isn't very nice, I know. There's more, but I can't remember it.'

'It'll do for the moment,' said Upjohn. Beside him, Matthews stared into space, and Ingersoll carried on scribbling.

F-J and Diana left them to it and went to sit in the Mess. 'If it is from somewhere else,' said Diana, slowly, 'I mean, if it's from a foreign embassy, and it's been stolen, the original could be anything, couldn't it? Any language at all?'

'Yes,' said F-J. 'That's the problem. One makes codes by adding on letters—so A becomes D and so on—or substituting them. Adding is comparatively simple, but with substitutions, the possibilities are endless. They'll start by looking for letter frequencies, common words...obviously that would be too straightforward for a military application—if that's what this is, of course—but that's the basic principle of the thing. But if anyone can crack it, this lot will. We'll just have to wait and see.'

After lunch—dreadful food, including an extraordinarily bright pink sponge pudding, but surprisingly good coffee—F-J and Diana strolled across the lawn to the pond. They watched the ducks for a while, then F-J said, 'A penny for your thoughts.'

Diana laughed. 'I doubt they're worth it. I was just thinking of something Jock Anderson said to me, about the hidden self— that's what he called it. He said that it's the part we don't reveal, sometimes because we don't dare to, and that the safest thing was to be exactly what one appeared to be.'

'"To thine own self be true,"'— quoted F-J, '"—and it must follow, as the night the day, thou canst not then be false to any man."'

'Hamlet?'

F-J nodded. 'Polonius.'

'It didn't do Ophelia much good, did it?'

'Laertes. Ophelia got all the stuff about how Hamlet was only after one thing and not to believe a word he said.'

'Oh.' Diana, whose mind had leapt immediately to Claude, hoped she wasn't looking as uncomfortable as she felt.

'I've always thought that "to thine own self be true" was a singularly useless piece of advice,' said F-J. 'What do you think Jock meant?'

I suppose,' said Diana, thoughtfully, 'that certain areas of one's life—inner life—have to be kept in separate compartments. Like clothes in a chest of drawers.'

'Very feminine. I forgot to ask, how was Hampshire?'

Diana sighed. It had to come sooner or later. 'Difficult. Evie—my mother-in-law—seems to have found out about my seeing Claude.'

She'd thought F-J might be angry, or at least allude to the fact that he'd warned her to be careful, but he merely said, 'Oh, dear.'

'She made me promise not to see him again, sir.'

'I know it must be hard for you,' said F-J, gently, 'but it's probably for the best.'

'Yes, sir.'

'Have you been keeping your promise?'

'Yes,' said Diana. After all, she thought, she *had* been keeping her promise—except after her disastrous visit to Apse's flat, and she couldn't tell F-J about that.

She felt as if she might be sick. She concentrated on breathing slowly, waiting for it to pass, horribly aware of F-J's scrutiny.

'I hope that's true,' he said. 'It's often tempting to think one is too sophisticated for these things to matter much, especially at times like this, but they do matter in the long run. The complications and their consequences can be disastrous, even fatal. One can live to regret a very great deal.' He paused to light a cigarette. 'You're probably thinking I sound like Polonius,' he said. 'Pompous platitudes. I don't mean to, but I am very fond of you, my dear, and I would hate to see you come to harm. It is always a possibility, now more than ever, but it would be a mistake to turn a possibility into a probability. In that event, I would be unable to help you.' He took her hand. 'Trust is important, my dear, and if you lie to me I cannot trust you...'

As Diana stared down at their linked fingers, the image of F-J staring down at his fly buttons came into her mind again, and with it, a desperate urge to snatch her hand away. Instead, she forced herself to look into his eyes as she said, 'I understand, sir.'

Although F-J's words had been delivered in the kindest of tones, she had heard the unmistakable suggestion of a threat, without—she thought—fully understanding how it was directed. At her behaviour with Claude, yes, but there was something greater—more personal—that she couldn't comprehend. And when F-J talked about 'living to regret', did he mean his own past behaviour? What had he said? The consequences can be disastrous, even fatal...

'I hope you do,' F-J let go of her hand. 'Why don't you stay down here for a while? I shan't need you for a couple of hours—got a few people to speak to.' He patted her on the shoulder and, turning, strolled back to the house.

It wasn't a game, and she'd always known that, but...For all his puggish charm, and apparent fondness for her, Diana knew that F-J would not, ultimately, put her first. His loyalties would—must— lie elsewhere. And he hadn't, she was sure, only been talking about loyalties within MI5. Dr Pyke, for instance. And Claude himself, who obviously knew a great deal more than he was letting on. Knowledge might be dangerous, but ignorance was dangerous, too. There's something happening here, thought Diana. Something I can't see. No-one will speak about it, but it's there all right.

She turned round and, watching F-J walk through the door of the great house, felt very frightened indeed.

CHAPTER

38

Stratton arrived home, on time for once but feeling thoroughly out of sorts, and was not best pleased to find Jenny and Doris sitting in the kitchen, with the unmistakable look of two women who had got together to sort out a man: him. Must be about talking to Johnny, Stratton thought. He *had* promised to speak to Johnny, he knew. It wasn't his fault that he hadn't had time. It had been at the back of his mind, but what with everything at work and going to visit the kids...Bloody hell, he thought, that's all I need.

He went upstairs to tidy himself before tea, trying to spin out his ablutions for as long as possible. When he came down about ten minutes later, he stood on the stairs for a moment, trying to pick up what Jenny and Doris were saying, but they spoke too softly. They must have heard him coming, because by the time he entered the kitchen, an animated discussion about Princess Elizabeth's broadcast to the children was underway. It sounded, to Stratton's ears, curiously unspontaneous, as if they'd already had that particular conversation and were repeating it now for his benefit. It's the etiquette of the thing, he thought. They're just trying to lull me into a false sense of security before they join forces and pounce. Accepting a cup of tea from Jenny, he thought, balls to that. He didn't have the patience to do it their way—what with the bishop's son and Sir Neville, he'd had quite enough pussy-footing around. 'What's up?' he asked.

Jenny and Doris looked disconcerted, and Stratton felt an altogether childish, but none the less enjoyable, pleasure at having thrown a spanner into the works. Then realising from their genuinely serious expressions that this was more than the usual feminine hokum, he softened. 'Please,' he said, 'I've had a hell of a day. Let's not go round the mulberry bush—just tell me. It's Johnny again, isn't it?'

'Yes,' said Jenny. 'Lilian was here this afternoon. She's out of her mind with worry.'

'Has she found out about the petrol coupons?'

'Yes, but it's worse than that, Ted. She thinks he's killed someone.'

'That's ridiculous,' said Stratton. 'Why?'

'She overheard him,' said Doris. 'He was talking to one of his friends. They were larking around, boasting—you know the sort of thing.'

'Yes,' said Stratton, 'but that doesn't necessarily mean anything.'

'Lilian thinks it does. She said she heard Johnny say to this young chap that he'd better be careful, because he'd killed someone—bumped off, he said—and then the other one said it was just some old woman, and—'

'An old woman?'

'Yes. "Some old girl up west," was what he said.'

'When did she hear this?'

'Yesterday.'

'Has she told Reg?'

'He thinks it's a joke,' said Jenny. 'Funny sort of joke, if you ask me, but all the same...We tried to tell Lilian it wasn't very likely,' she looked at Doris, who nodded in confirmation, 'but she's convinced it's true.'

'Why?' asked Stratton. 'She's usually the one who defends him.'

'That's what's so odd about it,' said Doris. 'Lilian said it was the *way* Johnny said it. His face. It seems she's known about the coupons for a while, and him losing his job, and she said she didn't tell Reg because she thought he'd be angry, and Johnny told her he'd got another job lined up. He kept saying she was worrying over nothing, and the business at the garage was all a mistake and nothing to do with him, and of course she believed him.'

'We tried to tell her, Ted,' said Jenny. 'I told her what Mr Hartree said, that Johnny had been fiddling the coupons, but she wouldn't listen. But this afternoon, well...'

'I've never seen her like it,' said Doris. 'She said things had never been right between Johnny and Reg and then she said she didn't know what she'd done wrong but it must be her fault for being a bad mother, and Reg had always thought she was stupid. When we asked her why she'd never said any of this to us before, she said it was because she didn't want to turn the rest of the family against Reg and Johnny more than they were already, but she couldn't bear the strain of keeping it to herself any longer. It was awful, wasn't it, Jen?'

Jenny nodded. 'We didn't know what to say, Ted.'

'What do you think?' asked Stratton.

Jenny and Doris looked at each other. 'We really don't know,' said Jenny. 'But it's like Doris said, we've never seen her like that before, so het up...She was crying.'

'She never does that,' said Doris. 'Jen and me were trying to remember if we'd ever seen her cry before, and we couldn't, even when we were little. Not over anything.'

'Really?' said Stratton, surprised. He'd always considered that Lilian's lack of emotional response must come either from being too cowardly to face up to the true horror of being married to Reg, or too dim to see that there was anything to be faced up to. It had never entered his head that her phlegmatic manner might be a sign of fortitude.

'Never,' repeated Jenny. 'That's what made us think there must be something in it. I know it sounds far-fetched, but...'

The unspoken end of the sentence seemed to buzz in the air between the three of them like an angry wasp. Stratton imagined that Jenny and Doris, like himself, were trying to swat it away. Was it so far-fetched, he wondered. He'd been worried about Johnny for some time—the whole family had, apart from his idiot of a father—but he'd assumed it was theft, looting from bombed premises, that sort of caper, not murder. Remembering Johnny shadow-boxing in the alley, Stratton thought, but he's still a child. Except he wasn't, not any more. Johnny was old enough to fight, and to kill, legally, for his country. And gangsters had to start somewhere...He thought of Joe Vincent's description of Wallace's boy companion: sixteen or seventeen, brown hair, pale, freckled face. Rogers had said he was medium height with dark brown hair. Johnny was eighteen, but otherwise both those descriptions, vague as they were, fitted him. Bumped off some old girl up west. Mabel Morgan had been forty-seven when she died, middle-aged but not old, though her scarred face, her wig, and the crimped, toothless mouth might have made her appear so...

But he *wouldn't*. Not his own nephew...Maybe Reg was right, for once—being a copper made you suspicious of everybody.

'On the other hand,' Jenny was saying, 'it's like you said, Ted. That sort of boasting doesn't really mean anything, and I know Johnny's always been a bit wayward, but I'm sure he'd never do anything really bad. Not like that, anyway,' she added, in an unfamiliar wheedling tone that suggested she was trying to convince herself as much as him and Doris.

'I don't know,' he said. 'And I won't know until I ask him. I'll go over there now.'

'Would you?' said Jenny. 'I know Lilian would be grateful.'

Walking down the road, Stratton wondered what he was going to say to Reg, failed to think of anything, and fervently hoped that he'd be off on patrol somewhere with the Home Guard. By the time he'd turned the corner of their road, he found himself hoping that Johnny wouldn't be at home, either. After all, it was one thing to question a person you'd only just met, quite another when the suspect was your own nephew, for God's sake.

When Lilian answered the door and let him in, Stratton inspected her face for signs of tears. Her eyes did look slightly red, but if he hadn't been alerted by Jenny and Doris, he honestly didn't think he would have noticed. She accepted his suggestion that he might go and have a word with Johnny, sent him upstairs and went back to the kitchen. Stratton knocked on the door of Johnny's room, got a grunted 'What?' and entered.

Johnny was lying diagonally across his bed, feet and head hanging off on either side, smoking and staring, upside down, at the bookcase on the other side of his small room. Seeing Stratton, he righted himself in a single movement, leant on his elbows, and stared up at him. 'What are you doing here?' he asked.

Looking round, Stratton saw a row of books, mostly from the library, by authors such as Sapper, Peter Cheyney, and Erie Stanley Gardener. 'I didn't know you liked detective stories,' he said.

'They're all right.'

Stratton picked up a book. 'Sabatini. I used to like him.'

'Soft,' said Johnny, scornfully, blowing smoke.

'I suppose they must be, to modern taste. I haven't read one for years.'

'You didn't come up here to talk about books, did you?'

'No,' said Stratton. 'I didn't. I've come for a chat.'

'I'm not scared of you.'

'I should hope not,' said Stratton, sitting down beside him on the bed. 'Move over.'

'Oi!' said Johnny. 'What you doing?'

'Making myself comfortable. I suggest you do the same.'

'Why?'

'Well, you don't want to be uncomfortable, do you?'

Johnny levered himself off the bed. 'I'm going out.'

'No, you're not,' said Stratton. 'Not till you've heard what I'm going to say.'

Johnny looked down at him. 'Supposing I don't want to?'

Stratton, who certainly wouldn't have accepted that sort of talk from Pete, decided to let it go. 'That would be a shame,' he said, mildly, 'because you're in trouble, and I'd like to help.'

'Arrest me, you mean.'

'Why would I want to do that?'

'You know.'

'The petrol coupons?'

'That wasn't me. You all think it was, but it wasn't.'

'Who was it, then?'

'The others.'

'What others?'

'At the garage.'

'Mr Hartree doesn't employ anyone else.'

'It was him and his pals doing it. They blamed me 'cause they was scared someone would find out.'

'I don't believe you.'

'I don't care. You always think the worst of me—all of you. Whatever I do, doesn't make no difference.'

'Your mother believes you.'

'Yeah...' Johnny's mouth curved in the suggestion of a smirk, before resuming its habitual sullen shape.

'And your father—'

'My *father*.' The word came out in a sneer, 'He's an old fool, and you know it.'

Stratton, caught off guard and cursing himself for mentioning Reg, stood up and went over to the window. Of course Johnny wasn't stupid, and anyone with half an eye could see that Reg was a fool.

'You think so,' said Johnny, driving home his advantage. 'And Uncle Donald. You despise him.'

Oh, Christ. Johnny had him, and Donald, bang to rights. I am making a complete balls-up of this, thought Stratton. He knew that the boy disliked his father, but he had no idea that his and Donald's feelings were so clear—but then, a determinedly straight face could be just as much of a giveaway as an eye-rolling grimace. What the hell could he say? Now Johnny had the upper hand, and he was the one caught on the hop. Feeling the boy's eyes boring into him, he said, in an attempt to salvage the situation, 'We don't despise him, Johnny, it's just...'

'I know how it is.' Johnny's tone was flat. 'If you're going to give me some speech about how grown-ups don't always get along and difficult times and all that, you can save it. Dad may be stupid, but I'm not.'

'I know you're not,' said Stratton, 'but—leaving aside your dad—you are in a fix.'

'Who says I am?'

'Your mother is very worried about you.'

'She's no need to be. I've told her I'm getting another job.'

'Are you?'

'Yeah. Next week.'

'What is it?'

'Dekker's.'

'Why would Dekker's employ you? Mr Hartree isn't going to give you a reference.'

'Trusts me, doesn't he? Unlike some. I'm going to train as a mechanic.'

'Why would Mr Dekker want another mechanic with everyone's car up on blocks?'

'His other bloke's been called up, that's why.'

'I can check, you know.'

'You do that. Like I said, I don't care.'

'Well, I do, and so does your Mum. She overheard you talking—boasting you'd killed someone. I'm sure it isn't true,' Stratton laughed, 'you wouldn't know the first thing about it, but all the same, it's not very clever to go around saying things like that.'

This stung, as Stratton had intended it to. 'I know more than you think,' said Johnny sulkily. 'You think I'm too young and too stupid to know things, but I'm not.'

'You're giving a pretty good impression of it.'

'I'm not.' Johnny glared at him.

'Yes,' said Stratton gently, 'you are. You don't want people to think you're a fool, do you?'

'They don't think I'm a fool,' said Johnny. 'They respect me.'

'Who does?'

'People.'

'People respect you,' repeated Stratton. 'I'm relieved to hear it. Is that because they're scared you're going to kill them, too?'

'I never said…' Johnny tailed off, uncertain now.

'You never said you didn't. "Some old girl up west". Easy to kill an old woman, was it? Good fun?'

'I didn't say that!'

'Your mother heard you. Telling your chums they'd better watch out because you'd done a murder.'

'I never meant it.'

'Didn't you? Then you were a fool to say you'd done it, weren't you?' Johnny hung his head. 'Tell me about this old girl,' said Stratton. "What was she like?'

'She wasn't…' The boy wasn't looking at him now. Instead, his eyes flitted round the room as if he were seeking a way of escape.

'Wasn't what?' Stratton prompted.

'Nothing. I told you. I didn't do it.'

'Then who did?'

'Nobody! I made it up. I never meant it.' Still, he didn't look at Stratton. 'I was being stupid,' he mumbled at the floor. 'Like you said.'

'Were you, Johnny? Look at me.'

Johnny raised his head a couple of inches, then dropped it again. 'I haven't done nothing.'

'Another mistake, was it? Somebody else's fault?'

'No…It wasn't anything. I never meant it.'

'Are you sure?'

'Yes! Look, Uncle Ted, I'm sorry, but I've got to go out now.'

He took his jacket from the hook on the back of the door. 'Going to see your friend Mr Wallace?'

Johnny froze, his hand on the door handle, then turned back to face Stratton. 'I don't know what you're talking about,' he said, then yanked the door open and clattered down the stairs and out of the house. Stratton watched him run down the street. The boy knew something about Mabel. He may not—God, let this be true—have had a hand in her death, but he did know something.

CHAPTER

39

$\mathcal{S}$tratton went downstairs to Lilian, who was sitting at the kitchen table. The oddness of this struck him immediately, but it took a bit longer for him to realise why: Jenny and her sisters were always doing something—drinking tea, talking, knitting, mending, cooking—they never just sat. Lilian appeared to be in a sort of trance of misery and flinched when he spoke to her. 'I'll be fine,' she said, in response to his question. 'Just being silly.'

'No, you're not.'

'I'm so worried, Ted.'

'I know. I've spoken to Johnny, and...' Stratton stopped, realising that there wasn't actually anything specific he could say by way of reassurance. 'It's true he's got in with a bad crowd, but I'm sure he'll see sense. It's hard for him, Lilian—he can't go in the forces like his dad, which must be a big disappointment for him. I don't know all the rights and wrongs of this thing at Hartree's, but he's obviously unsettled at the moment. He's not a bad lad—just needs a bit of time to sort himself out.' All right, he said to himself, as Lilian dabbed at her eyes with a screwed up handkerchief, the stuff about the services is probably balls, and he would happily put his last penny on the fact that the boy was involved in the coupon business, but he didn't really have a clue why Johnny was acting as he was, and his mother needed to hear something.

He was about to elaborate further when he heard the front door open, and Reg's voice issued from the hall. 'Anybody home?'

'Bloody hell,' muttered Stratton.

'Don't tell him,' Lilian said, just as Reg walked into the kitchen, wearing his Home Guard uniform.

'Don't tell him what?' he asked, rubbing his hands together vigorously. 'Got a surprise for me? Had a good day today, I don't mind telling you—orders for Christmas cards coming in left, right and centre, and an excellent parade this evening. The men are coming on a treat.'

'That's nice, dear,' said Lilian, automatically.

'Nice? It's a damn sight more than that! Honestly, women...' he rolled his eyes at Stratton. 'Any tea in the pot?'

'I'll make some fresh.' Lilian stood up and spent what seemed an unnecessarily long time busying herself with the kettle and cups, while Reg gave a demonstration of bayonet training which involved a lot of leaping about and blood-curdling yells. 'Still using broom handles, of course,' he panted, pulling up a chair, 'Weapons haven't arrived from HQ as yet. What's this surprise, then? Something good for tea?'

Stratton winced. 'No,' he said. 'It's Johnny.'

'Don't, Ted,' said Lilian, quietly. 'Let it alone.'

'Still fussing about the boy?' Reg asked. 'Storm in a teacup. I'm going to use my influence with the Major. Get him into the unit.' He made it sound like a commission in the Guards. 'Do him good. Discipline, exercise, fresh air—just what the boy needs.'

Christ, thought Stratton, he'll be talking about cold baths in a minute. 'Johnny's in trouble,' he said. 'He's been sacked from his job.'

'What?'

'He's been accused of stealing. Fiddling petrol coupons. It's serious.'

'When did this happen?'

'A couple of weeks ago.'

'Did you know about this?' Reg asked Lilian, who was standing by the stove, twisting a tea-towel in her hands.

'Yes, dear.'

'Why the hell didn't you tell me?'

'I thought...' Lilian faltered and stopped, staring down at the lino.

'You didn't think,' snapped Reg. 'That's your trouble. You never do. How do you *think* this makes *me* look? Stupid, that's what. If it got out...Have you told anyone?'

'Only Jen and Doris.'

'Only Jen and Doris,' Reg mimicked. 'You might as well put up a public notice.'

'I thought it would blow over, dear, and Johnny's getting another job.'

'For God's sake! Blow over? I suppose it never occurred to you to consider my position?'

Lilian flushed. 'I'm sorry,' she said.

'It's a bit late for that, isn't it? How am I going to look when people know that my son has been caught with his hand in the till? This is your fault! I've done my part, but you...' Reg spluttered to a halt, shaking his head. 'Time and time again, I've made it clear to her,' he told Stratton, 'but she doesn't listen. I might as well talk to the wall.'

Lilian had her hands over her face. Why she was still standing there, Stratton could not imagine. The man's egotism really was beyond belief. 'The point is,' he began, but Reg cut him off.

'I'll tell you what the bloody point is! Someone needs to sort that boy out, that's the point! Where is he?'

'He's gone out.'

'What did you let him go out for?' Reg bellowed at Lilian. 'What the hell's the matter with you?'

Lilian removed her hands from her face. 'I'm sorry,' she repeated. She looked dazed, as if someone had punched her.

'That's enough, Reg,' said Stratton, quietly. 'Losing your temper isn't going to help anyone.'

'Ted,' said Reg in a strangled voice. 'You're not going to...I mean, this isn't going to be taken any further, is it?'

Stratton shook his head. 'Mr Hartee seems to have decided not to report it, so no, not this time. But if it happens again, and I find out about it...' He shrugged.

'Thank you,' said Reg, then, with more confidence, 'I knew we could rely on you to do the right thing. After all, it's family, isn't it? And this sort of thing happens all the time, nowadays. I'm sure it's just a—'

Stratton, who was thinking that if Reg started on about boyish japes and the foolishness of youth, he might just have to hit him, interrupted. 'I'm not sure you appreciate the seriousness of this, Reg. Johnny's got in with a very bad crowd. I've spoken to him, and I hope he'll see sense, but you need to keep an eye on him from now on.'

'Don't worry!' said Reg. 'When I get hold of him he won't—'

'No,' said Stratton. 'Shouting at him won't do any good. You'll only make things worse. Just make it clear that you're not happy about what's happened. And,' he added, 'I shouldn't say anything about the Home Guard just yet—you don't want to antagonise him.'

'I think I can decide what to do for myself, thank you,' said Reg stiffly. 'I can see he's got you sticking up for him, as well.'

'It's just a suggestion,' said Stratton. 'If you don't want to take it, that's fine.' He pushed back his chair. 'I'd best leave you to it.'

Lilian accompanied him to the door. 'Thank you,' she whispered, when he was on the step. 'For not bringing up the other thing.'

'That's all right,' said Stratton. 'Don't worry, Lilian. I'm sure it was just some silly talk. You know what kids are like.'

❀ ❀ ❀

Stratton asked himself, as he walked slowly back home, what else he could have said. He hoped, against all his instincts, that Johnny's mention of killing someone had been mere boasting.

Besides, he had no evidence beyond the boy's reactions, especially to the mention of Wallace, that Johnny had anything to do with the death of Mabel Morgan or anybody else. Perhaps, he thought, I shouldn't have said anything at all to Reg, but the idea of keeping quiet while the bloody man downed around the kitchen playing soldiers had been too much...Besides, the wretched boy was his son, not Stratton's.

He had a sudden memory of putting his own son, Pete, then aged five, to bed after Reg, at some family outing or other, had spent the entire day talking—for reasons best known to himself—in an exaggerated French accent, confusing railway porters, waitresses in cafés, and everyone else they came across. Pete, lying down to be tucked in, had looked up at him solemnly, with big green eyes the spit of Jenny's, and said, 'Uncle Reg is mad, isn't he?' Stratton couldn't remember how he'd answered, but he knew that whatever he'd said had been pitifully inadequate. What he had never forgotten was the expression on Pete's face as he'd listened—serious and kindly, as if aware that his father was doing the best he could in the circumstances. Pete, Stratton thought, had probably forgotten the whole thing long ago, but he never would.

Perhaps mad was how Reg had seemed to Johnny, too, when he was young. He'd never really considered it before. It was bad enough having to see Reg at intervals, albeit fairly frequent ones, but what it would be like day after day...I should have talked to the boy earlier, Stratton thought. Instead of laughing about his stupid bastard of a father, I should have done something to help.

Later, lying in bed in the hope of a few hours' sleep in comfort before the raids started, he repeated this to Jenny. He'd given her an edited version of his talk with Johnny earlier—if he hadn't told Lilian and Reg about his suspicions, he was damned if he was going to upset her with them. She reproached him for not talking to Johnny before, but not too harshly, and then, after a decent pause, said, 'You can't take everything on yourself, love,' and then, 'Oh dear, I hope Reg isn't being too awful to Lilian.'

'He was pretty bad when I was there.'

'I'm glad I'm not married to someone like that,' said Jenny. She reached out and took his hand. 'You always do your best, Ted. That's one of the nicest things about you.'

Stratton smiled at her. He felt a profound sense of gratitude—although really, he supposed, it was a negative sort of gratitude, that she wasn't Lilian and he wasn't Reg and Johnny wasn't their son and they weren't arguing. 'Do you know something?' he asked.

'Not until you tell me.'

'If you weren't my wife already, I might just ask you to marry me.'

Jenny considered this for a moment. 'Well,' she said. 'I suppose that's better than a poke in the eye with a kipper.'

'Why a kipper?'

'Why not?' She thought for a moment, and said, 'Any kind of fish, really.' A moment later, she said, 'That's not a kipper.'

'That isn't your eye,' replied Stratton.

'Good heavens,' said Jenny in mock surprise. 'So it isn't.'

CHAPTER

40

'It turned out,' said Professor Ingersoll, 'to be much simpler than we first thought. The original was in English, not German.'

Diana stared over F-J's shoulder at the piece of paper. 'It's from President Roosevelt,' she said in surprise.

'They're having an election soon,' said Professor Upjohn. 'Judging by this, it sounds as if he wants America to join us.'

'That's not what's been in the papers,' said Diana. 'He keeps saying he'll make sure that they stay out of the war. Besides, that's what the people want. Mr Roosevelt won't get re-elected if they think he's going to get them involved in something that most of them consider to be none of their business.' She looked at F-J for confirmation of this.

'It's true,' he said, thoughtfully. 'This,' he waved the paper, 'is addressed to the ambassador, Mr Kennedy, so I suppose someone at the embassy must have got hold of a surplus copy.' Diana opened her mouth to say something, but F-J shook his head at her almost imperceptibly before turning back to the assembled boffins. His tone became brisk as he folded the paper, pocketed it, and began shaking hands all round. 'Well, gentlemen, we're most grateful for your assistance, and we shan't take up any more of your valuable time. Come, Diana.'

'Sir,' Diana said, the minute the door closed behind them, 'I know that—'

'Not now. We'll find somewhere for lunch and talk there.'

In a private room at the Swan in Newport Pagnell, Diana, at last able to speak, blurted out, 'I'm sorry, sir, I meant to tell you, but it didn't seem too...To be honest, it slipped my mind, sir. There's an American who comes to the Right Club gatherings at the tearoom. I've only met him once, but I know he's a friend of Lady Calne's daughter, Helen. I think he might work at their embassy.'

'What's his name?'

'Walter Wymark.'

'What does he do?'

'I don't know, sir.'

'Shouldn't be too difficult to find out. Judging from that message, the President has been corresponding with Mr Churchill for some time. Mr Kennedy must have been getting copies of the telegrams afterwards, so it must be someone from their embassy who stole the message—this man Wymark, perhaps. If he's got other telegrams, and he chooses to make them public, Roosevelt won't be re-elected, and Wilkie's an isolationist.'

'Wilkie, sir?'

'Wendell Wilkie, the Republican candidate. If he becomes President, the States will never come into the war unless they're attacked first, and the Germans are far too intelligent to do anything like that. Besides which, Wilkie's not keen on Churchill—thinks he's too self-assured. Dear God...' He sighed. 'You should have told me about this man before.'

'I know, sir. I'm sorry.'

'Well, tell me as much as you know.'

'I don't know much, sir. I know Lady Calne isn't very keen on him seeing her daughter. Helen's been quite upset about it. They're not engaged or anything, but Lady Caine doesn't think he's good enough, that sort of thing. I did find out that he was in Moscow for several years before the war, and he seems to have been a member of the Right Club for quite a while, so I suppose he must be an isolationist.'

'Have you ever heard that discussed?'

'No, sir.'

'Then we don't know for certain. If he's pro-Nazi, I don't suppose he's a Communist, but it's not impossible.'

Diana frowned. 'I don't understand, sir. I thought that Germany and the Soviets had a non-aggression pact.'

'They do, but it doesn't necessarily follow that because you're on the side of one you have to support the other. I should have thought a few years in Moscow would be enough to make anyone think twice about the Russians, but one never knows which way these chaps will jump.'

'What will you do, sir?'

'The first thing is to look into this man Wymark—his background and so on, and then we'll need to speak to the Ambassador. They're not going to be pleased we've gone behind their backs, but it can't be helped. If necessary, we can ask them to waive Wymark's diplomatic immunity, and there are a few other things that'll need to be followed up, too...'

Diana waited for F-J to continue, but he didn't, and after a moment, the landlord appeared with their lunch. F-J did not return to the subject while they were eating, but questioned her about Phyllis and her billet at Bletchley, so that the conversation became social rather than official. She tried, several times, to steer the talk back to the coded message, but F-J changed the subject. By the time they'd got to the lukewarm and very weak coffee, she decided to venture a direct question.

'What will happen to Apse, sir?'

F-J put down his cup and pinched the bridge of his nose. He screwed up his face for a moment, as if trying to force a thought, then said, 'It's a good question. Apse's position means that he has access to diplomatic channels, and the real risk, as I've said, is that if it becomes public knowledge that Roosevelt is intending to bring

America into the war, he'll lose the election. Of course, one doesn't know the extent of his intentions, but he's certainly shown himself willing to help in the matter of destroyers and so forth—albeit at a pretty high cost and despite a great deal of opposition. He's got to convince the people that they have a moral and practical stake in defeating dictatorship, and that isn't going to happen if Apse, or Wymark, or anyone else, has managed to get this sort of damaging stuff into the hands of people who will print or broadcast it.' F-J sighed. 'Apse knows too much, Diana, and too many people. It's complicated—we can't just remove him. And then there's the question of blackmail. I shouldn't be surprised if that was at the root of all this, but I don't see how...' He stopped, and stared at the sludge in the bottom of his coffee cup.

'How what, sir?'

'It doesn't matter,' said F-J. 'Just thinking aloud.'

F-J didn't elaborate while they were being driven back to London, either, but closed his eyes and appeared to be asleep for most of the journey. Diana stared out of the window and thought about Walter Wymark. Her impression had been of someone large, bland and sleek, with blond hair and the healthy look of a person who enjoyed exercise and spent a lot of time in the fresh air. Quite different from the pallid, tired faces of the British. She supposed he must be about thirty years old, and, if the rumours she'd heard were to be believed, Helen Pender was just one of several girl-friends. Did she, or Lady Calne, know what he was up to?

F-J, eyes still closed, shifted slightly, and Diana, turning to look at him, wondered if she could possibly have imagined the warning by the duck pond. She had a feeling of unreality, like the one she'd experienced on looking into the mirror at Apse's flat after finding the message. It would be so nice to find oneself back in a world where the expected and unexpected were exactly that, where one could take refuge inside one's own mind and not find that one's thoughts and instincts had somehow been booby-trapped. Suppose a miracle happened, she thought, and we woke up tomorrow to find that there hadn't been a war at all, and everything was back to the way it was before, wouldn't that be wonderful...Then, shivering at the memory of her sheer, fist-in-mouth horror in the cupboard at Apse's flat—her nearness to discovery a thousand times more terrifying than the air raid going on outside—she thought, things can never be the same again.

Stratton, arriving at work the following morning, found Constable Ballard in his office talking to DI Jones. 'Got a pal of yours downstairs,' said Jones. 'Name's George Wallace.'

'Oh yes?'

'Came in a couple of hours ago—caught with a van full of cigarettes. Seems he'd been following the driver while he made his deliveries, then took the lot while the thing was unattended. The man reported it, and Ballard here spotted him. Lobbed his truncheon through the windscreen.' Jones nodded appreciatively at the constable. 'Nice job.'

'Thank you, sir.'

'Anyway,' Jones turned back to Stratton, 'Ballard here had an idea that you might want to talk to him about another matter, so if you fancy it, he's all yours.'

Stratton glanced at Ballard, who seemed to be staring fixedly at a heap of files on the floor. 'Sounds like a good idea,' he said. 'Ballard, if there's a room free, you might bring him upstairs. I don't fancy suffocation so early in the morning.'

'Yes, sir.' Ballard grinned, and, carefully manoeuvred his way out through the chaos.

'Wallace does smell pretty strong, doesn't he?' said Jones. 'I had a word with him myself—he wasn't giving anything away, but I got the impression that he's been doing a bit of business on his own account. I've not had a lot of dealings with Abie Marks but I know that Wallace is one of his boys, and I had the distinct feeling,' Jones put his distinct feeling in inverted commas with two brisk raisings of the eyebrows, 'that this little consignment wasn't going Marks's way.'

'That's interesting,' said Stratton. 'Any idea where it was going?'

Jones shook his head. 'Can't be the Eyeties, and if the Malts are expanding their interests outside brasses, I think we'd have heard about it by now. So unless it's the Elephant lot, which is possible, I suppose, I'm guessing it's another Yiddisher, maybe the East End—Levy or Wilder. Someone who runs spielers, I'd say. Anyway, if Wallace is branching out a bit, you can bet he's keeping it quiet, and if Marks were to find out...' Jones drew a finger across his throat.

'I see,' said Stratton. 'Are you sure it's all right for me to go ahead? I don't want to tread on any toes.'

'You won't be,' said Jones. 'Strictly speaking, it's your patch, and I'm up to here with bollocks from Machin about everything else—we all are—so help yourself. He handed Stratton a piece of paper. 'Here. That's what we've got so far. It's quite a haul.'

❀ ❀ ❀

Ballard had put Wallace in the only available room, which was downstairs and very small. The man seemed to have ripened like a foreign cheese, and the single window, like the one in Stratton and Jones's office, refused to budge. For a moment Stratton contemplated leaving the door open in order to be able to breathe without feeling actually sick, but decided that, what with the aroma from the still-blocked lavatory, such fresh air as the corridor might afford was less important than the possibility of being overheard. At this point, he definitely did not want what he was going to say to Wallace to get back to Machin or Lamb or anyone else. He shut the door, pulled up a chair, and sat down facing Wallace across the table. Trying to breathe only through his mouth, he said, 'Hello, chum.'

Wallace glared at him. Stratton was quite pleased to see that he had the beginnings of a spectacular shiner round his left eye, but less delighted by the man's obvious determination not to speak at all if he could avoid it.

'I'm afraid our premises aren't as smart as Mr Marks's office,' Stratton said, 'but you can't have everything, can you? In fact,' he continued, when Wallace offered no response to this sally, 'you can't have much of anything, can you, George? Not now. Apart from what you'll get when Mr Marks finds out what you've been up to, of course, and I don't imagine that's going to be very pleasant.'

Wallace gave him a sour look, but said nothing. The fact that he didn't deny Marks's lack of involvement might, of course, mean that Wallace was protecting his boss, but Stratton, suspecting that Jones had been right, decided to continue in the same vein and see what happened. 'We reckon you had the best part of half a million cigarettes in that van. So that's...' Stratton did a rapid mental calculation, adding on black market value, 'about fifteen hundred quid, give or take. More, perhaps. That's a lot of money, George. Mr Marks won't like to miss his share of that, will he?'

'I just pinched the van,' said Wallace. 'I didn't know what was in the back.'

'Balls,' said Stratton. 'I don't believe that, and neither will Mr Marks when he hears about it.' He leant back in his chair and folded his arms. Wallace stared back at him, but with less assurance than before.

'Well,' said Stratton, 'Are you going to tell me about it?' He let the silence continue for several beats before continuing, in a conversational tone, 'You'll be going down for a good while, of course, but I'm sure Mr Marks's boys'll be waiting when you come out—if they don't get you while you're inside, that is.' He put his head on one side and contemplated Wallace, who was now looking dangerously pale. 'I don't suppose you're interested in my opinion, but it seems to me that you're fucked either way, George. Frankly, you're not a pretty sight now, but after they've carved you up, you'll be...' Stratton looked thoughtful. 'Well, I'd say you'll be a fair old mess. Of course, I don't know, but I'd say you'll be lucky—or you might not be lucky, depending on what they do to you—if you're still alive when they've finished. Mr Marks doesn't take kindly to people who do the dirty on him, does he?' Wallace stayed silent, but he was definitely looking as if he might puke at any moment. 'Or perhaps I'm wrong,' Stratton added. 'Perhaps he'll pat you on the head and feed you a sugar lump.'

Wallace swallowed. 'What do you want?'

Stratton pretended to consider this for a moment, then said, 'I want you to tell me what happened at Joe Vincent's flat.'

'I don't know.'

'Oh, I think you do. This is no time for modesty, George. You're fucked, all right, but you can still do yourself a few favours if you play your cards right.'

'What happens if I tell you?'

'Depends how good it is. I'm not a magician, I can't just make a van load of stolen cigarettes disappear into thin air.'

'They don't have to disappear into thin air.'

'What are you suggesting, George?'

Wallace gave him a meaningful look. 'If it's what I think you're suggesting,' said Stratton, 'I wouldn't say any more, if I were you. In fact, if I were *you*, I'd start telling me about Joe Vincent, pretty damn quick.'

'We wasn't thieving,' said Wallace.

'We?'

'Me and the boy.'

'What's his name?'

'Johnny Booth.'

Oh, fuck, thought Stratton. The stupid little toe-rag had been there, after all. But there was no proof that either Johnny or Wallace had been there on the day that Mabel Morgan died, only later, when they'd visited Joe Vincent, and Rogers had seen them on the stairs. 'If you weren't thieving,' he asked, 'what were you doing?'

'We was collecting something,' said Wallace. 'For Abie Marks.'

'What was it?'

'A box. A big one. With things in it.'

'What things?'

'I don't know.'

'How were you supposed to recognise this box?'

'It wasn't a big place. Not much there. Abie just said to get anything that looked likely, but we couldn't find it. He said the bloke who lived there was an iron—wouldn't give us no trouble or go to the police or nothing. He wasn't there when we started, but then he come in so I had a word with him because we never found anything, but that was no good, so we came away, didn't we?'

'Did you?'

Wallace nodded. 'We'd looked all over, and it was a lot of noise—'

'When you were hitting Mr Vincent, you mean?'

'Well, that—and before, bumping around.'

'And you say you thought Mr Vincent didn't know where this box was?'

Wallace shook his head. 'He'd of told us.'

'Why did you take the photograph of Mabel Morgan?' asked Stratton.

'That was for Abie. Said he liked her. Wanted a souvenir, didn't he?'

'So you knew that Mabel Morgan lived there?'

'Well, yes.' Wallace looked surprised. 'Abie told us. The box belonged to her, didn't it?'

'Did it?'

'"S what he said.'

'Who was the box for?'

'Abie.'

'No,' said Stratton. 'When I asked you about the photograph just now, you said, "that was for Abie." But the box was for someone else, wasn't it?'

Wallace looked at him warily. 'I don't know.'

'Sure about that, are you?'

Wallace inclined his head.

'That's a shame. A real pity. I was almost persuaded you didn't know what was in the back of that van, but now...'

'All right. Abie done a favour for a friend.'

'Who?'

'I don't know the name.'

'Are you sure?'

'Yes.' Wallace leant forward. 'Abie never said, but I think it was someone important.'

'What made you think that?'

'The way he said it—"Nobody you know"—made me think we was going to a place in Mayfair. I was surprised when he told us where it was.'

'But no name?'

'He never said. Just that he was doing this bloke a favour— and there'd be something in it for us if we got this box.'

'Which you didn't get.'

'No, we didn't. I told Abie what happened, and he said not to worry.'

'Nothing else?'

'No. Surprised me a bit.'

'What did?'

'Well, he just let it go, didn't he? Never said another word.'

'I see. Tell me about Johnny Booth.'

'He's just a kid.' Wallace shrugged. 'Abie said, take him with you, so I did. Never thought much about it.'

'Had you met him before?'

'Seen him around. He done a bit for Abie, here and there. Nothing much. Abie must of took a shine to him.'

'Local boy?'

'Don't know. Don't think so—only seen him a few times, the last couple of months maybe.'

'Did you kill Miss Morgan?'

'No! On my life. She jumped out of the window. It was in the paper.'

'Doesn't mean it's true.'

'But it was there! You can't...We wasn't there then, only afterwards.'

'So Abie told you she was dead, did he?'

Wallace stared at him. 'No...I don't remember. He just said if anyone was there it would be the iron. He never mentioned no-one else.'

'He asked you for a souvenir, George.'

'Yes, but he never said nothing about her—if she was dead or if she'd be there, or...After he said this bloke was important, I never asked nothing else about it.'

'He never said the bloke was important. You told me you just thought it.'

Wallace fidgeted for a moment, then muttered, 'He did say something about him being important. "Friends in high places", something like that. But he never said who it was.'

'I see. A man like Mr Marks might do a great deal for friends in high places, George. Might even organise it so that someone fell out of a high window.'

'We never! God's truth, Mr Stratton, I never laid a finger on her—never even saw her. I wouldn't kill an old woman, not for anyone.'

'She wasn't an old woman, George. She was forty-seven. Did she look old, without her teeth in?'

'She—' Wallace checked himself, then repeated, 'I never saw her.'

'I think you did, George. If you'd seen it in the papers, you'd know she wasn't old. They printed her age.'

'I never. And I did see it in the papers. You don't remember how old someone is, do you? Just slipped my mind.'

'That's possible, I suppose,' conceded Stratton. 'What about churches, George?'

'Churches?' Wallace's look of bewilderment, Stratton thought, was genuine.

'Our Lady and St. Peter in Eastcastle Street. Ever been there?'

'No. Never heard of it.'

'Are you sure about that? It might have been a while ago—February, perhaps? Spot of digging? Good way to keep warm on a cold night.'

'I'm quite sure,' said Wallace, firmly. 'I don't know what you're talking about.' Judging by the look on his face, he felt himself on secure ground.

'Fair enough,' said Stratton. 'Now then, you're going back to the cells while I decide what I'm going to do with you.' The colour, which had, in the last thirty seconds, begun to return to Wallace's face, drained away once more, leaving his skin the colour of putty.

'What are you going to do?' he muttered.

'I'm going to go and have a nice cup of tea and think about it,' said Stratton. 'I'll let you know when I'm good and ready. Best make yourself comfortable,' he added with a grin. 'I've a feeling you're going to be here for quite a while.'

Stratton returned to his office—now mercifully empty—and stood staring out of the window, a not very nice cup of tea provided by Cudlipp in his hand. He definitely needed to think, and fast.

The idea of turning in his own nephew—of what Jenny would say when he told her about Johnny, of Reg's reaction, of Lilian's tears—made him feel sick. I should have spoken to the boy earlier, he thought. Instead, he'd justified putting it off, telling himself he'd no business interfering in someone else's family, even if it was Reg's. Guilt, anger at Reg for being…well, for being Reg, and the thought of upsetting Jenny made his stomach churn.

There is nothing I can do about it now, he thought. He took out his notepad and pencil, shut everything to do with Johnny firmly out of his mind, and began going through the points from his interview with Wallace.

Wallace and Johnny had turned over Mabel Morgan's flat to find the box containing the films and letters because Abie Marks had asked them to do a favour for one of his friends. Given the subject matter of the films, that friend must either be Sir Neville Apse, or the unknown man with whom he was dancing. All right so far. If the friend was Sir Neville, whose handkerchief had been found on the body in the church, then it was a fair bet that Marks also had some connection with that murder. Although, thought Stratton, Wallace might not have; the man's surprise when he'd mentioned the place had seemed real, and in any case, Marks had plenty of other people to help him do his dirty work. But where on earth would Sir Neville and Abie Marks come across each other? It wasn't as if they moved in the same circles, unless…Boys, thought Stratton. That was certainly possible. Marks had a reputation for being able to get you anything you wanted—if you could afford to pay for it. And a man in Sir Neville's position could hardly be seen hanging about in Piccadilly looking for male tarts…

Stratton made some notes, then paused for a cigarette and, finding his packet empty, chewed on the end of his pencil and thought longingly of Wallace's van-load of fags, now presumably under guard at the garage.

Miss Morgan, he wrote, and then, *Wallace?* The man may have been telling the truth about the church, but Stratton was damn sure he was lying about never having seen Mabel. If Sir Neville wanted those films enough, and was prepared to sanction murder in order to get them, why not ask his friend Marks for help? If Mabel had been blackmailing him, it made even more sense. Had she, perhaps, had an accomplice? The unknown man in the church—perhaps he had been the one behind the camera, or even the dancing partner? But then, why kill him so many months before? Unless it was a scare tactic that hadn't worked, or the man had given the films to Mabel at some point before his death and Sir Neville hadn't known she'd got them until she'd asked him for money, or…Stratton rubbed his hands over his face. There was no proof of any of it, and anyway, he had to decide what to do about Wallace before he did anything else. If he charged Wallace with the whole boiling, Marks would undoubtedly do him serious harm. Marks could hardly afford to let such a thing go without damaging his reputation, especially now, when all the gangs were fighting for control of the Italians' old turf.

Stratton didn't give two hoots about Wallace himself, but without him, he seriously doubted that he'd ever be able to find out what had happened to Mabel. It was, of course, possible that her death was an accident, or that she'd been so terrified that she'd taken her own life, but the facts, so far as he knew them, didn't point to either of those things. Besides, Joe Vincent's description of Mabel in the days before her death hadn't made her sound like someone who was about to do herself in. He could ask Johnny—lean on him—but he wouldn't be much use as an informant, whereas Wallace, who'd been around longer and knew a great deal, would be able to yield far more.

He could choose to accept that Wallace had no idea of what was inside the van, and simply charge him with the theft of the vehicle. It was true that he hadn't admitted knowing that the cigarettes were inside, but nobody would believe it—and he'd have to square it with Ballard, somehow. Catching Wallace was a major feather in the constable's cap, and he wouldn't be pleased if it came to nothing. Still, like Stratton, and every other copper before him, the kid had to learn that police work was less a matter of Sherlock Holmes-type detection and intuition than of trapping or coercing people into incriminating themselves and others. Not nice, but that was the way of it. He'd simply tell Ballard that he'd had instructions from higher up.

Stratton groaned. Higher up. He'd have to talk to Machin again. And if Machin put the tin hat on it, he might as well just throw the book at Wallace and forget the whole thing. For that reason, he told himself, it would be best to keep Johnny's name out of it.

CHAPTER
42

As Stratton deposited the cabbage and the newspaper package of potatoes on the kitchen table, he spotted Jenny's note. She'd gone round to Lilian's, where she seemed to spend more and more time these days. Stratton felt relieved. He supposed he shouldn't, but he was glad not to have to deal with all the things she wasn't saying. She'd been tip-toeing round him all week—not literally, of course, but being more solicitous than usual about whether he'd had a nice day or liked his dinner or wanted more tea. She'd called him 'love' a great deal more often, too, which was a sign that she wanted him to talk to her about something. He knew damn well what it was, too—bloody Johnny—and there was absolutely nothing he could say without making the situation a hundred times worse.

On his way upstairs he spotted an envelope on the hall table, addressed, in Jenny's handwriting, to the children. Turning it over, he saw that it wasn't sealed, and wondered if this was deliberate. Pulling it out, he glanced through it and, spotting *Your Dad has been very busy with work so I have not seen much of him but he sends you his best...*decided it probably was deliberate. He didn't blame Jenny—God knew, she wasn't one to nag and fuss—but he felt irritated, all the same.

He wondered whether to go round and see if Donald fancied coming down to the Swan. That, at least, would take his mind off his disastrous interview with DCI Machin, who had heard him in tight-lipped silence, and pointed out that Rogers's evidence and Wallace's confession ('the circumstances of which are dubious') did not conclusively link Sir Neville with Abie Marks, that Joe Vincent was not around to press charges for the assault, and that Stratton still hadn't managed to discover the identity of the corpse found in the church. He had then reiterated that Stratton was not, under any circumstances whatsoever, to question Sir Neville, and that, frankly, he ought to be putting his time to better use. Added to which, he'd instructed Stratton to charge Wallace with the theft of both the van and its contents, which meant that he could kiss goodbye to any more information from that quarter.

Clearly, whichever bigwig Machin had spoken to about Sir Neville had sent him away with a flea in his ear. Still, not mentioning Johnny meant that at least he wasn't known to have a criminal in his family—hardly a recommendation for future career prospects—for the time being, anyway. God only knew what the boy would do next. So far, he'd been lucky, but that wouldn't last. Kids like him always got caught, and what that would do to his parents, and the rest of the family, didn't bear thinking about...

I need a bloody miracle, thought Stratton. He put Jenny's letter back in its envelope and stood for a moment, tapping it against the table. He wasn't going to get a miracle, but a couple of jars and an uncomplicated hour with his brother-in-law might brighten things up a bit.

With a defiant glance upstairs in the direction of the bathroom, he took out his handkerchief, wiped his muddy hands on it, and, slamming his hat back on his head, left the house.

CHAPTER

43

'Are you quite sure,' asked Lally Markham as they refreshed their make-up in the Ladies' Cloakroom at the 400, 'that you're not seeing Claude any more?' Diana sighed. She'd been having such a nice evening, dancing and laughing and enjoying herself with Lally and Jock and the others, until he'd walked in, alone. She'd pretended not to see him, but it hadn't worked—all the others had, and it was the work of a few moments to find him a seat at their table. She'd greeted him coolly, then carried on talking to Margot. She'd been painfully aware of his eyes on her and the memory of what happened on her last visit to the club—the raid, and going to bed with him for the first time—and of everyone else pretending not to pay attention but actually drinking everything in as if they were watching a play.

Finally, unable to stand the tension for a moment longer, she'd excused herself, only to find that Lally was following her. 'He's still pretty keen, isn't he?' she said, patting her hair back into place. 'He can't take his eyes off you.'

'I hadn't noticed,' said Diana. 'And I've *told* you—'

'Yes, you have,' said Lally calmly, 'but I don't believe you.'

Diana, who had expected to have to deal only with a spot of ragging from Lally, was disconcerted by the seriousness of her tone.

'As I told you, Diana,' she said, settling herself on one of the gilt chairs and lighting a cigarette, 'the last time Claude pursued someone like this, it ended badly.'

'I know that.' And I know a few things you don't, Diana thought. Dropping her compact into her evening bag, she added. 'I'm leaving.'

'He'll follow you,' said Lally.

'No he won't.'

'Of course he will. He only came because he knew you'd be here.'

'How?'

'Jock let on that you were coming with us. Stupid man, I told him not to.'

'Well, I'm going anyway. If he tries to come with me, I'll send him on his way.'

'Diana, wait. You don't know how serious this is.'

'I know perfectly well. That's why I'm not—'

'For heaven's sake! It's crystal clear to every single person round that table that he's crazy about you, and—whether or not you admit it— you are crazy about him.'

Diana made for the door, but Lally beat her to it and stood with her back to the panels.

'Please let me pass.'

'Not until you hear what I've got to say.'

'There's nothing more to discuss,' Diana said coldly. 'If you're saying these things because you're in love with him yourself, then...'

'Diana!' Lally looked hurt. 'That's an awful thing to say. I'm not in love with Claude, and even if I were, this is far too important for some petty piece of jealousy.'

'I'm sorry. I didn't mean that. But you're making a mountain out of a molehill, because there really isn't—'

'Please!' Surprised by the raw urgency in Lally's face, Diana took a step backwards.

'You don't know.'

'Know what?'

'Julia Vigo—that was the woman's name—she didn't commit suicide. She was killed.'

'Oh, nonsense.' Diana tried a laugh, but it was shaky. 'Honestly, Lally, if you're trying to put me off Claude—not that you need to bother—you'll have to come up with something better than that.'

'It's the truth.'

Diana sat down. 'How do you know?'

'I overheard part of a conversation between Claude and F-J.'

'F-J?'

'Yes. I didn't realise what it was about at first, but then I put two and two together, and...'

'Why on earth would F-J want to kill her? Or Claude, for that matter? It doesn't make sense.'

'That's why I didn't realise. They were talking about her, and F-J said, "I'm afraid your Mrs Vigo will have to go."'

'He probably just meant dismissal. If she was...unreliable, or something.'

'But then Claude said, "I'll see to it." If she was going to be dismissed, F-J would do it himself.'

'But if he said "your Mrs Vigo" perhaps she was reporting to Claude, so surely he'd be the person to do it.'

Lally shook her head. 'That's not how it works.'

'All right, but why kill her?'

'I don't know. Perhaps she was a double agent—working for them, I mean.'

'But surely...' Diana stopped. If Claude was telling the truth about Julia Vigo being a drug addict, she'd be a target for blackmail, or—if the drugs she craved were expensive—she might have been given them in exchange for information. Either was possible, and if either were the case, then silencing her might well be the only option. Presumably, an injection of drugs—obtained from the very-useful-on-certain-occasions Dr Pyke—would do the trick if it were strong enough. And if Claude had been lying and Julia wasn't a drug addict at all, it would have been equally simple to make up that story afterwards...Could he really have done it? Bewildered, Diana thought back to their conversation. No, she told herself. I believed him. He was telling the truth.

'What is it?' Lally was staring at her.

'It's impossible to believe. Claude was having an affair with her—you said yourself that he was pursuing her.' It struck her, then, for the first time, that Claude had expressed no remorse over the woman's death. Judging from his behaviour, it seemed not to have affected him at all. 'It seems so unnatural,' she concluded, with a helpless gesture. 'It's not normal.'

'None of this is normal. Having this conversation isn't normal. Everything we've always taken for granted—rules and values—is changing in front of our eyes. Black, white, right, wrong—they don't mean the same any more. Surely you understand that?'

'Yes, but...'

'You cannot afford to be naïve about this, Diana. Claude may be fond of women, but he doesn't take them seriously. You must have realised that by now.'

'I suppose I have.' Diana put her head in her hands. 'This is...It's...I'm so confused, Lally. I don't know what to think. I just want to go home. Would you mind telling the others? Say I've got a headache or something—apologise.'

'Would you like me to come with you?'

Diana stood up. 'No need. I'll take the bus. It's still early. I just...I'd like to be by myself.'

Lally looked at her doubtfully. 'You will be careful, won't you?'

'I promise.'

'Very well.' Lally embraced her. The look in her eyes was so heartfelt, and the gesture so very unexpected, that it made Diana want to cry. 'I know it's not easy, darling,' she murmured, 'but you must be strong.'

Diana stood on the crowded bus in a daze, scarcely registering where she was going. Was it possible that Claude had killed Julia

Vigo? Obviously, if he had, he could never discuss such a thing with her...And she couldn't ask him about it, either. Bringing Lally's name into it would get her friend into trouble—or worse...But if Claude had killed Julia Vigo, it wasn't because he was wicked, but because it was his job. She'd heard things about people disappearing, but never anyone she knew, and never more than the vaguest rumours. Surely, Lally had misunderstood what she'd heard? Really, it was no better than the dotty old ladies she visited with imaginary Germans under their beds. But what she'd said about right and wrong not being the same any more certainly rang true. And as for F-J's words at Bletchley Park: 'The consequences can be disastrous, even fatal...'

Diana dug her nails into her palms, remembering the vertiginous feeling she'd had when Claude walked into the 400, how she'd looked across the room and seen only him, as if he was lit by a sort of halo. He is like an addiction, she thought. A drug. She'd had two notes from him since her return from Bletchley Park and ignored them both, but managing not to think about him for more than five consecutive minutes was little short of a miracle. At least he hadn't had the temerity to telephone her at work, and the line at Tite Street had barely functioned since the bombing started. But I am in love with him, she thought. I can't help it.

There was no point in going round and round in circles, she told herself: I must never see him again. Ever. Following the beam of her torch along the Chelsea Embankment, her footsteps seemed to sound the words 'Never, ever, never, ever,' on the pavement. She turned the corner of Tite Street, desperate to get home, to sleep, to forget, 'Never, ever,' she muttered to herself. 'Never, ever, never, ev—' Yards away from her house, she was brought up short by the sight of a slim, elegant form leaning against the railings: Claude.

She stopped, her whole body buzzing as if she'd been wired to an electric socket. For a second, she considered running away, but the street was dangerously dark and besides, her limbs seemed to have turned to water. Before she had a chance to collect herself, Claude was coming towards her, and a moment later his arms were round her and he was kissing her on the mouth.

For a moment she was stupefied by the treachery of her body's reaction to his, then she pushed him hard, so that he staggered backwards. 'Stop it!'

'Not here, you mean?'

'Not anywhere. What do you think you're doing?'

'You know damn well what I'm doing. And I'm going to go on doing it.'

'No, you're not.'

'I think you'll find, darling,' Claude grabbed her arm, 'that I am.'

'Leave me alone!' Diana tried to push him away, but this time he was ready for her, and, shoving her against the railings, kissed her again.

'You disappoint me, Diana,' he whispered. 'You shouldn't let people frighten you so easily.'

'I'm not frightened!'

'Then why are you shaking?'

'I just don't want...'

His hand felt beneath her coat for her breast. 'You're lying,' he said, in a sing-song voice. 'If you want to have your cake and eat it, I don't mind. You're frightened, and you like being frightened, my angel. It excites you. You do want to. I know you do.'

There was too much truth in this for Diana to deny it, and she was appalled that he'd perceived it so clearly. 'All right,' she said, furiously. 'I do. But that doesn't mean I'm going to.'

'Oh, yes it does. Right here in the street, or upstairs.' His hand moved down between her legs. 'It's your choice.'

'Go away!' She beat at him with her bag, and he caught her hands and forced them to her sides, holding them there and laughing at her.

'Come on.' He began towing her towards the house. I must not allow this to happen, she thought, frantically. Never, ever. It's too dangerous. I *must* stop him—slap him or something, but I must not give in to him. Or to myself. She could hear all these things clearly in her mind, but suddenly it was as if someone else was speaking, far way. She wanted him so much...Helplessly she let herself be pulled up the front steps. Claude held her round the waist as she fumbled in her handbag for her latchkey, and she felt him caress her back and buttocks through her clothes as she opened the front door. 'Stop it,' she whispered, desperately, 'Someone will see.'

'Then hurry up.' Claude pushed her inside and, closing the front door behind him, half-dragged and half-carried her, unprotesting now, up the stairs to her flat.

CHAPTER
44

'Come!'

Stratton entered DCI Machin's office with a heavy heart. What had he done now? He'd charged Wallace as instructed, and received a mouthful of abuse. He hadn't asked Sir Neville any more awkward questions, but then again he was no nearer to identifying the body in the church. Presumably, he thought, it's just going to be a run-of-the-mill bollocking to keep me in line until Lamb gets back. All the same, he could have done without it.

Machin looked, if possible, even more uncomfortable than the last time Stratton had seen him. 'You're to report immediately to Colonel Forbes-James at Dolphin Square.'

Stratton thought afterwards that he wouldn't have been any more astonished if Machin had jumped up and kissed him. As it was, he just managed to splutter, 'Yes, sir,' before collecting himself enough to add, 'May I ask why, sir?'

'You'll be informed when you get there. DI Jones has been told to deal with anything that comes up in your absence.' Jones was going to love that; Stratton made a mental note to apologise to him the first chance he got. 'There's a car outside.'

'A car?' echoed Stratton.

'Yes,' said Machin impatiently. 'You'd better look sharp. Don't want to keep them waiting.'

Descending the steps, Stratton was surprised to see a FANY driver with stout calves who looked like a compressed (and consequently far less attractive) version of Policewoman Gaines, holding open the rear door of a dark Bentley. 'Good morning, sir.' She saluted smartly. 'Legge-Brock, sir. I'm to take you to Dolphin Square.'

The big car looked, felt and smelled more luxurious than anything Stratton had ever been in before. He stopped wondering what the hell was going on, in order to enjoy the feeling of riding in such a magnificent vehicle. He'd never been able to afford to run a car, much less one like this, but...perhaps I should learn to drive, he thought. Maybe, when the war was over—provided, of course that they weren't bombed to buggery and annihilated as a nation and all the rest of the stuff that didn't bear thinking about. But he might rather enjoy driving—certainly Stumpy-Leggy, or whatever her name was, was doing a grand job. Perhaps he and Donald could club together and get a small car. Easing himself back on the expensive leather, he closed his eyes and sniffed appreciatively.

A few minutes later, the car came to a halt outside the entrance to Dolphin Square. Stumpy leapt out of her seat, opened the rear door, and let him out, saluting again. 'Flat 19, sir,' she said. 'Nelson House. Second block on your left, sir.'

'Thank you,' said Stratton.

A different glacial blonde beauty (was there a factory somewhere?) answered the door and ushered him into Colonel Forbes-James's office. Stratton, who had been expecting boarded up fireplaces, khaki-drab and military precision, was relieved to see a room with a distinctly civilian air, which was almost as chaotic as his and Jones's office. He'd expected to be kept waiting again, but Forbes-

James was seated behind his desk, and actually looked at him, as opposed to just waving a hand in his general direction. He had a round, slightly squashed-looking face, with large bright eyes, and no neck to speak of, and his general appearance was neat—no, thought Stratton, not neat, dapper. That was the word.

'Thank you for coming at such short notice, Inspector. Do have a seat—if you can find one, that is. Bloody awful mess in here.' Forbes-James put a cigarette in his mouth and, bending his head, started peering under various piles of paper. Stratton, who had sat down after removing a stack of documents from the nearest chair, got up again to offer him a light.

'Thank you. Have one yourself—there's a box on the mantelpiece. Tea?'

'If it's no trouble, sir.'

'Of course not.' Forbes-James went to the door and gave instructions to the telephonist outside. A few minutes later, after a bit of general stuff about Great Marlborough Street—he seemed to know all about the bombing of West End Central—the woman called Diana, looking every bit as lovely, haughty and unassailable as Stratton remembered, came in with a tray. She was introduced as Mrs Calthrop (married then, but not, he thought, to the man she'd left Sir Neville's flat to have lunch with, which was interesting). As she leant over to hand him his tea, Stratton caught a whiff of scent, an expensive smell like the car. He expected her to leave the room after that but, to his surprise, she cleared some files from one end of the sofa and sat down.

'Well,' said Forbes-James, 'now we're all here, I'd better fill you in. This is, of course, of a highly confidential nature, and covered by the Official Secrets Act, so it is not to be repeated. Your boss at Great Marlborough Street has been told that he is handing you over for such time as we need you, and you are not, until further notice, to discuss your work with him or anyone else. Is that clear?'

'Yes, sir.'

'Good. The situation is this...'

Stratton listened with mounting astonishment as he was given a rundown of Diana Calthrop's infiltration of the Right

Club, the decoding of the message she'd found in Sir Neville's flat, and the involvement of Walter Wymark in purloining encrypted telegrams from the American Embassy. 'Wymark's a cipher clerk,' said Forbes-James. 'That's more important than it sounds—he's one of those responsible for coding and de-coding sensitive material as it enters and leaves the Embassy. We've got some background on him somewhere.' He rooted around on his desk for a few seconds before gesturing to Diana to come and sift through the muddle for the relevant information. 'We think he's motivated by isolationist sympathies. It's possible that he might have been working for the Soviets, but we shan't know until we've had a chance to question him. According to what we've learnt, he hates Communists—which may or may not be true—and he hates Jews. To be honest, we're not entirely sure how he received security clearance. There might have been some influence from elsewhere, but...' Forbes-James shrugged. 'These things happen sometimes. The American Embassy has agreed to waive his diplomatic immunity, and we're planning to arrest him at his flat this evening. You will be present. Any documents we may find will, of course, be confiscated and examined.

'Now—' he proffered the folder that Diana had handed to him. 'Is that clear?'

'Yes, sir,' said Stratton, taking the notes. On top of the pile was a photograph of a well-built, fair man, with the sort of heroic, athletic stance (head up, shoulders back, keen-eyed stare and so forth) that Stratton associated with pictures of sportsmen on ciga-rette cards.

'That's him,' said Forbes-James. 'Any questions?'

'Why me, sir? Why not Special Branch?'

'I suspect you already have some idea of the answer to that.'

'I assume that it's to do with Sir Neville Apse, sir.'

'Precisely. Diana,' said Forbes-James, turning to Mrs Calthrop, who had resumed her place on the sofa, 'perhaps you should leave us.'

'Yes, sir.' As she stood up, smoothing her skirt, and left, Stratton took a surreptitious look at her legs and decided that she could definitely give Betty Grable a run for her money. 'I thought,' said Forbes-James, as the door closed, 'that it would be easier if Mrs Calthrop were not present.'

'Yes, sir. Thank you.'

'I've had some information about your activities from Scotland Yard—who, as you probably know, are none too happy—but I'd like to hear it from the horse's mouth.'

Stratton swallowed. He had the distinct sensation of waters closing over his head. We're on the same side, he told himself. His Majesty's government, the common good...But the power of men like Forbes-James was more far-reaching than that of his superiors, especially now that, like an idiot, he'd blundered into something far beyond his ken. He tried to combat visions of arranged accidents (shot in mistake for German spy, run over by car in blackout) with the fact that he'd done nothing wrong—or rather, nothing really wrong, not in the grand scheme of things. But that, of course, might not be good enough—knowledge might be power, but it was also bloody dangerous. Was what he'd discovered about to blow up in his face?

As if reading his mind, Forbes-James leant forward and said, 'You can trust me, you know. We understand you've been doing some digging on your own account, and we thought we might as well put you to good use.'

Stratton had half a mind to ask who 'we' were, but decided it would be pointless. Here, 'we' meant people in power, who could do things—people more commonly known to him and his ilk as 'they'. Still, no suggestion of any kind of threat—yet.

'So,' said Forbes-James, 'tell me what's been going on.'

'Well, sir,' said Stratton, 'I don't know if you've ever heard of a film actress called Mabel Morgan...'

Forbes-James listened attentively while he talked. When Stratton had finished, he said, 'I see. And that's everything, is it?'

'Yes, sir. I gave the deed box containing the films to DCI Machin, at his request.'

'Mmm. And you didn't recognise the dancing partner?'

'No, sir.'

'Neither did we, unfortunately.'

'You mean you've seen the films?' asked Stratton in surprise. 'I mean, sir, they haven't been destroyed?'

Forbes-James shook his head. 'We're holding onto them,' he said, 'for the moment, at least. Does anyone, besides DCI Machin and your brother-in-law, Donald…'

'Kerr, sir.'

'…Donald Kerr, know of their existence?'

'My wife, sir. Or rather, she knows that we were watching some of Miss Morgan's films, but she has no idea what they were.'

'And Mr Kerr, what does he know?'

'Nothing, sir. I didn't mention Sir Neville's name.'

'Can you write down Mr Kerr's address for me—his home and his business.'

'Yes, sir.' Stratton jotted down the details in his notebook and tore out the page to hand to Forbes-James.

'It's just a background check, you understand. We shan't be questioning him—unless it's necessary, of course.'

'It won't be, sir.'

'That's good. What about the man who gave you the box?'

'Constable Ballard, sir. He has no idea what was in it. I broke the padlock myself, at home. He knew I'd been making some enquiries, and he thought it might be of use.'

'Well, that all seems pretty straightforward. We'll need copies of all your notes—Mrs Calthrop can see to that while we have a spot of lunch. There's a little place near here that's not bad at all.'

Stratton, having marked the relevant pages of his notebook for Diana's attention, accompanied Forbes-James to the restaurant. Uneasy in the unfamiliar surroundings, which were a good deal smarter than he was used to, with a waiter whose French accent would have put Maurice Chevalier to shame, he chose Dover Sole as being the simplest (and most recognisable) item on the menu. It turned out to be very good, although it would have been a lot nicer if he had been eating it with Jenny, and not Forbes-James who was gently but persistently questioning him about his background, family and work. He said little about Johnny other than that he'd been rejected for the services and was a bit of a tearaway, and hoped he'd delivered this information in the same matter-of-fact tone as everything else. Forbes-James paid close attention, occasionally prompting him with questions. The man must have a formidable memory, Stratton thought, because he hadn't taken a single note—unless, of course, he was equipped with some sort of listening device. Stratton had never heard of such a thing—rooms could be wired, of course, and telephones, but he'd never heard of anything small enough to be carried by a person.

Alone in the Gents, he took a moment to compose himself. Of course Forbes-James didn't have a listening device. Such things did not exist. All this cloak-and-dagger stuff was making him neurotic and, in any case, someone must surely have looked into his background a bit before they'd summoned him over? He couldn't pretend he wasn't excited about the prospect of the raid on the American chap's home, but all the same...One step out of line, and they'd have his balls in the wringer before you could say Jack Robinson, and then he could say goodbye to his career all right. Watch it, chum, he told himself. Just bloody watch out.

'Blast!' Diana yanked the paper out of the typewriter for the third time. Hopeless. Damn F-J, he knew she was no good at typing. Glancing at the clock, she saw that he and the policeman, Stratton, would soon be back from their lunch. Grabbing another piece of paper, she started feeding it into the machine, then remembered she'd forgotten the carbon. She wished she could ask Margot to help, but the stuff was confidential. She had read through Inspector Stratton's notes with mounting astonishment, especially when she'd come to the bit about Apse's handkerchief being found on an unknown corpse...That had been the real reason for Stratton's visit to him. Apse had denied all knowledge, but evidently he hadn't been believed. But could he really be associated with criminals, as the notes seemed to suggest? Thieves and murderers? She tried to imagine what these men—Marks and Wallace—might look like, but her mind could only conjure up a pair of large, hairy brutes with guns in one hand and bags marked 'Swag' in the other.

She re-aligned the paper and carbon and began again, wishing her hands weren't shaking so much. For heaven's sake, she told herself, get a grip. You're not going to be at Wymark's flat. Of course it would blow her cover as far as the Right Club was concerned, but she'd served her purpose, hadn't she? F-J was planning—indeed, had been given permission—to round up everyone concerned, so she'd be quite safe, apart from the fact, always in the back of her mind, of what she'd told Claude...He'd said he wouldn't tell anyone about Apse, but was it true?

Stop it, she said to herself. It was no good thinking about what *might* happen when she needed to get on with the task in hand. In any case, it wasn't as if she'd even have to see anyone from the Right Club again, except in court. Lally had got hold of the necessary information about Wymark, and she'd been instructed to give Mrs Montague a false address (a flat belonging to a fellow agent) for any post, so none of them—apart from Apse—knew where she lived. But he could tell them...

Casting around for a way to steady her nerves, she fixed on DI Stratton. She had not really noticed, when he came to see Apse, how big he was (but then she hadn't noticed much that morning, she'd been too busy thinking about having lunch with Claude). There was something solid about him, solid and comforting and all together right in a way she couldn't quite explain but which was very reassuring. He didn't seem like an ordinary policeman, but then, Diana reflected, she did not really know what ordinary policemen were like because she'd never met one—at least, not properly.

F-J hadn't been pleased when he'd discovered that Stratton had been digging about and found a film of Apse dancing with another man. He hadn't said much to her all week, deflecting any questions with a weary, preoccupied air. Surely, she thought for the umpteenth time, he must have had some suspicions about Apse? She supposed that her information had meant that he could no longer have it both ways—like pretending you thought someone was joking even though they weren't. Or sincere when you knew they weren't...Was Claude sincere when he said he loved her? Did he even know if he was being sincere or not? And now she really had broken her promise to F-J.

'Damn!' She'd typed a 'v' instead of a 'b'. That was—she counted—the fifth mistake in two lines. Telling herself to concentrate and not think of anything else until the thing was finished, she managed to peck out the rest of the page correctly and then, half way through the next one, found herself typing 'mp=pmr pg yjsy ms,r' instead of 'no-one of that name' because she'd been wondering whether Inspector Stratton was married and, if so, what his wife might be like. Big and solid like him, probably. Perhaps they had children...he looked as though he'd be a good father...As she put a line of x's through her mistake, she pictured him in a big old armchair with a small daughter on his knee. The only knees she'd ever sat on as a child were the bony protuberances of a succession of nannies, which was fine as far as it went but hardly the same as the comfort and security of a constant lap. She tried to imagine herself, a child again, sitting on her father's knee, but this, as far as she could remember, had only happened once, and then only for the duration of a photograph.

These musings were interrupted by the slam of the front door. Hell! They were back from lunch, and she hadn't finished. Determined that they shouldn't think her inefficient, she set about typing as fast as she could. Fortunately, F-J didn't call for her for another hour, by which time she had done almost all of it. When she'd handed him the copies and returned the notebook to Inspector Stratton, F-J told her she could go home, even though it was only quarter past four. She'd half expected this, but still felt downcast and rejected, as if she'd been dragged away from a party before the fun had really started. In spite of having no conscious desire to have anything to do with the raid on Walter Wymark's flat, she walked back to Tite Street knowing that she'd be too restless to settle to anything, and that the evening would be a time to get through, rather than enjoy.

Sitting alone in her bedroom, she picked up Guy's letter of the previous week. He was planning to come down to London for a couple of days before the regiment went overseas, and was—surely this couldn't be as ominous as it sounded—*looking forward to hearing what you've been up to*. She'd tried to put him off—*the flat is simply too tiny*—but he'd written back to say that he would be staying at his club—which, she supposed, must still be possible, because she'd heard nothing to the contrary.

There was another problem, too. Her doctor, who'd bent the rules for her once already, by giving her a contraceptive device without her husband's permission, was not likely to be so accommodating a second time.

It was overwhelming, and she was far too tired to think about any of it. The best way was to shut it out, to try and get some proper rest—at least until the raids started. She poured herself a small whisky—bad habit, drinking on one's own, but never mind—and curled up on the bed, cradling the glass.

CHAPTER
46

No-one spoke as the Bentley, the thin beams from its shuttered headlamps barely penetrating the blackout, nosed its way north past Hyde Park towards Walter Wymark's flat in Gloucester Place, tailed by a Black Maria. There were muffled bangs and crumps from raids in the distance, but nothing too close. Stratton sat between Forbes-James and a man from the American Embassy called Ritter, who sat, shoulders hunched, twisting a ring on his little finger.

Stratton and Forbes-James led the way to Wymark's flat, which was on the third floor of a large mansion block, with three constables in tow and Ritter and a policewoman bringing up the rear. The men lined up in the passage, truncheons at the ready, as Forbes-James knocked. There was no response. Forbes-James knocked again, and this time, there was a shout—'Go away!' When he knocked a third time, the voice—male—called out again, 'I told you, I'm busy. Come back later!'

'Police!' shouted Stratton. 'Open the door.'

'No!' The voice was louder now. 'You can't come in here!'

'Open the door, Mr Wymark.'

'No! I'm protected—you can't come in.'

'Mr Wymark, if you don't open this door, I'll have to—'

'No! Go away!'

Stratton looked at Forbes-James, who nodded. The last time Stratton had broken a door down his shoulder had ached like hell for a week afterwards, and he was buggered if he was going to let that happen again in a hurry. He beckoned to the largest of the constables. 'Off you go, lad.'

The man charged and burst the door open. A woman screamed shrilly, and, over the din of policemen's boots on the tiled floor of the hallway, Stratton heard a man's voice—'Shut up!'—and the crack of a slap, followed by the sound of a window being raised somewhere towards the rear of the flat. Barging past the constables, he dashed down the long central corridor, Forbes-James at his heels, and charged into the end room. Wymark, barefoot with pyjamas flapping, was straddling the window-ledge, and in the bed a dishevelled girl, blankets pulled up to her chin, was sobbing, a livid red wheal across one side of her face.

Stratton marched across the room and grabbed Wymark by the arm. The man tried to shrug him off, lost his balance and nearly fell out of the window. Stratton leant over and hauled him back inside. 'I wouldn't if I were you,' he said. 'It's a hell of a long way down.'

Wymark, sprawled on the floor, did not reply. Stratton had expected argument, protestation, even threats, but the man simply shook his head, as if disgusted by the whole business. Behind them, the girl in the bed began to howl wordlessly, like a trapped animal. 'Come on.' Seeing that the fight had gone out of Wymark, Stratton took hold of his elbow and pulled him to his feet. 'Let's go somewhere we can talk.' He put a hand on the man's back and propelled him into the corridor, where he stood passively and allowed two of the constables to button up his pyjama jacket and hand-cuff him before letting them march him away, head down, to the waiting van.

Stratton ushered the policewoman into the bedroom, with instructions to calm the girl down, and went through to the flat's small sitting room, where various pieces of male and female clothing discarded on the floor, or draped over items of furniture, marked the progress of Wymark and his paramour towards the bed. He called in the remaining constable and said, 'You'd better pick up this lot and take it to the bedroom.'

Scarlet-faced, the young man cleared his throat, 'You don't want me to go in there, Sir?'

'Of course not! Just tap on the door and leave them outside. And let me know when she's dressed.'

'Yes, sir.' Relieved, the man's voice was several tones lower. As Stratton turned away to hide his grin, Forbes-James appeared from the bedroom. 'We need to search the whole place.'

'Shouldn't take too long, sir.' The flat had an impersonal look about it, with tasteful modern furniture and few ornaments, and was, scattered clothing excepted, extremely tidy. Stratton watched as the constable picked up the remaining item of clothing—a brassiere—and, holding it out in front of him with his fingertips as if afraid it might burst into flames at any moment, left the room. 'You start in here,' said Forbes-James. 'I'll take the kitchen. We'll do the bedroom when we've dealt with the girl.'

The search, which was easy enough, was accompanied by hysterical shrieks from the bedroom, and the soothing tones of the policewoman, who was evidently having some difficulty coaxing the girl into her clothes. Stratton, having found nothing in the sitting room, went to find Forbes-James in the tiny kitchen. 'Nothing, sir.'

'Nor me. Must be in the bedroom.'

The young constable put his head round the door, 'She's ready, sir.'

'Right.'

The girl, pallid, tousled and tear-stained, was waiting in the corridor, the policewoman's arm around her shoulders. 'Please,' she said, 'let me go.'

'Sorry,' said Stratton. 'What's your name, miss?'

'The Honourable Helen Pender,' said the girl, with an attempt at dignity. 'My father is Lord Calne. You'll let me go now, won't you?'

'No, miss.'

'Please...' turning to Forbes-James, who clearly struck her as someone of the right sort, she said, 'Tell him to let me go.'

'Impossible, I'm afraid,' said Forbes-James.

'But my father—'

'Is Lord Calne,' finished Forbes-James, calmly. 'Nevertheless, we need to ask you some questions.'

'You can't arrest me!'

'We're not arresting you,' said Stratton. 'At least, not for the moment. Now, why don't you go in here'—he indicated the sitting room—'and sit down quietly.' Glaring at him through her tears, the girl consented to be led away. Forbes-James waited until the policewoman had closed the door, then beckoned Stratton into the bedroom.

'Did you know about her?' Stratton asked.

'We had an idea.' Forbes-James opened the door of the wardrobe and began lifting up piles of shirts and underwear. After a few seconds of this he said, 'Here we are,' and held up a leather briefcase. 'You might as well check the rest of the room,' he told Stratton, 'but I'm pretty sure it's all here. And not even locked.'

As Stratton pulled open the rest of the drawers, Forbes-James undid the clasps of the briefcase and slid the contents—a thick wad of papers—onto the bed. 'Must be over a hundred documents there,' said Stratton, appreciatively.

'At least. And,' Forbes-James thrust a hand into the bottom of the briefcase and produced a pair of keys, 'these. Duplicates, by the look of it.' He compared the edges. 'Same lock. And,' he fished in an inside pocket and pulled out a single sheet of paper, covered on both sides in handwriting, 'this.'

'What is it, sir?'

'It looks like a list of the Right Club members. Very useful.' He pocketed the paper and gave the keys to Stratton. 'Take these to Mr Ritter, would you? I imagine they're for the embassy code room.'

'Yes, sir.' Stratton went to find Ritter who was standing outside the door of the flat like a guardsman, but still, Stratton noticed, twisting the ring on his little finger. When he returned to the bedroom Forbes-James was shovelling the papers back inside the briefcase.

'Right,' he said. 'We can go.'

'What about the girl, sir?'

'I don't imagine she knows about this lot,' Forbes-James tapped the briefcase, 'but we'll have to make sure. I'm afraid you will have to arrest her. Regulation 18B. I'm sure you know the drill.'

Stratton, who had feared that this might be the case and who did know the drill, nodded glumly. More hysterics. 'Is the van still downstairs?' he asked.

Forbes-James shook his head. 'They've gone to Brixton. She'll have to come with us. You can drop her directly at Holloway—I'll let them know—and then the car can take you home.'

'That's very kind of you, sir.'

'Not at all.' Forbes-James smiled. 'Long day—and there'll be another tomorrow.'

CHAPTER
47

Jenny stood on the path and watched as the bulky shape of the car disappeared into the darkness. 'I've been so worried, Ted. And when I heard a car, and it stopped outside, I thought...'

'I know, love.' Stratton hugged her. 'It's all right, I'm here now.'

'Did you really come all the way home in that?'

'Yes. Aren't you impressed?'

'It was enormous! I couldn't think what it was doing here. When I heard it, I thought something terrible must have happened.'

'Well, it hasn't. Come on, you've left the door wide open. We'd better get inside before the warden rolls up and fines us for showing a light.'

They stumbled down the path, arm in arm, and went inside. 'Your dinner's all dried up,' said Jenny, 'but I can make you a sandwich. There's a bit of cheese left.'

'Don't worry, love. I'm too tired.'

'You must have some food, Ted.'

'I'm fine. I had Dover Sole for lunch.' Which, thought Stratton, felt like a very long time ago, to his brain if not to his stomach.

'Did you go to a restaurant?'

'Yes.'

'Why?'

'I can't talk about it, love.'

'But you can tell me about the food, can't you?'

'I suppose so. It was a very smart place. French waiters. We've still got a bit of that Scotch from last Christmas, haven't we? I wouldn't mind a spot of that. Put it in a mug and I'll take it out to the Anderson with me.'

Stratton lit a cigarette and waited on the back lawn for Jenny to come down from the bedroom. He stood in the darkness, sipping his Scotch and enjoying the warm sensation as it went down, although he wasn't that keen on the taste—not that he'd ever drunk any really good Scotch, not like the sort of stuff Colonel Forbes-James would have. Presumably, he must have felt Stratton had done all right or he wouldn't have offered the ride home. Stratton was surprised at how much this pleased him. There was definitely something about the man that made you want his approval. He wondered if Diana Calthrop felt like that, too.

Jenny shut the back door and joined him. 'It's all on the other side of London tonight, thank goodness. Let's hope they don't come this way.'

'It'd take more than the Luftwaffe to keep me awake tonight. Let's go in, shall we?'

As they readied themselves for bed, moving round each other in the narrow space down the middle of the Anderson, Jenny said, 'I do wish we had a telephone, Ted.'

'I know, love. It can't be helped. But even if we did, you can't always get through.'

'But if you did, then at least I'd know you were all right. It's horrible waiting and not knowing.'

Stratton bent over and kissed the top of her head. 'I'm sorry.'

'And you haven't told me about your lovely meal. Did you have a sweet?'

They chatted for a bit before Jenny fell asleep, but Stratton, who thought he'd be out like a light as soon as his head touched the pillow, found himself taking stock of the day's events. Hell of a turn-up for the books, being summoned like that. Colonel Forbes-James had clearly decided that he was more use working with them than blundering around on his own. Stratton wondered what DCI Machin and SDI Roper had had to say about it, and what Lamb would say when he came back. Good riddance, probably. When he returned to Great Marlborough Street—or to West End Central, assuming it was habitable—Lamb would take a great deal of pleasure in making sure he hadn't got too big for his boots working for MI5. Because that's who Forbes-James was, he was sure of it. The man hadn't said as much, just War Office, but he had to be.

The Honourable Helen Pender had been stunned when he'd unloaded her at Holloway, and Stratton couldn't blame her. All those brasses yelling their heads off, then the wardress had kept her in reception, in a tiny cubicle the size of a toilet, for over an hour. He had asked if the prison doctor could give her something to calm her, but he didn't suppose the woman would pass on his request. He hoped the doctor would be more sympathetic. It was pure spite on the part of the wardress because of who the Honourable Helen was and what she was in for. Stratton knew the girl would be horrified when she saw the filthy cells, with their lumpy mattresses and canvas sheets, and the air permeated with the stench of unemptied chamber pots—not to mention the appalling food, and the shock and helplessness at being locked in. Still, being held under Regulation 18B meant that she'd be able to wear her own clothes and receive parcels, and at least Holloway wasn't verminous, which was more than could be said for Brixton, which was where Wymark had been taken. Stratton sighed. He felt sorry for the girl because she was young, stupid and, in his opinion, had simply been in the wrong place at the wrong time. And Wymark had been all set to scarper and leave her to face the music, although he couldn't have hoped to get far in pyjamas and bare feet. Idiot, Stratton thought, trying to make himself comfortable on the narrow bunk. He must try to get some sleep. As Forbes-James had said, long day tomorrow...

CHAPTER 48

'Are you all right, Mrs Calthrop?' asked Stratton.

'I'm sorry.' Diana leant against the outer wall of the prison. Her face was pale, and, as she reached for the cigarette he offered, he saw that her hand shook. As they huddled together to shield the match from the November wind, she said, 'I've never been inside a prison before. It was rather a shock, that's all. And Helen's reaction—although I suppose I should have been prepared for that.'

Stratton, who'd been astonished at Forbes-James's insistence that Diana accompany him to Holloway to question Helen Pender, and frankly shocked that the Honorable Helen, such a well-brought up girl, knew so many filthy words, said, 'You mustn't take any notice of that. You were doing your job.'

'Sticks and stones, I suppose.' The laugh was weak, but it was a start. She's a tough one, Stratton thought. Tough as well as striking, standing there on those long legs with her hair, loosened from its pins where the hysterical Helen had made a grab for it, blowing round her face. 'You must get a lot of that sort of thing in your work.'

'Quite a bit,' he replied, surprised that she should think of him when she was obviously upset.

Diana picked a shred of tobacco off her lip, contemplated it for a moment, then said, 'Do you like being a policeman?'

Nonplussed, Stratton said, 'I suppose so. It's my job.'

'Are you glad you chose it? I mean, you wouldn't rather be doing some other kind of work?'

'Bit late for that now if I did. But it's all right. Good and bad, same as any job.' He knew this wasn't an adequate answer to her question, but couldn't think what else to say. He wanted to say something to comfort or at least engage her, to try and draw her thoughts away from the memory of the almost deranged girl who had snarled and spat and made incoherent threats, but he didn't know how to do it.

'I've led a jolly sheltered life,' said Diana. 'I suppose lots of people have, but the war's changed all that, hasn't it?'

About bloody time, thought Stratton, but aloud he said, 'Things are changing. They have to, you know.'

'Yes, they do,' she said, with a vehemence that surprised him. As they stood smoking in silence, he wondered what someone like her could possibly know about things needing to change. He thought of all the crumbling houses he'd been in, with fungus on the walls and shared toilets that flooded and stank, whose inhabitants existed on bread and margarine. What could she know about that? She probably had no idea such places even existed. Perhaps she was talking about something else.

Glancing in the direction of the prison gates, she said, 'They're bringing Mrs Montague in later.'

'Who's she?'

'Peverell Montague's wife.'

'The MP who founded the Right Club?'

Diana nodded. 'He's kept his distance since Mosley was arrested—it's been mainly her. But he'll be arrested, too.'

'Do you know her?'

Diana nodded. 'I know most of them. The worst thing, you know, is not being able to talk about it. I know what you're thinking—women can't keep secrets or resist gossip—but I don't mean that. I mean talking about how...well, about what it feels like, when you're scared and you don't know what to do, or whether what you're doing is right.'

Disconcerted by this unexpected intimacy, Stratton looked away and, glancing down the road, was relieved to see the Bentley approaching. Stumpy (he must ask her to remind him what her name actually was) pulled up, then leapt out to open the back door. 'I've been given instructions to take you back to Dolphin Square,' she said in a bright, isn't-this-jolly sort of voice, 'then I'm off to Brixton prison for F-J.'

'Have you seen Apse today?' Diana asked her.

She shook her head. 'I'm to be solely at F-J's disposal. Margot passed the message on.' She closed the rear door and settled herself in the driver's seat. 'I mean,' she gave a little moue in the rear-view mirror, 'Miss Mentmore.'

On their return to Dolphin Square, Margot-I-mean-Miss-Mentmore provided sandwiches and a bottle of very nice wine (Stratton had a quick squint at the label and made out the word Claret against a background of fancy scrollwork). While they ate, Diana, acting on written instructions left by Forbes-James, filled him in about the other members of the Right Club. 'There may be more,' she finished. 'F-J said you'd found a list in Wymark's flat.'

'Yes,' he said, 'but I didn't see it.' Christ knows who's on that, he wondered. The people Diana was telling him about were bad enough. He stopped eating about halfway through his sandwiches, too shocked and astonished to continue. He supposed his reaction was naïve—after all, what little he'd seen in the police force had shown him that plenty of skulduggery went on in high places, but now they were at war, for God's sake. Of course, no-one in his right mind would actually want a war, but circumstances had changed. He shook his head, baffled. Such people must know more than he did—why couldn't they see what was under their noses, especially after two months of air-raids? Perhaps they were simply too stupid, or too self-centred, to comprehend that the world had changed. The idea made him angry, and he sought relief from his feelings by focussing his attention on a small painting of some blotchy flowers on the wall behind Forbes-James's desk.

'It's an Odilon Redon,' said Diana. 'Do you like it?'

'I'm not sure,' he replied cautiously. He supposed he was meant to be impressed by the name, but it meant nothing. 'I don't know much about pictures.'

He'd thought that would get him a superior smile, but Diana said 'Neither do I,' and then gesturing, pointed out a larger painting beside the door, which was half hidden behind a stack of papers on top of a filing cabinet added, 'But I do know that that one is by a painter called Henry Scott Tuke.'

Stratton, who hadn't noticed it before, was surprised to see a nude boy—or, to be strictly accurate—half a nude boy, rear view, standing in front of a pool in a forest clearing. He liked the way the kid had his head bent, and one hand on his hip, as if he was considering how cold the water might be before jumping in. It reminded him of swimming in rivers with other farmers' sons when he was young, although there certainly hadn't been any pederasts with easels lurking on the banks. Come to think of it, there was something a bit queer about the whole thing. 'It's quite...' Stratton had been going to say, 'daring' but, seeing that Diana was blushing he said 'interesting', instead. He wondered why she'd drawn his attention to the painting if it embarrassed her.

'I asked him about it once,' she said. 'It was a present from Apse.'

'Oh,' said Stratton. That explained the choice of subject, although not why Forbes-James had chosen to display the thing, or why Sir Neville had given it to him in the first place.

He stared at the painting while Diana busied herself replacing the cork in the wine bottle and removing the plates. At least the boy looked like someone real, not like all those Renaissance women he'd seen in the National Gallery, who looked as if they'd had their tits whacked on with a ladle...'It's good,' said Stratton, when Diana returned from the kitchen with coffee. 'I like things that look like what they're meant to be.'

'So do I.' Diana set down the tray. 'Life's quite confusing enough as it is. Coffee?'

'Thank you.'

'What will happen to Helen, Inspector?'

Flattered that she thought he might know the answer to this, Stratton said he wasn't sure, but he didn't think it would be too serious.

'I think she was telling the truth this morning when she said she didn't know about the documents.'

Stratton nodded.

'So she hasn't really done anything, has she? Apart from being silly.' Diana appeared to be blushing again. Perhaps, thought Stratton, the idea of Helen in bed with Wymark shocked her. If so, it was prudishness of a type that didn't seem to fit with what he knew of her character, especially what he'd seen of her conduct towards the man who'd taken her out to lunch when he'd first met her, but he couldn't think of another explanation. He was about to agree that Helen Pender had been pretty silly, but not actually bad, when Forbes-James appeared.

'Successful morning?'

Diana took a step back, leaving the floor to Stratton. 'Miss Pender seems to be infatuated with Mr Wymark,' he said, 'but she says she had no idea he was stealing copies of documents. We questioned her all morning, sir, and she denies any knowledge.'

'Diana?'

'I agree, sir.'

'Good.'

'Have you had lunch?' asked Diana.

Forbes-James waved a hand. 'Later. Get me a drink, would you? Scotch will do.' He stuck a cigarette in his mouth and started shuffling papers on his overloaded desk. Stratton, recognising the beginnings of a fruitless search for a light, stepped forward with a match. Forbes-James inhaled deeply and when Diana placed his drink in front of him, sat back, contented. 'Sit down, sit down.' Obediently, they sat side by side on the sofa, and, as Diana smiled at him, Stratton found himself smiling in return.

'I've interviewed Wymark. He confirms what we thought—his interests are in keeping America out of the war. Came out with it straight away. Loyal servant of his country, acting in her best interests and so forth. Defiant. And he's refusing to say how he planned to get the documents across the Atlantic. Ritter, the chap from their embassy, says he doesn't have access to diplomatic channels, which may well be true. Unfortunately, we're not in a position to investigate—the Embassy is pretty browned off with us as well as with Wymark, and the last thing we need at the moment is an incident.' Forbes-James sighed. 'It seems likely, assuming it's true that Wymark doesn't have access via the American Embassy, that he was going to send the stuff through a neutral country. It's how these things have been done in the past. So, either he has a contact at another embassy, or...' He stopped and raised an eyebrow at Diana.

'Or it's Apse, sir.'

'Quite.' He looked at Stratton 'I think it's time that you and I had a chat with Sir Neville. A chat,' he repeated, pointedly. 'We're not going to arrest him unless he confesses.'

'But sir—'

Forbes-James held up a hand. 'We need more evidence. And allow me to do the talking. You're not to ask him anything unless I say so.'

Stratton opened his mouth to object, then closed it again.

'You stay here,' Forbes-James told Diana. 'Hold the fort.'

'Yes, sir.' She sounded, to Stratton, extremely relieved.

Forbes-James didn't speak as they went downstairs, but on the way across the garden to Frobisher House, he asked, 'How did Miss Pender react when she saw Mrs Calthrop?'

'She was extremely upset, sir, and angry. Called her a lot of names.'

'Genuine, would you say?'

'Yes, sir.'

'And how did Mrs Calthrop behave?'

'There wasn't much she could say because Miss Pender was shouting a great deal, and it took quite a while to calm her down. We had to send for the doctor. Mrs Calthrop was clearly shaken, but she didn't allow it to affect her—not outwardly, sir. Kept her cool.'

'I see. And how do you find her yourself?'

Stratton, surprised by the question, found he couldn't think of any reply that didn't contain words like gorgeous or knock-out.

'Apart from her looks, that is,' added Forbes-James, sounding amused. 'We'll take those as read.'

'She's very dedicated,' said Stratton, feeling foolish. 'Good at her job, I imagine.'

'Yes, she is, but she's vulnerable. Beautiful women always are.' They reached the front door of Frobisher House and Forbes-James paused. 'Before we go up, there's something I didn't mention. When Mrs Calthrop was copying the coded document she found in Apse's flat, he came back. Unexpectedly, of course. My fault, I'm afraid. He'd told me he was going to the country to visit his family, so I gave her permission to go to his flat in the evening. He arrived with a boy prostitute. Mrs Calthrop managed to hide and then make her escape, but—not to put too fine a point on it—she heard them in flagrante.'

'Blimey!' exclaimed Stratton. So, in pointing out the painting and telling him who the giver was, Diana had been trying to convey that she knew about Apse. No wonder she hadn't come straight out with it.

'Most unfortunate. I'm afraid it might have had rather a bad effect on her. One knows these things go on, but...' He shrugged. 'If only they'd be discreet.'

'I suppose he thought he was being discreet, sir.'

'Not by fouling his own doorstep. Makes the situation very difficult for all of us.' Forbes-James opened the door. 'Come on.'

Following Forbes-James down the hall, Stratton found that he didn't feel entirely sure whether 'all of us' referred to the

Secret Services, or to homosexuals in general. Obviously, Forbes-James had meant the former, but, remembering the painting of the naked boy, Stratton thought, surely he can't be one as well? And why ask him about Diana? He was only a copper, for God's sake—why should his opinion matter? Maybe he suspected her of something, too…Fucked if I know, he thought. I should stop getting carried away, it's just the way they all talk—makes you think everything has a double meaning. If I'd spent my life stabbing my old chums in the back for the greater good then I'd probably talk in riddles as well.

Suddenly, he wished himself back in his cluttered office at Great Marlborough Street. At least with the likes of Abie Marks you knew where you were. And they didn't make you feel stupid for not knowing about pictures and claret, either.

CHAPTER

49

$\mathbb{B}$y mutual agreement, Forbes-James and Stratton walked back to Nelson House without talking. The interview had been a waste of time. Apse had denied everything and claimed that Diana had secreted the coded message in his flat and then pretended to discover it. When they got back, Forbes-James dismissed both Diana and Margot, and they sat nursing large Scotches until the two women had left. Stratton had expected Forbes-James to launch into a review of their interview with Sir Neville, but instead, he put his elbows on his desk and leant forward. 'Well?'

'He's lying, sir. He's either pro-fascist, or he's being blackmailed by someone in the Right Club because he's a homosexual.'

'Very possibly. But we only have Mrs Calthrop's word for it that she found the document in his kitchen, and that she heard him with the boy.'

Stratton nearly choked on his drink—which was, as he'd suspected, far superior to the blended stuff he had at home—and said 'She couldn't have made that up, sir.'

'She wouldn't have made it up on her own, no.'

'You mean...'

'Her name was on Wymark's list of Right Club members,' said Forbes-James.

'But it would be, wouldn't it? You instructed her to infiltrate it.'

'Apse's name wasn't there. And that list, as far as we can tell, is comprehensive.'

'You didn't tell me that, sir,' said Stratton.

'No, I didn't. Perhaps I should have.'

Yes, thought Stratton, you fucking well should, if you want me to be any use. It might be the Secret Service way of working, but this whole business of telling people things at the last minute, or not telling them at all, was bloody unsettling.

'Apse said she made a number of pro-fascist comments while she was working for him.'

'But if she was trying to find out whether he...'

'Yes. But it is also possible that she might have planted that document. In fact, she didn't even need to do that—or to visit Apse's flat at all on that particular evening. As I said, we only have her word for it.'

'But if she was acting for the Right Club, what would be the point of incriminating Sir Neville? If it's blackmail, they could have put pressure on him. You've seen the film, sir.'

'Yes,' said Forbes-James, 'and so have you. But we don't know if anyone else has, do we? Diana's been spending a lot of time with members of the Right Club, and she has also been having an affair with one of my men—a double agent who arrived from Lisbon several months ago, briefed by the Abwehr, although she did begin the infiltration before she met him. And while this man has given me no reason to believe that he is anything but reliable, and Diana tells me she has broken off the liaison, one can't be absolutely certain about either of those things.'

So I was right, thought Stratton. The chap who took her out to lunch...

'As I mentioned earlier,' said Forbes-James, 'beautiful women are vulnerable.'

'But why would Mrs Calthrop tell you about a coded message in Sir Neville's flat? If she's acting for the Right Club, she'd know that the code could be broken and the whole thing could be traced back to Wymark. And if she's working in Germany's interests, surely that includes keeping America out of the war, and anything that would stop Mr Roosevelt from being re-elected would help that. It doesn't make sense.'

'You mean it doesn't seem to make sense,' said Forbes-James.

That's because I don't know what the fuck is going on, thought Stratton. 'What about Miss Pender this morning?' he asked.

'She may not have been aware of the situation.'

'But all the same...'

'The Right Club may have had other reasons for wanting to discredit Apse, and Diana may not have known how easily the code could be broken. Or—and this is entirely possible—she may have been given the wrong document by mistake.'

Stratton gaped at him.

'Believe me, such things have happened. It's quite astonishing how easily the best laid plan can turn into the most almighty cock-up,' said Forbes-James, blandly. 'Happens all the time, especially in war.'

'But if Mrs Calthrop is involved,' Stratton persisted, 'how would she have access to these neutral countries?'

'Through my double agent,' said Forbes-James. 'As I mentioned, his Abwehr contacts are in Lisbon. It's all a question,' he continued, 'of looking at things from every angle. It's unlikely, but not impossible. One mustn't take anything for granted.'

'Christ,' said Stratton.

'My sentiments exactly. More Scotch?'

'Thank you, sir. I feel as if I need it.'

They drank in silence for a moment, then Stratton said, 'May I ask something, sir?'

'Of course.'

'Why didn't you let me question Sir Neville about the body in the church?'

'He's already denied having anything to do with it.'

'But it was his handkerchief, sir. We made sure of it. It's all in my notes.'

'I know that, but there are ways of doing these things, and we need more information before we go any further. Softly, softly, and all that. Besides,' Forbes-James smiled, 'I could see you weren't particularly keen on him.'

'No,' he agreed. 'I wasn't.' Sir Neville's air of amusement—the mental shrug at the world in general and, Stratton felt, at him in particular, had rankled, as it had at their first meeting, but he hadn't realised he'd let it show. The all-too-visible chip on the shoulder: exactly what someone like Sir Neville—and Forbes-James and, when you came down to it, Diana Calthrop—would expect from a person of his class.

'You'll get your opportunity, I assure you,' said Forbes-James. 'But first, we need to go and talk to Peverell Montague. They'll have taken him in by now, and our driver will be waiting.'

'I imagine,' said Forbes-James, as they went down to the car, 'that you are thinking you'd like to strangle the lot of us with our old school ties.' This was pretty much exactly what Stratton had been thinking. He didn't see any real point in denying it, but before he could reply, Forbes-James continued, 'Incidentally, I agree that it is probably a question of blackmail. Although Mrs Calthrop is compromised, I think her involvement is highly unlikely.'

Then what the hell was all that about, Stratton wanted to ask, but said nothing. As they drove along the Embankment towards Albert Bridge, he thought of the Indian waiter in the ruins of West End Central Station. You think I know bugger all, Colonel, he mouthed silently, and you're right. I haven't got a fucking clue.

CHAPTER
50

Diana had gone home with nothing to look forward to but an evening of sitting alone and fretting, followed by an uncomfortable night in the basement shelter. Unlike the night before last...Seeing Claude like that, leaning on the railings, had taken the wind out of her sails, but that was no excuse for her pathetic capitulation. How could she, after what Lally had said to her? She had gone over and over it in her mind, trying to decide who and what to believe, but had come to no conclusion. She felt so guilty, convinced that everyone knew what she'd been up to, as if Claude's fingerprints were visibly stamped all over her skin. And when Helen Pender had shouted at her...she flinched at the memory of her voice, filling the small, drab room: *Bitch, traitor, turncoat, whore...*She'd told herself again and again that the girl was furious and upset, but she couldn't get that last word out of her mind. *Whore.* It seemed to reverberate all around her and, no matter how often she told herself that Helen could know nothing about Claude, it didn't do any good.

At half-past nine, after a couple of hours of trying, and failing, to concentrate on a novel, the siren sounded. Diana gathered her belongings and was just about to change into her slacks and go down to the shelter when the bell rang. Claude? She threw the slacks onto the bed and flew down the stairs to the door. But it wasn't Claude, it was Guy. His uniform was dishevelled, his eyes glassy, and he staggered as he crossed the threshold.

'What are you doing here?'

'That's a nice way to greet your husband.' He swung his kitbag off his shoulder and dropped it on the hall floor. 'Change of plan.' His voice was loud, with a sort of belligerent joviality. 'Got here a couple of days early. Want to see your flat.'

Diana backed away from him. 'You've been drinking.'

'Very osser...osservant. Is it upstairs?'

'Darling, I told you, it isn't big enough for two people.'

'Just one night, then I'll go to my club.'

'We can't, Guy. The raid's started.' The thought of taking him down to the shelter and facing the curious eyes of the other people in the house was unbearable. Supposing someone had spotted Claude leaving her flat? People talked. Again, she heard Helen's shrill voice shouting 'Whore!'

'Don't care,' Guy persisted. 'Want to see.'

'Please, darling...' Diana patted his arm, thinking to placate him. 'You can't stay here.'

'Want to stay here. Tired. Want to go to bed.'

'Very well. But we'll have to go down to the shelter.'

'No. Coming with me.' He caught hold of her wrist, and shook it like a dog worrying a bone. 'With me,' he insisted.

Defeated, and afraid of being overheard, Diana said, wearily, 'I'll take you upstairs.' Perhaps he'd go to sleep straight away, and she'd be able to escape.

'Come on.' Towing him upstairs, his kitbag banging against the banisters with each step, she tried not to remember her eager ascent with Claude.

While Guy dumped the kitbag on the bed, Diana looked wildly around for any evidence of Claude's presence. Mercifully, there seemed to be nothing.

'Nice li'l place,' Guy slurred. 'What's to drink?'

'Don't you think you've had enough?'

'No,' he said aggressively. 'I don't.' He plonked himself down on the stool in front of her dressing table and stared at her expectantly. Diana shrugged, poured him some whisky, and approached him cautiously, holding out the glass in her palm as if it were a sugar lump for an unpredictable horse. Guy lunged, grabbed her hips and pulled her towards him. Propelled forwards, she tottered, just managing to hold on to the Scotch. 'Don't. You'll spill it.'

'Put it down.'

Obediently, Diana deposited it on a corner of the dressing table. 'Please let go of me,' she said, quietly.

'No.' Guy's face, brick-red and loose-lipped, tilted up to hers for a moment, and then he closed his eyes and laid his head against her stomach.

'Stop it!' She jerked backwards, so that he pitched forwards, head down, almost falling off the stool. Righting himself, he picked up the whisky, peered in the glass as if considering some experimental brew, and drank.

'You're a bitch, Diana.'

Helen's abuse echoed again in her mind as she stood in the middle of the room. Her guilt, and her revulsion, overwhelmed her. She'd never thought of Guy here, in her little sanctuary, but his uncontrolled presence, leering and touching her and breathing whisky fumes over everything, was worse than she could have imagined. This man in front of her was her husband. How had it come to this? 'Maybe I am,' she said, wearily.

'You are a bitch. But...' Guy's face brightened, as if he'd been struck by a new and revolutionary idea, 'you're my bitch. My wife, in fact. My'—he belched—'woman. And you're here, and I'm here. Isn't that nice?'

'Yes,' Diana agreed, 'Lovely.' Surely, if she could just humour him, keep him talking for long enough, he would fall asleep? She wondered if she should try coaxing him onto the bed. He was bound to start pawing her, but if he were horizontal the alcohol might take effect more quickly...She wondered how much he'd had. Perhaps it was too soon to gamble on his passing out. She'd never seen Guy drunk before—tipsy, yes, but never like this—so she couldn't be sure what stage he'd reached. Some men fell asleep, she knew, but others got lecherous, or wanted to sing or fight, or even started to cry…It seemed extraordinary not to know what type one's own husband was.

She was just about to ask if he wanted more Scotch when he lifted up his hands like the paws of a begging dog. 'Won't you be kind to me?' he whined. 'Please?'

Diana felt sick. Guy pretended to pant, sticking out a yellow, furred tongue, then made a puppyish whimpering noise. Unable to stop herself, she turned away in disgust.

'No!' Her scent bottles clattered, then toppled over, as he pounded the dressing table with the flat of his hand. 'Christ's sake, Diana, 'smatter with you?'

It occurred to her that the easiest thing to do would be to take the line of least resistance—give him what he wanted, then he'd go to sleep and she could go downstairs. All she had to do was walk towards him—three steps—and then…And in any case, he might not be able to, so that would be that…But supposing he could, and she became pregnant? Without the device, there was every chance of that happening. Claude might be relied upon, but pregnancy was exactly what Guy wanted. 'What about another drink?' she asked. She was aiming for a light tone, but the words came out shrill and nervous.

Guy got to his feet and lumbered towards her. 'You're my wife,' he snarled, and, taking her by the shoulders, pulled her to him. Pinioned, she twisted frantically from side to side, shaking her head, elbowing and clawing, as they staggered together towards the bed. Pulling one arm free, she slapped him, hard, across the face. He tottered backwards for a moment, releasing her, then fell sprawling on his back, his eyes wide with shock.

Diana seized her handbag and ran from the flat, down the stairs, and into the darkness of the street where the raid was in full swing. Flares and flashes of light pierced the blackout, the drone of aeroplanes and the boom of guns sounded continuously, and the smell of escaping gas was coming from somewhere nearby. Keeping close to the railings of the houses, she made her way towards the tube station at Sloane Square. Judging by the length of the whistling sounds before the explosions, the bombs were falling a mile or so away, somewhere to her left—Knightsbridge? Paddington? For God's sake, Diana thought, don't come any closer. I don't want to die now, not like this, not in this state... What did Catholics talk about? A state of grace, that was it. Well, whatever the opposite of that was, she was in it.

Don't be idiotic, she told herself. No-one believes in hell any more, it's just something made up to frighten people. And, in any case, hell, if it existed, could hardly be worse than this. Concentrating hard on these thoughts, and on putting one foot safely in front of the other, she reached Sloane Square station, bought a ticket to Piccadilly Circus, and set about picking her way through the recumbent bodies on the platform, breathing through her mouth to minimise the smell of packed humanity and latrine buckets. Afterwards, she told herself that she hadn't known where she was heading, but it wasn't true. By the time she'd reached the King's Road she'd already known that she would go to Claude.

CHAPTER

51

Sitting on the sofa at Jermyn Street, Claude held Diana's hand while she gazed tearfully at the hulking furniture and dismal paintings that surrounded them, and tried to collect herself. 'He was drunk,' she said. 'He tried to rape me.'

'Impossible, darling,' said Claude, lightly. 'One can't rape one's own wife. One can only rape,' he stroked her thigh, 'other people's.' Even in her emotional state—she'd done nothing but sob for the first five minutes—Diana could sense the depth of his unease, his desire not to be drawn in.

'But he did,' she persisted. She needed comfort, vindication—anger on her behalf—not this superficial dismissal of her predicament.

'You can't really blame him, darling.' Claude stroked her arm. 'A warrior off to the war, and all that...Besides, I had the impression you rather enjoyed that sort of thing.'

'That's a horrible thing to say!'

'True, though. It means that you, my darling, can enjoy yourself without having to feel bad about it afterwards.'

'Don't!'

'Oh, stop making such a fuss,' said Claude, irritably. 'You're making a mess of your face. Still, it's nothing that soap and water can't fix.'

'I think,' said Diana, with as much dignity as she could muster, 'that I'll leave.'

'Don't be ridiculous. We're in the middle of an air-raid. Go and wash your face, and I'll fix you a drink.'

Diana got up and went to the bathroom. He doesn't want to know, she thought. She supposed she couldn't blame him for it; apart from anything else, there was the sheer impropriety of complaining to one's lover about one's husband, but the disappointment, on top of everything else, was hard to bear.

'That's better,' said Claude, when she returned, clean, with a freshly powdered nose. 'You look lovely in that dress. Mind you,' he added, handing her her drink, 'you'll look even better out of it.'

'You don't understand.' Diana was unable to contain herself, 'that's not why I——' The rest of the sentence was lost as the building shook and blast rattled the windows.

'It's getting closer,' said Claude, putting his arm round her waist. 'We'll be safer in bed, and much, much more comfortable.' He nuzzled her cheek with his lips.

Diana stared at him. Explanation would be pointless. He didn't, or wouldn't, understand. I shouldn't have come here, she thought. I should have gone to Lally. Why hadn't she? It hadn't even occurred to her. Am I really so in thrall to this man? She shook her head in self-disgust and, too tired to resist, allowed Claude to steer her into the bedroom. She stood, doll-like, and let herself be undressed, and then followed Claude to his mattress under the propped-up bed frame and let him do as he wanted.

When he'd finished, he rubbed her cheek with the back of his hand and said, 'There. That was what you needed, wasn't it?'

No, Diana thought. I needed something else entirely. She wanted to ask, is this all I am to you, but she didn't dare.

'He didn't accuse you of anything, did he?' asked Claude.

'Accuse me?'

'Of adultery.'

Wearily, Diana shook her head.

'Good,' said Claude. 'That means he doesn't know about us.' He patted her on the bottom with an air of satisfaction.

That's all he cares about, Diana thought. Lally's right, he doesn't take me seriously. Why should he? Lying awake while he slept beside her, it occurred to her, as she considered the evening's events, that Guy might have been drinking in order to get up the courage to see her—or, more than see her, to...That was horrible. *She* was horrible. Everything was horrible. Listening to Claude's breathing in the silence after the raid, she thought, *he* would never have to get drunk to face a woman. Did that make him better, or worse, than Guy? She didn't know. All she did know for certain, as she lay beside Claude, was that she had never felt so lonely in her entire life.

Returning to Tite Street from Claude's flat in the chilly grimness of early morning, Diana had found a scrawled, almost illegible note on her dressing table in the middle of a litter of hairpins, loose powder, and overturned boxes and bottles. *Sorry. Shouldn't have come. G.* She wondered, briefly, if Guy would try to contact her again before he went overseas, and decided it was unlikely. After all, she thought dully, what was there to say?

Claude had been asleep when she'd crawled out from the makeshift shelter of his bed just after dawn, and she hadn't woken him to say goodbye. She supposed she ought to have left him a note, but she'd been too dispirited. The worst thing about it was that the realisation of how little Claude was able to give her didn't make her love him any the less. You poor old heartbroken thing, you, jeered the worldly voice in her head, it can't come as a surprise. Which, Diana reflected, it didn't, really. From the beginning her intuition—not to mention warnings from F-J and Lally and, it seemed, everyone else—had told her that Claude was heartless. In any case, she thought, I'm the one committing adultery, not Claude. He's got nothing to lose.

You're a bitch, Diana. With Guy's slurred words echoing in her head, she slumped in the armchair, too depressed to cry. She wondered if Guy would write to Evie about what had happened and, if so, what he would say. At least he didn't know where she'd gone when she fled from the flat. Evie would, though, she thought. Evie would be bound to guess instantly. And then…

If this is the end of my marriage, thought Diana, why can't I *feel* something? Guy was right—she was a bitch. Well, she'd got what she deserved, hadn't she?

CHAPTER 52

Peverell Montague MP was a tall, thin man with a tallow-coloured face, an impressive white moustache and an expression that reminded Stratton of one of Jenny's mother's favourite sayings, about looking as if you were in the middle of a long chew on a dry prune. He also had a stoop that made it appear as if he had an invisible weight attached to the end of his long nose. The weight seemed to double in heaviness as Forbes-James explained about the raid on Wymark's flat, until the man's forehead was almost resting on his crossed arms. So inert did he seem that Stratton jumped in his hard prison chair when Montague jerked his head up and banged his fist on the table.

'This is an outrage! When will I be able to see my solicitor?'

'Tomorrow,' said Forbes-James.

'I shall say nothing until I have spoken to him.'

'It may be,' said Forbes-James, coolly, 'that your solicitor will be unwilling to act for you.'

'Nonsense. And I shall say nothing until I know what crime I am to be charged with.'

'I'm afraid that's not how it works,' said Forbes-James, calmly. 'Your case will be heard by an advisory committee, who will hear each prisoner held under Regulation 18B, and will advise the Home Secretary about the suitability of release.'

'So one man's whim is to be the law?'

'Your case will—'

'What case? If there is no charge, there is no case! If I cannot be properly charged with a crime, then I have committed no offence. The idea that an Englishman may be held indefinitely in prison, without any proper legal charge, is a monstrous perversion of justice. My cell is infested with lice. Keeping men in these conditions is not acceptable.'

'We are acting for His Majesty's Government, Mr Montague.'

'Exactly! For people who chose not to fight in the Great War. They are the traitors and cowards, not I.'

'Is Mr Churchill a coward and a traitor?'

'Greenwood, Morrison. You know very well who I am talking about. Yours is the treachery, gentlemen. It may be respectable, but it is still treachery.'

'We are acting in the interests of national security.'

'You are acting in the interests of an unprincipled bunch of Jew-ridden politicians who want to demolish everything this country stands for. What happened to freedom of speech? Gone! Habeas Corpus? Gone! And with it—'

'In a state of national emergency.'

'Which would never have arisen if we had had—as we still could have—a negotiated peace! It is perfectly possible, gentlemen, to negotiate with Herr Hitler, and quite insane to allow this lunacy to go on for one single moment longer than it has to.'

'Peace under what terms?'

'Herr Hitler is a reasonable man.'

'So reasonable, in fact, that he is currently raining down death and destruction on British women and children.'

'As we are doing to German women and children. *We* declared war on Germany, *we* bombed Berlin. An aggressor should not be surprised by retaliation, and you cannot, surely, be labouring under the illusion that we can do anything to help Poland now.'

Stratton couldn't see where any of this was getting them. Montague was a zealot. He talked and gestured as if he were addressing a rally, not sitting cooped up in a tiny, airless prison room, and he obviously wasn't going to help them.

'You don't deny,' said Forbes-James, 'that your organisation, the Right Club, exists for the purposes of disseminating pro-Nazi and anti-Jewish propaganda?'

'Our propaganda, as you call it, is wholly patriotic. Besides, I have very little to do with it.'

'Your wife does.'

Montague looked as if he were about to say something, but Forbes-James carried on, 'Would you be prepared to defend this country in the case of a German invasion?'

'I consider that question an insult.'

'Why?'

'Because I would do my utmost to defend my country. Nothing would induce me to harm Great Britain, or her Empire.'

'And yet you are acting in a manner which will harm them both.'

'No!' Montague thumped the table again. 'I am a loyal British subject.'

'I hardly think so.'

'If you think that everyone whose views are at variance with the government is disloyal, then—'

'A person is either loyal or disloyal, Mr Montague. Talking like a politician does not change that. Those are the rules of the game. You cannot begin to invent them.'

'Unlike you people, who can change the law at a stroke.'

'We are going round in circles, Mr Montague. Tell me, has your organisation received funds from Germany?'

'That is an outrageous suggestion.'

'Is it? You have, after all, met Signor Mussolini.'

'I have never denied it.'

'The British Union of Fascists is known to have received funds from Italy.'

'That is untrue.'

'How do you know that?'

'Sir Oswald has said so.'

'He has said he had nothing to do with the finances of the movement. That's not quite the same thing, is it?'

'He has stated that no money should be accepted except from British subjects.'

'But the origin of that money may be a different matter entirely. However, I am not here to talk about that.'

'Then why are you here, other than to insult me?'

'To ask for your help.'

Stratton shifted back in his chair and stared hard at his shoes. What the hell was Forbes-James playing at?

'My help?' echoed Montague.

'We will, of course, be speaking to your wife, and we wanted to clarify a few matters first.' Forbes-James paused and scrutinised Montague for a moment, before adding, in a casual voice, 'Before we go to Holloway.' The change in the atmosphere was as abrupt and shocking as if an electric current had been passed through the small room.

'*What?*' Montague, his face now blue-white, cords standing out in his neck and jaw working, stared at them.

'Of course,' Forbes-James continued, as if he had absolutely no idea of the devastating effect of his deftly primed grenade, 'if we don't have the necessary information from you, then...'

'Wait! Are you telling me that you have arrested my wife?'

'Yes,' said Forbes-James, blandly. 'Last night. I assumed you were aware of the fact.'

'I had no idea of it,' he said. 'You...you can't.'

'We can, Mr Montague. We have.'

'But that's...it's preposterous, it's...it's...'

'Surely you must have expected it?' said Forbes-James, smoothly. 'After all, Lady Mosley—'

'I want to see my wife.'

'I'm afraid that's impossible. At least, for the moment.'

'When will I be able to see her?'

'That rather depends on you. There's the issue of national security, but it may be possible for Mrs Montague to be removed from the confines of prison and kept under some form of house arrest...I don't know how long it will take the Advisory Committee to look into your wife's case, but I imagine it will be quite a while before they can prepare the necessary information. Treason is a serious business, Mr Montague.'

'My wife has not acted in any—'

'Mrs Montague and other members of the Right Club have been aiding the enemy by being party to the illegal transfer of confidential documents to people liable to be hostile to the interests of this country,' said Forbes-James flatly. 'That is treason.'

'Nonsense! Everything we have done is in the interests of this country. Unlike yourselves.'

'I hardly think that the people of this country will look kindly on an organisation which advocates any form of negotiation with a man who is trying to bomb us into submission. Anything less than the ultimate penalty would be an insult to them. Now,' Forbes-James stood up, and Stratton, taking his cue, pushed back his chair, 'if you have nothing else to say, we shall take our leave.'

'Wait! What is to happen to my wife?'

'I'm afraid I'm unable to say,' said Forbes-James, calmly. 'We have left a parcel of necessities for you at reception, and any other—'

'Under what circumstances,' interrupted Montague, 'would my wife be placed under house arrest?'

'I cannot make bargains, Mr Montague. I may, however, be able to make certain recommendations.'

'I see.' Montague stared down at his feet, then looked at Forbes-James. 'You said you needed my help.'

'It would be appreciated.' Forbes-James sat down again. His eyes met Montague's, and, for a long moment, neither man spoke. Once more, Stratton felt the sense of exclusion from a club, from the upper echelons—upbringing, public school, university—he could never be part of it. But Montague, treason or no treason, would always be a member. At least at Great Marlborough Street he, Stratton, was an inferior amongst equals. Here, despite the stale body odour and the faecal smells wafting from the corridor, he was a rank outsider.

Montague cleared his throat. 'I believe you have some questions for me.'

'We do,' said Forbes-James. 'The documents in Mr Wymark's possession: Have you seen them?'

'No.'

'But you have an idea of the contents?'

'Yes. I must reiterate that everything I have done has been in the interests of this country. For a power such as America to enter this war would cause death and destruction on a scale unparalleled in history.'

'If the United States comes to our aid, Mr Montague,' said Forbes-James, 'we will win.'

'At what cost?'

'Peace,' said Forbes-James. 'Peace, as Mr Chamberlain said in a rather different context, with honour. These documents came to our attention through the involvement of Sir Neville Apse. He has given us certain information...' Forbes-James stopped to light another cigarette, taking his time over it. 'Blackmail, Mr Montague. That is what we are talking about.'

'Blackmail would seem to be your speciality, Colonel, not mine.'

Forbes-James ignored this. 'Sir Neville isn't a member of the Right Club, is he? His name does not appear on the list we found in Mr Wymark's possession.'

'I have no knowledge of any such list.'

'I understand from Mr Wymark that you gave it to him for safekeeping. Or perhaps it came from your wife?'

'My wife,' Montague's voice shook slightly, 'has nothing to do with this.'

'I'm afraid we are not convinced of that. Perhaps you can assist us.'

'How?'

'A few facts...'

'I must say, gentlemen, that I consider your behaviour disgraceful. Shabby in the extreme.'

'This is war, Mr Montague, not a garden party. When did you first learn of Sir Neville's, ah—proclivities?'

Montague's face turned from pale to a mottled red. 'From a man named Chadwick.'

'Chadwick?' Stratton took out his notebook.

'Bobby Chadwick.' Montague pronounced the name with distaste. 'A revolting little pansy.'

'Is he a member of the Right Club?' asked Forbes-James.

Montague shook his head. 'Described himself as a friend to the cause. Ordinarily, of course one wouldn't have any truck with such people, but...' He paused.

'It's not a garden party,' murmured Forbes-James. Montague flushed a deeper red. 'Do go on.'

'He came to me,' Montague continued, 'said he wanted to help. He told me that Sir Neville had had a...liaison with a friend of his. Said there was evidence to prove it.'

'What sort of evidence?'

'Some sort of film.'

'Have you seen this film?'

'No. I had no desire to see it. Chadwick said he'd made the film himself—operated the camera—and that he knew where it was.'

'And the friend who was in the film with Sir Neville?' asked Stratton. 'What was his name?'

'I have no idea. Chadwick referred to him only by a nickname.'

'What was that?'

'He called him Bunny,' said Montague with a look of contempt.

Bunny, thought Stratton. The name in Mabel's letters, but it wasn't her. That, at least, explained the waspish tone and the comments about décor and orchids and so on. Did that mean that Sir Neville was the writer, Binkie? Perhaps, he thought, the next time they met, he ought to try calling Sir Neville a precious pinkle-wonk, just to see what happened.

'No surname?' asked Stratton.

Montague shook his head. 'I didn't ask. The thing made me sick—Chadwick was clearly an habitual sodomite, and utterly poisonous. I wanted as little to do with him as possible.'

'But nevertheless you were prepared to believe him. You took the information to Sir Neville,' said Forbes-James.

'I made use of it, yes.'

'And how did Sir Neville react?'

'He agreed to give assistance.'

'How?'

'To receive certain documents from Mr Wymark, and have them sent out of the country. He had a contact at the Portuguese Embassy.'

'This was in return for your silence?'

'Yes.'

'And Sir Neville didn't ask for proof—to see the film?'

'No.'

'Did you tell him that the source of your information was Chadwick?'

Montague shook his head.

'Do you know where Chadwick lives?' asked Stratton.

'No. He contacted me at my club.'

'When was this?'

'Sometime in February. I don't remember the exact date.'

'Did you offer him money?'

'Yes. Much to my surprise, he refused.'

Stratton noted this down. 'Can you describe him, sir?'

'Pansy. Effeminate. Looked as if he painted himself. Dyed his hair, that sort of thing.'

'What colour was it?'

'Dark red. Ridiculous.'

Dr Byrne, Stratton thought, hadn't mentioned anything about the corpse having dyed hair—just that it was brown. But there might be traces of the dye, even if it had been washed out... And in any case, Montague was prejudiced. Chadwick's hair colour might have been natural—assuming, of course, that he was the body in the church. 'How old was he?'

'About fifty, I suppose.' Montague made a dismissive gesture. 'It's hard to say with these people.'

'How tall?' Stratton asked.

Montague looked him up and down in a way that made him think of an executioner calculating a prisoner's height and weight for the drop. 'Under six feet,' he said. 'Five feet nine or ten, I should say. Fleshy,' he added, with an expression of distaste.

'Did you see him after that?'

'Never.'

'You didn't hear from him?'

'No.'

'Do you know a man called Abraham, or Abie, Marks?'

'No.'

'Have you heard of him?'

'I don't associate with Jews.'

Stratton, who had not really expected anything different, received this in silence, and, after a moment, Forbes-James said, 'If you have no further questions, Inspector...?'

Stratton shook his head. Turning to Montague, Forbes-James said, 'That will be all for the time being, Mr Montague. Thank you for your assistance.'

'What will happen to my wife?'

'That remains to be seen.' Forbes-James rose. 'However, you may rest assured that we shall inform the relevant authorities of your co-operation.' As he held out his hand, Montague placed both of his firmly behind his back.

'I would be sorry,' said Forbes-James, 'if we could not part like gentlemen.'

'I do not consider you a gentleman, Colonel.' Montague did not even bother to nod in Stratton's direction. 'Good day to you.'

CHAPTER 53

'I'm not sure,' said Forbes-James, as the car bore them away, 'how far you will be able to proceed with your enquiries. It may not be in the national interest to stir things up too much. I hope you understand that.'

Stratton sighed. 'Yes, sir, I do.'

'Interesting that Apse caved in so quickly to Montague's demands.'

'Fear, sir. Public disgrace.'

'I realise that,' said Forbes-James testily, 'but it's extraordinary that he should have done so without at least attempting to obtain a copy of the film. Especially if Montague didn't mention Chadwick.'

'Sir Neville knew it existed all right, though. Mr Montague said Chadwick had filmed them himself.'

'I suppose so, although the film might have been destroyed, of course...Never a good idea to put one's youthful indiscretions on the record, so to speak. Any idea who this man Bunny might be?'

'Yes, sir. From the letters Miss Morgan had.'

'Yes, I know about those, but I've not read them. We assumed they were unconnected.'

'So did I, sir, but they're addressed to someone called Bunny. I'd assumed it was Miss Morgan herself, but I suppose Bunny must be someone she knew. Otherwise, why would the letters be in her possession?'

'Hmm. Well, I suppose we'd better go and see Mr Chadwick—if you can find him, that is.'

'Yes, sir. And if he is the body in the church?'

Forbes-James sighed. 'We'd better cross that particular bridge when—or if—we come to it.'

'Yes, sir. What will happen to Mr Montague?'

'Well, I doubt if he'll be prosecuted—I shan't recommend it. I imagine he'll remain in detention for the duration. He'll manage pretty well. Public school men always do. It's the other chaps who have a rough time.'

'I'm surprised Mr Montague didn't realise that prison might be the outcome of his actions, sir.'

'Yes...' Forbes-James looked thoughtful. 'I must say he struck me as a rather unworldly individual. Didn't know him before, of course. A fantasist, perhaps, as well as a fanatic, and altogether cruder than Mosley, who has a fine mind, although there's an element of naivety there as well, of course...'

'What about Wymark?'

'I'd like to say that he will be first deported and then shot, but I don't know. Even if they'd agree to it, a public trial in America at the moment would hurt Roosevelt's chances of re-election, so I suppose we'll have to hang on to him—for the time being, at least.' Forbes-James fell silent. Stratton looked out of the window at men taking down railings beside a public air-raid shelter, its brick walls piled high with sandbags, and wondered if Abie Marks knew he'd been doing dirty work for a man in league (however unwillingly) with the Right Club. He couldn't see it. Marks had always made much of his arrest at Cable Street in '36, although, according to a friend of Stratton's who'd been on duty at the time, it wasn't, as he claimed, for beating up one of Mosley's henchmen, but for assaulting a policeman. But even if his part in the fighting—which was mostly, Stratton knew, between the Communists and the police—was exaggerated, Marks was hardly likely to get into bed with a Jew-hater like Montague ('Wouldn't give 'em the sweat off my balls, Mr Stratton.'). Sir Neville, however, was another matter: whatever his connections, money and friends in high places would always count for something with a man like Abie Marks. If Sir Neville had prevailed upon Marks to find and destroy Mabel Morgan's film, and he had managed it, what might he have expected in return? If that was what had happened, then Sir Neville had clearly known that the film was in Mabel's possession, which meant that, in all likelihood, his erstwhile dancing partner was Mabel's husband Cecil Duke. Otherwise, why should she have it at all?

'We'll drop you off at Great Marlborough Street,' said Forbes-James. 'See what you can do about locating Chadwick. I'll make sure you have all the assistance you need...Report to me as soon as you've got something, and make it quick.'

'Yes, sir.'

'Good. I'll arrange for a sample of Apse's handwriting to be checked with one of those letters. What did he call himself, by the way?'

'Binkie, sir.'

'Dear God,' murmured Forbes-James, and closed his eyes.

Stratton picked up a file and shook it. The office window, which had formerly refused to open, was now, thanks to Arliss's attempts at maintenance and the effect of further air-raids, stuck at half-mast, and consequently the November cold chilled the room and everything was covered in grey, gritty dust. He took a sip of his tea and made a face. In just a few days he'd managed to forget how vile Cudlipp's brews could be. He was lighting a cigarette to get rid of the taste when Policewoman Gaines put her head round the door. 'We've found him, sir. Robert Peregrine Chadwick. Address in Belgravia. Chester Square. As far as we know, he's still there.'

Bollocks, thought Stratton. Chadwick wasn't their corpse. That would have been just too easy, wouldn't it? Bollocks, bugger, fuck and shit. Aloud, he said, 'Well done. Does he have a telephone?'

'No, sir.'

'Right.' Stratton lifted the receiver and blew into it before dialling Forbes-James's number. Margot Mentmore's efficient voice told him to please hold the line, and then the Colonel said, 'Any luck?'

'Yes, sir. Robert Peregrine Chadwick. Lives at No. 96, Chester Square.'

'Not your corpse, then.'

'Doesn't look like it, sir.'

'Pity. I'll do a spot of digging. Meet me outside his house in…let's say two hours, shall we? That ought to give me enough time.'

Stratton caught a bus to Victoria and walked to Chester Square, where Forbes-James was waiting for him in the Bentley. The houses were huge, venerable, and very grand. If Chadwick was a professional blackmailer, thought Stratton, he obviously had a great many wealthy victims.

'The flat's over there,' Forbes-James gestured towards a house a few hundred yards away. 'It was left to him, apparently, by a man named Lionel Atwater. A life-long bachelor,' he added, sardonically. Bloody efficient, thought Stratton. He must have found that out in about ten minutes.

'Inherited the flat in 1938,' said Forbes-James. 'Fifty-three years old and, as far as we can ascertain, still alive.'

He certainly wasn't their corpse, though Stratton thought he was having a fair go at drinking himself to death. Montague's 'fleshy' was a good description, and the 'dyed hair' was, in fact, an unconvincing wig. He was wrapped in a silk robe with an oriental pattern of swirling, bug-eyed dragons. His features, which, like the rest of him, were submerged beneath a thick layer of fat, resembled blobs of molten wax. He stood on the threshold, blinking at them, one pudgy fist closed around a glass. Hysterical falsetto yipping and the sounds of paws scrabbling against the paintwork issued from behind a door further up the narrow hallway.

'Detective Inspector Stratton, CID, and this is Colonel Forbes-James. May we come in for a moment?'

Chadwick made a squawking noise and clasped his hands together, losing hold of the glass, which shattered on the parquet floor. Forbes-James and Stratton stepped back smartly to avoid being splashed, but Chadwick barely seemed to notice. He was too drunk, Stratton thought, to register fear, or even surprise.

His sitting room reminded Stratton of a posh brothel he'd raided some years ago, and it looked as if a particularly violent orgy had recently taken place. Pieces of flimsy gilded furniture seemed to be scattered about at random, there were cigarette burns and dark stains on the sofas and armchairs, ash on the pale carpet, and various bottles strewn about. One blackout curtain hung loosely, half off its rod as if someone had tried to swing on it, while dirty plates, soiled cushions, and several small turds seemed to indicate that neither the dog, nor, presumably, its owner had left the place for some days.

'Dreff'ly sorry.' Chadwick flapped a languid hand at the mess, subsided onto a sofa and closed his eyes. 'Can't get help these days.' Stratton wasn't surprised—although, given the level of squalor, he thought that Chadwick wasn't so much in need of a maid as a bunker, preferably one lined with rubber sheeting. Forbes-James went over to the broken and spilt remains of the drinks tray and picked up a jug. 'Some water, I think,' he said, holding it out to Stratton. 'And try to find some coffee.'

The kitchen wasn't in a much better state than the sitting room. Stratton filled the jug, found a bottle of coffee essence, and boiled some water. He almost dropped the kettle when a sudden series of hysterical shrieks issued from the sitting room, accompanied by frenzied yapping from the unseen dog. Hurrying through with the jug and a cup of strong black coffee, he found Forbes-James standing over Chadwick, who was curled up on the sofa. Stratton couldn't tell if the noises he was making were the result of genuine distress, or simply a tantrum. But then, he reflected, Chadwick was probably too pissed to know the difference himself. Forbes-James took the jug, wrenched Chadwick into a sitting position, and hurled the water in his face.

Shocked, Chadwick spluttered, hiccupped, and finally wiped his eyes on the sleeve of his robe. Forbes-James's manhandling had caused his wig to slide off and his bald pate, obscenely exposed, looked like a turtle without its shell. He made no attempt to retrieve it. Stratton held out the coffee cup. 'Drink this.'

Chadwick sipped, grimaced, and then, noticing the looks on the faces of the two men standing over him, gulped down the hot liquid. Stratton, catching Forbes-James's eye, took the cup and went back to the kitchen to fetch more. When he returned, Chadwick seemed more composed, and Stratton wondered what—if anything—Forbes-James had said to him in the interim.

Forbes-James waited until Chadwick had drunk the second cup, then pulled up a gilt chair and sat down in front of him, indicating that Stratton should do the same. 'Now then,' he said, 'I think we'd better start again. I am Colonel Forbes-James, and this is Detective Inspector Stratton of the CID, and you are going to tell us about your involvement with Sir Neville Apse.'

'I was never,' said Chadwick, with more dignity than Stratton would have thought possible under the circumstances, '*involved* with Neville Apse.'

'You made a film of him, dancing. With another man.'

Chadwick blanched. 'How do you know about that?'

'We've been to see Peverell Montague. In Brixton Prison.' Chadwick made a choking noise. 'That picture,' continued Forbes-James, blandly, 'wasn't intended to be seen by the public, was it?'

'It was a...a private...private entertainment. There was nothing...nothing...wrong in it.'

'Then why did you tell Mr Montague about it?'

'Are you going to arrest me?' Chadwick asked quietly.

'That depends on what you have to tell us.'

Chadwick stared past them at the violated room. His eyes looked dead, and Stratton wondered what he was thinking.

'Well?' said Forbes-James.

'Bunny asked me to film them together.'

'Bunny?'

'Bunny Duke.'

'Do you mean Miss Morgan's husband?' asked Stratton.

'Mabel...' Chadwick batted a hand in dismissal. 'I was his assistant.'

'Are you telling us that it was a marriage of convenience?' asked Forbes-James. 'A *mariage blanc*?'

'Of course it was. She didn't realise at the beginning, but she found out soon enough. Not that she was...Bunny was very successful in those days. She enjoyed herself, spending his money. And there were always plenty of men...'

'What was her attitude to Mr Duke's behaviour?'

'She was easy-going, I will say that. Just about the only thing I can say for her. I always told Bunny he should have chosen a better class of person, but he liked the vulgarity—the contrast...'

'Contrast?'

'With her looks. Utterly beautiful, sylph-like—and she talked like a docker. Common, coarse, drank like a fish...oh, you've no idea!' In Chadwick's priggish animation, Stratton caught a glimpse of the pretty, spoiled youth he must have been before age, booze and self-pity took their toll. 'Bunny thought she was a scream, but I could never see it. Of course, that's why she never worked in the talkies.'

'And the scars,' said Stratton.

'Well, that absolutely *finished* her.'

'So you knew Cecil Duke before he married?'

'Oh, yes. I'd worked with him from the beginning, you see. From the very start.'

'And you were...close?'

'We shared everything.'

'Until Sir Neville Apse came along,' said Stratton.

'Yes. Of course he wasn't *Sir* Neville then. I stayed, of course.' Stratton, who'd expected more malice, was surprised by the sadness in his voice. 'Bunny thought it was real. I could see that Apse was just amusing himself—he was the type—and I tried to warn Bunny, but he couldn't see it. Mabel didn't care—well, why should she? I've never blamed her for what happened. Besides, Bunny wouldn't have confided in her about something like that.'

'Why did you carry on working for him?' asked Stratton.

'What else could I do?' Chadwick sighed. 'I was in love. I always hoped...'

'We're touched by your fidelity,' said Forbes-James, sarcastically, 'but would you mind telling us why you chose to bring the film to the attention of Mr Montague?'

'Apse ruined my life,' said Chadwick, simply. 'If Bunny'd let me stay with him, he wouldn't have died. There wouldn't have been a fire—or, if there had been, I could have saved him.'

'Was Sir Neville with Cecil Duke on the night he died?'

Chadwick shook his head. 'Only Mabel, as far as I know. It was at their house in Sussex.'

'Where was that?' asked Stratton.

'Balcombe, near Haywards Heath.'

'When was the last time you saw him?'

'In May that year. We had a row, a bad one. I wrote him a letter afterwards, but he didn't reply.' Chadwick bowed his head. 'I never saw him again.'

'So,' said Forbes-James, 'you told Mr Montague about the film because you wanted to harm Sir Neville, because he'd come between you and Duke.'

'Yes.' Chadwick's voice was a whisper.

'Why not simply blackmail him? After all, Mr Montague offered you money, didn't he?'

'I would never resort to blackmail. Look at me, gentlemen. How could I?'

'Quite easily,' said Forbes-James. 'It's obvious what you are. You clearly have no reputation to lose.'

'I have my life,' said Chadwick. Then, glancing round the room, he added, 'Such as it is. Apse is a powerful man. If I had approached him for money—which, incidentally, I do not need, thanks to a generous legacy from a dear friend—he could easily have found me. I imagine some sort of accident or disappearance would have been arranged. But by involving a third party, I was protected...In any case, money makes it a paltry thing—sordid, commonplace—and, whatever you may think, gentlemen, it was never that. I wanted to hurt Apse as he had hurt Bunny—and hurt me. To put him in an intolerable position. It took me quite a while to see how that could be done, but in the end…And Bunny's dead, so what I did couldn't harm him.'

Hell hath no fury, thought Stratton. 'Do you have a copy of the film in your possession, Mr Chadwick?' he asked.

Chadwick shook his head. 'There's only one print.'

'And who has it?'

'I imagine it perished in the fire.'

'Are you telling us,' asked Stratton, incredulously, 'that you went to see Mr Montague with no evidence whatsoever?'

'Yes,' said Chadwick. 'I couldn't see how else to do it. Anyway, it worked.'

'And no-one has threatened you at any time?'

'No. I don't suppose,' he added, bitterly, 'that Apse even remembers my name.'

'Really?' said Stratton, sceptically. As far as he could see, just about the only thing homosexual society had going for it was that it was, relatively speaking, classless.

'Why should he?' Chadwick shrugged. 'He wasn't interested in me. I was just there. Unimportant. He didn't talk to me.'

'Did he talk to Miss Morgan?'

'I don't think they ever met. There was no reason for it. He wasn't often there when we were working. Apse knew Bunny was married, of course, and to whom, but that was all.'

'Did Sir Neville ever write to Mr Duke?'

'Oh, yes. I saw some of the letters. Bunny could be cruel like that. Not intentionally,' he added hastily, 'just leaving them around. Careless.'

'So Miss Morgan would have seen them, too?'

'She might have. It wouldn't have mattered, you see. Not to her. But it mattered to me.'

'Did you take any of the letters?'

Chadwick shook his head. 'You may search the flat if you wish.'

'We shall do,' said Forbes-James. 'Do you possess a photo-graph of Mr Duke?'

'I destroyed them all. You will find only his letters to me. Naturally, I would prefer it if you didn't read, them, but...' He shrugged resignedly.

'When you approached Mr Montague,' Forbes-James said, 'were you in any way influenced by a desire to aid his cause?'

Bending over with some difficulty, Chadwick plucked his wig from the carpet, set it on his head, and adjusted it. 'I am aware,' he said, 'that you find me both repulsive and ridiculous. I disgust myself—not for what I am, but for what I have become— but I am not a traitor. And I did love Bunny, very much.' Again, Stratton found himself oddly touched by the man's dignity, and felt himself rebuked, although for what, he could not say. After all, he told himself as he followed Forbes-James back to the car after searching the flat and narrowly escaping the evil attentions of Chadwick's tiny, beribboned dog, he was only doing his job.

CHAPTER
55

'I've had Apse's handwriting checked against those letters,' said Forbes-James on the journey back to Dolphin Square. 'It's identical.'

'Did you ask Sir Neville for a sample?' asked Stratton.

Forbes-James shook his head. 'Mrs Calthrop found one in my papers. We'll need a photograph of Duke—there wasn't one in that box of Miss Morgan's. Perhaps you could find out if the young chap she lived with had anything—you said he had the rest of her effects.'

'If he has, it'll be at his sister's,' said Stratton. 'She lives in the Clerkenwell Road.' He glanced at his watch—quarter past six. 'I could look in there now. She works for a dressmaker, but I should think she'd be home by the time I get there.'

'Good idea.' Forbes-James leant forward to instruct Stumpy. Stratton listened hard in case he used her name, but he didn't.

'Sir Neville must have been pretty frightened,' said Stratton, 'to have caved in so quickly to Montague. And Chadwick must have been fairly sure of his ground to have gone to Montague with nothing incriminating to produce.'

'I was thinking about that,' said Forbes-James. 'It rather depends on the individual, of course. There are some chaps everyone knows about—their proclivities—and of course if they're useful to us...' He shrugged.

'You mean you protect them in return for information?'

'I believe it sometimes happens,' said Forbes-James, disingenuously. 'Another sort of man might try to brazen it out, of course—take Oscar Wilde—especially if they're inclined to think they're above the law. At least Apse had more sense than that, and we can't afford a scandal.'

'We still don't know the identity of the corpse from the church, sir.'

'That may not be important.'

'Not to you, sir, but—'

'I know. But, as I said, it may not be in the national interest to pursue that particular line of enquiry any further. Sleeping dogs, muddied waters, frightened horses, and so forth. It's essential to keep things as simple as possible. Cigarette?'

Forbes-James got out of the car at Dolphin Square and Stratton travelled on to Clerkenwell, feeling gloomy. He was beginning to find the whole business intensely depressing, and the thought of Johnny being involved in it, not to mention the probable reaction of Lilian and Reg, was too horrible to contemplate. Of course, if he wasn't allowed to take it any further, then Miss Morgan's death would remain un-investigated, thus letting Johnny (and himself) off the hook—at least, until the next time. Because, for the Johnny Booths of this world, there always was a next time.

He thanked Stumpy and went into the courtyard of the Peabody Buildings and up the stairs to Beryl Vincent's small flat.

'Can I help you?' Beryl looked puzzled for a moment, then added, 'It's Mr Stratton, isn't it? How did you know Joe was here?'

'I didn't,' said Stratton, pleased. 'All right, is he?'

'Wait, I'll call him. Jo-oe!'

'It was you I came to see,' said Stratton. 'Why's he back?'

'He's on leave. Going abroad next week. But why did you want to see me?'

Noting the look of alarm on her face, Stratton said, 'It's nothing bad. I just wondered if I could have a look through Miss Morgan's belongings.'

Joe appeared in the doorway. He seemed larger, stronger and more confident than Stratton remembered. Must be the basic training, he thought. 'How are you?' he asked. 'Enjoying the army?'

'Don't know about enjoying it,' Joe shrugged, 'but it's not too bad. I heard what you were saying, Mr Stratton. Does it mean you're going to find out what really happened?'

'I hope so.' Beryl's face brightened as she stood back to let him into the flat.

'Well,' said Joe, 'I suppose Mabel's things belong to me now. At least, they aren't anybody else's, are they? No-one's come asking for them.'

'We're very grateful to you, Mr Stratton,' said Beryl. 'Looking after Joe like that. I haven't any tea—drunk it all, I'm afraid—but if you'd like a glass of water, or...'

Stratton, realising that there wasn't any 'or', said hurriedly that he was fine, thank you. 'If you could just show me where the things are?'

'I'll bring them,' Joe said. 'They're just through here. Why don't you sit down for a moment?'

Stratton waited while he brought in several battered-looking suitcases and a hat-box.

'Are you going to take them away?' Beryl asked.

Stratton shook his head. Officially, they weren't part of an investigation, so he couldn't very well take them back to Great Marlborough Street, and there didn't seem much point in carting everything over to Dolphin Square, either. As for taking the stuff home, he'd got into quite enough trouble for that already. 'If you don't mind,' he said, 'I'll look through them here.'

He knelt on the floor and opened the first case, wrinkling his nostrils at the smell of camphor. 'I think it's mostly clothes,' said Joe, leaning over, 'but there might be a few letters and things.'

'Have you looked through them?'

'No. Didn't seem right, somehow.'

Beryl leant forward and picked up a dove-grey jacket. 'I remember this. There's a skirt as well, and a green blouse she used to wear with it. What she called a rig-out.' She giggled. 'Madam Sauvin would have gone spare.'

Stratton fumbled his way through various garments, including an alarming salmon pink corset, but found nothing at the bottom of the case except a pair of brown lace-up shoes. The next case contained more clothing, an odd-looking collapsible wooden assemblage that Joe identified as a wig-stand, and a straw hat that looked as if someone had jumped up and down on it. In the bottom of the third case, he found a wooden box wrapped in a number of woollen shawls, a balding fox-fur knotted around it like a strap. Opening it, he saw that it contained several framed photographs and a small bundle of letters. 'Ooh,' said Beryl, leaning over to look. 'I recognise that one—it's from one of her films. She used to have it on the mantelpiece. And those.' Stratton held up the last photograph. Unlike the others, which were framed in silver, this one was mounted on thick cardboard.

'I've not seen that before,' said Joe. 'She never had it on show—I'd remember.'

'Do you recognise the man?' Stratton asked him.

'No.' It was a photograph of a dark-haired man in tennis clothes, eyes half-closed against the sun, holding a racquet.

'Maybe it's her husband,' said Beryl.

'Perhaps.' Stratton turned it over. The face didn't look familiar from the film, probably because he'd been paying too much attention to Sir Neville to take much notice of the features of the other dancer. He took out his penknife, cut carefully around the back of the card, and pulled out the photograph. 'There's something written on it,' said Beryl.

'Cecil,' Stratton read. '1938. It is her husband.'

'Are you sure?' asked Joe.

'That was his name.'

'Yes, but the date. Are you sure it's an eight and not a five?'

'Looks like an eight to me. Here.' Stratton passed him the photograph.

'Why?'

Joe and Beryl peered at it. 'It is an eight,' Joe said. 'But Cecil died in 1935. Mabel told me.'

'Perhaps she made a mistake.'

'I'm sure she didn't. I mean, you'd remember something like that, wouldn't you? And it seems odd to make a mistake writing it down. Sometimes you get confused in the New Year, writing letters and things, but you wouldn't be three years out.'

'What else did Mabel tell you?'

'Not much. Just that he'd directed her in films—that was how they met—and there was a fire at their house, which was how she got the'—Joe indicated his left cheek—'and how he died.'

'Look,' said Beryl, pointing to the frame, 'there's something else in there. Paper.'

'So there is. Let's have another go...' Stratton eased his penknife under the frame and wiggled it until the edges were loose enough for him to tug the paper free without tearing it.

'It's got writing on it!' Beryl knelt down beside him as he unfolded it.

Stratton grinned at her. 'You're enjoying this, aren't you, Miss Detective?'

Beryl looked abashed. 'Well, it's exciting—finding things. It might be important.'

'Or not.' Stratton glanced at Joe, who was beginning to look uncomfortable. 'Anyway, let's see what it says.' He began reading aloud:

Dear Mabel,
Are you surprised, after all this time? Perhaps you thought
I'd be gone forever, but it's the bad penny, I'm afraid.
I'd been planning to come back for a while, but it was

entirely by chance that I discovered what happened. Max Wolcroft. Remember him? What a shock if I hadn't known! I shall look you up very soon. We'll have lots to talk about, won't we, darling? In the meantime, here's a photograph to remind you, and I must reintroduce myself: Mr Symmonds, nowadays, but you may call me Arthur. By the by, who was the man in the fire? Or did you forget to ask his name? I'm sorry about the house, though. We had some fun there, didn't we? But all good things must come to an end. All best, C.

'It means he didn't die at all, doesn't it?' said Beryl, eagerly. 'He went away somewhere and someone else died in the fire and Mabel said it was Cecil, but it wasn't. But...' She frowned. 'Why would anyone do that? She couldn't have made a mistake, could she? I mean, you'd know who was in your own house, wouldn't you? Unless it was a burglar, of course, but I still don't see...'

'Do you know why?' Stratton asked Joe.

No. Unless...' Joe blushed. 'Well, Mr Stratton, she had quite a colourful past. Racy. And the letter...'

'Makes it sound as if she had a habit of taking up with other men,' finished Stratton thoughtfully. Chadwick had certainly implied that Mabel was promiscuous—perhaps he'd been wrong to put the remark down to spite.

'So that's why she was frightened,' Beryl continued. 'You said, Joe, remember?'

'I thought it was just the blackout,' said Joe. 'But if it was because of Cecil coming back...She must have thought he'd tell the police what had happened—but then why would he change his name? I don't understand.'

'Neither do I,' said Stratton, 'but I don't think he intended to tell the police.'

'Why not?' asked Beryl. 'Surely it's the first thing anyone would do. I mean, Mabel had sort of killed him, hadn't she, saying he was dead like that. And he'd have to prove he was alive to get ration books and things, wouldn't he?'

'Perhaps he wanted money,' said Joe. 'To keep quiet about it. But Mabel didn't have any. Do you think that's what it was, Mr Stratton?'

'I can't answer your questions,' said Stratton. 'Even if I did know the answers, I wouldn't be able to tell you because it's an official investigation. I shall have to take this.' He pocketed the letter. 'And the photograph. It's very important that you don't say anything about this to anyone—and I mean anyone. I don't mean to frighten you,' he added, more gently, 'but we don't want a repeat of what happened when those two men came to Joe's flat. Do you understand me?'

Joe and Beryl nodded, their eyes wide. 'Yes,' said Beryl. 'You can trust us. Can't he, Joe? We won't say anything. Nothing at all.'

Stratton hastened to the car and asked to be taken back to Dolphin Square. As the Bentley made its slow way through the blacked-out streets, he sat back, thinking of Mabel Morgan, all terrified white face and huge, anguished eyes, fleeing from a burning house in a fancy white nightdress which flared out behind her as she ran... But it wasn't a film, he thought. It couldn't have happened like that. Mabel must have stumbled from the house shrieking, her skin and hair on fire and her flesh melting like celluloid itself, while her lover, trapped perhaps, screamed in agony, or choked up his lungs until he was overcome by smoke. Who was he? Did his wife, or family, or parents, still wonder what had happened to him? They probably didn't have a hope in hell of finding out the poor bastard's name, but still...What a way to go.

Symmonds, though. That was familiar. He'd come across a Symmonds recently, but when? He switched on his torch and began thumbing through his notebook.

There it was. The scrawny woman who'd come to the station, looking for her husband. *Missing since February,* he read, *Lives at 14 Poland St, On business? 45/6, hair brown, straight, eyes brown, own teeth, corns. Bigamist? Statement taken (Gaines). Birth date given (26th April '94) incorrect. Chiropodist?*

'Bingo,' murmured Stratton. Dr Byrne had mentioned a dental plate, but that wasn't the same as false teeth, so it was entirely possible...it could have been dislodged at some stage, and not replaced.

For some reason—and insurance was the obvious one, if she was hard up—Mabel Morgan had identified an unknown and very burnt corpse, possibly one of her lovers, as her husband, Cecil Duke. And he obviously hadn't colluded because, according to the letter, he hadn't even known about it until he'd met this man Wolcroft. So where had he been at the time of the fire? Out of London? Mabel had taken a big risk if that was the case—he might have come back at any moment and blown the gaff. Abroad was more likely, and America seemed the obvious choice for a film director.

Stratton fished the letter out of his pocket and ran the torch over it. No date. A chance meeting...That must have been quite an encounter for both him and Mr Wolcroft, he thought. Mabel Morgan had seemed like a phantom on celluloid, but Cecil Duke was a living ghost. Mabel's fear would definitely make sense if she'd been looking out for Cecil-cum-Arthur, who had come back to England and—if Stratton was right—had palled up, bigamously, with Mrs Symmonds. 'I shall look you up very soon.' To demand money, presumably—money that Mabel hadn't got. But Cecil hadn't looked her up, had he? Had he been killed before he got the chance? Maybe there was something else...

Depositing the notebook and letter on the seat beside him, Stratton took out his penknife once more, and, holding his torch between his teeth, set to, sliding the blade into the gap he'd made in the cardboard frame and wiggling it up and down until... 'Yesss,' he said to himself. There was something else. More paper...

Unfolding it, he read the heading Weill, Blynde & Cartsoe, Solicitors. Of course, thought Stratton, remembering the label on the deed box. W. B. & C. It must have come from them. The letter was dated the twenty-seventh of August, 1935 and directed to Mabel at an address in Clapham. Stratton glanced through it: *Late husband's will...insurance...documents...personal effects lodged with us...Yours sincerely, Thos Blynde.* Even if Cecil Duke hadn't had much money to leave, there was still the insurance. If both Cecil and the house had been insured, that could have amounted to quite a tidy sum...What had Mabel spent it on, he wondered. Keeping body and soul together, certainly, but it must have been done in quite some style. Boyfriends, he supposed. Drink. Parties. It was certainly possible...Stratton wondered why Mabel had kept the letters. The one from the solicitor he could understand—it was, after all, an official document. But Cecil Duke's note? Most people's reaction to something like that would be to tear it up or throw it on the fire. 'Who knows?' he muttered. People were bloody odd...

He shrugged and turned back to his notebook: Mrs Symmonds, 14 Poland Street. He thought for a moment, then peered out of the window, trying to make out, from the dark shapes of buildings, where they were. Seeing nothing identifiable, he removed the torch from his mouth and leant forwards. 'Miss?'

'Yes, sir?'

'Where are we?'

'Pall Mall, sir. Detour. Unexploded bomb, sir. I'll go down Vauxhall Bridge Road.'

'Could you turn back? I need to go to Poland Street first. In Soho.'

'Yes, sir.'

'You don't mind?' asked Stratton.

'Course not, sir.'

'The raids'll be starting soon.'

'Shouldn't be bad tonight, sir. No moon.'

'That's true.' Pleased by her composure, Stratton decided that this was as good a time as any. 'I'm very sorry,' he said, 'I've been meaning to ask you...I didn't quite catch your name.'

'That's all right, sir. Legge-Brock. Rosemary.'

Legge-Brock, repeated Stratton to himself, as she turned the car round. Must remember. Rosemary Legge-Brock. Not much better, really. Oh, well...He wondered if Mrs Symmonds would be at home, or if she would already have headed for the shelter. He could always ask at the Wardens' Post.

'Here we are, sir. I'm afraid I'll have to get out and check the house numbers.'

'Don't worry,' said Stratton. 'I'll go. Wait for me here.'

Blundering along in the dark, shining his torch into doorways, Stratton illuminated a couple in a clinch, said 'I beg your pardon,' and decided that the blackout did, after all, have its uses. Cursing himself for not knowing which way the numbers went—he'd walked this beat so often he bloody well ought to remember—he was peering up at a shop sign when somebody grabbed his arm, roughly—'What are you playing at?'—and a beam of light hit him full in the face, almost blinding him.

'Unless you're asking me to dance, Arliss,' said Stratton, irritably, 'I suggest you let go of my arm.'

'Oh, sorry, sir. I didn't recognise you.'

'Obviously,' said Stratton. 'I don't suppose you can take me to number fourteen, can you?'

'Yes, sir. This way. It's only a few doors down.'

Mrs Symmonds stuck her thin face out of the door, a metallic fringe of curlers poking out from beneath her turbaned headscarf. 'What do you want?' she asked truculently.

'Detective Inspector Stratton, CID. You came to see me at the station. Just a few more questions about your husband. I shan't keep you long.'

'I should hope not. I was on my way down to the shelter—they're bound to start any minute.'

'We could talk there, if you like.'

'And have everyone knowing my business? No thank you. Have you found him yet?'

'That's why I'd like a word, Mrs Symmonds.'

She opened the door a grudging few inches to admit him, and motioned him to follow her upstairs. Closing the door of her flat after him, and leaning against it, arms crossed over her non-existent bosom, she said, 'Well?'

Stratton glanced round the poky room. It was none too clean, with yellowing lace curtains and balls of dust beneath the chairs, but there were no obvious traces of male occupancy apart from a greasy-collared coat that lay across the end of the thread-bare sofa. 'I'd like to show you a photograph, if I may,' he said.

'Fair enough.' She twitched the picture out of his hand, glanced at it, and said, 'That's him. What you done with him, then?'

'Nothing, Mrs Symmonds. We haven't found him yet.'

'Where'd you get that, then?'

'Have you seen it before?' Stratton parried.

'No. Must have been when he was in America.'

'When was that?'

'Before we met. He was English, of course. Down to the bone. Went to America on business.'

'What business was that?'

Her expression and tone changed from vinegary shrewdness to vague uncertainty. 'Couldn't rightly say.'

'When did you first meet him?'

'A year or so ago. October.'

'Before the war?'

'That would be right, yes.'

'You told me you'd been married for eighteen years, Mrs Symmonds.'

'I...' Mrs Symmonds's eyes re-focussed, but not on Stratton. She was staring hard at the linoleum, and harsh red spots had appeared on her cheeks. 'I must have made a mistake,' she said, haltingly.

'Rather a big one,' agreed Stratton genially, sensing victory. 'When were you married?'

'I couldn't rightly—'

'Are you married, Mrs Symmonds?'

'Not...as such.'

'I see. How long have you been calling yourself Mrs Symmonds?'

'That's my name!' she said, indignantly.

'So who is Mr Symmonds?' asked Stratton.

'My husband. My late husband, that is.'

'And his name was Arthur Symmonds, was it?'

'Yes.'

'And you'd been married for eighteen years before he died?'

'Yes. He passed away last August.'

'Where was this?'

'Here, in this very room.' She looked around as if she expected to see the late Mr Symmonds, glass-eyed and stuffed with horse-hair, standing in a corner to provide confirmation.

'Did you report his death?'

'What do you mean by that?'

'Did you report it to the proper authorities?'

'I couldn't very well leave him here, could I?' she said, tartly.

'I meant, all the proper authorities.' Mrs Symmonds glared at him, the red spots on her cheeks now intensified to an almost luminous glow. 'It can easily be checked,' Stratton added. 'Fraud is a serious matter.'

'How could I manage?' she burst out. 'I've no children—my boy died when he was six. Tuberculosis. Arthur had a small pension, because he was an invalid, you see, so I just...'

'Carried on drawing it?'

'I didn't know what else to do! I thought of getting a job, but my nerves wouldn't stand it—I'd never done anything like that, only looked after Arthur, and my boy, and I've no family—my sister's in Canada—so I didn't know which way to turn. I didn't mean to do wrong, only the pension was there, so I just went on fetching it, because when he got ill, you see, it was me that collected it, and I never thought...'

'And then you met the man who now calls himself Arthur Symmonds. What did he call himself then?'

'Twyford. Mr Henry Twyford. Wasn't that his real name?'

Stratton hedged. 'We're not sure. Did he have an identification card in that name?'

Mrs Symmonds shook her head. 'He said he'd become an American citizen, so he couldn't get one. He said it was for business. He was going to take me back to America with him, only the war broke out. He said we could be married there.'

Stratton, could see that to a woman like Mrs Symmonds, who clearly revered 'business' in all its nebulous glory, this was an entirely plausible explanation. It was pitifully easy to imagine the dreams that 'business' had conjured for her—men in top hats smoking cigars, with herself, outfitted in artificial silk and a fur coat, on her husband's arm...And with Cecil Duke being educated—or having the semblance of it—and better spoken than she, all he would have had to do was draw a sketchy picture in a few words, and the credulous woman would have filled in the details for herself with very little prompting. She'd been widowed and lonely and a man like Duke must have been the answer to her prayers. And—once he realised that she was able to provide him with a new identity—she was the answer to his. 'Did Henry Twyford know about your husband's pension?' he asked.

'Yes. I told him.'

'And the rent book is in your late husband's name?'

'Yes.'

'And you had his birth certificate?'

Mrs Symmonds nodded.

'And then you obtained an identification card and a ration book in his name.'

'Yes, for Henry. What's going to happen to me?' she wailed. 'I'm so frightened, with him leaving like that, and all this'—she gestured at the sky—'with me on my own. I can't stand it!'

'Why don't you come and sit down,' said Stratton, indicating the sofa. Mrs Symmonds followed him, picking up the coat and sitting crouched over in silence, hugging it to her bony chest. Stratton positioned himself in the chair beside the gas fire, and concentrated on his notebook for several minutes. 'He'll be feeling the cold without this,' she said, suddenly, stroking the coat. 'I was mending it for him. And his poor feet! I've still got that corn plaster. I'm keeping it for him.' Stratton winced inwardly. It was

now almost a certainty—unless some sort of miracle occurred—
that he, or some other poor bugger, would have to tell her that
both the coat and the corn plaster were redundant. 'It's strange
to think I don't really know who he was,' she said, thoughtfully.
'I was ever so fond of him. All these months, it's been terrible.
And when he never came back, I didn't know what to do but I
thought, if he had his cards, you'd be able to find him.'

'The date of birth you gave us.'

'That was his birthday—what he told me.'

'And your husband's date of birth?'

'September the third, 1896.'

'So he was, what…forty-four, when he died?'

'Yes, sir. Consumption, like my boy.'

'I see. And the description you gave at the station, for Mr
Twyford, brown hair and eyes, was that correct?'

'That's right…You will still try to find him, won't you?
Now I've told you. Only I couldn't…Oh, poor Arthur!' Mrs
Symmonds buried her face in the coat.

Watching her weep Stratton felt only pity, and disgust
with Cecil Duke for having aimed at so low and easy a mark.
'I'll do my best,' he said, grimly. 'You can be sure of that.' He
cleared his throat. 'There's one more thing I have to ask you, Mrs
Symmonds, and I'm afraid it's rather…well, indelicate.'

Mrs Symmonds peered at him over the coat, looking
alarmed. 'I'm very sorry,' said Stratton. 'But did you and Mr
Symmonds—Mr Twyford, that is—enjoy a full married life?'

She looked bewildered, then flushed scarlet as she realised
the implication of his words. 'But that's not…not against the law,
is it?'

'No.' Stratton grinned. 'If it was, we'd have to arrest half the
people in London.'

'Oh…' Mrs Symmonds put her hand up to her mouth. 'Oh,
dear…'

'So the answer to my question…?'

'Well,' said Mrs Symmonds, coyly, 'as a matter of fact,
the answer is yes.' Interesting, thought Stratton. A husband to

women and a wife to men: if Duke was Symmonds, then his marriage to Mabel Morgan obviously hadn't been as 'blanc' as Chadwick had thought.

'Thank you,' he said. 'And now, I suggest you go down to the shelter and get yourself settled for the night.'

As they were leaving the flat, Mrs Symmonds put a tentative hand on Stratton's arm. 'What will happen to me, sir?' she asked.

'Well, I'm afraid you can't go on collecting Mr Symmonds's pension, but apart from that, I think we'll call it a lesson learnt, shall we?'

Even in the dark corridor, Stratton could see the relief on her face. 'I don't know how to thank you,' she said. 'I'll write to them about the pension tomorrow morning, I promise.'

'Make sure you do,' said Stratton.

'Oh, I will. And will you let me know if you find Arthur? Even though I'm not...' she lowered her voice, 'not really his wife?'

'Yes. But it might not be good news.'

'Whatever it is,' she said, firmly, 'I'd like to know. It's not knowing makes it so hard.'

Stratton, hearing an echo of Jenny—it's horrible, waiting and not knowing—put his hand over hers. 'I understand,' he said.

At the street door, she turned to him and said, 'You know, it's been a relief to get it off my chest. I'm not...not a wicked person, and I've been ever so worried, going against the regulations. Still,' she brightened, 'you know what they say, One door opens, another closes.'

'Shouldn't that be the other way round?' asked Stratton.

Mrs Symmonds looked puzzled for a moment, and then her face cleared. 'Oh! I see what you mean.' After a moment's thought, she added, 'No, I don't think so. Not in my life.' With that, she disappeared into the blackout.

CHAPTER

57

The sirens sounded as Stratton trudged back to the car. 'Everything all right, sir?' asked Miss Legge-Brock. Rosemary, thought Stratton. Nice name. It suited her.

'Fine,' he said. 'No, don't get out. I can manage.'

'Yes, sir. Where to now?'

'Great Marlborough Street, please. The police station. It's only round the corner.'

'Of course, sir.' Starting the car, she added, 'Colonel Forbes-James says I'm to take you wherever you want to go.'

'Does he indeed?'

'Yes, sir. I'm at your disposal.'

I could get used to this, Stratton thought, as he settled back for the short journey.

Arliss was in the lobby, slurping tea and chatting to the desk sergeant. Seeing Stratton, he stood up and saluted. 'Just stopping off, sir.'

'It's fine, Arliss.'

Stratton leant on the desk and wrote a note to Ballard, requesting a check on Cecil Duke. He wrote down the birthdate, and then, remembering that Dr Byrne had given the dead man's age as around fifty, put, *Try same date back to 1885.* To be on the safe side, he asked Ballard to do the same for Henry Twyford. People in pictures sometimes changed their names, he knew, so that might have been the one he was born with. Stratton wrote this down, then added, *Also need to establish date of death for Duke/ Twyford, August 1935 in house fire at Balcombe, Surrey. Obtain details from local station.* He signed it, adding, at the bottom, *This is most urgent. Request help from Policewoman Gaines if necessary.* He'll like that, he thought, handing it over to the desk sergeant. Arliss, who had been hovering at his elbow throughout, said slyly, 'DCI Machin's not happy, sir.'

'That's a shame,' said Stratton, as affably as he could manage.

'Not happy at all,' repeated Arliss, with some satisfaction. 'Doesn't understand, sir, why they didn't get someone from Special Branch. Doesn't like officers here being taken off essential work. Says it upsets the routine of the station, sir.'

Stratton, who was certain that Arliss hadn't heard Machin say anything of the sort, and equally certain that the desk sergeant was lapping this up, said mildly, 'Hadn't you better be going?'

'Yes, sir.' Arliss put down his mug and straightened his tunic. 'Right away, sir.'

'Off you go, then,' said Stratton. Arliss left, casting a resentful glance back from the doorway when he spotted the Bentley waiting at the kerb. Stratton, hearing him mutter something that sounded suspiciously like, 'All right for some,' spent a brief moment weighing his desire to give Arliss a boot up the arse against the fuss it would undoubtedly cause, and decided with regret that it wasn't worth it. 'I need to make a telephone call,' he told the gaping desk sergeant. 'Right away. Tate 3289.'

The telephone was answered not by the dulcet tones of Miss Mentmore, but by a male voice—younger than Forbes-James, Stratton thought, but of similar background. 'One moment, please.'

A second later, Forbes-James spoke. 'Yes?'

'Something to report, sir.'

'You'd better come over. Still got the car?'

'Yes, sir.'

'Then I hope to see you shortly. Tell Miss Legge-Brock to come up as well, will you?'

It was Handsome who answered the door. When he greeted Rosemary Legge-Brock, Stratton (who had received only a curt nod) recognised the voice he'd heard on the line. 'I'm just off,' he told the FANY, 'F-J says to make yourself some supper.'

You cunt, thought Stratton, seeing her beam as he patted her on the bottom. He was disturbed by the vehemence of his dislike for the man—who might, after all, be perfectly all right—and told himself that it was only because Handsome had undoubtedly bedded Diana, but that didn't help. The plain fact was that Diana, like all the other women that Handsome had unquestionably seduced, wouldn't be available to Stratton, even if he wasn't married. He watched as Handsome donned his coat and hat, kissed Miss Legge-Brock on the cheek (if she'd had a tail she'd have wagged it) and left the flat.

Forbes-James appeared at the door of his office. 'Come in, come in. Would you like something to eat? I'm sure Miss Legge-Brock can rustle up some food for you.'

'No thank you,' said Stratton. 'My wife will have something for me at home.'

'Well then, I mustn't keep you too long. Help yourself to a drink.'

'Thank you, sir.' Stratton went to the tray and poured himself a modest shot of whisky.

'Excellent. Sit down. What news?'

'Well, sir, we thought that Cecil Duke was killed in a fire at the house he shared with Mabel Morgan in 1935, but that isn't the case. There was a body—unknown, but presumably male—which Mabel falsely identified as Duke. Duke was in America at the time, and didn't know anything about it until quite recently.' Stratton produced the letter and waited while

Forbes-James read it. 'It seems, sir, that Duke returned to England using the name Henry Twyford. When he met Mrs Symmonds, who was fraudulently collecting her late husband's pension and rations, he simply took over Mr Symmonds's identity. I think he meant to confront Mabel with what he knew, with a view to obtaining money. It would certainly explain why he didn't involve the police.'

'As I see it,' said Forbes-James, 'all this raises three questions.'

'Only three, sir?'

'Only three that need concern us. Who killed Cecil Duke?' Forbes-James held up the photograph, 'assuming, of course, that your body is Duke. Why was he killed, and what does it have to do with the rest of this business?'

'Quite a lot, I'd say, sir.'

'I'm afraid you're probably right. As you know, I rather wished to avoid all this, but it seems that Mr Chadwick has landed us in the middle of it.'

'You can say that again, sir.' Stratton leant forward, elbows on knees, and stared at the carpet, thinking. He knew he'd have to come clean about Johnny, but not now. He must tell Jenny first, and another few hours could make no difference...The thought of it made his stomach lurch, and he set down his drink, feeling a sudden rush of nausea.

'Do you think,' said Forbes-James, 'that Miss Morgan could have been blackmailing Apse over the film?'

Stratton forced his attention back to the matter in hand. 'As well as Montague, you mean?'

'Yes.'

'No,' said Stratton, 'I don't. According to her friend Joe Vincent, she didn't have any money.'

'Fair enough. But, assuming that Duke is the body in the church, she may have had something to do with his death. The position, as I understand it, is this: Mabel and Duke have become estranged—not surprising if he's been behaving like a nancy—and he's gone, and as far as she's concerned he's never coming back. When the house catches fire—presumably by accident—she takes advantage of the situation to identify the dead man as her husband and claim the insurance. She thinks she's quite safe, and she is—until Duke returns and threatens to expose the fraud.' Forbes-James tapped the solicitor's letter that Stratton had given him, 'So: she has him killed before he can say anything.'

'I suppose that's possible, sir, but I don't see how she could have done it on her own.'

'Someone could have helped her.'

'One of Marks's lot, you mean? That doesn't make sense, sir. They don't do favours, and she had nothing to give them.'

'She had the film and the letters.'

'But then why not hand them over? Why hide them? She'd hidden them pretty well because Joe Vincent told me they'd pulled the place apart, looking. And she was frightened, sir. Joe told me. If she knew that Apse was going to send someone to fetch them...'

'I see what you mean. I was thinking that if Apse hadn't been willing to pay her, she might have put the handkerchief on the body in order to incriminate him.'

'If she ever had the handkerchief in the first place. As far as we know, sir, Mabel and Apse never met. I don't think there's any connection between her and Marks, either. I think that the key to this is Duke, not Mabel. If Duke had been to see Sir Neville on his own account, he might have got the handkerchief that way—or had it given to him. That seems far more likely.'

'Perhaps. What a muddle.' Forbes-James sipped his drink thoughtfully. 'Now, I don't think there's anything more we can usefully do this evening, so I suggest you cut off home. Will your man Ballard have come up with some answers by tomorrow afternoon, do you think?'

'I hope so, sir. I told him it was urgent. There's also the matter of who did perish in the house fire, sir, if it wasn't Mr Duke.'

'I think we can leave that to the local constabulary—if they wish to investigate. Why not meet me here at, say, one o'clock. I'll see if Miss Mentmore can't rustle up a spot of lunch.'

Sitting in the car on the way home, Stratton stared through the window into the darkness. Here and there he could make out the edge of a building, but not much else. What a muddle, indeed. Just thinking about it made his head spin. And he was going to have to tell Jenny about Johnny. There was no getting round it—Wallace had named him, and Rogers might well be able to identify him, if called upon. He felt guilty about the boy—not spotting the danger signals earlier and acting before—but angry as well. If it weren't for Johnny, at least he'd be going back to a peaceful home and a half-decent night's sleep. Now it was ruined, and Jenny was bound to think he didn't trust her because he hadn't told her before, when in fact he'd been trying to spare her the worry of it—she had enough of that with Monica and Pete. If only they were at home, Stratton thought. He longed to go up to their bedrooms, to watch them as they slept, to kiss their foreheads, to be able to talk to them and hug them and keep them safe from harm. Not just bombs, but all the harm in the world. He put his hand in his pocket and took out the little knitted scarf he'd taken from Monica's doll. Holding it in his palm and stroking the nubbly pink wool with his thumb, he thought of his daughter, black haired and blue eyed like himself, but with her mother's pretty face, and felt utterly helpless. Like Jenny said—waiting and not knowing. And she'd be waiting now: he could picture her dozing in an armchair, cheek resting against the anti-macassar, a piece of mending or the Picture Post lying unattended on her lap.

'Sir? Are you all right?'

He wasn't aware of making a sound, but he must have done. 'Oh…yes. I'm sorry. Just thinking aloud.'

'That's all right, sir. Be home soon.'

Yes, thought Stratton, and I'm going to lob a grenade into it. He wondered if 'home' would ever feel the same again.

CHAPTER

58

'I'm sorry, love.'

Jenny pulled her handkerchief from the sleeve of her cardigan and blew her nose. 'Why didn't you tell me before, Ted? You said there was nothing to worry about. Every time I've asked you about it, you've acted as if I'm fussing over nothing.'

'I was hoping it would blow over. And I didn't know for certain! Honestly, Jenny—'

'You told Lilian it was just boasting. And me! Silly talk, you said.'

'I thought it might have been boasting. I didn't think there was any point in worrying you about it.'

'Worrying me! Johnny could...He could be...' Jenny started to cry again.

'Please, love...' Stratton leant across the kitchen table to touch her face, but she batted his hand away.

'I knew there was something wrong!'

'Then...' Stratton felt bewildered. 'Why didn't you ask?'

'I've tried! You wouldn't talk about it! And you've been working late with this...whatever it is, and coming back in that big car, and telling me about having lunch in restaurants—'

'Once.'

'You've been so far away, Ted.'

Stung, Stratton said, 'Well, you've been pretty busy yourself, working at the Rest Centre till all hours.'

'That isn't true! There's always supper on the table—I haven't neglected anything here, so don't say I have.'

'I wasn't saying you had. Just that we haven't had much time to talk, that's all.'

'It's not just time, Ted. It's because it was about Johnny, wasn't it?'

'Not entirely, love, I've had a lot—'

'Don't you care?'

'Of course I do.'

'And poor Lilian! What are we going to do? You should have told me, Ted.'

'I had to be sure, love.'

'You said he denied it.'

'He did deny it, but he knows about it, Jenny. He knows this man George Wallace, he knows Miss Morgan. "Some old girl up West", remember.'

'But that could have been anyone—anything!'

'He was there, Jenny. Even if he didn't kill Miss Morgan, he certainly threatened Joe Vincent, and lent a hand beating him up, and helped Wallace turn over the flat. Wallace told me.'

'And you'd take the word of a criminal over your own nephew?'

'Wallace didn't just pluck Johnny's name out of the air, Jenny. And he doesn't know he's my nephew, either.'

'How do you know?'

'He'd have said so. A man like that, if there's something he can use to his advantage, he won't hesitate.'

'But there must be lots of people called Johnny Booth. And you said this...Joe Whatsisname...is going overseas, so how can he say?'

'There was another witness, love. One of the lodgers. He described both of them.'

'But that was when they went to burgle the flat, not when the lady was killed.'

'I know. But the two things are connected, and the same man—Abie Marks—is almost certainly behind both of them.'

'But you don't know that for sure, do you?'

'No. We've been piecing it together. I wanted to be sure.'

'But you're not absolutely sure, are you? Not about this murder—if that's what it is?'

'It's a bit more than just a few petrol coupons, Jenny.'

'Johnny wouldn't kill anyone! And anyway, they said it was suicide, didn't they? You told me. The coroner said.'

'Yes, but—'

'This is all to do with those old films, isn't it, and that man you had lunch with.'

'I really can't talk about it, Jenny.'

'Why did you have to bring those things home? Why didn't you just leave it alone?'

'Believe me, I've been thinking the same thing. But that wouldn't have been right. Miss Morgan deserves better than that. Everyone does.'

'What about Lilian having her son branded a murderer? Doesn't she deserve something, too?'

Stratton sighed. 'Of course she does. But I'm afraid this is bigger than just one family.'

'But it's your own family!'

'I know that. But if I know something about Johnny, and I don't say anything, then I'm breaking the law. I've kept quiet for as long as I can.'

'Supposing it was Pete?'

'It isn't Pete. It won't ever be Pete, not if I have anything to do with it. This is Reg's fault, Jenny, and mine as well.'

'No!' Jenny sat upright, her eyes glistening. 'It's not your fault. You're always trying to be responsible for the whole world, and you can't.'

Stratton didn't know what to say to that. 'I'll have to tell them tomorrow. That's why I'm telling you now. I shouldn't, but I wanted you to understand the position.'

'Will they arrest him straight away?'

'He'll be brought in for questioning. That'll be the local police. It won't be me doing it.'

'That's something, at any rate.' Jenny blew her nose again, and said, more hopefully, 'Then Lilian and Reg won't have to know you had anything to do with it.'

'I don't think that's going to work, love. It's my case. Well, partly my case. It's complicated.'

'But you won't have to carry on with it, will you? Not when it's someone in your family?'

'Ordinarily, I'd say not, but as I say, it's complicated. If it came to court, I'd have to give evidence, and—'

'Oh, Ted!'

Stratton went around the table and knelt down beside her. He hugged her, and stroked her hair while she sobbed into his shoulder. Hearing her weep, and powerless to comfort her, he felt like the worst person in the world.

CHAPTER 59

Diana stopped beneath the gateway of Dolphin Square, her heart pounding, and feeling as if she had just been punched in the stomach. Apse was coming straight towards her, and he'd seen her. There was no doubt about that. She stood rooted to the spot, trying to think of something to say. Ever since that terrible night in his flat she'd avoided thinking about him as much as possible, but the reality, close to, haggard, with bitter eyes, shocked her and overwhelmed her with guilt. One more step, and he'd be beside her—she must speak. She worked saliva into her dry mouth. 'Good morning,' she managed, then ducked her head to avoid his gaze. Was he going to shout at her, too, and call her a bitch? She braced herself for the onslaught. If it happens, walk away, she told herself. Walk away, and keep walking. She raised her eyes to his.

'Diana.' He nodded curtly, and made as if to move past her, then stopped. 'I thought I could trust you,' he said.

Diana opened her mouth, realised she had nothing to say, and closed it again.

'You know I'm not helping them by choice?'

Diana, taking 'them' to mean the Right Club, said, 'Yes, sir.'

'F-J sanctioned it, didn't he?'

'I don't think,' said Diana, trying to keep her voice steady, 'that I ought to be speaking to you, sir.'

'Probably not. But this is a dangerous game, Diana. You may think of yourself as F-J's creature, but he won't help you.'

Diana took a pace backwards. 'Help me?'

Apse shook his head. 'Nor will Ventriss. If you're lucky, you'll get a warning, but then you'll be on your own and you'll realise what a—' He stopped, turning his head sharply as footsteps sounded on the path. Following his gaze, Diana knew she'd seen the man somewhere before, although she couldn't think where.

'Dr Pyke,' said Apse, curtly. That was it—F-J's neighbour, who'd taken his blood pressure. Who'd 'dealt with' the corpse of Julia Vigo. And God knows what else, thought Diana.

'Sir Neville,' said Dr Pyke, formally, 'And Mrs Calthrop, isn't it?'

'Yes,' said Diana, feeling slightly sick. 'How do you do?'

'Very well, thank you.' Dr Pyke was looking not at her but at Apse, who was staring at him so intently that she had the impression he had forgotten her existence. She was aware of an almost tangible change in the atmosphere and stared, uncomprehending, from one man to the other. Apse's curt, 'Good morning' sounded so harsh that she almost flinched at the words. Now, with another nod to her, he turned and walked away down Grosvenor Road in the direction of Westminster.

Dr Pyke remained beside her, watching Apse until he was out of sight. Diana cleared her throat. She wanted to thank him for rescuing her, but that wouldn't be appropriate...or would it? Had he, in fact, rescued her, or had he been trying to prevent Apse from telling her something? He knew F-J, and clearly, he knew Apse: the way the two men had looked at each other suggested he might know rather a lot about Apse and, unless she'd imagined it, she'd had a sense of something shared between them. Her mind raced, picking up and discarding possibilities.

'Mrs Calthrop?'

'I'm so sorry,' said Diana, 'Wool gathering...'

'I was merely remarking that it was a pleasant day for November.'

'Yes, very—er—mild.' She made a show of looking at her watch. 'Oh dear, I must hurry along. F-J will be wondering where I've got to.'

'I'm sure he will. Can't expect him to do without his Girl Friday.'

'Oh, hardly that.' Diana forced a smile. 'But I ought to be going.'

'Of course.' Raising his hat, Dr Pyke left the square. Diana paused long enough before walking across the garden to note that he'd gone in the opposite direction to Apse. On the face of it, it was more uncomfortable than actually important, but she had an odd, prickling feeling that Dr Pyke would inform F-J even if she didn't. He obviously knew about her—the way he'd called her F-J's Girl Friday—unless that was just an attempt to be pleasant...It occurred to Diana that perhaps it hadn't been pure chance that he'd arrived at that exact moment. She didn't know which flat he lived in, but perhaps you could see the gateway from the window? It seemed fanciful to think that he'd be looking out for either her or Apse, but nothing would surprise her. And what had Apse meant about F-J and Claude not helping her, and about getting a warning if she was lucky?

With a heavy heart, and the feeling that the waters were closing over her head, Diana made her way slowly towards Nelson House.

CHAPTER
60

'Remember that chap in the barber's shop a couple of months ago? The business over the hairbrush and the spectacles?'

'I'm not likely to forget it in a hurry, sir.'

'His name's Mr Rogers. He was one of the residents of the bombed house at Conway Street where Mabel Morgan lived. He's a potential witness, so we need to find him.'

Ballard looked as if he'd like to ask several questions about this, but merely said, 'I've got the details in my notebook, sir, but as to where he is now…'

'Try the Wardens' Post first. If they can't help, try the Assistance Board. Someone must know.' Stratton lit a cigarette, hoping it would help him concentrate. He was exhausted. He'd spent the night pent up in the narrow bunk in the Anderson, listening to Jenny weep and desperately searching for some reason, however slender, not to tell Forbes-James about Johnny. Around four o'clock in the morning, when Jenny's sobs had subsided, he'd fallen into a troubled doze and dreamt that Jenny, Lilian and Doris were ranged in front of him like judges in a court, while he stood in the dock and Reg pronounced the death sentence, and Pete and Monica up in the gallery turned their backs and would not look at him.

He'd tormented himself during the bus ride to work, wondering what the children would say when they discovered their cousin had been arrested. Monica had never seemed to like Johnny much ('He's rude, Daddy. Rude and nasty.') but Pete, he suspected, would be rather enamoured of the idea of becoming one of his gang. Several times, Stratton had caught him imitating Johnny's swaggering walk, and he'd once pinched a packet of cigarettes for the purpose of currying favour with his cousin. Stratton had given him hell for that and he'd promised never to do it again, but all the same…Supposing his children never forgave him? That would be hardest of all. There was also, as Jenny had reminded him while they were preparing for bed, the matter of Mrs Chetwynd, who might well decide that she didn't want the relatives of a criminal under her roof.

Thinking of all this made Stratton want to grab Johnny by the scruff of the neck and thrash him to within an inch of his life. The stupid little fucker had messed things up for everyone, himself included. He cast the whole issue from his mind—dwelling on it could do no good at all—and turned his attention back to Ballard.

'How are you getting on with the rest of it? Gaines giving you a hand, is she?'

'Yes, sir.' Ballard ventured a grin, leading Stratton to wonder if he should utter a word of warning about keeping things discreet. Before he had time to pursue the thought, Ballard had stuck a sheaf of notes under his nose.

'Here's what we've got so far, sir. Nothing for Henry Twyford for the date you gave me, but we found a Cecil Henry Duke, born sixteenth April 1888 in Torquay, died thirteenth August 1935. That was in the fire, sir. Identity confirmed by his wife Mabel Morgan. A neighbour saw the smoke and called the fire brigade, but they were too late to save him, or the house. Body was in quite a state, apparently.'

'So she wouldn't have been able to identify it by looking at it?'

'Not by the features, sir, but she said it was him. Wasn't it?'

'I very much doubt it,' said Stratton.

'They're sending us the report, sir, but I don't think there'll be much there. As far as they were concerned, it was an accident. They didn't investigate.'

'They'd no reason to,' said Stratton. 'You'd better see if you can track down Duke's dentist in Sussex—assuming he had one—and give Dr Byrne a call. We'll need photographs of the teeth from the body in the church. Those,' he scribbled the address, 'are the details, but I imagine he'll remember it well enough. Even if a dentist doesn't have Mr Duke's records, they can often identify their own handiwork. You'll also need to contact the major shipping lines and check passenger lists to America—see if Cecil Duke travelled there between...' Stratton thumbed through his notes to find the interview with Chadwick, 'May 1935, when we know he was in England, and mid-August, when he's supposed to have died. And see if you can find evidence of a return passage, either for Cecil Duke or the other name he used, Henry Twyford, in '39, up to October.'

'I'll do my best, Sir. Will that be all?'

'For the moment, yes.'

Stratton looked at his watch, found that it was almost midday, and wondered what, apart from miserably turning things over in his mind, he'd been doing all the morning. In the absence of Miss Legge-Brock and the Bentley, he decided to walk down to the Embankment in the hope that it might help to clear his head, and then catch a bus to Dolphin Square.

The fresh air, such as it was, did not have the desired effect. Everything he saw—buildings, shelters, people, even bloody sandbags—seemed to remind him of Johnny or Jenny or the kids. Looking into Suffolk Place as he passed down the Haymarket, he caught sight of a bombed house, the outer wall and stairs collapsed across the pavement and the lavatory, complete with cistern and chain, perched precariously on the landing above. Down the pan to nowhere: it was a suitable picture of where his career seemed to be heading. And, he thought, I'm on my way to pull the plug and land not only myself but my whole family, up to our necks in shit. He bent his head and, hands in pockets, trudged on towards Whitehall.

'Most unfortunate, your meeting Apse like that.' Forbes-James sounded matter-of-fact. 'I'm very sorry, my dear, but I suppose it was bound to happen sooner rather than later. What did he say?'

'Just that he'd thought he could trust me,' said Diana. 'And he looked so bleak.'

'Did he say anything else?' asked F-J.

'Not really, sir,' lied Diana.

'He didn't threaten you in any way?'

Diana shook her head. 'I think he might have done, sir, but Dr Pyke came along and rescued me.'

'Did he indeed? What happened?'

'Nothing, really. They just sort of stared at each other. I didn't know Dr Pyke knew Apse, sir.'

'No reason why you should...But living in the same place, especially hugger-mugger like this, it's hardly surprising.'

'I suppose not, sir. But the way they were...It's probably nothing, sir, but you did say to tell you everything—it made me think that Dr Pyke might know something about it.'

'About what?'

'About Apse, sir.'

'What about him?'

'Well...the whole business.'

'Did he say anything to indicate that?'

'No, sir. But I just thought—well, you know him, sir, and perhaps...' Diana tailed off, then tried again. 'I know it sounds foolish, sir, but...'

'Yes,' said F-J, 'it does. I've warned you about getting yourself so worked up that you imagine the whole world to be one vast conspiracy, but that really isn't the case. It's a bad state of mind to be in. Dangerous. This meeting with Apse has obviously rattled you more than I thought it would, but you're stronger than that, Diana. Now, stop being a silly girl and we'll say no more about it.'

'Yes, sir,' said Diana.

'But,' F-J continued, 'while we're on the subject of being silly, I understand you've been seeing Ventriss again.'

'I—'

'Don't bother,' said F-J. 'I overheard some conversation between Lally and Margot. I doubt very much if they were making it up.'

'It was a chance meeting, sir, at the 400 Club. Nothing more.'

F-J made a dismissive gesture. 'I've warned you once, Diana.'

Diana stared down at her lap, Apse's words, If you're lucky, you'll get a warning...echoing in her mind. 'I know, sir.'

'I'm disappointed in you, Diana. Please see that it doesn't happen again.'

'Yes, sir.'

'Right. Now we've cleared that up, I'd better fill you in on what's been happening before Inspector Stratton gets here.'

CHAPTER 62

'I've brought Mrs Calthrop up to date with the latest developments,' said Forbes-James. Stratton, watching Diana as she cleared up the plates of cold meat and salad, thought she looked pale and tired, and there was an air of fragility about her that could not, he felt, be entirely explained by Forbes-James's news. Perhaps, he thought, darkly, it had something to do with Handsome, and was again taken aback by how angry the thought of this made him.

'—any news for us?' The question—which, by the sound of Forbes-James's voice, was being asked for the second time—brought him back to the matter in hand.

'Yes, sir.' Stratton got out his notebook and passed on Ballard's findings and his further instructions.

Forbes-James sighed. 'I won't deny,' he said, 'that this is all getting rather too complicated for my liking. Too many people involved. However, there seems to be nothing we can do but press on.'

Stratton took a deep breath. 'Actually, sir, there's something else.'

'Oh?' Forbes-James, who had accepted coffee from Diana, stopped in the act of drinking, his cup in mid-air. 'Serious?'

'I'm afraid so, sir. At least, it is for me. It concerns Miss Morgan. As you know, sir, I never thought she was a suicide, and

Joe Vincent—the man whose flat she lived in—had a visit from a couple of thugs after her death.'

'Looking for something, yes.'

'Well, from the description Vincent gave me, I knew that one of them was a man called George Wallace, who works for Abie Marks. I also have descriptions from another lodger. I've made some further enquiries, and it appears that the other person is my nephew John Booth.'

Forbes-James looked at him intently. 'I see. That's most unfortunate. I assume that no-one else knows about this?'

'Only my wife, sir. I've told her not to say anything.'

Forbes-James raised his eyebrows. 'She won't, sir.'

'Can you be sure it's your nephew?'

'Wallace admitted it. We're holding him, sir—a van-load of stolen cigarettes. It's a bit irregular, but I decided not to charge him with anything until I'd worked out his part in this business.'

'Well, that makes things a bit easier...I take it that this character Wallace doesn't know about the family connection?'

'No, sir. But I think that Wallace and my...and Booth... may have had something to do with Miss Morgan's death.'

'Pushed her, you mean? Killed her?'

'I wouldn't go as far as that, sir. But I think they were present when it happened. Something my nephew said.'

'Rather hard to prove, I should have thought. Unless one has a confession, of course...And the man in the church? Did they have anything to do with that?'

'Wallace denies it, sir.'

Forbes-James shrugged. 'He would, wouldn't he? What do you think?'

Stratton rubbed a hand over his face. 'I honestly don't know, sir. Marks has a lot of people besides Wallace to do his dirty work for him. And if Sir Neville—'

'I must remind you,' said Forbes-James, severely, 'that there is no proven connection between Apse and this man Marks.'

'I'm aware of that, sir.'

Forbes-James sighed again. 'Well,' he said, 'it looks as if we all have a reason for wanting this wrapped up as quickly and as quietly as possible. How do you suggest we proceed?'

'The easiest way to get Marks to talk,' said Stratton, 'would be getting a confession from George Wallace, but I'm afraid I've used up my credit there, for the time being, at least. Booth should be more co-operative, but he may not know very much about Marks.'

'Better talk to him first, then,' said Forbes-James. 'I realise this is going to be pretty difficult for you.' Stratton thought, but did not say, that that was as masterly an understatement as he'd ever heard. Instead, he said, 'I didn't want to do anything without your say-so, sir, because it's not an official investigation. Not for us, anyway.'

'Of course not. Your nephew's not a member of any right-wing organisation, is he?'

Stratton shook his head. 'No interest in politics at all, as far as I know.'

'Shame. We could have had him detained under Regulation 18B, but that would seem to be taking things a bit far.' Forbes-James lit a cigarette and stared into space for a moment. 'I think,' he said, 'I'd better telephone the Yard and explain the situation. Why don't you take a turn round the square? Spot of fresh air. Take Mrs Calthrop with you.'

Stratton and Diana gravitated to the nearest bench. 'I'm so sorry,' she said. 'It must be awful for you and your poor wife.'

'He's her sister's son,' said Stratton, 'So it's worse for her. You know, Mrs Calthrop,' he added, 'I thought he'd tell me to leave.'

'That F-J would?'

'Yes.'

Diana shook her head. 'That's not how it works. Anyway,' she added, 'he likes you.'

'Does he?'

'Definitely. And please, Inspector, don't call me Mrs Calthrop. It's Diana.'

'Ted,' said Stratton. Diana looked surprised.

'I wasn't christened Inspector Stratton, you know.'

'No, of course not. How silly of me. Ted. Ted...' She put her head on one side and contemplated him. 'You know, Inspector, I really think you're more of an Edward. May I call you that instead?'

'If you prefer it,' said Stratton, nonplussed by her sudden flirtatiousness.

'I didn't mean to offend you,' Diana said quickly, lowering her eyes. 'If you don't like being called Edward...'

Stratton thought for a moment. He couldn't have said exactly why, but it seemed right, coming from her. 'It's fine,' he said. 'Cigarette?'

'Why not? I'm sure F-J will give us a wave when he wants us back.'

As Stratton leant over to give her a light, he was conscious of her delicate perfume, the closeness of her face and hair. Was his desire to kiss her, he wondered, because of Diana herself, or because of his need for comfort, or merely something to take his mind off whatever might be unfolding upstairs?

She seemed aware of it—or of something, anyway—because she drew back with a nervous laugh and said, 'Of course, we're assuming the worst about all this, but we don't know what's going to happen.'

'It won't be good, though,' said Stratton.

'No, I don't suppose it will. You know...' She looked at him oddly, her head on one side again. 'When I was young, I had a nanny—a lot of different ones, but this one was older than the others and stayed longer. If anyone talked about the future—you know, something that would happen or might happen—she'd say,'—Diana gave a reasonable imitation of an elderly woman—'"Well, I shan't be here to see it". As if that satisfied her. I used to think she could see into the future, that there was going to be a disaster and we'd all be killed or something. When I got older I felt sorry for her because she didn't have anything to look forward to, but now I'm beginning to dread things. Not the bombs—one's used to that—but...' She looked round the garden, then up at the window of Forbes-James's flat, '...all this. People not being who you thought they were. Nothing feels secure any more...I'm sorry, it's probably all nonsense, and in any case, I shouldn't be troubling you with it.'

'That's all right,' said Stratton, then, after a pause, and without really knowing what prompted him, other than a strong feeling that her comments were more wide-ranging than she was letting on, added, 'May I ask you something?'

'If you like. Of course, I might not know the answer.'

'Are you in love with him?'

Diana gave a muted shriek. 'With F-J?'

'No,' said Stratton. 'The man I saw in there.' He nodded in the direction of Nelson House. 'The one who took you out to lunch on the day that we first met.'

'When you came to see Apse, you mean?'

'That's right.'

'Oh, him.' Stratton thought she was about to dismiss the suggestion as laughable, but instead she said, solemnly, 'How did you know?'

'I didn't. But I thought the two of you seemed friendly.'

'Yes,' said Diana. 'That's the difficulty. Rather more than a difficulty, actually. What did you think of him?'

'I only saw him for a moment.'

'You only saw me for a moment. You must have formed an impression.'

Stratton was tempted to tell her the truth, which was that he'd been too busy looking at her to bother much about Handsome, but he knew this wasn't what was wanted. He thought that—in so far as he was capable of judging these things—she wanted an honest answer, so he said, 'I thought he seemed dangerous.'

'That's what everyone kept telling me,' Diana said. 'A breaker of hearts.' She laughed again, and added, 'I am, by the way. In love with him.'

'And that's not...' Stratton hesitated. 'Not good?'

'No, it isn't. NBG, in fact.'

'Because?'

'Because, Inspector,' she said, lightly, 'as you've already gathered, I'm married, because F-J is furious about it and has forbidden me to see him again, and because Claude—'

'That's what he's called, is it?' asked Stratton, thinking that the wretched man would have to have a matinée idol sort of name.

'Yes. Claude Ventriss. He's one of F-J's.'

'So I gathered,' said Stratton. 'He was coming out of his office when I went up last night.'

'Was he?' Diana frowned. 'Claude isn't the sort of person one ought to fall in love with if one wants to keep one's sanity.' She stood up. 'I can't imagine why I'm telling you all this.'

'Because I asked you.'

'You won't say anything to F-J, will you? I mean, I honestly have stopped seeing him—not that anyone seems to believe it—but...' She grimaced.

'Of course not. I hope you didn't mind my asking.'

'No, I ought to mind, awfully, but I don't.' Glancing upwards, she said, 'Look, F-J's summoning us. We'd better go back.'

Following Diana up the stairs, Stratton wondered if she'd meant what she said about keeping her sanity. There was nothing melodramatic about the way she'd said it, and yet it hadn't seemed altogether a joke—that wouldn't fit with her clarity about her situation or her apparently passive acceptance of it. But then again, you couldn't choose who you fell in love with, any more than you could stop loving them if it proved inconvenient or dangerous. But if Claude—Stratton's lip curled in disgust—Ventriss wasn't... how had she put it...The person she thought he was, then surely that would change her feelings about him? NBG, she'd said, but she wasn't married to the man, so she didn't have to resign herself to having backed the wrong horse. Stratton eyed her ankles and wondered what her husband was like. Like Ventriss, probably: a man who expected, and took, a woman like Diana as no more than his due. But she'd betrayed him, hadn't she?

Standing behind her on the landing as she opened the door, Stratton felt the discomfort of disloyalty to his wife. He wondered, gloomily, if he and Jenny would ever be the same again. Would he be condemned forever, with Johnny always between them, and constant, silent accusation—far more effective than shouting— reducing him to an outsider in his own home, a man who was there to pay the bills, to be fed and watered, and nothing more? Reg and Lilian would think that he'd betrayed them, all right... And suppose Donald sided with them? If Doris took Lilian's part, he'd probably have to as well, to keep the peace, and that would mean he'd lost not only his best friend, but his ally. Christ, he thought, I could do with a drink. Numbness, that was what he needed, a good, thick buffer between himself and the whole bloody mess. He wanted to turn round and go back down the stairs, find some spit-and-sawdust place where no-one knew him, sit by himself, and get stewed.

'Here.' Forbes-James handed him a large brandy. 'You look as if you might need it. Diana?'

'No, thank you, sir.'

'Well, sit down. I'll need you to take notes. I've spoken to Roper. He's going to instruct the station at Tottenham, but he won't mention your name, Stratton. They'll bring the boy in—attempted burglary, threatening behaviour and so forth— and I'll see him tomorrow. I want you to take me through the details again, and you'd better tell me a bit about the lad, too. After that, I suggest you get yourself home.'

CHAPTER
63

It was chilly and raining when Stratton left the pub. He stood in the doorway and peered out at the dark street. When he'd left Dolphin Square, he'd chosen the place deliberately, drawn by the look of it—a grim Victorian building with a funereal aspect, drab and comfortless inside, with a skinny, sour faced barmaid. When he'd asked for whisky, she'd jerked her thumb at a crudely chalked sign saying No Spirits and said, 'Sorry', in a voice that sounded anything but.

The bar had been almost empty when he'd arrived, but it had filled up remarkably quickly. A sluttish girl with tow-coloured hair and a loud, nasal voice had her large, flat bottom pressed right against the edge of the small table where he sat, his back to the wall. She was surrounded by four men, but as she seemed to treat them all with the same combination of familiarity and disdain, Stratton couldn't tell which one was 'with' her. Next to this group stood two hefty, masculine looking women, dressed in trousers and armbands, and beside those a large number of soldiers, as well as older men in suits and overcoats, huddled in twos and threes, and a sprinkling of young couples.

After almost three hours spent intermittently fighting his way to the bar and back, Stratton was tipsy, but nowhere near as drunk as he wanted to be. Normally a two or, at most, three-pint man, he hadn't reckoned with the difficulty of getting tight on nothing but watered-down beer, even if it was chasing Forbes-James's generous brandy.

'Christ,' he muttered, turning the collar of his overcoat up against the spitefully gusting wind. It was absurd—the only occasion of his life, so far as he could remember, when he'd actually tried to get a skinful, and he couldn't manage it. At least, he thought, as he walked, only slightly unsteadily, towards Victoria station, he might be spared a hangover, although, given the circumstances, the nausea and general dreariness of it would probably come as a blessing if it dulled the pain of his situation.

By the time Stratton reached home, he felt sober once more. Dreading his reception, he tried to make his entry as quiet as possible, but Jenny must have heard him fumbling with his key because the door was suddenly yanked open and she threw herself into his arms. 'I've been so worried!'

'It's all right, love.' Stratton half-carried her the few steps into the hall and closed the door with some difficulty, as she refused to let him go. 'I'm sorry, I've been…'

'Drinking.' Jenny looked up at him, half-sobbing, half-laughing. 'You smell like a brewery, but it doesn't matter. You're here, thank God! It's been terrible. Lilian came round this afternoon. I was upstairs but I knew it was her because she called through the door, so I pretended I wasn't here. I was sure she was going to let herself in, but she didn't, thank God. I felt so bad about it, and then Doris came about half-past seven, when they took Johnny—she was at Lilian and Reg's, her and Donald, and Lilian told her to come round and fetch you…I didn't know what to say to Doris, Ted. She said Lilian was in hysterics, and she kept telling her you'd said the boy'd done nothing wrong and she wanted you to go to the station and get it all cleared up so he could come home. Doris wanted me to go over there, but

I couldn't, Ted, I just couldn't! Not knowing...She kept asking what the matter was, and in the end I had to tell her—about the burglary, not the other. I'm sorry, Ted, but I had to.'

'It's all right,' said Stratton, rubbing her back. 'I understand.'

'Doris didn't speak to me, Ted. Didn't say a word, just looked at me and then she left. Such a look...And now she'll tell Lilian, and Lilian'll know I didn't answer the door to her and they'll never speak to me again...And then when you didn't come back, I thought...I don't know what I thought. I was just so worried, and thinking about Lilian, and Doris, and Reg...I thought I was going mad!'

'I should have been here,' said Stratton, helplessly. 'I'm sorry.'

'No,' said Jenny, through tears. 'It's all right. I understand why you didn't come back.'

'Do you?'

Jenny nodded. 'You did what was right. I know it wasn't easy for you.'

'Are you on my side, then? You don't hate me?'

'Course not.'

Stratton planted a kiss on her forehead. 'Thank you, love.' They stood there, embracing, looking at each other, looking away, and holding each other tighter still, until Stratton felt like crying too, from sheer relief. Jenny, her face buried in his chest, heard him clear his throat and poked a finger in his ribs. 'Don't you start,' she whispered. 'Can't have both of us turning on the waterworks, or we'll drown.'

A loud bang on the door behind them made them both jump. 'It's Donald. Can I have a word?'

Stratton and Jenny exchanged glances, then Stratton released her, and went to open the door. Donald's face, half in shadow, gave Stratton no idea what he was thinking. Bracing himself for recrimination or abuse, he was taken aback when Donald said, quietly, 'I don't blame you, mate. It's not your fault.'

Stratton could tell that he meant it. 'Thanks, Don. Why don't you come in?'

'Can't stay long.' Donald followed him into the kitchen. 'Doris is still with Lilian. She's in a hell of a state.'

'I'm not surprised,' said Stratton, grimly. 'Have a seat. How's Reg?'

'Never seen him like it,' said Donald, pulling out a chair. 'I thought he'd…' he glanced at Jenny, who had sat down next to Stratton and put her hand in his, 'well, you know…when the police came, but he didn't. Not a word. As if he'd been struck dumb. Poor Lilian was crying her eyes out, but he just stood there as if he couldn't really take it in. I don't blame him, poor chap. What a business.'

'I couldn't—' Stratton began, but Donald cut him off.

'It's all right. You don't have to explain, Ted. It's your job. If Johnny's been stealing, that's—'

'It's worse than that,' Jenny interrupted. 'You might as well tell him, Ted. Everyone's going to know soon enough.'

'Worse?' Donald looked at Stratton for confirmation.

'I think I'll leave you to it.' Jenny squeezed his hand. 'I'll go upstairs and lie down till the siren goes.'

They watched her go, then Stratton said, 'I don't blame her not wanting to hear it all again. It's knocked her for six.' Donald listened closely to his explanation, his eyes narrowed. There was a long silence after Stratton had finished, then Donald said, 'Bloody hell.'

Stratton nodded.

'I mean, what was he playing at? I know he's got himself into a few scrapes in the past, but I never thought…something like that…I don't know how I'm going to tell Doris.'

'Best not say anything to Reg or Lilian. They'll know soon enough.'

'It's going to be bloody difficult, Ted. I can see why you didn't…Why you were keeping it quiet. Sets everyone against each other…Jesus, I never thought I'd feel sorry for Reg, though. Properly, I mean, not just sorry for him because he's Reg and a…' Donald rolled his eyes, then added, 'Not that it isn't mostly his fault, how the boy's turned out.'

'That's another thing,' said Stratton. 'When I was talking to Johnny, I said something about Reg, and he said he was an old fool and he knew how much we—you and me—despised him.'

'Christ,' said Donald, with feeling.

'I didn't know what to say to him. No point denying it.'

'No.'

'Johnny hates him.'

'Christ,' said Donald, again. 'Do you think we should have done something?'

'I keep asking myself that. But we couldn't have done anything about Reg being Reg, could we?'

Donald shook his head. 'I can't imagine it, though,' he said, thoughtfully. 'Feeling that way about your dad.'

'Me neither. I liked the old boy. Bit set in his ways, perhaps, but...'

'Yeah. What'll happen to Johnny? I mean, will they charge him with burglary, or with this other...'

'Don't know yet. It's complicated.' Stratton didn't elaborate, and Donald didn't ask him to, just sat there muttering 'Christ,' to himself at intervals, while Stratton, without asking, poured the last of the Christmas whisky into a couple of glasses.

They drank in silence for a moment, then Donald said, 'They won't hang him, will they?'

'I doubt it'll come to that. Not enough evidence. And if he can give them something else...'

'Information, you mean?'

'Yes.'

'But he's going to need a solicitor and all that, isn't he? That'll cost a bit."

'Yes, it will.'

'We've got a bit put by, so perhaps we could...'

'I was thinking that, only Reg might not take it from us once he knows.'

'Where were you when Doris came round? Still at work?'

'Pub near Victoria. Trying to get drunk.'

'Don't blame you.'

'Couldn't manage it. No spirits, and the beer was piss.'

'Bloody typical.'

They were staring glumly into their respective glasses when the air raid warning started and Jenny called out to Stratton from the bedroom.

'Bugger,' said Donald. 'I'd better go.' He finished his drink. 'Ted, I can't go back to Doris and Lilian with this on my breath. You haven't got any peppermints, have you?'

'No, but there's parsley.'

'Parsley?'

'Had the last of it from the allotment a couple of days ago. Jenny hasn't got around to drying it yet. Cleans your breath.'

Donald raised his eyebrows. 'If you say so.'

Stratton produced the bunch of parsley from the cupboard. 'I'd better have a bit, too.'

They stood side by side, munching solemnly. 'Christ, I feel like a horse,' said Donald. 'Oh, well...' He went to the front door. 'I meant what I said,' he told Stratton, quietly. 'I'm on your side.'

'Thanks.' Stratton expected Donald to open the door, but he stood on the mat and stared at him, clearly feeling that something more was needed. Stratton didn't know what to say.

'Pack up your troubles in your old kitbag, eh?' Donald murmured.

'There wouldn't be room in an elephant's kitbag for this lot.'

'No...Stupid thing to say. But if...look...you know...' Donald gave up and buffeted Stratton clumsily on the shoulder by way of explanation.

'Thanks,' he said. 'I do know. I appreciate it.' They looked at each other quickly, then down at their shoes, before Donald cleared his throat and said, 'Well, best be off, then.'

'Right you are.' Stratton opened the door. ''Night.'

''Night, Ted.'

Stratton closed the door and stood for a moment in the hall, aware of feeling a little better, and quite relieved—he hadn't realised how much Donald's support would mean to him until

LAURA WILSON

he'd heard it voiced. He spent a further moment leaning against the door and trying, vainly, to marshal his thoughts into some sort of order, before trudging upstairs to resume comforting Jenny and prepare for whatever sleep he might be able to snatch in the shelter.

CHAPTER

64

In neither the basement shelter, where she'd spent half the night, nor in her bed, had Diana been able to sleep. The raids hadn't kept her awake—she was used to them. It was her own fears, which had intensified into lurid paranoia as the small hours dragged on towards morning, that caused her to sit upright, sweaty and shaking with fear. The airless darkness, full of panic, seemed to close around her so tightly that she felt as if she could barely breathe. When the sun rose and the blackouts could be taken down, she told herself that she was being ridiculous, but she still couldn't shake off the sense of dread. It was very early, but unable to bear the claustrophobia of the flat any longer, she decided to take herself off to work.

At least there had been no letter from Evie. Walking down Tite Street towards the river in the grey morning, she wondered if Guy had told Evie yet about his surprise visit to her flat. Any normal person would suppose that embarrassment would prevent this, but then, she thought sourly, any normal person wouldn't have a mother who behaved more like a familiar than a parent. The image of Vinegar Evie, complete with yellow eyes and feline ears and whiskers cheered her up momentarily. Then the ever-present net of painful, confused feelings—anguish, anxiety and guilt—closed around her once more, and she began to speculate, as she had done countless times over the last twenty-four hours, about what nice Inspector Stratton—Edward—had said about Claude's visit to F-J. When he'd asked her if she was in love with Claude, she'd been too amazed to be angry. He'd been so kind, so genuinely concerned, and it had been a relief to say out loud how she felt.

Why, she asked herself for the umpteenth time, had F-J summoned Claude? Of course, there were any number of reasons that had absolutely nothing to do with her, or it could have been a purely social call, but, no matter how much she tried, she couldn't make herself believe either of these things. Could Claude have mentioned what she'd told him about Apse? He'd said he wouldn't—promised, in fact. You're not at school now, chided the jeering voice in her head. Promises mean nothing—like your marriage vows.

If F-J had ordered Claude to stay away from her, it would certainly explain why she hadn't heard from him since the night of Guy's surprise visit. It's for the best, she told herself. And it probably wasn't even true—after all, F-J had far more important things to worry about than her. And as for poor Inspector Stratton, who must be going through absolute hell because of his beastly nephew...Her problems were nothing in comparison to his. Or, she thought, as she stared at the wreckage of four or five houses on a small street adjoining Grosvenor Road, to the problems of whoever had lived there. Several rescue men in bluette overalls were crawling about in the rubble, listening for survivors, periodically shouting, 'Quiet, please!' at the gaggle of spectators who stood smoking on the opposite pavement, apparently oblivious to the strong smell of gas.

Tears pricked Diana's eyes. Uncertain whether they were for herself, the people buried—possibly dead or dying—in the wreckage, or for humanity in general, she turned away towards the river so that no-one should see, and stared at the gulls on the mud flats and the grey bulk of Battersea power station on the opposite bank. This is what it's about, she told herself firmly.

London. People. Not you, but all this. In the great scheme of things, you are nothing.

All the same, she thought, surreptitiously wiping her eyes with a corner of her handkerchief, my problems may be insignificant, but they're happening to me. And she had a feeling that they were about to get a whole lot worse.

She glanced at her wristwatch. It was half-past eight—earlier than she'd thought. Too early for Margot to be there, and too early for her, too, really, but it was getting nippy, and she had plenty of paperwork to sort out, so she might as well...

Diana was unlocking the door when she heard voices coming from F-J's office. He didn't usually arrange meetings so early in the day...She'd better start by making them some coffee. She put her handbag down on Margot's desk outside the office door and listened for a moment. She frowned, then put her ear closer to the door. It was F-J, but sounding so emotional that she almost hadn't recognised his voice...

'Why, Claude? Why did he do it?'

Her eyes widened. 'Why?' F-J repeated.

'Because,' Claude spoke slowly, almost drawling, 'he thought he could get away with it. After all, most of his friends do.'

Diana's heart missed a beat. They must be talking about Apse, she thought. There's no other explanation. Claude must have told him what I said...Except that couldn't be right, because F-J sounded unhappy, not angry. There was silence for a moment, then Claude said, 'They do get away with it, don't they Charles?'

Charles! No-one, ever, called F-J by his first name. What was going on?

'You're being idiotic.' F-J sounded waspish.

'Not idiotic, Charles dear,' said Claude in an affected tone. 'Simply truthful. And while we're on the subject of uncomfortable truths, you made damn sure that Evie Calthrop got to know about Diana and me, didn't you? A word here, a word there. Very smart work. Your quickest yet, I'd say.'

'For God's sake, Claude,' said F-J, sharply. 'The woman's married. I told you to keep your hands off her.'

'Oh, yes, so you did. Silly me. But I don't think you're in any position to preach morality, are you? I know exactly why you like to surround yourself with beautiful women.'

'You take advantage of them fast enough.' F-J's voice shook.

'You shouldn't put temptation in my way. But at least I'm honest, Charles. I'm not using them as camouflage.'

Camouflage, thought Diana. What...? And making sure Evie knew. Why would F-J do that? He couldn't...He couldn't... A split second image, lit as if by a photographer's flashbulb inside her head, came to her, of F-J looking down to check his fly buttons. Heart racing, she grabbed her bag, made for the front door, and ran down the stairs, through the garden, and back into Grosvenor Road, where she bolted round the corner and into the mews where the cars were kept. She looked wildly around, saw no one, and crept down a narrow passage beside one of the garages. She'd be safe there—no-one could see her.

Trembling all over, she leant against the brick wall and tried desperately to collect her thoughts. F-J hadn't denied that he'd made sure Evie got to hear about her affair with Claude...And Claude said he'd done it before—your quickest yet. Everything F-J'd said about not wanting her to get hurt was nonsense. He doesn't care about me, the person he cares about is Claude. He's jealous. And Claude knows it. Why else would he take such liberties? Because he can get away with them. And whatever happens, F-J will protect Claude. And if Claude is a double agent, and not as reliable as F-J presumably thinks he is, then F-J is in a very, very dangerous position. Did Apse know that? Was that what he'd been about to tell her? My God, she thought, how must he be feeling now? Of course, F-J had no choice but to throw him to the wolves—in whatever form that might take—but F-J was at risk himself. Although—Diana shuddered, remembering what she'd overheard while hiding in Apse's cupboard—surely F-J wouldn't pay a young man to come home with him? And what about Dr Pyke? Where did he fit into it? Could he be F-J's lover? If so, did he know about F-J's feelings for Claude?

Head spinning, knees buckling, Diana slid down the wall and sat on her haunches in the filthy, narrow alleyway. If F-J ever found out she knew...The consequences can be fatal...His words at Bletchley Park. 'My God!' She clutched at her throat. Was that why Julia Vigo had died? Because, if so, it meant that Claude would have no hesitation in...'Help me,' she whispered. 'God...Have mercy on me. Lord, have mercy on me, Christ have mercy on me...'

CHAPTER 65

Stratton, walking towards the Tottenham High Road to catch a bus to work, was experiencing a similar feeling of dread, coupled with a dull, but persistent headache. Jenny, who had insisted vehemently that she would be fine and he wasn't to worry about her, had almost pushed him out of the door. Stratton guessed that, despite her protestations that she agreed with him and supported him, she needed him to go out so that she could work out how best to deal with Lilian, Reg, and possibly—Donald's affirmation notwithstanding—Doris as well.

After a journey that could have been far worse but was nonetheless quite irritating, uncomfortable and slow enough, he arrived at Dolphin Square and was admitted by Margot Mentmore. She ushered him into the office with a message to wait for Forbes-James, who had gone to Tottenham police station to interview Johnny. At his request, she put him through to Jones at Great Marlborough Street.

'Have we still got George Wallace?'

'Yes, we bloody well have. Came up yesterday, refused bail. Supposed to go to Pentonville, but they couldn't get through— HE bomb or something—so he ended up at Brixton, and they sent him back here this morning. Fucking shambles. Don't ask

The Innocent Spy

me why. I've spoken to them, but no-one seems to know what's going on.'

'Can you hold onto him?'

'I suppose so,' said Jones, wearily. 'Another twenty-four hours, anyway. Machin's fit to be tied as it is—one more thing's not going to make much difference.'

'What's upsetting him?'

'You, chiefly.'

'But I'm not directly responsible for this.'

'That's not the point. It's the fact that we're up to our eyes in shit and you've swanned off to join the toffs—that's what's really put his nose out of joint. Enjoying yourself, are you?'

'Not really. Tell you the truth, I'd rather be back at the station.'

'I'm touched. Was that it?'

'Not quite. Is Ballard around?'

'No. Hang on, there's a message somewhere...Here we are. He's spoken to Dr Byrne—lucky chap—and now he's gone to see him about some teeth. The lovely Miss Gaines is working on passenger lists. I haven't got a clue what any of it means, but Ballard says you'll know all about it.'

'I do. Sounds like good news.'

'Well, I'm glad you're happy. Now, if that's all, I've got to go and see Machin. I tell you, Stratton, I won't half be pleased to see your ugly mug again.'

'The feeling's mutual. Can you let Ballard know he's to telephone me as soon as he gets back?'

'Certainly, Your Lordship. I'll stick a broom up my arse and sweep the floor at the same time, shall I?'

'Why not?' said Stratton. 'Might stop you talking out of it. By the way, I don't suppose they gave Wallace a bath, did they, at Brixton?'

'No, they bloody didn't, and I've had complaints about that from downstairs, too, which is saying something. I'm buggered if I'm going to be responsible for the fucker's personal hygiene, so bring your gas mask.'

As Stratton replaced the receiver, Diana, who looked as if she might have been crying, appeared with a cup of coffee, and beat a hasty retreat in the direction of the kitchen before he could say any more than 'thank you'. Stratton wondered if it was that bastard Ventriss, or bad news about her husband, or both, but her manner suggested that neither questions nor sympathy would be welcome, so he decided not to pursue it.

He cleared some papers off the sofa and sat down. Somehow, he didn't think that Johnny's bravado would last long. Policemen were one thing, but Forbes-James, the man from the War Office with his smart clothes and educated voice, was something else entirely: a manifestation of the full weight and majesty of law, government and authority. Stratton could picture the scene; Johnny's night in the cells might have begun in a mood of defiance, but he'd lay good money that it was ending in one of abject submission. He felt almost sorry for the boy. Men like Forbes-James made him feel out of his depth, and Johnny, with his head full of celluloid gangsters and no real experience of the world, wouldn't stand a chance.

At some point—he didn't know exactly when—he must have nodded off, because the next thing he heard was a woman's voice saying, 'Edward,' and, when he opened his eyes, Diana's beautiful, troubled face was inches from his own. For a moment, before he remembered where he was, he thought he must be dreaming, and was just starting to enjoy it when she shook his arm and said, 'Wake up, Edward. F-J's back.'

'Oh. Yes. Right. Sorry.' Stratton sat upright, blinked, and felt like an idiot.

'It's all right.' Diana gave him a wan smile. 'We thought you must be terribly tired to go off to sleep like that, so we left you.'

'What's the time?' asked Stratton.

'Quarter to eleven. I'll make some more coffee.'

'Wait...' Stratton put out a hand to stop her. 'Are you...I mean, you looked—before...' Diana's smile became fixed, and he stopped, embarrassed.

'It's nice of you to ask,' she said, briskly, 'but I'm quite all right. You mustn't worry about me.'

No, thought Stratton, watching her neat ankles as she left the room, I mustn't.

Forbes-James arrived a few minutes later, his round face haggard with fatigue. Stratton wondered how long he'd been at the station, but before he could ask, Forbes-James tugged a typed carbon out of his briefcase, thrust it at him and said, 'Here. Booth's statement.' He disappeared without waiting for a reply, and a second later Stratton heard him asking Diana to find him a clean shirt.

He settled down to read what his nephew—or rather, the presiding officer, since it was full of police words and phrases—had to say. It was a long statement, four or five hours' worth, Stratton thought. *I have been cautioned by Chief Inspector Naughton, and told that I am not obliged to say anything unless I wish to do so...* Then a long preamble about how Johnny had lost his job at Hartree's Garage and was looking for other work and how he had met George Wallace in a café in the West End and been taken to see Abie Marks at the billiard hall on the promise of some employment. *On the 13th June I accompanied Mr Wallace to a house in Conway Street, to visit a woman I know now to be Miss Mabel Morgan. This was between 4pm and 5pm. Miss Morgan admitted us to the premises. The visit was undertaken on behalf of Mr A. Marks. Miss Morgan had incurred a debt from him and he wished to obtain the money. She told Mr Marks that she had some valuable pieces to give him to defray the cost of the money owing, and Mr Wallace and I went to the premises where she lived for the purpose of collecting these goods.*

It might have been what Johnny was told, thought Stratton, but it sounded like bollocks to him. Why would Abie Marks lend money to Mabel Morgan without first making sure of his security? And if Mabel knew of their visit in advance, she would surely have put her teeth in...unless they'd fallen out of her mouth when Wallace hit her. Byrne hadn't mentioned any bruising to her face, but then he hadn't been looking for it, and what with the scars and the thick make-up, it might not have been particularly obvious. He carried on reading:

Mr Wallace asked Miss Morgan if she had the goods, and she said she did not. She said, 'I think you are mad. I do not know what you are talking about.' Then she started a terrific argument with Mr Wallace and tried to slap his face so he pushed her. She was standing near the window at that time, and she fell back. We saw her go out of the window. I did not touch or push her and Mr Wallace did not touch her again after pushing her once. We left the house quickly after that. We could see her where she was over the railings and I said to Mr Wallace that she looked in a bad way.

No kidding, murmured Stratton.

I asked if we should do something but Wallace said 'No, leave it,' so we returned to the billiard hall to see Mr Marks. He went with Mr Wallace to a room at the back to speak to him. I was not present but I heard shouting and I heard Mr Marks say 'What is this rubbish you are telling me?' Then he said, 'It is no good. When they came out of the room Mr Wallace said he was sorry. Mr Marks told us that the matter would be concluded another way and he would speak to Mr Wallace later. I went home to Tottenham after that.

Mr Wallace and myself returned to the house in Conway Street on the 17th June to speak to Mr Vincent about the goods as Mr Marks had told us to do. We were admitted by a man. (Rogers, thought Stratton.) *It was after 10pm but Mr Vincent was not there so we waited until he came back which was at about 11pm. Mr Wallace asked Mr Vincent if he had some things for us to take away. Mr Vincent said 'You have made a mistake.' He said he had nothing for us and that we should leave. He was in a temper and pushed Mr Wallace out of the way. Mr Wallace said a few words to him, which I could not hear, before we left the house. I have not seen Mr Wallace since that time. I have seen Mr A. Marks. I received £10 from him. I have read this statement and everything I have said is the truth.*

Pull the other one, thought Stratton. Joe got the black eye by magic, did he? Johnny claimed that Wallace had not instigated violence on either occasion, there was no mention of threats, or damage to Joe Vincent's flat, and the statement suggested that he himself had been merely an onlooker. That part of it, Stratton reflected, might well be correct, and the thing was, he felt, generally right. Johnny, lured by the glamour of gangs and the prospect of easy money, had become, for a short time, a minor henchman. He sincerely hoped that the stuff about Mabel falling from the window—which was pretty damn vague—was at least accurate where the boy was concerned. They'd probably never know the truth about her death, but, judging by Johnny's report of the exchange between Wallace and Marks at the billiard hall, it hadn't been part of the original plan. Maybe Mabel had...what was it? Stratton looked through the statement again: *She started a terrific argument with Mr Wallace and tried to slap his face...*Beryl Vincent, the first time he'd met her, had described Mabel as not afraid to speak her mind. Poor woman. He hoped she'd put up a good fight, but she must have been terrified, especially in those last few seconds, when she realised she was falling, and then the impact...It didn't bear thinking about. Good job Johnny isn't here now, he thought savagely. I'd give him something to think about, all right...

Stratton read through the statement once more, and then again, squeezed his eyes shut, then opened them wide and rubbed his face violently, trying to force himself to concentrate. If only he wasn't so bloody tired.

'Finished?' Forbes-James was standing in the doorway with Diana, holding a tray of coffee, behind him.

'Yes, Sir.'

'He wants to see you.' Stratton could imagine how that conversation had gone: tell me what I want to know and you get a visit from Uncle Ted. Otherwise, forget it. Coupled with being woken up in the middle of the night—if he'd managed to sleep at all, that is—questioned for hours, and then the relief when it was over and they left you in peace. He'd orchestrated this enough times to know how it worked. 'We'll see Wallace first,' Forbes-James added. 'This time, you can do the talking. Do you have any more information?'

'Only that Wallace is at Great Marlborough Street.'

Forbes-James frowned. 'Not Pentonville?'

'Some sort of cock-up. Sorry, Mrs Calthrop,' he said to Diana, who was bending over the coffee cups. 'An HE bomb or something. I've got a constable checking passenger lists for Duke.

He's also trying to find a match from the teeth for the body in the church.' It occurred to Stratton, as he said this, that if Forbes-James thought Wallace was in Pentonville, he must have engineered a refusal of bail. These people really do have fingers in every pie, he told himself. Just do as you're told, mate, or you're fucked.

'Good,' said Forbes-James. 'If you wouldn't mind finishing your coffee outside, I have to speak to someone before we go.'

As Stratton made for the door, he heard Forbes-James say, 'Ask Margot to place a call to this number, will you?' and an intake of breath from Diana. It was such a small sound he thought he might have imagined it, but when Diana appeared her face was dead white, and her voice shook slightly as she spoke to Miss Mentmore, who stared at her in consternation, but made no comment.

Stratton hastily gulped down his coffee and followed her into the kitchen. 'Was it Ventriss's number?' he asked. Diana nodded without looking at him, then grabbed an already dry wine glass, and started buffing it vigorously with a tea towel. They stood tense and silent, side by side, listening. If she had asked, Stratton would have pretended disinterest, and he'd no doubt she'd have done the same, but Forbes-James must have been speaking quietly, because he couldn't make out any words and nor, judging from her strained expression, could Diana.

When Forbes-James called her name, Diana left the kitchen without looking at Stratton, and a few moments later he heard her leave the flat. He picked up the glass she'd deposited on the draining board. When he held it up to the light, he saw that it was cracked.

At Great Marlborough Street, Machin—presumably alerted by the desk sergeant—bustled through to Stratton and Jones's office, where he greeted Forbes-James with a level of obsequiousness which, Stratton thought, masked an equally high degree of loathing. He assured Forbes-James that the resources of the station were at his disposal, making it sound as if he could whistle up champagne and dancing girls at the drop of a hat. By the time Machin backed out of the room, Jones—ostensibly minding his own business throughout—was shaking with suppressed laughter and Stratton felt ready to burst.

Machin was replaced a moment later by Arliss, who said, 'Wallace is ready for you downstairs, Your Lordship,' and began ushering them through the door in a series of curious salaaming motions which nearly caused him to fall flat on his arse in the corridor. Stratton, who was behind Forbes-James, turned in the doorway and mouthed, 'Fuck off,' at Jones, who was, by that time, doubled up, helpless with silent mirth.

Stratton's dangerous feeling of hilarity was abruptly and revolt-ingly quelled by the sight and smell of George Wallace. He wasn't surprised there'd been complaints—the man was even riper, if that were possible, than before. As Arliss led them through the door, he heard a strangled 'Good God,' from Forbes-James.

'Sorry, sir, should have warned you,' Stratton murmured. 'A stranger to soap.'

Wallace glared at them as Forbes-James introduced himself and they sat down on the opposite side of the small table. Stratton lit a cigarette, hoping it might help to mask the smell, and Forbes-James did likewise. 'Good news, Georgie-boy,' said Stratton, cheerfully. 'We're going to forget about that van-load of cigarettes after all. Provided, of course, that you're prepared to co-operate.'

Wallace's expression changed from sullen to suspicious. 'How?'

'The last time we spoke,' said Stratton, 'you told me that Abie Marks sent you and Johnny Booth to collect a box from Miss Morgan as a favour to one of his friends, but that you didn't know the friend's name.'

'That's right.'

'And you talked to Mr Vincent—knocking him about a good bit in the process—but you didn't get the box.'

'That's what I said.'

'However,' Stratton continued, 'According to Booth, the pair of you had visited the flat before, and on that occasion you pushed Miss Morgan out of the window.'

Wallace looked from Stratton to Forbes-James and back again. 'He's lying.'

'Why would he do that?'

'Scared him, didn't you? Threatened him. Knocked him about.'

'George.' Stratton shook his head reproachfully. 'I'm sorry you have such a low opinion of us. As a matter of fact, he told us of his own free will. He said that Miss Morgan attacked you, and you acted in self-defence.'

'Bollocks.'

'We have witnesses, George.'

'What witnesses?'

'You were seen leaving the house.'

'You said that before.'

'About the other time, you mean?'

'Yes.'

'So you did go there twice.'

'I never said that.'

'Oh, well...' Stratton crushed out his cigarette and pushed back his chair. 'Looks like we'll have to proceed with the charges. It's a shame.' He stood up. 'You see, Colonel Forbes-James is quite a magician. One wave of his wand and all this could go away—provided, of course, that he likes what you've got to tell him. But if you're not prepared to talk to us, then...Well, I'm afraid they're changing the law, George. Looting's going to be made a capital offence, and by the time your case gets to court I should think they'll be about ready to make a nice big example out of somebody, and with your record...' Stratton shook his head sorrowfully. 'I don't hold out much hope.'

Forbes-James rose. 'Time to go, I think, if you've nothing more to say to us, Mr Wallace...'

'Don't make no difference,' said Wallace, bitterly. 'You're saying you'll drop the charges if I say I done the Morgan woman. You must be joking.'

Stratton furrowed his brow. 'Why would we do that?'

'Because murder's a topping offence, too—in case you'd forgotten.'

'Who said anything about murder?' Forbes-James sounded genuinely puzzled. 'Did you, Inspector?'

'Heavens, no.' Stratton shook his head in bewilderment. 'Accidents happen, George. You know that. Anyone can make a mistake.'

Wallace stared at them. 'I don't understand.'

'Come, Mr Wallace,' said Forbes-James, gently. 'We just want a spot of information. Surely that's not too much to ask—in the circumstances?'

'Wait a bit. You're saying that if I tell you what you want to know, you'll drop the jump-up, and you won't charge me with nothing else?'

'That's right.' Forbes-James made an expansive gesture.

Bloody hell, thought Stratton. 'There is the matter of breaking and entering at Mr Vincent's flat,' he said.

'I'm sure we can all forgive and forget,' said Forbes-James, smoothly. Machin won't, thought Stratton. When he finds out, he's going to have my head on a plate. Never mind squaring the station at Tottenham over Johnny...By the time it was all finished, his name was going to stink worse than Wallace. Of course, from his family's point of view, Johnny's release was a good thing—a spell in Borstal would, in all likelihood, make him worse, not better—but all the same, the copper in him couldn't approve of riding rough-shod over the law. 'We don't want you to confess to anything, Mr Wallace,' continued Forbes-James. 'As I said, we simply want information. And if you give us what we want, you'll be free to go.'

Wallace stared at him in disbelief. 'Just like that?'

'Just like that. Once we've established you're telling the truth, of course.'

'Hold up,' said Wallace, 'Never mind me telling the truth—how do I know if you are? He,' Wallace jerked his head at Stratton, 'give me all that before, how he'd help me, then look what happened.'

'Circumstances change, Mr Wallace. You're a lucky man. You've come to the attention of higher authorities.'

'You mean I'm talking to the organ grinder, not the monkey?'

'I shouldn't have put it quite so crudely myself, but...' Forbes-James shrugged. Charming, thought Stratton. Kick me in the balls while you're at it, why don't you?

Wallace stared at them both, then shrugged. 'Fair enough.'

'Good,' said Forbes-James. 'Now that we all understand each other, let's have that little chat, shall we?'

'I never meant it to happen,' said Wallace. 'Straight up. She fell. Like I told him,' his eyes flicked towards Stratton, 'and I don't know who Abie was collecting the stuff for.'

'Did you know what was in the box?'

'No...Well, I knew it was something to do with her, but—'

'Her?'

'Mabel Morgan. Her films. She thought we was coming to buy the stuff off her, you see.'

'Stuff?'

'Film stuff. She thought we was coming from some rich bloke who liked old films and that. For a private cinema or something. I said to Abie, she'll never believe that, but Abie said she'd fall for it, and she did.'

'So she was expecting you?'

'That's right.'

'Who set it up?'

'Abie. Sent someone round to the Wheatsheaf, all respectable and that.'

'If she was expecting visitors,' Stratton interrupted, 'why didn't she have her teeth in?'

'I don't know. Perhaps they didn't fit.'

'She was wearing make-up,' said Stratton. 'She'd have had her teeth in.'

'Well...' Wallace looked towards Forbes-James for guidance.

'Answer the question, please.'

'Fell out, didn't they?'

'What, they dropped out of her mouth onto the floor? Pull the other one, it's got bells on.'

'Well, she got nasty, didn't she? All smiles at first, then when I said we wouldn't give her nothing, she said we couldn't have the stuff, so...' Wallace shrugged. 'I had to...you know...'

'Hit her?'

'I might of given her a tap. That's when the teeth came out.'

'Both sets? That's more than a tap.'

'I didn't say I liked doing it,' said Wallace defensively. 'It was business.'

'Whose business?' asked Forbes-James.

'I don't know. On my life.'

'You don't seem to know much, Mr Wallace,' said Forbes-James. 'Or not enough, anyway. Perhaps I should leave you alone with Inspector Stratton for a few minutes to refresh your memory.'

'Won't make no difference.'

'Won't it? Well, let's try a few more questions and see what you make of those. Inspector?'

'McIntyre Brothers,' said Stratton, hiding his irritation at being reduced to the status of a heavy. 'Firm of builders. Premises in Cleveland Street. Heard of them?' Wallace stared at a spot on the wall above their heads, apparently deep in thought. 'In particular, a man named...' Stratton leafed through his notebook for the name of the shifty-looking labourer. 'Curran. Thomas Curran.'

'I might know him.'

'Might?'

'He done some business with Abie. Supplies and that. Bit of redistribution.'

'Recently?'

Wallace shook his head. 'Not that I know. It was back...' He screwed up his face in thought. 'February, March...I was minding the shop.'

'The billiard hall?'

'That's right. I was there. Abie's told me he's got to see someone about a job, and then he comes back—that was late, after we'd closed, so I let him in.'

'Was he alone?'

'Yes.'

'What happened?'

'Abie's told me to take the motor round to the garage—round the back—and clean it up inside.'

'Why?'

'It was just a bit of dirt in the back and on the seat, and a few footmarks and that, and a bit in the boot. When I come back, Abie'd cleaned himself up.'

'What do you mean?'

'There was mud on his shoes when he come in. Earth and that. Lime. He asked me to wash the floor.'

'Nothing else?'

'Such as what?'

'Such as blood.'

'Nothing like that. Just a bit of dirt.'

'How did you know he'd been to see Curran?'

'Abie told me. Said he'd had some stuff off him—wood, I think he said—and put it in the car. Mucked up his clothes.'

'Come off it, George. Abie's not going to bother going out for a few sticks of wood.'

'That's what he told me.'

'Did he say anything else?'

'Nothing. Just asked me if I done the car all right, then told me to get off home.'

'Right.' Forbes-James, who'd had his eyes closed for most of this exchange, suddenly sat up and pushed back his chair. 'That will be all—for the time being, at least.'

Wallace half-rose, but at a gesture from Stratton sat down again. 'What's going to happen to me?' he asked.

'You're staying put,' said Forbes-James. 'We're not finished with you yet.'

CHAPTER

67

Stratton followed Forbes-James up the stairs to the front of the station, where they stood outside, smoking. Further along the street he could see Arliss, moving along slowly with one of the reservists. Arliss's demeanour and measured walk gave off an air of dignified, disciplined patience, but Stratton knew a state of stupefied boredom when he saw one. He found himself grinning, despite his annoyance. 'Nice to have some fresh air,' commented Forbes-James.

'Yes, sir.'

'Do you know this man Curran?'

'I interviewed him after we found the body.'

'Well, you'd better go and see him again. See if you can't confirm Wallace's story. I don't imagine,' he added, raising his eyebrows, 'that Curran's employer knows what he's been up to.'

'Highly unlikely,' agreed Stratton. 'It depends if he's prepared to drop Marks in it in exchange for a bit of leeway, but I don't hold out much hope. Abie Marks isn't the sort of man you want to cross.'

Why, Stratton asked himself for the hundredth time as he trudged back inside, was everything so bloody complicated? He was used to witnesses who were too scared to talk, but at least he normally knew the aim of what he was doing: catching villains and putting them away. Simple. Forbes-James, he was sure, had other ideas, and if that meant guilty men walking free, then so be it. He could imagine Johnny, his statement having mysteriously been discarded, newly released and regaling his friends with tales of how the cops hauled him off to the station in handcuffs and worked him over, but he hadn't talked…It would raise his stock in their eyes, make him cock of the walk, and whatever authority old Uncle Ted possessed would be gone, placing him on a level with the despised Reg. Two pathetic little men, powerless cogs in the world's machinery like flies in a spider's web, whereas he, Johnny, would be someone to be reckoned with, looked up to…Stratton groaned.

'You all right?' Jones looked up from a pile of papers as he entered the office. 'You look bloody terrible.'

'Thanks. You're not much of a matinée idol yourself.'

'I've got too much to do, and I can't find anything. We had two soldiers come in this morning saying they robbed a hotel back in 1938 and now they've seen what the army's like they'd rather be in prison. Of course, the army's not going to want them back, so we're stuck with them. Second time it's happened this month. And there's another jeweller been turned over, and a furrier, a jump-up in Hanway Street, and another tom's got herself killed, and for all the good I'm doing I might as well wipe my arse with this lot.' He lifted up a handful of papers and let them flutter to the floor. 'A good half of it's yours, by rights.'

'I wish I could help,' said Stratton, sincerely. 'You haven't come across a man called Thomas Curran, have you? Works for a building firm called McIntyre Brothers.'

'Never heard of him.'

'Never mind.' Stratton picked up the telephone. 'I thought it was too much to hope for.'

Learning from the clerk at McIntyre Brothers that Curran was working on a site in Covent Garden, Stratton went over there and found him sitting on an upturned fruit box, smoking and reading a paper with a bunch of other workmen, none of whom he recognised. 'Remember me, chum? Detective Inspector Stratton, CID.'

Curran turned pale, but said nothing. Stratton addressed his comrades. 'I'm here to speak to Mr Curran, and we'd like a bit of privacy, if you don't mind.' With studied nonchalance, the men drifted away just far enough to re-position themselves within earshot, where they pretended to talk amongst themselves. 'I'm sure you've got work to do,' Stratton said to them. 'Now scram. Unless, of course,' he added to Curran, who was looking extremely worried, 'you'd prefer to accompany me to the station.'

Curran shook his head. 'Can't do that, sir. Get myself in trouble.'

'You're already in trouble,' said Stratton. 'But,' he smiled at Curran, who was sagging on his box, twisting his cap in big, freckled hands, 'this is your lucky day, because I'm going to give you the chance to get yourself out of it. Now I've been hearing a lot about you and your activities. Got yourself a nice little earner, I understand, selling building materials on the side.'

'I never.' Curran's face wore a look of virtuous denial. 'On my life.'

'That's not what I heard. I heard you'd been doing business with the big boys. Or rather, one big boy in particular, a Mr Marks. Known to his friends as Abie.'

'Not me. Never met the man.'

'I think you have,' said Stratton. 'You've been selling him stuff you've knocked off. And in February or March, you helped him with something else as well, didn't you?'

'Not me, sir. I'm telling you, I've never heard of him.'

'Come off it,' said Stratton easily. 'I appreciate that you might be a little worried about talking to me, Thomas, but I can assure you it'll be better in the long run.'

Curran didn't even look up, just shook his head. Feeling an utter shit, Stratton said, 'Where are you from, Thomas?'

'Camberwell.'

'Not here. Your family, in Ireland.'

'County Clare, but my father fought in the last war. London Irish, First Battalion.'

'Good for him.'

'He was at the Battle of Loos.'

'Kicking a football over the top, was he?' Stratton stared at Curran, who blinked and lowered his eyes. 'People can change their minds, Thomas. If we look hard enough, we might find that you're pals with the IRA as well as with Mr Marks.'

Curran looked up, eyes wide with alarm. 'You can't do that.'

'Oh yes I can. New rules, Thomas. Defence of the Realm. Regulation Number 18B to be precise. We don't need to charge you, we just get our friends in high places to sign a piece of paper, and then we've got you for as long as we want. And don't tell me you'll be safe in prison. Marks has friends in there, too, and you'll be a sitting duck. You'll be walking like a duck, too, when they've finished with you. If you're walking at all, that is.'

Curran stared at him. His face had taken on a greenish tinge. 'You wouldn't.'

'I shouldn't bet on it if I were you.'

'You bastard,' said Curran, thickly. 'You fucking bastard.'

Stratton looked shocked. 'Do you kiss your mother with that mouth?' he asked.

'My mother's dead.'

'Died of shame, did she?' He put his head on one side and looked at Curran. After a moment, he squatted down beside him, and took out his notebook. 'Now, you just cast your mind back to February, and tell me what happened with Mr Marks.'

Curran glared at him, and for a moment, Stratton thought he was going to chance it. 'The church,' he prompted. 'Eastcastle Street. The body.'

'Look,' pleaded Curran. 'I had to help, didn't I? Mr Marks come to fetch me himself, said I had to go with him.'

'Where was this?'

'Holloway Road. About nine o'clock. I was on my way to the Nag's Head, pitch dark and I never spotted the car till Mr Marks comes and tells me I've got to go with him.'

'Did he threaten you?'

'Didn't need to, did he?' Curran looked resigned. 'You don't argue with Abie Marks.'

'Do you remember what day it was?'

'Friday night, but I don't remember the date. We'd been on the church job for a week—started on the Monday so it must have been…sometime round the beginning of March. That's as near as I can remember.'

'What happened?'

'I went to the car with Mr Marks and he told me to get in. I asked where we was going, and he said I'd see when we got there, or something like that, so I thought I'd better keep quiet.'

'Was anyone else there?'

'No. Just him. We went up through Camden to the West End, and I thought we was going to McIntyre's yard. I told him I didn't have no keys or nothing, but he said it didn't matter. Then we go into Soho, and he stops in Romilly Street. I asked what was going on, but he just said to get out of the car, so I did, and he takes me to this flat…'

'What number was it?' asked Stratton.

'Don't know. It was too dark. Middle of the street some-where. First floor. Small place, poor looking.' Curran ran his hands over his face. 'I'll never forget it,' he muttered, staring at the ground. 'It was horrible. I've never seen anything like it.'

'Like what?'

'Horrible.' Curran shook his bowed head slowly. 'We'd gone up there in the pitch dark. Wasn't no light on the stairs. Then we get inside, and the blackouts was done, but when Mr Marks turns on the light, I can see there's a man in there. There was some chairs and a table at the side of the room, and he was sort of wedged up in one of the chairs, slumped against the wall. I could see he was dead. I must of said something—"What's going on?"—and Mr Marks said, "You're going to give me a hand with this." I thought I was going to be sick when I see the top of the bloke's head, all slimy looking, like liver or something. Horrible.'

'He'd been hit on the head, had he?'

'I suppose so. I don't know. It looked like it must have been done with something big.'

'You didn't see a weapon?'

'No, but it must of been an iron bar or a spade, something like that. There was blood on the wallpaper, all round his head.'

'Was there any sign of a struggle? Other bloodstains?'

'Not really. I saw some blood on the skirting under the table, and on the floor, but apart from that...'

'Was the other furniture disturbed?'

'There wasn't much in the room. Just an armchair, and that looked all right to me. I asked Mr Marks what we was doing, and he said he wanted to get the body down into the car. I was shaking. I didn't know what to do—I mean, I'd seen it, hadn't I? I thought if I didn't help Mr Marks it would be me next, my head bashed in. I couldn't...' Curran swallowed and wiped his mouth with the back of his hand. 'Next thing, Mr Marks went into the other room, that was off to the side—a kitchen or something—and he come out with a couple of blankets.'

'What sort?'

'Brownish. Khaki. Army blankets, I thought...I don't know. Mr Marks tossed one of them over the bloke's head, sort of wound it round. You know, for the blood, so it wouldn't...'

'Was the blood fresh?'

'Not really. Sort of dull. Not dripping, nothing like that.'

'Did the body smell at all?'

'I didn't notice it.'

'What did the man look like?'

'Just an ordinary bloke. He was wearing a suit. I was trying not to look. His hat was on the floor—it was just boards, no lino or nothing—Mr Marks picked it up and put it on the table. Upside down.'

'Then what?'

Curran swallowed again. 'Christ...Mr Marks told me to stand him up. I got my arms round him and pulled him upright.'

'How did the body feel, when you were holding it?'

'Jesus...Lumpy and heavy. Like a sack of potatoes. Flopping all over me it was. Mr Marks put the blanket round him. I said, what about his feet, because it wasn't long enough and they were sort of sticking out. He said it was all right—told me to get hold of the ankles. He give me some rope to tie them together, and he took the head end...We got him across the room and down the stairs. Then Mr Marks said to leave him by the door and he'd check it was all clear. The car was stopped right outside, so he went and opened the boot and we got him in there.'

'Did anyone see you?'

'No-one about. Even if there was...' Curran didn't bother to finish the sentence: even if they had seen something, none of the locals would dare to let on.

'Mr Marks told me to wait in the car while he went back up, so I sat there. He come back down and opened the boot again, for the bloke's hat, then he got in and just drove off. Never said anything. We went across Oxford Street, and when he stopped I could see the church where we'd been working, so I knew...There was this hole in the wall, where we'd put planks across to get in and out—'

'So Marks knew you were working in the crypt of Our Lady and St. Peter?'

Curran nodded. 'He come there the week before, when I was delivering the tools. I was by myself, thank God. I thought he wanted something, but he never said—just looked around a bit, asked me what we was doing...He put some money in the box—a note. I thought that was a bit odd with him being Jewish. I thought maybe it was for good luck or something, but after what we done I thought it was more his idea of a payment.'

'What happened next?'

'Mr Marks told me to move the planks, then we get the body out—that took a bit of doing. We get it through the gap and down the bit of slope to the crypt. There'd been a door there, but we'd had it off its hinges before because of the job, and it was propped against the wall. Then Mr Marks said to put the...' Curran gestured at an invisible corpse at his feet, 'on the floor, and go and get the shovels. He gives me a torch to go and fetch them, then he showed me the slabs he wanted digging up.'

'In the dark?'

'He was holding the torch first, then he saw I need help, so he's put the torch on the ground. They was big slabs, heavy, and it took a while. I don't know how I done it—I'm shaking, and there's this thing lying there on the ground...We done it in the

end. There was soil underneath so I dug a hole, then Mr Marks
said he wanted lime putting in. I said it wouldn't work—'

'What do you mean?'

'He wanted it destroyed, didn't he? I tried to tell him it
wasn't the right sort of lime, but he said to shut my trap and get
on with it, so I did. Then we took the blankets off...Couldn't see
too clearly, thank God, just touching him was bad enough...We
got him covered up with earth, and put the slabs back, but it was
like I could still see him. I thought I'd never sleep again, after.'

'What happened to the blankets?'

'Mr Marks told me to put them back in the boot. Said he
was going to burn them. And the hat. He said...' Curran stared
at Stratton, hollow-eyed. 'Said he'd burn me, too,' he whispered,
'if I told anyone.'

'He won't,' said Stratton. 'Did he say anything else?'

'No. He drove off. I took a bus home.' Curran put his head
in his hands. 'What the fuck do I do now?'

'Have you got a family?' asked Stratton.

'Two boys. Just babies.'

'What about brothers and sisters?'

'Two sisters. One here, one in Liverpool.'

'Then I suggest you go and stay with her.'

'What about the wife and kids?'

'Take them with you.'

'Mr Marks'll come after me.'

'No he won't. You have my word.'

Curran shook his head.

'Don't you trust me?'

'You?' Curran looked incredulous. 'Joking, are you?'

'No.' Feeling even more of a shit, Stratton added, 'You may
not believe it, but I'm sorry about all this. Needs must, I'm afraid.
You go up North for a few months, and I guarantee you'll come
to no harm.'

'You can't guarantee nothing,' said Curran.

'On this occasion, I can,' Stratton hoped this sounded as true
as he desperately wanted to believe it was. 'But you'd better piss

off sharpish. And when you come back, no more pilfering, or I will have you.'

'No choice, have I?' said Curran sourly. 'What about my work?'

'Hand in your notice,' said Stratton. 'There'll be work in Liverpool, if you decide to stay. In any case, you'll probably be called up with the next lot, won't you?'

Walking away, Stratton felt sick with self-disgust. He wasn't a saint, and God knows, he'd threatened enough people, done enough deals—that was commonplace to get a result—but *this*?...Fucking hell. He had no illusions about being a copper but the Regulation 18B business really stuck in his craw. Forbes-James, he thought, wouldn't have turned a hair, but it made him sick. Needs must, he'd said to Curran. The end justifies. Does it really, he wondered, shaking his head. I'm buggered if I know.

Suddenly feeling he couldn't bear to go back to Dolphin Square without having a bit of time on his own, he went into a café on Monmouth Street and ordered a cup of tea. Curran had said that the dead man flopped all over him, so the body must have been fairly fresh. Abie, presumably, had lured him into the flat in Romilly Street on the pretext of receiving money from Sir Neville, and bludgeoned him to death. Wallace hadn't mentioned any blankets in the car, or a hat, but perhaps Abie had disposed of them before taking the car to him for cleaning. He wouldn't have had to burn them—just dump them on a bomb site somewhere and no-one would be any the wiser. Wallace had said the car seat was dirty, but he'd denied seeing any blood. There must have been traces, and unless Abie had organised a clean-up job there would be blood at the Romilly Street flat, too. Not that he held out much hope of being authorised to go and check. Perhaps he should go on his own. No, he thought. I landed myself in this because I used my initiative, and I'm buggered if I'm going to do it a second time. It occurred to him then that he could, quite legitimately, return to Great Marlborough Street to check on Ballard's progress with the Sussex dentists. At least it would put off his trip to Dolphin Square for another hour, which was better than nothing.

CHAPTER

68

Jones broke off his conversation with the desk sergeant as Stratton entered the station. 'Had a good time with Wallace, did you?'

Stratton curled his lip. 'Haven't had so much fun since my Auntie Annie caught her tits in the mangle.'

'Well, you've got more delights in store. Ballard was just asking for you. You'll catch him if you're quick.'

'Thanks.' Dashing down the corridor, Stratton heard laughter coming from his office, and, opening the door, almost collided with Ballard's backside, which was sticking out because he was leaning over Gaines, who, seated in the desk chair, had her arms about his neck. Hearing the noise, they leapt apart, smoothing their tunics, scarlet with embarrassment.

'I'm glad some people are enjoying themselves,' said Stratton.

'I'm sorry, sir,' Ballard stammered. 'We were just...'

Stratton raised an inquiring eyebrow. 'Just...?'

Ballard stared at the floor. Gaines coughed. 'Actually, sir, we were celebrating.'

'Celebrating what? Your engagement?'

'No, sir. Constable Ballard's made a discovery.'

'Evidently,' said Stratton, dryly. 'But I'd prefer it if he didn't examine his findings in my office.'

'No, sir,' said Gaines, who had turned, if possible, even redder than before. 'It's the dentist.'

'Turn up for the books, sir,' said Ballard, when Gaines had been despatched to fetch a cup of tea and Stratton, promising discretion, had delivered a short lecture about not carrying on like love's young dream in front of all and sundry as he—or, more probably, Gaines—risked dismissal if found out. 'I contacted the dentists in the Haywards Heath area and there was one—Joseph Dwyer— who'd had Cecil Duke as a patient. Recognised the photographs. Marvellous how they can do that, sir—know their own handiwork. It all matches up with the notes, so we've found our man.'

'That's excellent. Well done. Any luck with the passenger lists?'

'Not yet, sir. Miss Gaines,' Ballard's cheeks, which had returned to their usual colour, turned slightly pink again, 'is working on it. We've found your man from the barber's shop, though. Mr Rogers. He's in a boarding house in Bloomsbury.'

For all the good it'll do, thought Stratton. Aloud, he said, 'Splendid. Keep up the good work. But remember, no more canoodling.'

'No, sir.'

'No sir is right. Now bugger off.' Ballard grinned and exited, leaving Stratton shaking his head. All right, he thought, Cecil Duke was killed by Abie Marks, who was acting on instructions from Sir Neville. And Marks had sent Wallace to retrieve the films from Mabel Morgan for Sir Neville. Damage limitation. But it hadn't done any good because they'd failed, and in any case Bobby Chadwick had gone to Montague to get his revenge…Left to himself, Stratton would get to work on Sir Neville—tell him Marks had confessed and implicated him, and then sit back and watch the dominoes come down, one by one, but he was willing to bet that Forbes-James had no intention of giving him the chance to do any such thing. A surge of frustration at his impotence made him slam a fist on his desk, then jump up and kick it. 'What's the point?' he said, between gritted teeth. 'What is the fucking point?'

'Inspector?' Stratton turned to see Policewoman Gaines in the doorway, teacup in hand, looking startled. 'I'm sorry,' she said. 'I didn't mean to interrupt.'

'It's all right.' Stratton cradled his bruised hand. 'Just... letting off steam, that's all.'

'I've brought your tea.' Gaines held out the cup gingerly, as if offering a treat to a dog of uncertain temperament. Stratton told her to close the door behind her, and repeated the lecture he'd given Ballard, using slightly different words and with a good deal more awkwardness. He opted for what he hoped was avuncular jocularity in place of the men-of-the-world tack he'd taken with Ballard, but Gaines refused to meet his eye, and seemed to be near tears by the time he'd finished. 'Don't look so worried,' he said. 'This isn't an official reprimand. Just be careful, that's all. Ballard's a nice chap,' he added, and then, realising that if he wasn't careful he'd turn into the father of the bride (I hope you'll be very happy together), said, 'It's not the end of the world.' Gaines, who clearly thought it was, stifled a sob and fled. Stratton collapsed in his chair, feeling that, despite the mildness of his tone and the rightness of his observations, he'd somehow been a bully and a brute. Men were so much easier to deal with... Apart from Forbes-James and his ilk, of course.

He was still wondering about the man who had died in the fire and been wrongly identified as Duke. He supposed he could ask the Sussex police to come up with a list of missing persons for 1935, but they'd probably never find out who the stranger was. It would remain a mystery, like the true cause of Mabel's death... Bollocks. And he couldn't even go and see Abie Marks without asking Forbes-James's permission first...It was no good. He couldn't put off Dolphin Square any longer. As he was swilling down the rest of his tea, the telephone rang.

'I was hoping I'd catch you,' said Forbes-James. 'How did you get on?'

'Curran confirmed Wallace's story, and he said Marks asked for his help removing a body from a flat in Romilly Street in his car, burying it in the crypt of Our Lady and St. Peter. And it's definitely Duke, sir. The dental records confirm it.'

'In that case, I'd like to speak to Marks this evening. We need to get this wrapped up as soon as possible. Do you know where he's to be found?'

'He's got a billiard hall in Soho. Does most of his business from there. Do you want me to bring him in?'

'No. Wait for me at Great Marlborough Street. I've got a couple of things to see to, and then I'm on my way. We can discuss how to handle him when we're in the car.'

CHAPTER 69

Abie Marks looked as plump and shiny as ever as he ushered Stratton and Forbes-James into his office at the back of the billiard hall. Hastily altering the look of apprehension on his face to an overdone expression of eager friendliness, he despatched one of his boys for decent chairs and made a great play of offering drinks and telling them what an unexpected pleasure it was to have a visit from such company. He kept calling Forbes-James 'Brigadier', and would probably have promoted him to Field Marshal if Stratton hadn't told him to put a sock in it. Forbes-James himself remained silent, managing to convey by his expression that he found all this mildly amusing, but not enough to bother with any sort of response. It reminded Stratton of Sir Neville, and he wondered, not for the first time, how it was achieved. Perhaps, he thought, it was something you learnt at public school, or maybe you inherited it from your parents in the same way as a lesser person might get, say, freckles or brown eyes.

While they were waiting for the chairs, he glanced round the office and noted, with surprise, that the large blonde doll he'd noticed on his visit back in June was still staring glassily from her position behind the bottles on the filing cabinet. 'Got attached, did you?' he asked Marks, nodding at it.

'Eh?'

'Goldilocks there. You told me your daughter's birthday was back in the summer.'

'That's right. It's a different one. For Christmas.'

'Starting a collection, is she?' said Stratton.

'She likes them. Plays hospitals.' Abie rubbed his hands together. 'Nothing but the best for my baby girl.'

'So I see.'

'You got kids, Inspector?'

Stratton was prevented from answering by the arrival of a sulky looking youth carrying two gilt chairs. Abie made a great fuss of positioning them exactly and dusting the padded seats with a large silk handkerchief before inviting Stratton and Forbes-James to sit down. By way of a counter to this, Stratton twirled his chair round with a flick of his wrist and straddled it, as he had seen American cops do in films, arms across the top. It was bloody uncomfortable, but, he felt, worthwhile.

'Now, gentlemen,' said Abie, leaning back in his own chair, 'What can I do for you?'

Forbes-James accentuated his faintly amused look by raising an eyebrow. 'Actually,' he said, pausing to take out a cigarette, and tapping it thoughtfully on the silver case before transferring it to his mouth, 'at this point, it's rather more a question of what you can do for yourself.'

'Oh?' Abie seemed nonplussed for a moment, then, looking around him, said, 'It may not be a palace, but I rub along.'

'Yes,' said Forbes-James meditatively, 'but for how much longer?'

'We none of us know that, do we?' Abie made an expansive gesture, then cast his eyes to the heavens, adding, 'If it's got your number on it, well...' and shrugged. 'These are troubled times, gentlemen.'

'They are indeed,' said Forbes-James. 'However, I was talking about matters rather closer to home than the Luftwaffe.'

Abie chuckled. 'A bomb in the bedroom is a bit too bloody close for my taste, Brigadier. If you don't mind my saying so.'

'I was referring to Sir Neville Apse. He is, I'm afraid, no longer in a position to protect you.' Stratton, who'd been aware that this was coming, was none the less impressed by the finality with which it was uttered.

Abie stared at him. 'I'm afraid I don't know what you're talking about.'

'What I'm talking about, Mr Marks, is treason.'

'*Treason?*' The facsimile of bewilderment on Marks's face was replaced by the real thing. 'I may have pulled a few strokes in my time, but I'd never—'

'Aiding an organisation known as the Right Club, which—'

'Here, wait a minute!'

Forbes-James held up his hand for silence. 'Which is a pro-fascist body whose members are known to have engaged in acts prejudicial both to the public safety and the defence of the realm by abetting and giving succour to the enemy, Mr Marks.'

'Pro-fascist? Listen, I don't want nothing to do with those bastards. I fought them when they come in the East End in thirty-six. We knew they was evil before you lot did. I did time for it, too—for doing what the whole country's doing now, fighting the Fascists! It was us and the Communists saw them off. Champion of the Jews, that's what they called me.' He thumped his chest with a fist.

There was a moment's silence, and then Forbes-James said, almost to himself, 'And what will they call you now, one wonders, when they find out?'

'Find out what? There's nothing to find out. I hate those bastards.' He put out his hands in a gesture of appeal. 'Come on, Mr Stratton, you know that.'

Stratton, who did indeed know that, folded his arms, shook his head, and stared back in silence. 'Surely,' he lied, 'you knew that Sir Neville was a leading member of the Right Club?'

Abie shook his head emphatically. 'Course I didn't. He's not going to tell me that, is he? If I'd known, I'd never...'

'You'd never...?'

'I wouldn't have anything to do with him, would I?'

'And what exactly did you have to do with him, Mr Marks?' asked Forbes-James.

'We was friends, that's all.'

'Friends?' Really, thought Stratton, Forbes-James couldn't have injected the word with more disbelief if Abie had claimed to be pals with the Pope.

'Acquaintances, then. Business acquaintances.'

'I see. And the nature of this business was what?'

'I've had nothing to do with those bastards. You ask anyone.'

'We've asked Sir Neville. He's made a full confession.'

Stratton blinked, glad that Abie was fully occupied with staring at Forbes-James and so hadn't noticed the astonishment that must have shown on his own face. Christ, he thought. He himself had played fast and loose with the truth often enough to get a confession, but he'd never have dared pull a stunt like that over a suspect with such connections. Unless, of course, it were true—which was, he reflected, entirely possible, but it would have been nice if Forbes-James had told him.

'It's lies,' said Abie.

'How do you know it's lies when we haven't told you what he said?'

'If it's anything to do with those fuckers, it's lies. He's a fascist, I'm a Jew. Of course it's lies.'

Forbes-James put his head on one side, as if he were thinking. 'That's a point, of course. However, your best chance— in fact, your only chance—of avoiding a charge of treason, is to tell us the truth about your association with Sir Neville. You can't save him—although, if what you're saying is true, I can't imagine why you should want to—but you can save yourself.'

Abie narrowed his eyes. 'How do I know you're telling the truth?'

'You don't. But I advise you to trust us, because right now, Mr Marks, we're the only friends you've got.'

'Balls!'

'I wouldn't be so sure about that. Inspector Stratton here is empowered to arrest you here and now, without charge, under Defence Regulation 18B, and to hold you for as long as we deem necessary. And if we do decide to charge you with treason, well… I'm sure I don't need to tell you the penalty for that. Of course, we may not, but surely it's occurred to you that once the news of your arrest—and the reason for your arrest—becomes common knowledge, your business interests will be, let us say, jeopardised at the very least. Inspector Stratton has been kind enough to furnish me with a few details of how your…enterprises…work, and it seems to me that your colleagues, or perhaps I should say, ex-colleagues, will, not unnaturally, wish to form other allegiances, and as for your competitors, well…I imagine, like all good businessmen, they will relish the opportunity of expanding their empires.'

'You can't do that,' said Abie, hoarsely.

'My dear fellow,' said Forbes-James, silkily, 'I assure you I can.'

Abie cast a pleading look at Stratton, who nodded. 'You must ask yourself ' continued Forbes-James, 'whether it is worth taking such a gamble. If everything I have been saying is, as you say, balls, then you have nothing to fear. But if it should—as it will—turn out to be true, then…' Forbes-James shrugged. 'It is, of course, entirely your decision.'

'That's bending the law. Perverting the course of justice.'

'We are at war, Mr Marks. The course of justice has altered. It's a serious decision and we shall be happy to wait while you consider. However,' he added, as Marks stood up, 'We would prefer it if you were to remain seated.'

Watching Abie, who had resumed his seat and had his head in his hands, Stratton felt almost sorry for him. He glanced at Forbes-James, who was staring impassively ahead and, feeling that he couldn't just sit there—apart from anything else, sitting the wrong way round was crippling him—he got off the chair and wandered across the room to lean against the wall. Feeling in his pocket for his cigarettes, his fingers closed around the little scarf that Monica had knitted for her doll. A scarf and knickers to match, he thought, eyeing the doll on Abie's filing cabinet and remembering his visit to his daughter's room. Except that this doll probably had silk knickers...Like its predecessor, Abie's doll had yellow hair and blue eyes—perhaps all dolls did, but the hard pink sheen of the skin seemed less glossy. Perhaps it was made of a different material. Moving closer, he saw that it was covered with dust, which had settled in the folds of the frock and clung, in a grey film, to the face and the pudgy, toddlerish limbs. Noting, out of the corner of his eye, that Abie had lifted his head and was watching him, he raised his hand and, very deliberately, ran a finger over the wooden surface of the filing cabinet before holding it up for inspection: clean. Then, reaching over, he picked up the doll and, smoothing the dust from its skirt, which was made from some sort of stiff material, raised it a modest half-inch to look at the petticoat beneath, and the—yes—silk bloomers. Not a bad hiding place, thought Stratton.

Slowly, with the doll in his arms, he turned to face Abie. 'Nothing but the best, indeed. Only she's not very clean, is she? I think she's been here for quite a while.' He thought afterwards that he wouldn't, for the life of him, have been able to describe Abie's expression at that moment, but it certainly made the hairs on the back of his neck stand to attention. He was aware, also, that Forbes-James, who had been staring at him with incredulity, had become very still. 'Oh, you beautiful doll,' he murmured, 'you great big beautiful doll.' Raising his voice, he said, 'Shame you've let it get so dirty, Abie. You really ought to buy that boy of yours a feather duster.'

'Take your hands off that!' Abie rose to his feet and stood, puce and rigid with fury, his eyes bulging. 'It's for my little girl. You've got no right.'

'Oh,' said Stratton, turning the doll upside down so that its skirts fanned out around its midriff and its legs stuck up in the air, 'I think I have. This might have started off as a present, but now—if I'm not very much mistaken—it's evidence.'

'You dirty bastard!' Abie stormed round the desk towards Stratton and was about to lay hands on the doll when Forbes-

James stood up and said calmly, 'Sit down,' and Stratton saw that he had a gun in his hand. Astonished, he looked from the gun to Forbes-James's set face. He'd been quite prepared to restrain Abie, and, if necessary, slap him about a bit, but he had no idea that his new superior carried, and was prepared to use, firearms.

Forbes-James motioned with the gun for Abie to return to his chair, which he did, walking backwards, his face draining of colour until it was the shade and sheen of unflavoured junket. 'You going to shoot me?' he asked.

'Not,' said Forbes-James, in a matter-of-fact voice, 'unless it becomes necessary.'

Stratton waited until Abie was seated—Forbes-James had remained standing—then reached under the doll's skirts and pulled down her drawers. Underneath, he found several pieces of thick, buff-coloured paper: identity cards and a ration book. 'Well, well,' he said, holding them up. 'Full house! In the names of Eunice Holroyd, Gordon Marchant, and...one Arthur Symmonds. And a ration book for him, too.' He glanced at Forbes-James, and received an almost imperceptible nod telling him to continue. 'I've been hearing quite a lot about Mr Symmonds lately, Abie. What do you know about him?'

Abie shook his head. 'You've got the man's papers hidden in your office,' said Stratton. 'Or did they just fly up the doll's skirt when you weren't looking and tuck themselves in of their own accord?'

Abie's breathing was audible now. 'Well?' said Stratton. 'Let's have it.'

'I don't know anything about him.' Abie coughed. 'Chap I know sells identity cards...'

Stratton returned the doll to the filing cabinet. 'Pack it in, Abie. You made a big mistake keeping Symmonds' documents. You should have burnt them along with the hat and the blankets, but you got greedy, didn't you? Thought you'd make a little extra by selling them on.'

'I don't know what you mean. Bloke wanted to sell, so I obliged him. Same as the others.'

'I'm not interested in the others, Abie—though,' Stratton added, pocketing the cards, 'I'll keep them all the same. Just tell me about Mr Symmonds.'

Watching the man's face, Stratton was reminded of how, as a boy, he'd seen the body of a decapitated hen continue to run around the farmyard, the movements—or, in Abie's case, the words—purely reflexive. Even the threat of death didn't stop him ducking and weaving; the habit was too ingrained.

'We know,' said Forbes-James, 'that you killed Cecil Duke, also known as Arthur Symmonds, sometime in March, and buried his body under some slabs in the crypt of the church of Our Lady and St. Peter in Eastcastle Street. Sir Neville's handkerchief was found on the body. He's told us all about it. So, Mr Marks,' Forbes-James glanced momentarily at the gun in his hand, 'I shall not ask again: what have you got to tell us?'

Abie's face, which had turned from junket to an unhealthy cheesy colour, was sweating, but his tone was still insouciant. 'He asked me for help,' said Abie. 'Friend in trouble...What would you do?'

'When,' asked Forbes-James, 'did you become acquainted?'

'At my club.'

Forbes-James coughed.

'Nightclub,' added Abie.

'Would that be the Blue Lagoon?' asked Stratton.

Abie inclined his head. 'That's right. We got talking.'

Forbes-James looked pained. 'What was he doing there?'

'What anyone does at a nightclub. Enjoying himself.'

'What did you talk about?' asked Forbes-James.

'Mutual interests,' said Abie.

'Such as...?' asked Forbes-James. 'I can't imagine you found much in common.'

'Oh...' Abie shrugged. 'This and that. You know how it is, gentlemen.'

Even when he's cornered, thought Stratton, he still can't resist...Any more front and he'd need a pier. 'Goods and services?' he suggested.

'I believe that came into it.'

'Boys?'

'Now, Mr Stratton.' Abie assumed an expression of the utmost virtue. 'You know I've never had nothing to do with that.'

'With what?'

'Kiddies.'

'Young men, then. At a price.'

Abie shook his head in a sorrowful manner.

'Stop pissing about, Abie,' said Stratton. 'Did you, or did you not, procure boys for Sir Neville Apse?'

'I never—'

'The truth, Mr Marks, if you will,' said Forbes-James. 'As you know, we already have a full confession from Sir Neville, and I'm sure you'll agree that his word is likely to carry rather more weight than yours. So...' he gestured for Marks to speak.

'We had some...mutual acquaintances, yes.'

'Mutual acquaintances as well as mutual interests?' said Stratton. 'Very cosy.' Deciding to step up the pace, he strode to the desk and thumped it with his fist. 'This isn't a fucking Rotary Club!' Leaning towards Abie, he grabbed his tie and yanked it so that the man's face was an inch from his own. 'Get on with it!'

Released, Abie fell back into his seat, coughing.

'Did you, or did you not, supply Apse with male whores?'

Spluttering, Abie nodded.

'Yes or no?'

'Yes.'

'You had an arrangement?' asked Forbes-James.

'Yes, sir.'

'And did you send George Wallace and John Booth to collect a box from Miss Morgan on Sir Neville's instructions?'

'Yes.'

'And, also on his instructions, did you kill Arthur Symmonds—whose papers we have here—and dispose of his body?'

'On my life...'

'Your life, Mr Marks, will be entirely worthless unless you tell us the truth. After all,' Forbes-James's voice softened, 'it's Sir Neville we're interested in, not you. As you yourself said, you would never knowingly consort with an organisation such as the Right Club. In fact, you mentioned that you are regarded as something of a... Champion, I believe you said, amongst your own people...' Forbes-James paused to make sure that Abie had registered this. 'I am sure that they, more than most, would wish you to help us in removing the Nazi menace, and in the absence of Sir Neville I am sure you will appreciate having other friends in similarly advantageous positions. After all, who knows what benefits might accrue...?' Forbes-James waved his hand airily, as if summoning imaginary ranks of dignitaries to lay honours and privileges at Abie's feet. Very clever, thought Stratton. First the big stick, then the promise of a carrot. 'As I said,' continued Forbes-James, 'we are your friends.'

'Friends,' Abie repeated sourly. 'You're no friends of mine.'

'I understand your distrust, Mr Marks,' said Forbes-James, gently. 'You've told us Sir Neville was your friend—or that you thought he was—but it has proved otherwise. We, on the other hand, share a purpose. We are all acting in the national interest against a common, and very dangerous, enemy. Your help in such an endeavour would not be forgotten.'

For a moment, Stratton thought Forbes-James's appeal wasn't going to work—after all a confession was a confession, however you dressed up the reason for it, and Abie wasn't stupid...As he watched the man's face, he almost fancied he could hear his thoughts: knowing he was fucked both ways, Abie was trying to disregard his instincts and calculate which was the lesser of two evils.

Finally, he spoke. 'I don't know about you two gentlemen, but I could do with a drink.'

Recognising this as capitulation, Forbes-James said, 'Of course. Mr Stratton, would you mind?'

'Scotch,' said Abie.

'Make it a double,' said Forbes-James, generously. 'And I'll have the same, if I may.'

As he went to the filing cabinet and poured the drinks, including one for himself (thanks for asking), Stratton reflected that this was as strange as it got.

'Excellent,' Forbes-James sniffed his whisky appreciatively.

Stratton slid Abie's glass across the desk, where it was seized and gulped, and took a sip from his own. It was, unsurprisingly, as good as Forbes-James's. Stratton wondered, briefly, if it came from the same source, albeit by a circuitous route. Forbes-James produced his cigarette case and offered it first to Abie, and then to him.

'Now,' he said, 'if we're all quite comfortable, I think we may proceed. You were telling us about Mr Symmonds.'

'Sir Neville asked me as a favour,' said Abie. 'Back in February. Symmonds had been to see him. They'd been friends in the past. Close friends, if you take my meaning. Sir Neville told me Symmonds had been in films, and he'd gone to America to try and get work because he wasn't doing any good here, but he never had no luck there either, so he come back. He gives Sir Neville this sob story, how he was broke and all the rest of it, you see?' That, Stratton thought, must have been when Sir Neville gave him the handkerchief. He could just imagine the man regarding his washed-up old lover down his long, patrician conk and flicking out the linen square with the very tips of his fingers in the man's direction. 'Well,' Abie continued, 'Sir Neville wasn't having it, so this Symmonds got shirty, saying he'd got letters and some old film—evidence of the two of them—and he'd make things nasty for him if he didn't cough up. Sir Neville sends him packing, but then he gets worried, and that's when he comes to me and asks me to sort it out.'

Abie stopped for another slurp of whisky, and Forbes-James said, 'How did he intend you to sort it out?'

'Said he'd leave that to me.'

'Did he pay you?'

Abie nodded.

'How much?'

'Three thousand. It wasn't hard to find Symmonds—the silly bastard had only told Sir Neville where he was living, hadn't he, cause he thought he was going to help him—Sir Neville led him on a bit, see, at first...So I find out where Symmonds drinks and arrange to run into him, and I tell him Sir Neville's changed his mind and I've got what he wants, and he comes along with me, good as gold. We go to this place I've got in Romilly Street— I've told the girls I don't want them around for the night—and then I get down to business.'

'Business?'

'I've shown him the money, and then I ask him—nicely— where the film is, and the letters, and we banter a bit, and then he tries to get nasty with me and says he won't hand the stuff over because it's not enough. So then *I* get nasty, and, well...' Abie spread his hands. 'I think you know the rest.'

'Did he tell you where the stuff was?'

'I didn't give him much choice.'

'You tortured him?'

'I persuaded him.'

'I see,' said Forbes-James. 'And what did he tell you?'

'About the Morgan woman. So I do the necessary, and—'

'You mean, you disposed of the body?'

'I done that, then I go back to Sir Neville. I told him we ought to sort it out, but he says that the Morgan woman never knew about him and Symmonds.'

'That's what Sir Neville called him, is it? Symmonds?'

'Yes. Why?'

Forbes-James shook his head. 'Not important. Let's keep to the matter in hand. You say Sir Neville wasn't concerned about the fact that Miss Morgan had these things in her possession?'

'Not then. That was later.'

'When?'

'May sometime. He said some other bloke had been on to him, and he wanted me to get the stuff from Miss Morgan, so I send Wallace and the boy.'

'And Miss Morgan ends up dead,' said Stratton.

'I wasn't happy about it,' said Abie. 'Not happy at all.'

'Leaving that aside,' said Forbes-James, 'this "other bloke"... Did Sir Neville mention any names?'

Abie shook his head. 'Not a dicky bird. I thought it must be a pal of Symmonds, and I asked him why not go after him, but he said it might happen again with some other bloke, and he wanted me to get hold of the stuff so we could destroy it.'

'And he paid you?'

Abie nodded.

'He can't have been very happy,' said Stratton, 'when you told him you'd failed to get it back.'

'He wasn't. But I told him, that's the way it is.'

'You didn't return the money?'

'What do you think?'

'I think you kept it, and you threatened him with what you knew.'

'Mr Stratton! I told you, we was friends.' Abie drained his glass, and was about to put it back on the table when a thought appeared to strike him. 'Wait a bit. It wasn't one of Symmonds's chums, was it? It was that fascist lot. They done it.'

'Now, Mr Marks.' For a moment, Forbes-James looked almost roguish. 'We really can't discuss that. National security, and so forth.' He turned to Stratton, 'If you've finished your drink, Inspector, I think we can leave Mr Marks in peace.'

CHAPTER
70

Walking back to Tite Street, Diana barely noticed the ruins of the morning. She fled upstairs—no post, thank God—and stood in her tiny kitchen, lighting cigarette after cigarette with shaking hands. F-J had told her to go home at five, rest for a few hours, and be back at Dolphin Square by ten o'clock. He'd told Rosemary to collect her in the car. And—even more disturbing—he'd telephoned Claude again. Could he have heard her in the flat that morning? She'd asked herself this a thousand times in the course of the day. She'd thought she'd left quietly, but she couldn't really remember. She'd just fled. If F-J had looked out of the window at the right moment he would have seen her as she ran across Dolphin Square, and it would hardly take a genius to put two and two together.

Or if Claude had looked out of the window…Diana desperately wanted to believe that if he'd seen her running across the garden he wouldn't have told F-J, but she didn't. Although it didn't have to be Claude; someone else—Dr Pyke, for instance—could have seen her and told F-J. It had taken her the best part of an hour to summon up the courage to return to his flat, and Margot had been there when she arrived. She'd excused her lateness with a story about air-raid damage to the windows at Tite Street, which F-J had, apparently, believed. As soon as she'd had the chance, she'd asked Margot, as casually as possible, whether there had been any visitors. Margot had said no, but all that really meant was that Claude must have left before she'd got there.

It didn't prove anything, Diana thought. If Dr Pyke did see me, he could have told F-J before Margot arrived. Why did F-J want her back at such a late hour? He'd said he was going to Soho with Inspector Stratton to visit the gangster Abie Marks, and then he'd be back. If he did know she'd been listening, that could only mean one thing…except that he'd told Rosemary to pick her up, hadn't he? So if the worst happened and she disappeared into thin air (she'd been trying so hard not to imagine the ways in which this might be engineered that her entire upper body was rigid with tension), Rosemary would be a witness of sorts. At least, she'd be the last one to see her…

She'd been avoiding F-J as much as she could all day. He hadn't said anything, or hinted—but he wouldn't, would he? He wouldn't want her to panic. She was cornered. She'd gone over and over the possibilities for escape in her head, but the plain fact was, there was nowhere to run. She couldn't tell Lally because that would put her in danger, and in any case, it wasn't as if Lally could do anything to help her. Claude was out of the question. Perhaps she should bolt, get on a train to Hampshire and throw herself on Evie's mercy. Diana hauled her dressing case and valise from under the bed and started throwing bits and pieces into them, then remembered Claude's accusation of the morning: You made damn sure Evie Calthrop knew…F-J hadn't denied it. Even if F-J didn't know Evie personally, he knew people who did, and he had influence everywhere. Running to Hampshire would simply delay the inevitable and, besides, it wasn't as if she could offer a credible explanation for suddenly turning up out of the blue. Diana dropped the pile of clothes onto the armchair and went back to the kitchen for her cigarettes and a cup of tea.

It occurred to her, as she waited for the kettle to boil, that the only person she hadn't actually lied to was Inspector Stratton. Edward. How peaceful he'd looked, asleep on F-J's sofa, the lines in his face smoothed out…Surely he was someone she could trust? But what good would it do—she barely knew him, and anyway, despite his rank and experience, he was just as powerless against F-J and Claude as she. He might not even believe her.

Not that she could blame him. The whole thing was fantastic. She paced up and down, and then abruptly turned off the gas. Tea was no good—she needed something stronger. She sloshed some whisky into a glass, took a large swallow and felt slightly calmer.

Perhaps she was worrying needlessly; perhaps F-J and Claude had no idea about her eavesdropping, but then why, she asked herself for the umpteenth time, did F-J want to see her at such a late hour? Perhaps it was something to do with Apse. She remembered overhearing F-J that morning, asking Claude why Apse had done it. Such a risk…But perhaps that was part of it. She turned the glass between her palms, thoughtfully.

The sound of the siren interrupted her reverie. The sheer helplessness of her situation—encapsulated by the relentless warbling tone—made her furious, and, looking heavenward, she said aloud, 'You could make me stop loving Claude, at least. Even if you won't do anything else.'

She drained the rest of her whisky. Ridiculous to blame God—if he existed—for something that was entirely her own fault. 'For heaven's sake,' she muttered. Moving purposefully, she collected her things together, donned her fur coat and descended briskly to the basement shelter, where she sat in a deckchair and avoided eye-contact by opening a book and turning a page from time to time.

Returning to her flat at half-past nine—it was a moonless night and very quiet, and pretending to read when she couldn't concentrate was making her head ache—Diana repaired her make-up and sat on the bed to wait for the car. By the time she heard the horn at quarter to ten, fear had given way to numbness. With the dead weight of resignation in her stomach, she left the house and settled herself in the Bentley's passenger seat next to Rosemary Legge-Brock, who proffered a hipflask. 'Want some?'

'Thanks. I must say, it was jolly nice of F-J to send you.'

'Nice for you, you mean.' Rosemary started the engine. 'I was supposed to be meeting my chap. When I've delivered you I've got to go back to Soho for F-J and the Inspector. Have you been listening to the wireless? Mr Chamberlain's terribly ill. Such a pity. But Daddy always said he was too much of a gentlemen to deal with a lot of thugs and gangsters.'

'I suppose he did his best,' said Diana. 'Poor man.' Taking another sip from the flask, she added, 'Munich seems such a long time ago, doesn't it? A different world.'

Pulling up outside Dolphin Square, Rosemary said, 'F-J says can you go up to Apse's flat and—'

'Apse's?' Diana's stomach lurched. *If you're lucky, they'll give you a warning...*

'Yes. To collect some documents he's left on his desk. F-J says they'll be clearly marked. I offered to go myself, but he said they wouldn't be ready.'

'Where is Apse?' Diana asked. She thought she'd managed to keep any trace of fear out of her voice but Rosemary said, 'Gone home for a few days. Why, what's up?'

'Nothing. But how will I get in? I don't have a key anymore.'

'Spares.' Rosemary took them out of her handbag. 'From F-J. Oh, and he said to tell you he's quite sure this time. No idea what he meant, but he said you'd know.'

'That's what he said? That he's quite sure?'

'Yes. Is something the matter, Diana?'

'Did he say anything else?'

'No. Look, I can come up with you if you like.'

'No, really.' Diana opened the door.

'Are you sure?'

'Yes. I'm fine. Anyway, F-J's expecting you, isn't he?'

Walking slowly and feeling shaky, Diana followed the beam of her torch along the garden paths and hoped F-J was right about

Apse not being there. The memory of their last meeting in the gateway made her shudder. She stood at the outside door of Frobisher House, took some deep breaths and tried to compose herself with only limited success. She let herself in and ascended the stairs, pausing on every landing because her heart was beating like a tom-tom and her throat was dry. It occurred to her, as she leant against the wall trying to calm down, that F-J might have asked Claude to follow Apse, hence the telephone conversation. That, she thought, would make sense. After all, Apse must know that the net was closing around him, so...Yes, that would be it. Claude was keeping an eye on him. That was how F-J could be sure that Apse was not at home. Relax, she told herself. You are being a silly girl. All you have to do is keep going up these stairs, one step at a time, and, when you get to the top, open the door and collect the package.

*If you're lucky, they'll give you a warning...*Was it Apse's confession she was being sent to collect? What would he do after that? Would he...Stop it, Diana, she muttered. It's a simple task, no need to turn it into a melodrama. Head down, she began to climb the final flight. Reaching the top, she turned right to the corridor, and right again, until she was standing outside Apse's front door.

Sticky with perspiration, she squared her shoulders, took a deep breath, and fumbled, clammy-handed, with the key until she managed to insert it into the lock.

'Oxford Circus please, Miss Legge-Brock, then on to Dolphin Square.' Forbes-James settled himself in the back seat of the Bentley and proffered his cigarette case as Stratton sat down beside him. 'Well done with that doll. Very observant, and useful. I think we make rather a good double act, don't you?'

'Yes, sir,' said Stratton, remembering his parting glimpse of Abie's face, wearing the intense, bitter expression of a man who knew he'd been well and truly done over. He felt sick. 'Perhaps we ought to go on the halls,' he said sourly, then, 'I suppose there's no question of charging Marks with anything?'

'I know it goes against the grain, not bringing him in.'

'He's confessed to murder, sir. My job is to solve crimes, not sweep them under the carpet.'

'I know that. But it's a question of priorities. National security and public morale are more important.'

'What about law and order, sir?'

'Also important. But it's not as if Mr Marks hasn't broken the law before and got away with it, is it?'

'With respect, sir, that's hardly the point.'

'Be that as it may,' said Forbes-James, heavily, 'we simply cannot have any more breaches of security coming to light. And this business about Apse is thoroughly sordid, boys and gangsters and so forth. We can't risk it, Stratton.'

'*Do* you have a confession from Sir Neville, sir?'

Forbes-James waved a dismissive hand. 'Let's get back to the subject in hand. What have we got?'

Fuck it, thought Stratton, if he wants me to behave like PC Plod, I will. 'Well,' he said, 'Marks admitted to procuring boys for Sir Neville. He's also admitted acting on his orders by sending Wallace to fetch the incriminating films from Miss Morgan, and by killing and disposing of Cecil Duke, also known as Arthur Symmonds. Incidentally, sir, I believe Marks was telling the truth when he said he didn't know Symmonds's true identity, because there was no reason for Sir Neville to take him into his confidence—unless, of course,' he added, pointedly, 'Sir Neville has told you otherwise, sir.'

Forbes-James shook his head. Realising that he was not going to be told anything further, Stratton continued, 'Wallace can't have been telling the truth about there being no bloodstains in the car, but I suppose, as the body was wrapped, they might have been negligable. Marks said he killed Duke in the empty flat in Romilly Street. We know from Curran that he was then loaded into the boot, so there must have been something left in the car, blanket or no blanket. It's a miracle no-one saw the two of them, but even if they did, it's not surprising they didn't come forward. Local shops and businesses know better than to get on the wrong side of Abie Marks. In the normal course of events, we'd take the car away for examination and inspect the flat for bloodstains and so on, but I assume it would be—'

'Best to let the matter drop,' finished Forbes-James. 'We've got what we need. I know you don't like it, Stratton, but it can't be helped.'

'And what about Sir Neville, sir? Presumably,' said Stratton, sarcastically, 'the national interest will not be served by allowing him to remain in his current position.'

'That,' said Forbes-James, 'is being taken care of.'

Stratton was too angry to heed the little voice in his head that was telling him to button it. 'May I ask how?'

'I'm afraid not,' said Forbes-James, calmly. The car slowed to a halt. 'Oxford Circus, I think.' As Stratton leant over to open the door, he added, 'You may rest assured that we are giving the matter our full attention.' Leaving the car, he heard Forbes-James say, 'Dolphin Square, Miss Legge-Brock, quick as you can. We don't want to keep Mrs Calthrop waiting.'

Stratton wondered what Diana might be doing at Dolphin Square at such a late hour. It wasn't until he had bought a ticket and was standing on the platform, trying not to stand on the grimy blankets of the shelterers, many of whom were already asleep, that he began to wonder exactly what 'giving our full attention' to Sir Neville Apse might mean. The turn-up with the doll in Abie Marks's office had pleased him, as had Forbes-James's praise of it, but when he thought about the two men in whose company he'd spent the evening, Abie, despite his criminality, seemed the more human. With a feeling of dread, he considered what the news might be at Dolphin Square the following morning. He boarded the train and, swaying in a packed crowd of shabby, exhausted workers, turned his mind to the more immediate—and even more depressing—prospect of what would be in store for him when he eventually arrived home.

It had begun to rain while Stratton was walking from the tube station to the bus stop, and by the time he'd got off the bus and was walking home it was pelting down, drenching and relentless. The darkness made it almost impossible to avoid puddles, and by the time he reached his house, both his feet were soaked. He stood for a moment on the slippery pavement next to his sodden front hedge, afraid—despite a strong desire to be warm and dry—to enter. The late hour meant he had no alternative but to go in, since the pub was closed.

Jenny must have been listening for the creak of the gate, because she'd opened the front door before he was halfway up the garden path. She stepped out onto the porch, and, catching a brief glimpse of her face from the light in the hall before she pulled the door to, he saw fear.

'Where have you been?' she whispered. 'It's Reg. He's in the kitchen. He came over after his Home Guard parade and parked himself at the table. He's been here for hours, just sitting there, staring at nothing. I've tried talking to him, but he hasn't said a word, and when I gave him a cup of tea it was as if he didn't even see it. He's not himself, Ted. He's got this horrible look on his face, it's like he's not right in the head or something. I'm frightened. I didn't know what to do. I didn't want to leave him—he's got that great big sword with him, and I thought—'

'He hasn't tried—'

'Keep your voice down!' Jenny hissed. 'He hasn't done anything with it, not threatened me or anything, but I've been so worried, I'm sure he's—'

'Where's Lilian?'

'I don't know. I'd have gone round there, only—' She grimaced and jerked her head in the direction of the kitchen.

'It's all right. You did the right thing staying here. Now listen, we'll go into the kitchen—just act as if everything's normal—then you go and fetch Donald and bring him back here. Tell Doris to go round to Lilian and make sure she's all right.'

'They'll be asleep, Ted, it's very late.'

'Doesn't matter. Tell Donald Reg's here, and he's in a bad way. And tell Doris not to say too much to Lilian. We don't want to upset her more than we need.'

'All right.' Jenny opened the front door again, and launched into a fair, if slightly shaky, impression of concerned wifeliness, exclaiming over Stratton's wet clothes, helping him off with his mac and fetching slippers and clean socks. During this, Stratton glanced several times into the kitchen, and saw Reg sitting inert, head bowed, apparently unaware of anything around him. 'Got your torch?' he asked, as she put on her coat.

'Yes. I'll be as quick as I can.' Pulling her umbrella from the hall stand, she added, 'Be careful.'

'Don't worry.' Stratton pushed her out of sight of the kitchen, planted a quick kiss on her cheek and propelled her out of the door. 'We'll sort this out, I promise. Go.'

Reg didn't look up when Stratton entered the kitchen. 'Hello,' he said, in a cheerful, glad-to-be-home sort of voice. 'Coming down like stair-rods out there. Lucky you missed it. Any tea in the pot?' Lifting the lid, he peered inside. 'Bit stewed, but it'll do. No sense in wasting it.' He saw, with a slight shock, that Jenny had left her empty cup on the table, and it was this, plus the lack of a cloth and the sight of the milk bottle, that made him realise quite how frightened she must have been. He knew why: the sink was on the same side of the room as Reg, and she clearly hadn't wanted to get too close. He sat down, picked up Jenny's cup, poured what was left of the tea into it, added some milk and half a spoonful of sugar, then stirred and drank. 'That's better. Cigarette?'

Still, Reg did not respond. This was even more worrying—never, in all the years Stratton had known his brother-in-law, had he seen him refuse a smoke. He lit up and put the packet on the table, within Reg's reach. 'How was the parade? Still making good progress?'

He had no idea what was wrong with Reg, but the first thing to do, he decided, was to get him talking on some general and safe topic, and the second was to remove the sword. This, he thought, could be done without too much difficulty, even if it involved a modicum of force—Reg was, after all, older than he, smaller, and considerably flabbier. But where was the sword? He leant his elbows on the table and, continuing the small-talk about the Home Guard, deliberately shifted his right arm so that it pushed a box of matches to the floor. Still speaking, he bent to retrieve it, ascertaining at the same time that the weapon was leaning against Reg's chair. 'It's a good job they've got chaps like you, with some experience,' he concluded, righting himself.

Reg didn't look up, but frowned slightly and pursed his lips. Stratton was beginning to wonder if Jenny's comment about him being not right in the head was not, in fact, spot on. Could the business about Johnny have distressed him to the point of causing some sort of nervous breakdown? Stratton would have liked to be able to reassure him of Johnny's imminent release without charge, but in the first place he didn't want to alert Reg to the extent of his involvement, especially while the man was in this frame of mind; and in the second, until he had spoken to Machin (some fun that was going to be) and Machin had spoken to the Tottenham station, it wasn't really on the cards. For all he knew, the local lads were taking advantage of Johnny's presence to pursue their own enquiries. It was, after all, a fair bet that Johnny had rubbed up against some of the neighbourhood villains, and information was always welcome. He'd just have to hope that they didn't come up with any reason to charge him with something.

He was considering what he might say next, something about the allotment, perhaps—though not much of a gardener himself, Reg could never resist giving advice—when he noticed that his brother-in-law was moving his head to one side in a peculiar corkscrew motion, ending in a place that Stratton thought must surely be uncomfortable, if not downright painful, with his nose almost touching his shoulder.

Reg gazed malevolently at him out of the corner of his eye. 'Damn you,' he said, his tone giving the impression that the words had been forced out by great pressure, much like a jet from a punctured hose.

'What's that?' asked Stratton, in what he hoped was a slightly puzzled, but otherwise entirely neutral voice.

'Damn you!' Reg's head swivelled round, and then, in a second distinct movement, returned to its usual position. His eyes widened, and he moistened his lips with his tongue. 'You bastard.'

'Reg...'

'Bastard!' Reg got to his feet stiffly, clutching the sword to his leg as if he was standing to attention. The hand holding it, Stratton saw, was trembling. He decided that it was best, for the moment, to remain seated. He didn't want to make the situation worse, and the sword was so cumbersome that he could easily duck out of the way if Reg started swinging it about.

'I know you're upset, Reg,' he said cautiously. 'I'd feel the same way myself if it was Pete, but I don't see how—'

'You're a shit!' The last word came out in a projectile of spit, some of which hit Stratton's cheek. 'Interfering! You think being a policeman makes you superior to the rest of us, and you can come and take my son away as if he's a criminal, and lock him up, and make me look bad.'

Stratton could see how this had been arrived at: no son of Reginald Booth could possibly be a criminal, therefore Stratton—standing for the entire police force—must have acted out of malice. Malice aimed not at Johnny, of course, but at Reg himself. 'I didn't take Johnny away,' he said. 'He's at the local station, isn't he? I don't have any control over their activities.'

'You spoke to him! You came to my house, without being asked, and—'

'I spoke to him because Lilian asked me to,' said Stratton, reasonably.

'I didn't ask you to! I'm the lad's father, not you. I can look after my own family!'

'I'm sorry, Reg,' said Stratton, 'I thought it would help, but now I see that it wasn't a good idea. I had no intention of interfering.'

'You barged into my house without my permission, and… and…' Displaying his lower teeth like a bulldog, Reg made a sudden groaning noise, like an ancient piece of machinery grinding suddenly into action, and, lifting the sabre, swung it in front of him like a golf club. 'How do you like it, eh? People barging into your house, taking—'

Stratton, who had leapt from his chair and was holding it in front of him like a shield, legs to the fore, retreated to the doorway. He lost the rest of the sentence in the smash of crockery as the edge of the camel sword hit the top of the teapot.

'Let's see how you like it,' Reg screamed, brandishing the camel sword with an effort, 'Come on! Come on, then!'

Before Stratton could reach him, Reg used both hands to swing the sabre over his head. It clanged against the light fitting as he brought it down on the table as if he meant to cleave it in two. The force with which this was done meant that the blade stuck a good inch into the wood. Reg, unable to remove it, was left red-faced and panting, grasping the handle as if caught in the middle of some strange suburban ritual of sacrifice. Stratton closed in and gently eased Reg's hands from the hilt. Then he put one arm around his waist and lowered him, slumped and unresisting, into the nearest chair, where he burst into noisy, gulping tears.

Jenny gasped at the sight of the smashed teapot and the sword sticking out of the table, but Stratton, standing beside Reg who was blowing his nose into a tea towel, put a warning finger to his lips and gestured towards the kettle, which was about to boil. Putting her hand across her mouth, Jenny nodded, took off her coat and put on her apron. Donald, contenting himself with raising his eyebrows so that they almost disappeared into his hair, set to work prising the blade out of the wood. Stratton, feeling awkward, remained next to Reg, one hand on his shoulder, while he carried on making snuffling, slurping noises. He didn't look up until five minutes later when, with the sabre removed to the garden, the broken china swept up, the soggy tea leaves wiped away, and a cloth spread over the damage, Jenny served tea from the battered tin pot they kept for picnics. 'Come on, Reg,' said Stratton, 'Drink this. It'll do you good.' He'd stirred three spoonfuls of sugar into it. Jenny had frowned slightly at this depletion of the ration, but said nothing.

'Thank you,' said Reg. He still didn't sound quite like himself but he was clearly over the worst. Donald, who'd sat quietly, looking at Reg with great attention while he downed his tea, said gently, 'That's a bit better, isn't it?'

'I went to see him,' said Reg, suddenly. 'At the station. He told me to go away. He said...' his eyes became moist again. 'Said he hated me.'

'I'm sure that's not true,' said Jenny. 'He was upset, that's all. People often say things they don't mean when they're upset.' Reg looked at her, and then at Stratton and Donald, who nodded in silent confirmation.

'The thing is,' Jenny continued, 'that Johnny's in trouble, and we must all rally round to help. All pull together—just like Mr Churchill says.' Invoking the prime minister, Stratton thought, was inspired, and, sure enough, Reg sat up a little straighter at the mention of his name.

'It's a difficult age,' said Donald. 'When I think back to what I was like...' He shook his head remorsefully. 'I know my old Dad used to despair of me.'

Stratton, though fairly certain that this wasn't true, or, at least, wasn't *that* true, nevertheless nodded in agreement, and allowed himself to emit what he hoped was a rueful chuckle. 'With guidance from you and Lilian, he'll turn out just fine,' continued Donald. This, Stratton felt, was verging dangerously into the territory of outright lies, but Reg seemed to be swallowing it pretty well.

'These things happen in families,' Jenny said, with a firm wisdom that suggested years of experience. 'Even the best ones.'

Reg gave her a grateful look. 'So you don't think...'

'Of course not,' said Stratton, heartily. He was about to add something along the lines of seeing it all the time at work, but thought better of it. The last thing they needed was for Reg to be reminded that his son was a common criminal like the rest of the rabble Stratton dealt with on a daily basis. Instead, he said, 'No need to worry. Now, why don't you get off home and get some rest. It sounds like it's stopped raining, and I'm sure Lilian will be wondering where you are.'

Donald finished his tea and stood up. 'I'll walk round with you. I could use a bit of fresh air.'

Reg, limp and exhausted, allowed himself to be helped to the door. He didn't enquire into the whereabouts of his camel sword, and no-one suggested fetching it. Stratton drew Donald aside. 'I shouldn't say too much to Lilian.'

His brother-in-law nodded. 'Good job it's pretty quiet out there.'

'Better hope it stays that way. Last thing we need's an air-raid on top of all this.'

Donald acknowledged this with a brief lift of the chin and, pulling his torch from his coat pocket, escorted Reg out of the door and down the path.

'Thank God for that.' Stratton returned to the kitchen to find Jenny using the laundry tongs to pick up the sodden tea towel on which Reg had blown his nose. Dropping it into the copper, she said reproachfully, 'You might have fetched him a handkerchief.'

Stratton, recognising that this wasn't a genuine rebuke, said, 'Sorry, love. It all happened rather fast.'

'I suppose so,' she conceded.

Stratton hugged her. 'You were brilliant, talking about Churchill like that. It was just the right thing to say.'

'I was so relieved to see you still in one piece. Oh, Ted...'

'Don't be upset, love. It's all right.'

Jenny stroked his lapel for a moment in silence, then broke away and started clearing up the tea things. 'Don't worry about that,' said Stratton. 'You go on up. I'll tidy away.'

'Will you? Properly?'

'Yes, properly.'

'I need to do the hot water bottles.'

'I'll do them. Go on.'

Jenny took off her apron and patted her wet hair. 'I must look a real sight. I'll have to put curlers in. And don't you stay down here too long—you need to get out of that damp suit before you catch your death.'

'All right, Bossyboots.'

When she'd gone, Stratton sat down, lit a cigarette, and spent some considerable time gazing into space in a sort of trance. He'd managed to heave himself to his feet and was just drying up the last of the cups when there was a quiet knock on the front door. Donald was standing on the step. Stratton opened the door wide to let him in, but he stayed where he was.

'Thought you might still be up.'

'I was just going to bed. Jenny's gone up already. How's Reg?'

'Not too bad. We managed to get him to bed all right. Gave him some of the stuff that Lilian had for her nerves when the raids started. Doris is going to stay the night.'

'What about Lilian?'

'Oh, you know...Christ, though.'

'Yeah...'

'Poor bastard. Crying like that. I know we...you know... about Reg, but all the same...Felt like when I was a kid at school. Only kid I ever hit—don't mean the usual sort of scrap, but he said something or other, and I punched him. He was a bit of a sissy, we used to laugh at him. When I did it, he sat down on the floor and started crying. I felt terrible about it. Still do, when I think of it.'

'Yeah.' Stratton avoided Donald's eyes, aware that the other man was doing the same. A thought struck him, and he said, hastily, 'I didn't hit him.'

'I know you didn't, Ted. I didn't mean that, but...'

'Yeah. It's all right, I know what you meant.'

'I just wanted to say, you know...I know you can't tell me about what happened with Johnny, but...Look, I'd better go. It was just...Well, just that, really.'

'Yeah.'

Donald looked relieved. 'Better not stand out here all night, or the warden'll be round. 'Night, then.'

''Night.'

Stratton undressed upstairs and put on his pyjamas and dressing gown. Then he boiled the kettle for the hot water bottles, wrapped them in towels, and took them out to the Anderson. He couldn't tell from Jenny's breathing whether she was really asleep, or just pretending. She gave a little grunt as he slid her hot water bottle under her covers, and, after looking down at her for a moment, he knelt down on the ground beside her and squeezed her shoulder. 'Jenny?' he whispered.

After a moment, she said, drowsily, 'Yes, love?'

'You all right?'

'Mmm. Tired.'

'Can I have a kiss?'

Jenny turned her face, framed in curlers, towards him, and pecked him sleepily on the cheek.

'You're all spiky.'

'Sorry.' Jenny blinked at him, then sat up, looking horrified. 'Ted! Get up off that damp floor. You'll get piles.'

'I'm not sitting on it.'

'Well, rheumatism, then.'

'All right, I'll get up. As long as you're OK.'

'Wait a minute.' Jenny leant over and hugged him. 'I'm OK. You did so well tonight, love...I'm proud of you.'

'I'm proud of you, too. Let me up, then.' Stratton kissed her again, on the nose, and struggled to his feet. He got into his own bunk and settled himself as best he could. ''Night, Jenny.'

''Night, love. Sleep tight.'

The door of Apse's flat creaked slightly as Diana pushed it open, and she stopped, holding her breath. It was silent, and, but for the triangle of light from the corridor, very dark, the air heavy and still. Hoping that Apse had done the blackouts before leaving, Diana switched on her torch. She tiptoed into the office and shone the beam onto the desk. It was bare of papers.

Diana willed herself not to panic. Rosemary had said the documents would be on the desk, but Apse might have forgotten...She turned the beam onto the coffee table—nothing there—and then, moving slowly, advanced around the room, checking the bookshelves and mantelpiece. Diana made herself stand still and count to ten. Something was odd...The place was too neat. Where was all the paperwork? Apse was nearly as untidy about it as F-J, and yet the desk, coffee table, sofa and armchairs were entirely free of files and documents. Unless he'd cleared up himself, which didn't seem likely, someone had been there already and taken everything away. As quietly as she could, she began opening the desk drawers, checking the contents. Stationery, pens...nothing of any importance.

She closed the last drawer and retreated to the hall, where she stood, trembling, her back to the front door. She listened intently, but could hear nothing but the beating of her heart and the blood in her ears, magnified in the dull, thick silence.

Did F-J know someone had already been there? If he did, what was it that she was meant to find? If it was a confession— something of a personal nature—it might be in the bedroom. Was this, she wondered, some sort of test? If it is, she thought, it's my only chance to prove my loyalty. I mustn't fail it, or...Fear of what might happen if she did fail drove her forward once more. She'd look in the bedroom—perhaps whoever had been there before had searched only the office. It seemed a forlorn hope, but she must do something...

She stood at the end of the corridor pointing the torch beam at the floor, willing herself forward. It's a document, she told herself. Rosemary had said so, hadn't she. A piece of paper, nothing more. She took a few cautious steps, then stopped dead. There was a draft of cold air from her right. Shining her torch through the kitchen doorway, she saw, with a hastily stifled gasp, that the door to the fire escape was ajar. She stood still, letting the beam play over the cupboards, the sink and the oven before advancing, very slowly, into the small room. She nudged the outer door open a few more inches, and shone her torch onto the fire escape, keeping it angled down-wards for fear of attracting the notice of one of the ARP wardens. She looked along the railings, and was about to retreat back inside when, at the very edge of the pool of light, she caught sight of an elongated shape, dangling in midair a few feet from her.

Diana jumped and the torch fell out of her hand and clattered on the floor, rolling across the metal slats, throwing its feeble light into the gloom of the alleyway beyond. Lunging after it, bent over, Diana's face smacked into something hard, which swung away and then back, thudding against her temple. Clutching the torch, she shuffled backwards on her knees until she felt the side of the door frame. Then she pointed the torch at the object. In the thin, jiggling beam, she saw a pair of shoes. Men's shoes with feet in them, rotating gently, left to right and back again. Clapping one hand across her mouth to stop herself from screaming, she angled the beam upwards. Apse was hanging from the upper banisters of the fire-escape, suspended from the neck by what appeared to be a pair of braces. His long body was hanging, sack-like, his face barely recognisable with bulging eyes, mottled blue cheeks, and a swollen tongue bursting obscenely from the mouth like the end of a blood pudding.

'Oh, my God!' Diana dropped the torch again as she crawled back into the kitchen on her hands and knees. 'No, please, no...' She tried to stand, but her legs refused to obey her, and she was forced to grab a drawer handle and haul herself upright. She staggered back to the hall, out of the front door and down the main corridor, crashing against the walls as she went, then fled down the stairs and out into the garden, wide-eyed and shaking.

It was pitch dark. She stumbled on the side of the path, felt soft earth beneath her feet and something scratching at her legs as she lurched and fell, sideways, onto the grass, her breath coming in loud gasps. A sudden light shone down from above, blinding her, and someone slapped her hard across the face, knocking her backwards. 'Shut up!' A man's voice, loud and hard.

Diana put her hands up to shield herself. 'Please—'

'Shut up!' It was Dr Pyke. She shut her eyes, unable to bear the light, as he grabbed her by the upper arms and hauled her upright, then shook her hard, so that her teeth rattled. 'You're coming with me.'

She was as floppy as a rag-doll, with no choice but to obey him, as, with a heavy arm bearing down on her shoulders, he steered her across Dolphin Square towards F-J's flat.

F-J opened the door, tie loosened, brandy glass in hand, frowning. 'Get her through here.' Dr Pyke pushed Diana in front of him, and F-J took her elbow and pushed her into a chair. After the darkness outside, the room seemed bright and too highly coloured.

'Some brandy, I think,' said F-J. His voice was calm, almost avuncular.

Dr Pyke handed her a glass. 'Good for shock.'

Both men were standing over her. Diana looked from one to the other. Dr Pyke's face was flushed, but F-J looked quite composed. 'Go on, drink it.' He nodded encouragement. Diana tried to comply, but the glass banged against her teeth and she couldn't swallow. She coughed, then started to choke.

'Lean forward.' Dr Pyke gave her a sharp slap on the back and Diana spat some of the liquid onto her coat, noting through watering eyes that her stockings were laddered and her shoes muddy. 'That should do the trick. Have you got a handkerchief?'

Glancing down again, Diana realised that her handbag was missing. 'I left my bag,' she said, 'when I—' She stopped, abruptly, realising that neither man had asked why she was in such a state. 'It's Apse,' she said. 'I found him. He's...'

'Take this.' F-J proffered a neatly folded square of white linen. Diana dabbed at her mouth and began again. 'Apse—'

'Not now,' said F-J. 'Finish your drink.'

The two men withdrew to the hall, and Diana sat clutching her glass, straining to hear what was being said. She heard the words, 'in the garden, screaming her head off.'

Had she been screaming? She couldn't remember. Perhaps she had. Dr Pyke had told her to shut up...This was the second time that he had come—or had seemed to come—to her rescue. Maybe he'd heard her in the garden and gone out to see what the matter was. But no-one else had, and if she'd been making that much noise...What was it Claude had said about him? *I believe F-J finds him very useful on certain occasions.* Was this one of them? Had he been waiting for her to leave Apse's flat?

The brandy, she thought suddenly. Something in the brandy. It hadn't tasted odd, but they'd been very insistent that she drink it. She could still hear the voices from the hall, though not the actual words. She took off her muddy shoes, tiptoed over to a pot plant, poured the remainder of the drink into it, and returned to her chair.

❈ ❈ ❈

A few minutes later, F-J returned alone and sat down behind his desk. 'Apse,' he said. 'Tell me.'

'He's dead,' said Diana, flinching at the memory of his purple, violated face. 'Hanging from the fire escape. There weren't any documents.'

'I see.' You knew, thought Diana, staring at him. You already knew. 'I suppose I should have guessed something of the sort might happen,' he continued, dispassionately. 'I'm sorry you had to be the one who found him. Did you have a chance to search the flat before...?'

'Only the office,' said Diana. 'I was going to the bedroom when I noticed the door to the fire escape was open, and that was when—'

F-J held up a hand. 'That's all right. You don't need to say anymore. We'll sort it all out.'

That's where Dr Pyke has gone, thought Diana. Gone to work his magic...She was beginning to feel woozy. 'The police,' she began, then halted, struggling to make a sentence. The words wouldn't seem to get into order. 'They'll want to know what happened, and my handbag...' She stopped. Judging by the look on F-J's face, it wasn't coming out as intended.

'Try again,' said F-J.

Diana groped for the right words. 'Police,' she said, finally. 'Handbag.'

'We'll deal with that. And...' F-J's voice seemed to be fading away. His words weren't reaching her, and the ones that did seemed to be coming out at the wrong speed. Julia...Julia Someone...the words seemed to jab into her as if someone was prodding her with a finger, but she couldn't think why they were significant. She was aware of her body against the soft cushions of the armchair, of the hardness of the glass in her hand, slipping away from her fingers...There was a dull thunk from somewhere by her feet, then F-J was bending over her, his face softened to a blur, and then...nothing at all.

CHAPTER
74

Stratton stopped at the corner of Aylesford Street and blew his nose. Hoping he wasn't coming down with anything, he turned up his collar against the wind. Across Grosvenor Road, the Thames was the colour of khaki, and the sunless November sky made the buildings look forlorn and shabby. Tired, he thought. We're all tired, even the bricks. Jenny had reminded him, over breakfast—mainly, he thought, in an effort to talk about something unconnected to Reg and Johnny—that Sunday was Armistice Day. Well, the last war had been futile...was this one really going to be any different? Our Glorious Dead—brother Tom—all for nothing. God, it had better be worth it, this time.

As he climbed the stairs to Forbes-James's flat, the thing he'd been trying very hard not to think of all morning—what Donald had said afterwards—came back to him. That was the trouble with people like Reg: feeling sorry for them made you despise them more, not less, than you did already, and that, in turn, made you feel a complete and utter shit. Caught suddenly by a wave of self-disgust, he stopped in his tracks and stood for a moment before—not entirely successfully—shrugging it off and continuing upwards. At least, he reflected, the events of last night had stopped him worrying too much about what might happen this morning.

The minute Miss Mentmore answered the door, he knew that something had happened. The telephonist's manner, though just as pleasant and friendly as on previous occasions, had a tightness about it, and her normally brisk knock on the office door was, he thought, distinctly tentative.

Forbes-James was seated behind his desk as usual, but there was none of his normal preamble of burrowing fruitlessly amongst his papers for his lighter or grumbling about his office harem moving his things. Instead, he said, 'You're here. Good. Sit down.' Stratton did so. 'Bit of bad news, I'm afraid. Sir Neville Apse has committed suicide.'

Allowing this to sink in, Stratton found himself not entirely surprised, and wondered if he had, subconsciously, been expecting something of the sort. Unable to voice any of this, he said, 'I see.'

'It happened last night,' said Forbes-James, 'In his flat. I've made the necessary arrangements. The body will be sent home, and I shall travel up to see his wife this afternoon.'

'What makes you sure it was suicide?' asked Stratton. 'Surely, a postmortem will—'

'Apse hanged himself,' said Forbes-James. 'My neighbour, Dr Pyke, has performed the necessary inspection. Under the circumstances, we naturally wish to spare Lady Violet further distress.'

'I see,' said Stratton, again. 'Who found him?'

'Unfortunately, it was Mrs Calthrop. She was extremely upset.' I'm not bloody surprised, thought Stratton. 'I blame myself for that,' continued Forbes-James. 'It was my understanding that Apse had gone home for a few days, and I sent her over there to collect some papers. There was no reason to think...With hindsight, I should have gone myself. I realised what must have happened as soon as I saw her face.'

'What time did she find him, sir?' They hadn't left Soho until around nine o'clock, and Forbes-James's last words suggested that she'd made the discovery and come straight to him with the news.

'About ten o'clock. She'd been working late.'

'Where is she now?'

'Here. Asleep, I hope. Dr Pyke gave her a sedative. Fortunate that he was here.'

Yes, thought Stratton, wasn't it just? 'Did Sir Neville leave a note?' he asked.

'If he did, we haven't found it yet. It's possible that he may have put something in the post for Lady Violet, of course, but I doubt it.'

'What will you tell her?'

'I certainly shan't go into details,' Forbes James replied. 'Strain. War nerves. That sort of thing. Could happen to anyone.' He shook his head. 'Bad business.' Or maybe not such a bad business, thought Stratton, depending which way you looked at it.

'Of course,' Forbes-James continued, 'It does mean that we may safely conclude our investigation. I shall, of course, be making a full report, and your co-operation will be noted.'

'Thank you, sir.'

'On the matter of your nephew, who I am told will be released this morning without charge, the police at Tottenham are not—unless the lad has told them himself, of course—aware of the family connection, and neither are your superiors at Great Marlborough Street. I am sure you would not wish them to be apprised of it, and I can see no reason why they should be.' Forbes-James looked intently at Stratton before adding, 'All things being equal, that is.'

'I understand, sir.'

'Good. I hardly need remind you that you are a public servant, and that confidentiality is vital, especially at the moment. As I say, your co-operation has been noted, and I shall give a favourable account of your work to your superiors. However, you must be clear that in the event of any…dispute, shall we say, over the facts of the case, my word would, of course, be accepted in preference to…' He made an open handed that's-just-how-things-are gesture. 'I'm sure you understand this.'

'Yes, sir.'

'Just as you also understand that there is no question of charging Mr Marks, Mr Wallace or Mr Curran with anything connected to our recent activities. We cannot risk any part of this matter coming to public attention. Mr Duke's body must, of necessity, remain unidentified. After all,'—here, the corners of Forbes-James's mouth turned up slightly in what might or might not have been a smile—'a funeral service has already been conducted for his benefit, if not for his corpse.'

'What about Mrs Symmonds?' asked Stratton.

'Mrs ? Oh, you mean the woman who claimed to be his wife. I'm afraid you'll have to tell her that the identification—which in any case had not been officially made when you spoke to her— proved to be incorrect. I don't imagine she'll make any trouble.'

No, thought Stratton, remembering the pathetic room, the torn coat and the corn plaster, the wretched woman will simply go on hoping that one day her man will turn up and marry her.

'Miss Morgan's unfortunate demise has been officially pronounced upon, so there's no difficulty there. If Marks or Wallace show any inclination to complain about the treatment they have received, which I rather doubt, you may refer the matter to me, but otherwise I think we can safely say that our business is concluded.'

'Yes, sir.'

'Have you any questions about what I have said?'

None that can be answered, thought Stratton, you've just made quite sure of that. Forbes-James, he was certain, would be entirely ruthless about protecting his own reputation as well as Sir Neville's, and one toe out of line would see his own reputation, such as it was, go up in smoke, taking his career along with it. But a desire to salvage something of his pride, however small—to let Forbes-James know that two could play at this game—made him look the man in the eye and say, 'No, sir. You need have no concerns about my ability to remain discreet,' before turning his head for a moment to gaze at the Henry Scott-Whatsit painting of the naked boy bather, and adding, 'I fully understand the delicacy of the situation.'

Forbes-James's eyes widened very slightly, but otherwise his expression did not alter. 'Splendid,' he said, heartily, and rose from his chair to shake Stratton's hand.

CHAPTER 75

Stratton was, on the whole, happy to be back at Great Marlborough Street. It was nice—last week's meeting with poor Mrs Symmonds aside—to return to something like the old routine. He'd had a word with Johnny, who seemed, temporarily at least, sobered by his experience, and Reg was giving every indication of having forgotten his outburst. Jenny, who'd been greatly cheered up by the funny letters they'd received from Monica and Pete, had guessed that Reg would act as if the incident had never happened, and so far she'd been right. When Stratton had, with some misgivings, agreed to return the camel sword, Reg had received it as if it had merely been left behind.

He'd worried, afterwards, about his reckless parting shot to Forbes-James and the effect it might have on his report, but clearly the man thought he was far beyond threats, or rather, intimations of threats, from such an insignificant being as himself. And judging by DCI Lamb's grudging praise at the Scotland Yard debriefing yesterday, it must have been a bloody good write-up.

In the ten days that had passed since he left Forbes-James's office, Stratton's thoughts had circled round and round the subject of Sir Neville's death, crossing and re-crossing the same territory, never coming to any conclusions. The problem was that it wasn't just a matter of what had happened, it was also a matter of what he wanted to *think* had happened. He was painfully aware that these two things might be contradictory, although he didn't know whether he would be able to articulate—with, say, a gun to his head—exactly what it was that he did want to think.

Nothing would, or could, be proved about Sir Neville's suicide and, Stratton thought, it might well have been exactly that, given the man's predicament. That he hadn't left a note didn't necessarily mean anything; some people didn't. Sir Neville had known that they were closing in on him, and known, too, how much he had to lose. Not that there would have been any public disgrace—the Forbes-Jameses of this world didn't allow that to happen to their own kind if they could possibly help it—but his loss of status, the accompanying rumours and a gradual but remorseless inching out would have been just as impossible to bear. So perhaps he had chosen, in order to make it easier on his family, to take the quickest way out...

But there were odd things—Forbes-James's manner, for one. Mind you, as Stratton had often thought over the last couple of months, that might be due to the fact that Forbes-James worked in a place where the culture of secrecy was so strong that people didn't tell you things even when you actually needed to know them. Of course, he hadn't expected the man to be flinging himself about in hysterics, but all the same...And then there was the convenient presence of the doctor, another old school chum, presumably. And the telephone call to Ventriss before they went to Great Marlborough Street to see Wallace, and the 'couple of things' Forbes-James had said he needed to see to before they spoke to Abie Marks, and his telling Abie a) that Sir Neville wouldn't help him, and b) that he'd made a full confession. Not to mention the fact that Forbes-James wouldn't answer Stratton when he'd asked later if that were true...

Forbes-James had said that Diana found Sir Neville's body at 'about ten o'clock'—after he'd returned from Soho. But supposing she'd found it before, and Forbes-James hadn't mentioned it? Stratton could understand why he didn't want

Abie to know, but why not tell *him*? Or…Had Forbes-James known that it was going to happen? Had he, perhaps, spoken to Sir Neville, or had Ventriss been entrusted with the job of ensuring that Sir Neville took the gentleman's way out? Helped him, even? It wasn't impossible.

But then, why arrange matters so that Diana was the one to find the body? Why not 'discover' it himself? If he'd sent her over to Frobisher House deliberately, making an excuse about collecting some document or other…Forbes-James seemed genuinely fond of Diana. Would he really have done anything quite so callous?

He didn't know. He wished he'd had a chance to speak to Diana, but there'd been no question of asking her what she thought. He remembered how he'd last seen her, glimpsed through a half-opened door on the way to the bathroom, lying in bed in Forbes-James's guest room, clad only in a slip, face pale and hair spread across the pillow. Poor Diana. What was going to happen to her?

'Good news about West End Central.' Jones dropped a pile of papers on Stratton's half of the desk, curtailing his reverie. 'Looks as if you'll be back in your own little office come Christmas.'

'Just when we were getting along so well, too.' Stratton pointed at the new addition to the muddle. 'What's this?'

'More witness statements from that shooting last week. The soldier who came home on leave and found his missus in bed with the lodger. I must say, I shall miss our cosy chats…Speaking of which, how did you get on at Scotland Yard yesterday?'

'Well, I certainly wouldn't describe SDI Roper as cosy. It was a lot more palaver about the national interest and public morale—in other words, keep your mouth shut if you know what's good for you.'

'So it's all done with?'

Stratton nodded. 'The best thing was that DCI Lamb, who has just returned from his convalescence, actually had to congratulate me, because of Colonel Forbes-James's report. I thought for a second he was going to have a heart attack from the strain, but he just managed to force the words out.'

'Bad, is he?'

'Horrible. I thought being bashed on the head might improve him, but it hasn't. You wait—he makes Machin look like a ray of sunshine.'

'Crikey. By the way, have you noticed that love is in the air? PC Ballard and our Miss Gaines.'

'I told them to keep it under wraps.'

'Oh, don't worry, I shan't say anything. But it's a bit much you lot coming in here and pinching our girls.'

'Had your eye on her yourself, did you?'

'Certainly not, I'm a married man. Mind you, I'd rather sleep with her with no clothes on than you in your best suit, any day. She's the only decent looking bit of spare we've got.'

'You've obviously never had the pleasure of seeing Arliss do his Carmen Miranda impression.'

'No, thank God.'

'It was in a revue for the Widows and Orphans. The memory still haunts me. And then he got all fed up because he left the hat lying about and someone pinched his bananas.'

'Did you know they're going to stop importing them?' asked Jones.

'Hats?'

'No, bananas. Apparently they take up too much room in the ships.'

The telephone rang, and Jones stopped talking to pick it up. Stratton, who'd been about to busy himself tidying his desk, looked up when he heard Jones say, sharply, 'When?' and then, 'Yes. Right away.'

Jones banged down the receiver and stared at Stratton without speaking for a moment. 'This is not good,' he said.

'What isn't?'

'Abie Marks,' said Jones. 'Killed last night. And Wallace. They've gone and got themselves murdered.'

Stratton felt as if he'd been punched in the gut. He remembered Forbes-James's words the previous week about doubting that Marks or Wallace would complain of their treatment, and thought, I should have expected this. 'How?' he asked.

'Single shot to the head, both of them. Blindfolded. Hands bound behind their backs. Sounds like an execution, doesn't it?'

Stratton, unable to meet Jones's eye, merely nodded.

'They found them at the billiard hall, so it's on your patch, not mine. And,' Jones added, meaningfully, 'you're welcome to it.'

'Jesus.' Stratton ran his hands over his face.

'Yes, well...' Jones reached for his coat. 'Look, I don't know what the fuck is going on, and I don't want to know. But this isn't a gang thing, is it?' Seeing Stratton hesitate, he added, 'I wasn't born yesterday, old son. Like I say, I don't know what's been going on, but I don't believe in coincidence.' He shrugged. 'I'll leave you to it.'

'Thanks,' said Stratton dourly.

Jones turned in the doorway. 'They'll all be trying to muscle in on Marks's territory, now,' he said. 'As if we didn't have enough trouble.'

Left alone, Stratton slumped in his chair, feeling utterly defeated. Now he, poor fool, would have to go through the motions of trying to solve the case...Fuck it! Furious, he swiped a hand across his desk, knocking the telephone and a slew of papers onto the floor. God knows, he thought, I've got few enough illusions left about the job, but this takes the biscuit. He jumped up, kicked the debris out of the way, grabbed his coat and hat, and strode out of the station.

CHAPTER

76

Three days later, Stratton was just about to leave the office for another round of entirely pointless interviews about the deaths of Marks and Wallace, when the telephone rang, and Cudlipp's voice said, 'A Mrs Calthrop on the line for you, Sir.'

. 'Thank you.' He sat down abruptly, feeling slightly breathless. 'Hello? Are you there?'

'Edward.' Diana spoke so quickly that he lost the first part of what she said. '...and I know I shouldn't, but I just...I wanted...Look, do you think we could meet?'

'Meet? Well, I don't know if that's really...'

'It's just,' Diana hesitated for a moment, before the rest of the sentence poured out in a desperate gabble. 'You're the only person I can talk to about this. I know we're not supposed to, but I'd really like to...Please, Edward. After all, nobody's actually said we shouldn't, have they?'

'Not in so many words, no, but I'm sure they would have done if it had occurred to them.'

'But they haven't *actually*...I know I shouldn't have telephoned you. I've been trying to get up the courage for days, and now it's no use.' She sounded close to tears. 'I knew you'd be too—'

'Diana, wait. Where are you?'

'In a telephone box in Piccadilly.'

'Are you on your way somewhere?'

'I have to be back at Dolphin Square by four, but...'

Stratton glanced at his wrist watch: quarter past two. 'There's a café in Denman Street, Dorleac's, first on your left off Shaftesbury Avenue. It's the only one in the street. I'll meet you there.'

Stratton hurried down Regent Street. He'd wanted to see Diana, hadn't he? He'd been worried about her. He was certain that this was a bad idea, but all the same...His elation at the thought of meeting her again was tempered with guilt that he should feel quite so pleased about it. And she wanted to tell him something. About Apse, perhaps, or Marks? Not that he could do anything about either, so there wasn't a lot of point, but still...

His first thought, as he glimpsed her through the criss-cross of tape on the plate glass of the café door, was how utterly out of place she looked, seated at a battered plywood table in a grubby room filled with the greasy fug of mingled cigarette smoke, steam, fried kipper and rancid sausages. At least, he thought, as he hung up his hat and coat on the row of pegs by the door, none of her smart friends would be likely to drop in for a cuppa.

Even in the short time he took to get from the door to her table, his awareness of her was intense. In an effort not to stare he fixed his eyes on a printed notice on the wall behind her: *There is NO depression in this house, and we are not interested in the possibilities of defeat. THEY DO NOT EXIST.* Jesus, he thought. As if being constantly exhorted to Dig For Victory, Register, Save Money, Spend Money, Be Cheerful, Enrol, Volunteer, and Not Talk Carelessly wasn't enough, now they're trying to tell us what to think.

The breathless feeling—she was, if possible, even more beautiful and elegant than he'd remembered—was back in spades by the time he pulled out a chair and sat down opposite her. 'I'm sorry about the place. It was the only one I could think of that was close.'

'It's fine. I can't honestly recommend the tea, but it doesn't matter, I'm just glad...' Diana ducked her head, and continued in a voice so quiet that Stratton had to lean forward to catch what she was saying, 'It's been vile. F-J insisted on packing me off to my mother-in-law's for a week, but I couldn't bear it, so I came back.'

'But you're back at work now, are you?'

'Yes, from Monday. No-one's mentioned it, of course. Lally—she's another of F-J's girls—has been very kind. I think F-J must have told her to keep an eye on me. She says it's best to try and forget the whole thing as quickly as possible. I daresay she's right, but...'

'But what?' Stratton, realising this sounded rather brutal, attempted to soften it with what he hoped was an encouraging smile.

'Not you as well,' said Diana, sadly. 'I hoped that you, at least, would...' She tailed off and stared miserably down at her cup and saucer. 'I feel as if I'm in gaol.'

'Would you like to tell me what happened?' asked Stratton. 'If you think it might help, that is.'

'Yes, I would. You see, I went to Apse's flat, and I found him—well, you know about all that—and then I ran out into the garden...Dr Pyke was there. I don't know if you know, but he's a neighbour of F-J's, and I think he works for us, although I've never been told that officially. He took me up to F-J's flat, and then they gave me something to make me sleep. They already *knew*, Edward. They knew Apse was dead. The next thing I remember is waking up in F-J's flat, in bed,' here she turned slightly pink, 'in my underclothes, so I suppose Dr Pyke must have...F-J came in to see me, and when I asked about what happened—about Apse—he said it was all being taken care of. I had to make a statement about it. A policeman came to the flat to talk to me—I wanted to get up, but F-J wouldn't let me, and he stayed there all the time. He kept saying "I'm sure that will do", and that I needed to rest, which was nonsense because I felt fine by then, and when the policeman tried to ask me a question, he wouldn't let him.' At this point, she was interrupted by the waitress taking Stratton's order. When the woman had gone, she said, 'I tried to ask F-J about it again, after the policeman had gone, but he just patted my hand and said that it was probably all for the best.'

'It was certainly convenient,' said Stratton wryly.

'There's something else, too. About Claude. That morning, I got to the office early and I overheard F-J talking to him.'

'To Ventriss?'

'Yes.' Diana leant forward and whispered, 'I think F-J's in love with him, Edward.'

'What?'

'They were talking about Apse—what he'd done—I'd told Claude about it, which I shouldn't have, but now I think he must have known anyway. Some of it, at least. He was taunting F-J, saying he and his friends thought they could get away with... you know...what they do...I thought F-J would be furious, but he wasn't. He just seemed to accept it. And,' she continued in a rush, 'I think Dr Pyke may be one of them as well, because once I came into F-J's office when he wasn't expecting me and F-J's shirt buttons were undone. F-J said it was a medical check but afterwards, when I pointed out about the buttons, he looked down at his trousers, as if...I thought perhaps it was more than just blood pressure, because you wouldn't have to...would you? Not for that. This happened before I found out about Apse, and it didn't occur to me until much later that perhaps...'

'Do you remember that afternoon in Colonel Forbes-James's office when you pointed out the painting of the naked boy? I wondered then if you were trying to tell me something.'

'I...I don't really know what was going through my mind. I suppose I just wanted to see if you thought it was strange. I mean, I know there are lots of nudes in art galleries, but they're older, aren't they? When I asked F-J about it and he said that

Apse had given it to him, I thought...Well, I don't know what I thought exactly, just that it would be silly to have a picture like that hanging on your wall if you were that way inclined, I suppose...'

'The picture certainly surprised me,' said Stratton.

'I couldn't believe, I didn't *want* to believe that...that, you know...about F-J, until I heard him talking to Claude, and then...'

'Then there was little doubt. I take it his...fondness for Ventriss is not reciprocated?'

Diana shook her head. 'Claude uses it. But he's loyal to F-J. He's done...things...for him.'

'Sir Neville?'

'I don't know. But certainly other things. And F-J telephoned him that afternoon, didn't he? We heard him. And why was Dr Pyke in the garden? That evening, when I came back to Dolphin Square, it was dark, and—'

'Wait a minute. You say you went back?'

'Yes. That afternoon, F-J told me to go home, but to be ready by ten and Rosemary Legge-Brock would collect me in the car.'

'He told me you were working late.'

Diana shook her head. 'I went home and came back. Rosemary had a message from F-J that I was to go up to Apse's flat and fetch some documents. Rosemary told me she'd volunteered to do it, but F-J said they wouldn't be ready. But there weren't any papers, Edward, just—him.'

'Did Colonel Forbes-James say why he wanted you to return to Dolphin Square? Apart from collecting the papers, that is.'

Diana shook her head. 'I assumed it must be something to do with your meeting with Mr Marks. He gave Rosemary a message for me about Apse not being there, because of him coming back that first time. I think,' she added, 'that F-J made me find Apse as a sort of...well...'

'Warning?'

'Yes. I don't know if he knows that I know about him, but—'

'He knows I know,' said Stratton.

Diana's eyes widened. 'How?'

'I told him.'

Diana gasped. 'Edward, you didn't!'

'Not in so many words. But he knows I know. Not that I can prove anything. Neither of us can. That's why we've got to keep quiet about this. Abie Marks is dead, Diana. He was found three days ago, with one of his henchman. Shot. I'm supposed to be investigating, but we won't find anyone.'

Diana blanched. 'Claude,' she said.

'I don't know,' said Stratton. 'Possibly. It'll be chalked up as the result of a turf war between rival gangs.'

'I daren't ask him,' said Diana.

'Ask *Ventriss*?' Stratton experienced an instantaneous and nauseating jolt of jealousy, and before he had time to check himself he had asked, in the tones of a suspicious husband, 'Have you been seeing him again?'

Diana blinked, then bowed her head.

'What about your husband?'

'Abroad. I can't bear to think about him.'

'Are you mad, Diana?'

'Probably,' Diana whispered. 'It's awful. I don't know what to do. He wants us to carry on seeing each other. He treats it like a game, and now that I know about F-J's feelings for him...I haven't told Claude about that, of course,' she added, hurriedly. 'I'm not completely insane.'

'But you're still in love with him, aren't you?'

'Yes, I am. I can't help it.' This was said with an implacable, almost defiant certainty that infuriated him.

'For God's sake!' Stratton exploded. 'You'll have to bloody well *try* to help it. He'll destroy you, Diana. Between the two of them, him and Forbes-James, you haven't got a chance. You don't matter to either of them, any more than I do. Can't you see that?' Diana, her eyes glistening with tears, nodded.

'I'm sorry,' said Stratton, more gently. 'I know I've no business...' Impulsively, he reached across the table and took Diana's hand. She didn't respond, but neither did she make any move to extract herself. 'I'm concerned about you, that's all.'

Diana blinked rapidly for a moment, then withdrew her hand. 'Don't be kind to me, or I really shall cry.'

'All right.' Stratton attempted a reassuring smile. 'I'll try not to be. But,' he added, unable to stop himself, 'I can't help it.'

'You must.' Diana attempted a smile. 'I'm not worth it. As you can see,' she gave a resigned shrug, 'a hopeless case.'

'Ventriss is dangerous. You of all people should know that. He's playing with fire, and so are you, if you have anything to do with him. Please, Diana,' he added, desperately, aware that her face was becoming glacial and mask-like. 'I'm sorry if I've overstepped the mark. But you did ask to see me, and all I can do is give you my advice.'

Diana continued with the haughty stare for a moment before her face broke up and her mouth began to tremble once more. 'Yes,' she whispered, fumbling in her bag and drawing out a handkerchief. 'I know. And you're right. I'm sorry, Edward. It's just that so much of life seems to be about people not telling one things. It's always because something can't be mentioned, or isn't done, or isn't quite nice, or is unsuitable, or—' she nodded towards the sign on the wall '—like that notice, telling you something doesn't exist when it does, because it's bad for morale. There's always some reason why people can't say what they really mean. Especially now.' This was said very quickly, in an attempt, Stratton thought, to beat the tears that were gathering in her eyes. Putting the handkerchief to her face, she said, 'Oh, dear. NBG again, I'm afraid.'

'Well, they do say truth is the first casualty of war,' said Stratton, feeling helpless. 'But,' he added, 'you can help yourself. About Ventriss, I mean. Be careful, Diana. Remember what I said.'

'Yes.' Diana dabbed at her eyes again, then produced a compact from her bag and powdered her nose. Stratton, who had hoped for at least some intimation that she wasn't going to see the bloody man again, felt disappointed, although he knew he had no right to expect any such thing. He was hardly in a position to offer an alternative and besides, they were both married, for God's sake. Diana shut her compact with a snap and gave him a watery smile. 'How's that?'

'Lovely,' he said. 'Beautiful, in fact.'

'You know,' said Diana, 'I really should be going.'

'I think you'd better go first, then. Just as a precaution.'

'All right. Here.' She took out her purse.

Stratton held up his hand to stop her. 'It may not be much of a treat, but it's my treat.'

'Thank you.' Diana stood up. 'And thank you for your advice.'

Stratton stood up, too, and they shook hands for what seemed like a long time, but probably wasn't. 'Goodbye, Diana. And good luck.'

Diana leant over, and—to the great interest of two elderly charwomen at a nearby table—kissed him on the cheek.

'I shall never forget you, you know. Goodbye, Edward.'

Stratton watched as she walked between the tables towards the door, but she didn't look back. He didn't know if she would, or could, take his advice, but he hoped, just as he hoped he would one day see her again. That was all you could do really, about anything, when you came down to it.

Sighing, he turned round and picked up his cup. Noticing, for the first time, the marks of a previous drinker's lipstick on the part of the rim nearest to his mouth, and hoping, as he rotated the cup to a clean spot, that Diana had not observed them, he drank the remains of his tea.

LAURA WILSON

A VERY BRIEF NOTE ON HISTORICAL BACKGROUND

Part of the storyline for this book is based on true events, although I have taken some liberties with chronology.

The character of Colonel Forbes-James is based, in part, on the spymaster Charles Maxwell Knight (1900-1968). Knight was recruited to MI5 in 1925, and rose to the position of head of Department B5(b), with responsibility for domestic counter-subversion. The demands of fiction necessitated widening this remit in order to make Forbes-James responsible for agent Claude Ventriss, whose work takes him abroad. It is, however, entirely true that for much of its existence, B5(b) was based at Dolphin Square, London SW1 (though not in Nelson House).

Knight was responsible for the interning of Oswald Mosley, the British Fascist leader, in May 1940, and for uncovering a plot to prevent America's entry into the war. Author of several crime novels, he is thought to be one of the models used by Ian Fleming for James Bond's boss, 'M'.

Agents working for Knight included Tom Driberg, Olga Gray and Joan Miller (who provided a 'springboard' for the character of Diana). Miller (1918-1984), an attractive, upper-class girl, successfully infiltrated an anti-semitic organisation known as the Right Club in the early months of 1940. The Right Club—one of many similar organisations, most of which were disbanded or pared down at the start of the war—had originally been set up in May 1939 by Captain Archibald Maule Ramsay MP (1894-1955) on whom the character of Peverell Montague is loosely based.

The aim of the Right Club was to rid the City and Whitehall of Jewish influence and to capitalise on national antipathy towards Jews and Communists. When Britain declared war on Germany on the 3rd of September 1939, Ramsay's stated aim became the maintenance of 'an atmosphere in which the "phoney war" might be converted into an honourable negotiated peace'. Members distributed propaganda in the form of adhesive labels and leaflets that bore slogans such as 'This is a Jew's war' and claims that 'this war was plotted and engineered by Jews for world-power and vengeance'.

In May 1940, Miller's infiltration resulted in the unmasking of Tyler Kent (1911-1988), a cipher clerk at the US Embassy in London. Kent, like Walter Wymark in this novel, had been passing on copies of secret communications between Roosevelt and Churchill to members of the Right Club in the hope of damaging Roosevelt's bid for re-election to the Presidency. Kent was charged with obtaining documents that 'might be directly or indirectly useful to an enemy' and tried at the Old Bailey in October 1940. He was convicted and sentenced to seven years' imprisonment. At the end of the war he was released and deported to the US.

Miller was also instrumental in the arrest and detention of Ramsay under Defence Regulation 18B. Ramsay was eventually released in September 1944 and immediately returned to the House of Commons. He did not defend his seat in the election of 1945.

While researching *Stratton's War*, I consulted dozens of books. Amongst the most helpful were: *One Girl's War* by Joan Miller (Brandon, 1986), *The Man Who Was M: The Life of Maxwell Knight* by Anthony Masters (Grafton, 1986), and *Debs at War* by Anne De Courcy (Weidenfeld & Nicholson, 2005). The Mass Observation Archive at the University of Sussex proved, as it always does, to be an invaluable resource, as did the reference library at the Imperial War Museum.

The church in Eastcastle Street, London W1 is, in fact, Welsh. Its architecture is nothing like the Victorian polychromatic brick described in the text (that belongs to the church of All Saints, in nearby Margaret Street). I have also taken a couple of minor architectural liberties with the buildings at Dolphin Square.